THIS WORLD AND OTHERS

"Disch returns us from our contemplation of his now macabre, now comic machinations to face our real world with eyes set at a slightly different focus, our ears attuned to a progression of tones different from the major and minor scales we are used to, our whole imaginative range sensitized to patterns, oh, very much there in the workaday about us, but which we would not be so ready to notice had we not spent time gazing at the meticulously wrought vision of his maniacally altered constructions."

—SAMUEL R. DELANY,
from his Introduction

FUNDAMENTAL DISCH

DISCH

THOMAS M. DISCH

BANTAM BOOKS · TORONTO · LONDON · NEW YORK

FUNDAMENTAL DISCH

A Bantam Book / October 1980

ACKNOWLEDGMENTS

"Descending," copyright © 1964 by Ziff-Davis Publishing Co.
First appeared in Fantastic. *"The Squirrel Cage,"* copyright ©
1967 by New Worlds. *"The Asian Shore,"* copyright © 1970
by Thomas M. Disch. First appeared in Orbit 6. *"Casablanca,"*
copyright © 1967 by Thomas M. Disch. First appeared in
Alfred Hitchcock Presents: Stories That Scared Even Me.
"102 H-Bombs," copyright © 1965 by Ziff-Davis Publishing Co.
First appeared in Fantastic. *"Angouleme,"* copyright © 1971
by Michael Moorcock. First appeared in New Worlds 1.
"Bodies," copyright © 1971 by Coronet Communications, Inc.
First appeared in Quark 4. *"Et in Arcadia Ego,"* copyright ©
1971 by Coronet Communications, Inc. First appeared in
Quark 3. *"The Double-Timer,"* copyright © 1972 by Ziff-Davis
Publishing Co. First appeared in Fantastic. *"Dangerous Flags,"*
copyright © 1964 by Ziff-Davis Publishing Co. First appeared in
Fantastic. *"Doomsday Machines,"* copyright © 1974 and 1975
by The Crawdaddy Publishing Co. Inc. First appeared in
Crawdaddy. *"Assassin & Son,"* copyright © 1964 by Galaxy
Publishing Corporation. First appeared in If. *"White Fang
Goes Dingo,"* copyright © 1965 by Galaxy Publishing Corpora-
tion. First appeared in If. *"Master of the Milford Altarpiece,"*
copyright © 1968 by Thomas M. Disch. First appeared in
Paris Review. *"Getting into Death,"* an abridged version first
appeared in Antaeus, copyright © 1974 by Antaeus. The
present version copyright © 1976 by Thomas M. Disch. *"The
Uses of Fiction,"* copyright © 1975 by New Fiction Society.
First appeared in New Fiction Society. The introduction to
"Et in Arcadia Ego" copyright © 1974 by Harry Harrison.
First appeared in Author's Choice 4.

ISBN 0-553-13670-4

Published simultaneously in the United States and Canada

---

*Bantam Books are published by Bantam Books, Inc. Its trade-
mark, consisting of the words "Bantam Books" and the por-
trayal of a bantam, is Registered in U.S. Patent and Trademark
Office and in other countries. Marca Registrada. Bantam
Books, Inc., 666 Fifth Avenue, New York, New York 10103.*

PRINTED IN THE UNITED STATES OF AMERICA

0 9 8 7 6 5 4 3 2 1

Contents

Introduction

Thomas M. Disch writes tales that stand away and above most contemporary narrative production. The writers to whom, in my mind, he is most closely related (not in style or subject matter, but in that indefinable quality, sensibility) are England's Ian McEwan, America's Lynda Schor, and the American-born but finally international Harry Mathews. Among the riches Disch shares with these writers is a two-sided coin of extraordinary value: in one polished slightly convexed face you can discern reflected an astonishing social range over which the writerly vision remains precise. The other face, somewhere concave, presents a slightly askew mirror, often blatantly comic though not necessarily so, which focuses on psychosocial points in such a way that the lyric surround traditionally accompanying such details is suddenly replaced by a harsh, articulating light under which the traditional "sense of beauty" is revealed for the cliché it too often is, and a certain artistic control appears as the true source of aesthetic illumination. All four writers revel in a fantasy now weaker, now stronger through the flux of their astonishingly accurate perceptions. Disch as well writes science fiction. We could dwell at length on generic distinctions; but we all have an intuitive sense of what these distinctions are. The best such an analysis could do is dispel just a bit more of the popular prejudice that most serious readers (as opposed to merely pompous ones) have long abandoned anyway.

Thomas Michael Disch was born in Iowa in 1940, an eldest child, followed by three brothers and a sister. Eventually he came to New York to study at New York University, majoring in history. Briefly he worked in advertising. Many, if not most, of his early stories appeared in the professional science fiction magazines of the times, but soon his publications had branched out to include *Playboy* and *Harper's* at one end of the spectrum and *Paris Review* and *New American Review* at the other. In the last decade and a half Disch has lived the kind of peripatetic life which lends romance to many writers' biographies: a handful of months in Mexico, two years in London, three years in New York, a year and a half in Rome, now back in London, now again in New York—punctuated by longer or shorter stays in North Africa, Spain, Austria, and Istanbul. Also he is the author of a pseudonymous novel, lavishly researched and elegantly written, that was briefly a small *cause celebre:* While Disch was living in England, an American critic in a midwestern journal claimed that, from internal evidence, the mystery of the novel's true authority was now solved. It was obvious the book could have come from only one contemporary writer: Gore Vidal.

"Slaves" is one of my favorite Disch short stories, the more so because I suspect its excellences make themselves flagrantly available to our emotions but still hide from our analytical faculties—unless we are willing to dig. The story begins with a brief, gentle deception. Someone called "the Baron" is living with a pair of young, troubled lovers in a Riverside Drive apartment. But through the opening half dozen pages we learn (bit by bit, if we're alert) that this "Baron" is not the refined European aristocrat *manqué,* a complex of literary associations initially demands we inscribe over our imaginative vision. Our enlightenment/disillusion presents us with a modulated displacement from that traditional lyric surround we spoke of in our opening paragraph. Thus, at the tale's end, when the three characters plunge into precisely this lyric *weltsmertz* from which to launch their final, aerodynamic gesture toward freedom, Disch has already moved us out to the most ironic of distances from which to observe it: square in the bleachers with the harshest of suns burning down. Lyricism, always so carefully skewed, may at first strike a reader as awkward. Examine that "awkwardness" in Disch, and you find all the necessary signs of a high writerly intelligence wrestling with the aesthetic problems of our numerous conflicting writerly traditions that run from Gertrude Stein through modern poets like Koch and O'Hara to ... well, among the best contemporary fiction writers, Disch.

If the skewly lyric, within which so much post-modern beauty locates itself, describes the field effect of Disch's fiction, the displaced name (*e.g.*, the Baron in "Slaves," Alyona Ivanovna in "Angouleme," Yavuz in "The Asian Shore," Hansel and Gretel in "Minnesota Gothic") is certainly one of the rhetorical figures which Disch employs to adjust that lyricism to the desired angle—and uses frequently enough for us to comment on it. The narrative of "Angouleme," for example, is comparatively simple: some precocious youngsters in New York City, c. 2024, decide to commit the gratuitous murder of an old man who wanders about in Battery Park, begging or talking to himself. But a complexity that flickers from beginning to end of the story, that made and continues to make the story obsessive for me, that has pulled me back to reread it many times and will no doubt go on pulling me in the years to come, is the number of ways in which the tale demonstrates the variety by which a name may not quite stick to the thing or person it is supposed to indicate. "Little Mr. Kissy Lips," aka Bill Harper, and the code name for the intended victim, "Alyona Ivanovna," are only the two most blatant examples. But the image of the slightly inappropriate name runs throughout the story, from the name on the stolen credit card, "Lowen, Richard W.," which does not quite name the school that the would-be murderers attend, to Miss Kraus ("Why, if she were Miss Kraus, was she wearing what seemed to be the old fashioned diamond ring and gold band of a Mrs.?"), to the mis-labled chickadees in the park aviary (". . . Celeste, who'd gone to the library to make sure said they were nothing more than a rather swank breed of sparrow."). But in this brief story one can find at least half a dozen other misdirecting names ("Mrs. *Anderson,* of course she lives there, Mrs. Alma F. Anderson" . . . "Miss Nomer, Miss Carriage, and Miss Steak") if not more. Once one begins to pay attention to this use of names in Disch's stories, at least half the tales here provide something to comment on in that department, from the opening story, "Descending," whose main character has no name at all, to the final story in the collection, "Getting Into Death," whose protagonist, a writer of successful genre fictions, publishes under two different pseudonyms, Cassandra Knye and B. C. Millar, suggesting volumes of schizoid commentary. But like so many of the most interesting patterns in post-modern matters writerly, precisely at the point where the pattern becomes most fascinatingly complex the critic is least able to be sure that pattern is not simply a manifestation of the heightened critical attention itself.

The first Disch I ever read was "Descending," which appeared in Cele Goldsmith's *Amazing Stories* for October, 1962. The story stayed with me tenaciously over the next years. (I didn't actually meet Disch for the first time until Christmas, 1966, in London, when I accidentally encountered him baby-sitting one afternoon at a mutual friend's house where I had stopped off to deliver some Christmas presents.) During those first years and many times since, I've brought the story up in dozens of conversations with writers and editors, as one of the most economical jobs of character sketching I know. Disch paints his character largely through the use of lists, in one case a list of items in an almost empty kitchen cabinet and, a page or so later, a shopping list. It struck me then and still does as a marvelously Chekhovian triumph that certainly singles out the tale for any writer with interest in the technical side of the craft. Rereading it today, I am struck as well with its overall lucidity that holds not only these but a number of other technical turns to proportion so that they contribute to the chilling overall effect.

Disch's novel *Camp Concentration,* serialized in the British magazine *New Worlds* in 1967, secured the reputation Disch's short fiction had already won him with a circle of readers whose interests embraced both science fiction and post-modern experimental writing, as a most consummate writers' writer. The series of stories, revolving around two families living in an overpopulated New York City at about the first quarter of the twenty-first century in a huge apartment complex at 334 East 11th Street (collected as *334,* Avon Books, New York, 1974), extended that reputation; this series, from which two of the stories in this collection ("Angouleme" and "Bodies") are taken, also provides one of the most dazzling meditations on the urban future in the range of contemporary imaginative writing. His most recent novel, *On Wings of Song,* moves back and forth from the midwest to New York to cast a marvelous comic indictment at our cultural repressions and pretensions.

I know of many readers for whom Disch is an unquestionably important writer in their particular pantheons, and I have put this collection together under the assumption that he may well become important to many more in some of the particular ways that I find him so. There are a number of ways to be interested in a writer one finds consistently, even insistently, important. The various pieces here are included for various reasons that range over the various ways one can be interested in such work. "102 H-Bombs" is here because it is moving, and because it is the earliest presentation of an image that haunts three of Disch's booklength fictions, *Echo Rounds His Bones, Camp Concentration,* and *334:* the image of the endless, useless war, an image ceded to many people whose youth passed through (or over) the Viet Nam War. In a notable number of Disch's works, this image hangs just beyond the foreground, a backdrop of all possible arbitrary violence. Firsts are often interesting, if not in terms of their precise accomplishment, then in terms of what they presage. And Disch's first sold story, "The Double Timer," is also here. The novella "White Fang Goes Dingo" is here because the novel it was later expanded to become (*The Puppies of Terra*) threatens to drive the shorter, and in some ways both mellower and crisper, version from easy access. "Dangerous Flags" is here because Disch himself finds the story particularly intriguing—and all of Disch's writing more or less intrigues me. "The Roaches" and "Casablanca" are here because a general readership has found these stories eminently praiseworthy over the years (if, before, you have read any Disch, chances are it was one of these two), and I happen to agree. "The Squirrel Cage" and *"Et in Arcadia Ego"* are here because they are among the stories I have read, reread, and enjoyed the most, and a general readership, given a chance, might well concur. Three of Disch's brief non-fiction pieces make up a first appendix because it's interesting to read what writers who are important to you have written about their own writing and writing in general. Disch's libretto for Greg Sandow's opera, *The Fall of the House of Usher,* based on the Poe story of the same title, is here as a second appendix because it is always elegant, frequently witty, and you can't find it anywhere else.

Any number of Disch's stories stand up to detailed examination. And though a brief introduction to a general collection is not the place for a concerted examination of every tale, I would still like to close with a slightly more intensive look at a section of one of the outstanding stories here, *The Asian Shore.* This extraordinary modern horror tale dissects a kind of insidious racism so muted as to be barely perceptible and begins with a young American art historian sitting alone in a room in Istanbul while a woman in the street calls to him by—yes—the wrong name. The part I quote, however, describes the aesthetic theory embodied in the protagonist's first, fictive volume, written sometime before the story begins, *Homo Arbitrans:*

> It was the thesis of his first book that the quidity of architecture, its chief claim to an esthetic interest, was its arbitrariness. Once the lintels were lying on the posts, once some kind of roof had been spread across the hollow space, then anything else that might be done was gratuitous. Even the lintel and the post, the roof, the space below, these were gratuitous as well. Stated thus, it was a mild enough notion; the difficulty was in training the eye to see the whole world of usual forms—patterns of brick, painted plaster, carved and carpentered wood —not as "buildings" and "streets" but as an infinite series of free and arbitrary choices. There was no place in such a scheme for orders, styles, sophistication, taste. Every artifact of the city was anomalous, unique, but living there in the midst of it all you could not allow yourself too fine a sense of this fact. If you did. . . .

The rest of the story presumably fills in the concluding ellipsis. Throughout the tale this notion of the arbitrary controls a metaphorical system that finally generates an intense parallelism between the theory itself and the protagonist's decomposing psychology. Not to acknowledge the strong irony in the passage above would clearly mark a misreading: from its place in the story, one could hazard that Disch sees the theory not as a revelatory insightful success, but rather as an insidiously fascinating, even hypnotic failure. As a means, it is certainly a useful way to begin to see new patterns—and one suspects that, as a means, Disch has trained his own eye in precisely this way, on much of the world about him. As an end in itself, however, it makes of everything a vast ruin, among whose shadowy wreckages lurks the most energumenical fantasy. Its dangers—as an end—are the fantastical focus of the tale.

It is tempting to read some sort of extension of this critique over the breadth of Disch's fictive world—or rather over the plurality of his artfully contrasted worlds. (His work in science fiction makes him heir to many more than one.)

We can see such suggestions nestling among the near slapstick calamities of "Bodies"; we can scry them just beneath the anomie of "The Squirrel Cage"; we can read them into the genocidal catastrophe of *"Et in Arcadia Ego."* But Disch, as do all the great writers of the post-modern fantastic, returns us from our contemplation of his now macabre, now comic, machinations to face our real world with eyes set at a slightly different focus, our ears attuned to a progression of tones different from the major and minor scales we are used to, our whole imaginative range sensitized to patterns, oh, very much there in the workaday about us, but which we would not be so ready to notice had we not spent time gazing at the meticulously wrought vision of his maniacally altered constructions.

The intensity of that vision is one with the intensity of pleasure to be garnered among the stories here. And that is vision and pleasure indeed.

—*S. R. Delany*
New York, 1980

DESCENDING

Catsup, mustard, pickle relish, mayonnaise, two kinds of salad dressing, bacon grease, and a lemon. Oh yes, two trays of ice cubes. In the cupboard it wasn't much better: jars and boxes of spice, flour, sugar, salt—and a box of raisins!

An empty box of raisins.

Not even any coffee. Not even tea, which he hated. Nothing in the mailbox but a bill from Underwood's: *Unless we receive the arrears on your account. . . .*

$4.75 in change jingled in his coat pocket—the plunder of the Chianti bottle he had promised himself never to break open. He was spared the unpleasantness of having to sell his books. They had all been sold. The letter to Graham had gone out a week ago. If his brother intended to send something this time, it would have come by now.

—I should be desperate, he thought.—Perhaps I am.

He might have looked in the *Times*. But, no, that was too depressing—applying for jobs at $50 a week and being turned down. Not that he blamed them; he wouldn't have hired himself himself. He had been a grasshopper for years. The ants were on to his tricks.

He shaved without soap and brushed his shoes to a high polish. He whitened the sepulchre of his unwashed torso with a fresh, starched shirt and chose his somberest tie from the rack. He began to feel excited and expressed it, characteristically, by appearing statuesquely, icily calm.

Descending the stairway to the first floor, he encountered Mrs. Beale, who was pretending to sweep the well-swept floor of the entrance.

"Good afternoon—or I s'pose it's good morning for you, eh?"

"Good afternoon, Mrs. Beale."

1

"Your letter come?"

"Not yet."

"The first of the month isn't far off."

"Yes indeed, Mrs. Beale."

At the subway station he considered a moment before answering the attendant: one token or two? Two, he decided. After all, he had no choice but to return to his apartment. The first of the month was still a long way off.

—If Jean Valjean had had a charge account, he would have never gone to prison.

Having thus cheered himself, he settled down to enjoy the ads in the subway car. *Smoke. Try. Eat. Give. See. Drink. Use. Buy.* He thought of Alice with her mushrooms: Eat me.

At 34th Street he got off and entered Underwood's Department Store directly from the train platform. On the main floor he stopped at the cigar stand and bought a carton of cigarettes.

"Cash or charge?"

"Charge." He handed the clerk the laminated plastic card. The charge was rung up.

Fancy groceries was on 5. He made his selection judiciously. A jar of instant and a 2-pound can of drip-ground coffee, a large tin of corned beef, packaged soups and boxes of pancake mix and condensed milk. Jam, peanut butter, and honey. Six cans of tuna fish. Then, he indulged himself in perishables: English cookies, and Edam cheese, a small frozen pheasant—even fruitcake. He never ate so well as when he was broke. He couldn't afford to.

"$14.87."

This time, after ringing up his charge, the clerk checked the number on his card against her list of closed or doubtful accounts. She smiled apologetically and handed the card back.

"Sorry, but we have to check."

"I understand."

The bag of groceries weighed a good twenty pounds. Carrying it with the exquisite casualness of a burglar passing before a policeman with his loot, he took the escalator to the bookshop on 8. His choice of books was determined by the same principle as his choice of groceries. First, the staples:

two Victorian novels he had never read, *Vanity Fair* and *Middlemarch;* the Sayers translation of Dante, and a two-volume anthology of German plays, none of which he had read and few he had even heard of. Then the perishables: a sensational novel that had reached the best seller list via the Supreme Court, and two mysteries.

He had begun to feel giddy with self-indulgence. He reached into his jacket pocket for a coin.

—Heads a new suit; tails the Sky Room.

Tails.

The Sky Room on 15 was empty of all but a few women chatting over coffee and cakes. He was able to get a seat by a window. He ordered from the à la carte side of the menu and finished his meal with espresso and baklava. He handed the waitress his credit card and tipped her fifty cents.

Dawdling over his second cup of coffee, he began *Vanity Fair*. Rather to his surprise, he found himself enjoying it. The waitress returned with his card and a receipt for the meal.

Since the Sky Room was on the top floor of Underwood's there was only one escalator to take now—Descending. Riding down, he continued to read *Vanity Fair*. He could read anywhere—in restaurants, on subways, even walking down the street. At each landing he made his way from the foot of one escalator to the head of the next without lifting his eyes from the book. When he came to the Bargain Basement, he would be only a few steps from the subway turnstile.

He was halfway through Chapter VI (on page 55, to be exact) when he began to feel something amiss.

—How long does this damn thing take to reach the basement?

He stopped at the next landing, but there was no sign to indicate on what floor he was, nor any door by which he might re-enter the store. Deducing from this that he was between floors, he took the escalator down one more flight, only to find the same perplexing absence of landmarks.

There was, however, a water fountain, and he stooped to take a drink.

—I must have gone to a sub-basement. But this was not too likely after all. Escalators were seldom provided for janitors and stockboys.

He waited on the landing watching the steps of the escalators slowly descend toward him and, at the end of their journey, telescope in upon themselves and disappear. He waited a long while, and no one else came down the moving steps.

—Perhaps the store has closed. Having no wristwatch and having rather lost track of the time, he had no way of knowing. At last, he reasoned that he had become so engrossed in the Thackeray novel that he had simply stopped on one of the upper landings—say, on 8—to finish a chapter and had read on to page 55 without realizing that he was making no progress on the escalators.

When he read, he could forget everything else.

He must, therefore, still be somewhere above the main floor. The absence of exits, though disconcerting, could be explained by some quirk in the floor plan. The absence of signs was merely a carelessness on the part of the management.

He tucked *Vanity Fair* into his shopping bag and stepped onto the grilled lip of the down-going escalator—not, it must be admitted, without a certain degree of reluctance. At each landing, he marked his progress by a number spoken aloud. By *eight* he was uneasy; by *fifteen* he was desperate.

It was, of course, possible that he had to descend two flights of stairs for every floor of the department store. With this possibility in mind, he counted off fifteen more landings.

—No.

Dazedly, and as though to deny the reality of this seemingly interminable stairwell, he continued his descent. When he stopped again at the forty-fifth landing, he was trembling. He was afraid.

He rested the shopping bag on the bare concrete floor of the landing, realizing that his arm had gone quite sore from supporting the twenty pounds and more of groceries and books. He discounted the enticing possibility that "it was all a dream," for the dream-world is the reality of the dreamer, to which he could not weakly surrender, no more than one could surrender to the realities of life. Besides, he was not dreaming; of that he was quite sure.

He checked his pulse. It was fast—say, eighty a minute. He rode down two more flights, counting his pulse. Eighty almost exactly. Two flights took only one minute.

He could read approximately one page a minute, a little less on an escalator. Suppose he had spent one hour on the escalators while he had read: sixty minutes—one hundred and twenty floors. Plus forty-seven that he had counted. One hundred sixty-seven. The Sky Room was on 15.

167—15=152.

He was in the one-hundred-fifty-second sub-basement. That was impossible.

The appropriate response to an impossible situation was to deal with it as though it were commonplace—like Alice in Wonderland. Ergo, he would return to Underwood's the same way he had (apparently) left it. He would walk up one hundred fifty-two flights of down-going escalators. Taking the steps three at a time and running, it was almost like going up a regular staircase. But after ascending the second escalator in this manner, he found himself already out of breath.

There was no hurry. He would not allow himself to be overtaken by panic.

No.

He picked up the bag of groceries and books he had left on that landing, waiting for his breath to return, and darted up a third and fourth flight. While he rested on the landing, he tried to count the steps between floors, but this count differed depending on whether he counted with the current or against it, down or up. The average was roughly eighteen steps, and the steps appeared to be eight or nine inches deep. Each flight was, therefore, about twelve feet.

It was one-third of a mile, as the plumb drops, to Underwood's main floor.

Dashing up the ninth escalator, the bag of groceries broke open at the bottom, where the thawing pheasant had dampened the paper. Groceries and books tumbled onto the steps, some rolling of their own accord to the landing below, others being transported there by the moving stairs and forming a neat little pile. Only the jam jar had been broken.

He stacked the groceries in the corner of the landing, except for the half-thawed pheasant, which he stuffed into his coat pocket, anticipating that his ascent would take him well past his dinner hour.

Physical exertion had dulled his finer feelings—to be precise, his capacity for fear. Like a cross-country runner in his last laps, he thought single-mindedly of the task at hand and made no effort to understand what he had in any case already decided was not to be understood. He mounted one flight, rested, mounted and rested again. Each mount was wearier;

each rest longer. He stopped counting the landings after the twenty-eighth, and some time after that—how long he had no idea—his legs gave out and he collapsed to the concrete floor of the landing. His calves were hard aching knots of muscle; his thighs quivered erratically. He tried to do knee-bends and fell backward.

Despite his recent dinner (assuming that it had been recent), he was hungry and he devoured the entire pheasant, completely thawed now, without being able to tell if it were raw or had been pre-cooked.

—This is what it's like to be a cannibal, he thought as he fell asleep.

Sleeping, he dreamed he was falling down a bottomless pit. Waking, he discovered nothing had changed, except the dull ache in his legs, which had become a sharp pain.

Overhead, a single strip of fluorescent lighting snaked down the stairwell. The mechanical purr of the escalators seemed to have heightened to the roar of a Niagara, and their rate of descent seemed to have increased proportionately.

Fever, he decided. He stood up stiffly and flexed some of the soreness from his muscles.

Halfway up the third escalator, his legs gave way under him. He attempted the climb again and succeeded. He collapsed again on the next flight. Lying on the landing where the escalator had deposited him, he realized that his hunger had returned. He also needed to have water—and to let it.

The latter necessity he could easily—and without false modesty—satisfy. Also he remembered the water fountain he had drunk from yesterday and he found another three floors below.

—It's so much easier going down.

His groceries were down there. To go after them now, he would erase whatever progress he had made in his ascent. Perhaps Underwood's main floor was only a few more flights up. Or a hundred. There was no way to know.

Because he was hungry and because he was tired and because the futility of mounting endless flights of descending escalators was, as he now considered it, a labor of Sisyphus, he returned, descended, gave in.

At first, he allowed the escalator to take him along at its own mild pace, but he soon grew impatient of this. He found that the exercise of running down the steps three at a time was not so exhausting as running *up*. It was refreshing, almost. And, by swimming with the current instead of against it, his progress, if such it can be called, was appreciable. In only minutes he was back at his cache of groceries.

After eating half the fruitcake and a little cheese, he fashioned his coat into a sort of sling for the groceries, knotting the sleeves together and buttoning it closed. With one hand at the collar and the other about the hem, he could carry all his food with him.

He looked up the descending staircase with a scornful smile, for he had decided with the wisdom of failure to abandon *that* venture. If the stairs wished to take him down, then down, giddily, he would go.

Then, down he did go, down dizzily, down, down and always, it seemed, faster, spinning about lightly on his heels at each landing so that there was hardly any break in the wild speed of his descent. He whooped and halooed and laughed to hear his whoopings echo in the narrow, low-vaulted corridors, following him as though they could not keep up his pace.

Down, ever deeper down.

Twice he slipped at the landings and once he missed his footing in mid-leap on the escalator, hurtled forward, letting go of the sling of groceries and falling, hands stretched out to cushion him, onto the steps, which, imperturbably, continued their descent.

He must have been unconscious then, for he woke up in a pile of groceries with a split cheek and a splitting headache. The telescoping steps of the escalator gently grazed his heels.

He knew then his first moment of terror—a premonition that there was no *end* to his descent, but this feeling gave way quickly to a laughing fit.

"I'm going to hell!" he shouted, though he could not drown with his voice the steady purr of the escalators. "This is the way to hell. Abandon hope all ye who enter here."

—If only I were, he reflected.—If that were the case, it would make sense. Not quite orthodox sense, but some sense, a little.

Sanity, however, was so integral to his character that neither hysteria nor horror could long have their way with him. He gathered up his groceries again, relieved to find that only the jar of instant coffee had been broken this time. After reflection he also discarded the can of drip-ground coffee, for which he could conceive no use—under the present circumstances. And he would allow himself, for the sake of sanity, to conceive of no other circumstances than those.

He began a more deliberate descent. He returned to *Vanity Fair,* reading it as he paced down the down-going steps. He did not let himself consider the extent of the abyss into which he was plunging, and the vicarious excitement of the novel helped him keep his thoughts from his own situation. At page 235, he lunched (that is, he took his second meal of the day) on the remainder of the cheese and fruitcake; at 523 he rested and dined on the English cookies dipped in peanut butter.

—Perhaps I had better ration my food.

If he could regard this absurd dilemma merely as a struggle for survival, another chapter in his own Robinson Crusoe story, he might get to the bottom of this mechanized vortex alive and sane. He thought proudly that many people in his position could not have adjusted, would have gone mad.

Of course, he *was* descending. . . .

But he was still sane. He had chosen his course and now he was following it.

There was no night in the stairwell, and scarcely any shadows. He slept when his legs could no longer bear his weight and his eyes were tearful from reading. Sleeping, he dreamed that he was continuing his descent on the escalators. Waking, his hand resting on the rubber railing that moved along at the same rate as the steps, he discovered this to be the case.

Somnambulistically, he had ridden the escalators further down into this mild, interminable hell, leaving behind his bundle of food and even the still-unfinished Thackeray novel.

Stumbling up the escalators, he began, for the first time, to cry. Without the novel, there was nothing to *think* of but this, this. . . .

—How far? How long did I sleep?

His legs, which had only been slightly wearied by his descent, gave out twenty flights up. His spirit gave out soon after. Again he turned around, allowed himself to be swept up by current—or, more exactly, swept down.

The escalator seemed to be traveling more rapidly, the pitch of the steps to be more pronounced. But he no longer trusted the evidence of his senses.

—I am, perhaps, insane—or sick from hunger. Yet, I would have run out of food eventually. This will bring the crisis to a head. Optimism, that's the spirit!

Continuing his descent, he occupied himself with a closer analysis of his environment, not undertaken with any hope of bettering his condition but only for lack of other diversions. The walls and ceilings were hard, smooth, and off-white. The escalator steps were a dull nickel color, the treads being somewhat shinier, the crevices darker. Did that mean that the treads were polished from use? Or were they designed in that fashion? The treads were half an inch wide and spaced apart from each other by the same width. They projected slightly over the edge of each step, resembling somewhat the head of a barber's shears. Whenever he stopped at a landing, his attention would become fixed on the illusory "disappearance" of the steps, as they sank flush to the floor and slid, tread in groove, into the grilled baseplate.

Less and less would he run, or even walk, down the stairs, content merely to ride his chosen step from top to bottom of each flight and, at the landing, step (left foot, right, and left again) onto the escalator that would transport him to the floor below. The stairwell now had tunneled, by his calculations, miles beneath the department store—so many miles that he began to congratulate himself upon his unsought adventure, wondering if he had established some sort of record. Just so, a criminal will stand in awe of his own baseness and be most proud of his vilest crime, which he believes unparalleled.

In the days that followed, when his only nourishment was the water from the fountains provided at every tenth landing, he thought frequently of food, preparing imaginary meals from the store of groceries he had left behind, savoring the ideal sweetness of the honey, the richness of the soup which he would prepare by soaking the powder in the emptied cookie tin, licking the film of gelatin lining the opened can of corned beef. When he thought of the six cans of tuna fish, his anxiety became intolerable, for he had (would have had) no way to open them. Merely to stamp on them would not be enough. What, then? He turned the question over and over in his head, like a squirrel spinning the wheel in its cage, to no avail.

Then a curious thing happened. He quickened again the speed of his descent, faster now than when first he had done this, eagerly, headlong, absolutely heedless. The several landings seemed to flash by like a montage of Flight, each scarcely perceived before the next was before him. A demonic, pointless race—and why? He was running, so he thought, toward his store of groceries, either believing that they had been left *below* or thinking that he was running *up*. Clearly, he was delirious.

It did not last. His weakened body could not maintain the frantic pace, and he awoke from his delirium confused and utterly spent. Now began another, more rational delirium, a madness fired by logic. Lying on the landing, rubbing a torn muscle in his ankle, he speculated on the nature, origin and purpose of the escalators. Reasoned thought was of no more use to him, however, than unreasoning action. Ingenuity was helpless to solve a riddle that had no answer, which was its own reason, self-contained and whole. He—not the escalators —needed an answer.

Perhaps his most interesting theory was the notion that these escalators were a kind of exercise wheel, like those found in a squirrel cage, from which, because it was a closed system, there could be no escape. This theory required some minor alterations in his conception of the physical universe, which had always appeared highly Euclidean to him before, a universe in which his descent seemingly along a plumb-line was, in fact, describing a loop. This theory cheered him, for he might hope, coming full circle, to return to his store of groceries again, if not to Underwood's. Perhaps in his abstracted state he had passed one or the other already several times without observing.

There was another, and related, theory concerning the measures taken by Underwood's Credit Department against delinquent accounts. This was mere paranoia.

—Theories! I don't need theories. I must get on with it.

So, favoring his good leg, he continued his descent, although his speculations did not immediately cease. They became, if anything, more metaphysical. They became vague. Eventually, he could regard the escalators as being entirely matter-of-fact, requiring no more explanation than, by their sheer existence, they offered him.

He discovered that he was losing weight. Being so long without food (by the evidence of his beard, he estimated that more than a week had gone by), this was only to be expected. Yet, there was another possibility that he could not exclude: that he was approaching the center of the earth where, as he understood, all things were weightless.

—Now *that,* he thought, is something worth striving for.

He had discovered a goal. On the other hand, he was dying, a process he did not give all the attention it deserved. Unwilling to admit this eventuality and yet not so foolish as to admit any other, he side-stepped the issue by pretending to hope.

—Maybe someone will rescue me, he hoped.

But his hope was as mechanical as the escalators he rode—and tended, in much the same way, to sink.

Waking and sleeping were no longer distinct states of which he could say: "Now I am sleeping," or "Now I am awake." Sometimes he would discover himself descending and be unable to tell whether he had been waked from sleep or roused from inattention.

He hallucinated.

A woman, loaded with packages from Underwood's and wearing a trim, pillbox-style hat, came down the escalator toward him, turned around on the landing, high heels clicking smartly, and rode away without even nodding to him.

More and more, when he awoke or was roused from his stupor, he found himself, instead of hurrying to his goal, lying on a landing, weak, dazed, and beyond hunger. Then he would crawl to the down-going escalator and pull himself onto one of the steps, which he would ride to the bottom, sprawled head foremost, hands and shoulders braced against the treads to keep from skittering bumpily down.

—At the bottom, he thought—at the bottom . . . I will . . . when I get there. . . .

From the bottom, which he conceived of as the center of the earth, there would be literally nowhere to go but up. Probably another chain of escalators, ascending escalators, but preferably by an elevator. It was important to believe in a bottom.

Thought was becoming as difficult, as demanding and

painful, as once his struggle to ascend had been. His perceptions were fuzzy. He did not know what was real and what imaginary. He thought he was eating and discovered he was gnawing at his hands.

He thought he had come to the bottom. It was a large, high-ceilinged room. Signs pointed to another escalator: *Ascending.* But there was a chain across it and a small typed announcement.

"Out of order. Please bear with us while the escalators are being repaired. Thank you. The Management."

He laughed weakly.

He devised a way to open the tuna fish cans. He would slip the can sideways beneath the projecting treads of the escalator, just at the point where the steps were sinking flush to the floor. Either the escalator would split the can open or the can would jam the escalator. Perhaps if one escalator were jammed the whole chain of them would stop. He should have thought of that before, but he was, nevertheless, quite pleased to have thought of it at all.

—I might have escaped.

His body seemed to weigh so little now. He must have come hundreds of miles. Thousands.

Again, he descended.

Then, he was lying at the foot of the escalator. His head rested on the cold metal of the baseplate and he was looking at his hand, the fingers of which were pressed into the creviced grille. One after another, in perfect order, the steps of the escalator slipped into these crevices, tread in groove, rasping at his fingertips, occasionally tearing away a sliver of his flesh.

That was the last thing he remembered.

CASABLANCA

In the morning the man with the red fez always brought them coffee and toast on a tray. He would ask them how it goes, and Mrs. Richmond, who had some French, would say it goes well. The hotel always served the same kind of jam, plum jam. That eventually became so tiresome that Mrs. Richmond went out and bought their own jar of strawberry jam, but in a little while that was just as tiresome as the plum jam. Then they alternated, having plum jam one day, and strawberry jam the next. They wouldn't have taken their breakfasts in the hotel at all, except for the money it saved.

When, on the morning of their second Wednesday at the Belmonte, they came down to the lobby, there was no mail for them at the desk. "You can't really expect them to think of us here," Mrs. Richmond said in a piqued tone, for it had been her expectation.

"I suppose not," Fred agreed.

"I think I'm sick again. It was that funny stew we had last night. Didn't I tell you? Why don't *you* go out and get the newspaper this morning?"

So Fred went, by himself, to the newsstand on the corner. It had neither the *Times* nor the *Tribune*. There weren't even the usual papers from London. Fred went to the magazine store nearby the Marhaba, the big luxury hotel. On the way someone tried to sell him a gold watch. It seemed to Fred that everyone in Morocco was trying to sell gold watches.

The magazine store still had copies of the *Times* from last week. Fred had read those papers already. "Where is today's *Times*?" he asked loudly, in English.

The middle-aged man behind the counter shook his head sadly, either because he didn't understand Fred's question or

13

because he didn't know the answer. He asked Fred how it goes.

"Byen," said Fred, without conviction, "byen."

The local French newspaper, *La Vigie Marocaine*, had black, portentous headlines, which Fred could not decipher. Fred spoke "four languages: English, Irish, Scottish, and American." With only those languages, he insisted, one could be understood anywhere in the free world.

At ten o'clock, Bulova watch time, Fred found himself, as though by chance, outside his favorite ice-cream parlor. Usually, when he was with his wife, he wasn't able to indulge his sweet tooth, because Mrs. Richmond, who had a delicate stomach, distrusted Moroccan dairy products, unless boiled.

The waiter smiled and said, "Good morning, Mister Richmon." Foreigners were never able to pronounce his name right for some reason.

Fred said, "Good morning."

"How are you?"

"I'm just fine, thank you."

"Good, good," the waiter said. Nevertheless, he looked saddened. He seemed to want to say something to Fred, but his English was very limited.

It was amazing, to Fred, that he had had to come halfway around the world to discover the best damned ice-cream sundaes he'd ever tasted. Instead of going to bars, the young men of the town went to ice-cream parlors, like this, just as they had in Fred's youth, in Iowa, during Prohibition. It had something to do, here in Casablanca, with the Moslem religion.

A ragged shoe shine boy came in and asked to shine Fred's shoes which were very well shined already. Fred looked out the plate-glass window to the travel agency across the street. The boy hissed *monsieur, monsieur,* until Fred would have been happy to kick him. The wisest policy was to ignore the beggars. They went away quicker if you just didn't look at them. The travel agency displayed a poster showing a pretty young blonde, rather like Doris Day, in a cowboy costume. It was a poster for Pan American airlines.

At last the shoe shine boy went away. Fred's face was flushed with stifled anger. His sparse white hair made the redness of the flesh seem all the brighter, like a winter sunset.

A grown man came into the ice-cream parlor with a bundle

of newspapers, French newspapers. Despite his lack of French, Fred could understand the headlines. He bought a copy for twenty francs and went back to the hotel, leaving half the sundae uneaten.

The minute he was in the door, Mrs. Richmond cried out, "Isn't it terrible?" She had a copy of the paper already spread out on the bed. "It doesn't say *anything* about Cleveland."

Cleveland was where Nan, the Richmonds' married daughter, lived. There was no point in wondering about their own home. It was in Florida, within fifty miles of the Cape, and they'd always known that if there were a war it would be one of the first places to go.

"The dirty reds!" Fred said, flushing. His wife began to cry. "Goddamn them to hell. What did the newspaper say? How did it start?"

"Do you suppose," Mrs. Richmond asked, "that Billy and Midge could be at Grandma Holt's farm?"

Fred paged through *La Vigie Marocaine* helplessly, looking for pictures. Except for the big cutout of a mushroom cloud on the front page and a stock picture on the second of the president in a cowboy hat, there were no photos. He tried to read the lead story but it made no sense.

Mrs. Richmond rushed out of the room, crying aloud.

Fred wanted to tear the paper into ribbons. To calm himself he poured a shot from the pint of bourbon he kept in the dresser. Then he went out into the hall and called through the locked door to the W.C.: "Well, I'll bet we knocked hell out of *them* at least."

This was of no comfort to Mrs. Richmond.

Only the day before Mrs. Richmond had written two letters—one to her granddaughter Midge, the other to Midge's mother, Nan. The letter to Midge read:

December 2

Dear Mademoiselle Holt,

Well, here we are in romantic Casablanca, where the old and the new come together. There are palm trees growing on the boulevard outside our hotel window and sometimes it seems that we never left Florida at all. In Marrakesh we bought presents for you and Billy, which you should get in time for Christmas if the mails are good. Wouldn't you like to know what's in those packages! But you'll just have to wait till Christmas! You should thank God every day, darling, that you live in America. If you could only see the poor Moroccan children, begging on the streets. They aren't able to go to school, and many of them don't even have shoes or warm clothes. And don't think it doesn't get cold here, even if it is Africa! You and Billy don't know how lucky you are!

On the train ride to Marrakesh we saw the farmers plowing their fields in *December*. Each plow has one donkey and one camel. That would probably be an interesting fact for you to tell your geography teacher in school.

Casablanca is wonderfully exciting, and I often wish that you and Billy were here to enjoy it with us. Someday, perhaps! Be good—remember it will be Christmas soon.

Your loving Grandmother,
"Grams"

The second letter, to Midge's mother, read as follows:

December 2. Mond. Afternoon

Dear Nan,

There's no use pretending any more with *you!* You saw it in my first letter—before I even knew my own feelings. Yes, Morocco has been a terrible disappointment. You wouldn't believe some of the things that have happened. For instance, it is almost impossible to mail a package out of this country! I will have to wait till we get to Spain, therefore, to send Billy and Midge their Xmas presents. Better not tell B & M that however!

Marrakesh was terrible. Fred and I got *lost* in the native quarter, and we thought we'd never escape! The filth is unbelievable, but if I talk about that it will only make me ill. After our experience on "the wrong side of the tracks" I wouldn't leave our hotel. Fred got very angry, and we took the train back to Casablanca the same night. At least there are decent restaurants in Casablanca. You can get a very satisfactory French-type dinner for about $1.00.

After all this you won't believe me when I tell you

that we're going to stay here two more weeks. That's
when the next boat leaves for Spain. Two more weeks!!!
Fred says, take an airplane, but you know me. And I'll
be d——ed if I'll take a trip on the local railroad with
all our luggage, which is the only other way.

I've finished the one book I brought along, and now I
have nothing to read but newspapers. They are printed
up in Paris and have mostly the news from India and
Angola, which I find too depressing, and the political
news from Europe, which I can't ever keep up with.
Who is Chancellor Zucker and what does he have to do
with the war in India? I say, if people would just sit
down and try to *understand* each other, most of the
world's so-called problems would disappear. Well, that's
my opinion, but I have to keep it to myself, or Fred gets
an apoplexy. You know Fred! He says, drop a bomb on
Red China and to H—— with it! Good old Fred!

I hope you and Dan are both fine and *dan*-dy, and I
hope B & M are coming along in school. We were both
excited to hear about Billy's A in geography. Fred says
it's due to all the stories he's told Billy about our travels.
Maybe he's right for once!

Love and kisses,
"Grams"

Fred had forgotten to mail these two letters yesterday
afternoon, and now, after the news in the paper, it didn't
seem worthwhile. The Holts, Nan and Dan and Billy and
Midge, were all very probably dead.

"It's so strange," Mrs. Richmond observed at lunch at their
restaurant. "I can't believe it really happened. Nothing has
changed here. You'd think it would make more of a difference."

"Goddamned reds."

"Will you drink the rest of my wine? I'm too upset."

"What do you suppose we should do? Should we try and
telephone to Nan?"

"Trans-*Atlantic?* Wouldn't a telegram do just as well?"

So, after lunch, they went to the telegraph office, which
was in the main post office, and filled out a form. The
message they finally agreed on was: IS EVERYONE WELL
QUESTION WAS CLEVELAND HIT QUESTION RE-
TURN REPLY REQUESTED. It cost eleven dollars to send

off, one dollar a word. The post office wouldn't accept a traveler's check, so while Mrs. Richmond waited at the desk, Fred went across the street to the Bank of Morocco to cash it there.

The teller behind the grille looked at Fred's check doubtfully and asked to see his passport. He brought check and passport into an office at the back of the bank. Fred grew more and more peeved, as the time wore on and nothing was done. He was accustomed to being treated with respect, at least. The teller returned with a portly gentleman not much younger than Fred himself. He wore a striped suit with a flower in his buttonhole.

"Are you Mr. Richmon?" the older gentleman asked.

"Of course I am. Look at the picture in my passport."

"I'm sorry, Mr. Richmon, but we are not able to cash this check."

"What do you mean? I've cashed checks here before. Look I've noted it down: on November 28, forty dollars; on December 1, twenty dollars."

The man shook his head. "I'm sorry, Mr. Richmon, but we are not able to cash these checks."

"I'd like to see the manager."

"I'm sorry, Mr. Richmon, it is not possible for us to cash your checks. Thank you very much." He turned to go.

"I want to see the manager!" Everybody in the bank, the tellers and the other clients, was staring at Fred, who had turned quite red.

"I am the manager," said the man in the striped suit. "Good-bye, Mr. Richmon."

"These are American Express Travelers' Checks. They're good anywhere in the world!"

The manager returned to his office, and the teller began to wait on another customer. Fred returned to the post office.

"We'll have to return here later, darling," he explained to his wife. She didn't ask why, and he didn't want to tell her.

They bought food to bring back to the hotel, since Mrs. Richmond didn't feel up to dressing for dinner.

The manager of the hotel, a thin, nervous man who wore wire-framed spectacles, was waiting at the desk to see them. Wordlessly he presented them a bill for the room.

Fred protested angrily. "We're paid up. We're paid until the twelfth of this month. What are you trying to pull?"

The manager smiled. He had gold teeth. He explained, in imperfect English, that this was the bill.

"*Nous sommes payée*," Mrs. Richmond explained pleasantly. Then, in a diplomatic whisper to her husband, "Show him the receipt."

The manager examined the receipt. "*Non, non, non*," he said, shaking his head. He handed Fred, instead of his receipt, the new bill.

"I'll take that receipt back, thank you very much." The manager smiled and backed away from Fred. Fred acted without thinking. He grabbed the manager's wrist and pried the receipt out of his fingers. The manager shouted words at him in Arabic. Fred took the key for their room, 216, off its hook behind the desk. Then he took his wife by the elbow and led her up the stairs. The man with the red fez came running down the stairs to do the manager's bidding.

Once they were inside the room, Fred locked the door. He was trembling and short of breath. Mrs. Richmond made him sit down and sponged his fevered brow with cold water. Five minutes later, a little slip of paper slid in under the door. It was the bill.

"Look at this!" he exclaimed. "Forty dirham a day. Eight dollars! That son of a bitch." The regular per diem rate for the room was twenty dirham, and the Richmonds, by taking it for a fortnight, had bargained it down to fifteen.

"Now, Freddy!"

"That bastard!"

"It's probably some sort of misunderstanding."

"He saw that receipt, didn't he? He made out that receipt himself. *You* know why he's doing it. Because of what's happened. Now I won't be able to cash my travelers' checks here either. That son of a bitch!"

"Now, Freddy." She smoothed the ruffled strands of white hair with a wet sponge.

"Don't you now-Freddy me! I know what I'm going to do. I'm going to the American Consulate and register a complaint."

"That's a good idea, but not today, Freddy. Let's stay inside until tomorrow. We're both too tired and upset. Tomorrow we can go there together. Maybe they'll know something about Cleveland by then." Mrs. Richmond was prevented from giving further council by a new onset of her illness. She went out into the hall, but returned almost immediately. "The door into the toilet is padlocked," she said. Her eyes were wide with terror. She had just begun to understand what was happening.

That night, after a frugal dinner of olives, cheese sandwiches, and figs, Mrs. Richmond tried to look on the bright side. "Actually we're very lucky," she said, "to be here, instead of there, when it happened. At least, we're alive. We should thank God for being alive."

"If we'd of bombed them twenty years ago, we wouldn't be in this spot now. Didn't I say way back then that we should have bombed them?"

"Yes, darling. But there's no use crying over spilt milk. Try and look on the bright side, like I do."

"Goddamn dirty reds."

The bourbon was all gone. It was dark, and outside, across the square, a billboard advertising Olympic Bleue cigarettes (*C'est mieux!*) winked on and off, as it had on all other nights of their visit to Casablanca. Nothing here seemed to have been affected by the momentous events across the ocean.

"We're out of envelopes," Mrs. Richmond complained. She had been trying to compose a letter to her daughter.

Fred was staring out the window, wondering what it had been like: had the sky been filled with planes? Were they still fighting on the ground in India and Angola? What did Florida look like now? He had always wanted to build a bomb shelter in their back yard in Florida, but his wife had been against it. Now it would be impossible to know which of them had been right.

"What time is it?" Mrs. Richmond asked, winding the alarm.

He looked at his watch, which was always right. "Eleven o'clock, Bulova watch time." It was an Accutron that his company, Iowa Mutual Life, had presented to him at retirement.

There was, in the direction of the waterfront, a din of shouting and clashing metal. As it grew louder, Fred could see the head of a ragged parade advancing up the boulevard. He pulled down the lath shutters over the windows till there was just a narrow slit to watch the parade through.

"They're burning something," he informed his wife. "Come see."

"I don't want to watch that sort of thing."

"Some kind of statue, or scarecrow. You can't tell who it's meant to be. Someone in a cowboy hat, looks like. I'll bet they're Commies."

When the mob of demonstrators reached the square over which the Belmonte Hotel looked, they turned to the left, toward the larger luxury hotels, the Marhaba and El Mansour. They were banging cymbals together and beating drums and blowing on loud horns that sounded like bagpipes. Instead of marching in rows, they did a sort of whirling, skipping dance step. Once they'd turned the corner, Fred couldn't see any more of them.

"I'll bet every beggar in town is out there, blowing his horn," Fred said sourly. "Every goddamn watch peddler and shoe shine boy in Casablanca."

"They sound very happy," Mrs. Richmond said. Then she began crying again.

The Richmonds slept together in the same bed that evening for the first time in several months. The noise of the demonstration continued, off and on, nearer or farther away, for several hours. This too set the evening apart from other evenings, for Casablanca was usually very quiet, surprisingly so, after ten o'clock at night.

The office of the American Consul seemed to have been bombed. The front door was broken off its hinges, and Fred entered, after some reluctance, to find all the downstairs rooms empty of furniture, the carpets torn away, the moldings pried from the walls. The files of the consulate had been emptied out and the contents burned in the center of the largest room.

Slogans in Arabic had been scrawled on the walls with the ashes.

Leaving the building, he discovered a piece of typing paper nailed to the deranged door. It read: "All Americans in Morocco, whether of tourist or resident status, are advised to leave the country until the present crisis is over. The Consul cannot guarantee the safety of those who choose to remain."

A shoe shine boy, his diseased scalp inadequately concealed by a dirty wool cap, tried to slip his box under Fred's foot.

"Go away, you! *Vamoose!* This is your fault. I know what happened last night. You and your kind did this. Red beggars!"

The boy smiled uncertainly at Fred and tried again to get his shoe on the box. *"Monsieur, monsieur,"* he hissed—or, perhaps, *"Merci, merci."*

By noonday the center of the town was aswarm with Americans. Fred hadn't realized there had been so many in Casablanca. What were they doing here? Where had they kept themselves hidden? Most of the Americans were on their way to the airport, their cars piled high with luggage. Some said they were bound for England, others for Germany. Spain, they claimed, wouldn't be safe, though it was probably safer than Morocco. They were brusque with Fred to the point of rudeness.

He returned to the hotel room, where Mrs. Richmond was waiting for him. They had agreed that one of them must always be in the room. As Fred went up the stairs the manager tried to hand him another bill. "I will call the police," he threatened. Fred was too angry to reply. He wanted to hit the man in the nose and stamp on his ridiculous spectacles. If he'd been five years younger he might have done so.

"They've cut off the water," Mrs. Richmond announced dramatically, after she'd admitted her husband to the room. "And the man with the red hat tried to get in, but I had the chain across the door, thank heaven. We can't wash or use the bidet. I don't know what will happen. I'm afraid."

She wouldn't listen to anything Fred said about the Consulate. "We've got to take a plane," he insisted. "To England. All the other Americans are going there. There was a sign on the door of the Con—"

"No, Fred. No, not a plane. You won't make me get into an airplane. I've gone twenty years without that, and I won't start now."

"But this is an emergency. We have to. Darling, be reasonable."

"I refuse to talk about it. And don't you shout at *me*, Fred Richmond. We'll sail when the boat sails, and that's that! Now, let's be practical, shall we? The first thing that we have to do is for you to go out and buy some bottled water. Four bottles, and bread, and— No, you'll never remember everything. I'll write out a list."

But when Fred returned, four hours later, when it was growing dark, he had but a single bottle of soda, one loaf of hard bread, and a little box of pasteurized process cheese.

"It was all the money I had. They won't cash my checks. Not at the bank, not at the Marhaba, not anywhere." There were flecks of violet in his red, dirty face, and his voice was hoarse. He had been shouting hours long.

Mrs. Richmond used half the bottle of soda to wash off his face. Then she made sandwiches of cheese and strawberry jam, all the while maintaining a steady stream of conversation, on cheerful topics. She was afraid her husband would have a stroke.

On Thursday the twelfth, the day before their scheduled sailing, Fred went to the travel agency to find out what pier their ship had docked in. He was informed that the sailing had been canceled permanently. The ship, a Yugoslav freighter, had been in Norfolk on December 4. The agency politely refunded the price of the tickets—in American dollars.

"Couldn't you give me dirham instead?"

"But you paid in dollars, Mr. Richmond." The agent spoke with a fussy, overprecise accent that annoyed Fred more than an honest French accent. "You paid in American Express Travelers' checks."

"But I'd *rather* have dirham."

"That would be impossible."

"I'll give you one to one. How about that? One dirham for one dollar." He did not even become angry at being forced to make so unfair a suggestion. He had been through this same scene too many times—at banks, at stores, with people off the street.

"The government has forbidden us to trade in American money, Mr. Richmond. I am truly sorry that I cannot help you. If you would be interested to purchase an airplane ticket, however, I can accept money for that. If you have enough."

"You don't leave much choice, do you?" (He thought: *She will be furious.*) "What will it cost for two tickets to London?"

The agent named a price. Fred flared up. "That's highway robbery. Why, that's more than the first-class to New York City!"

The agent smiled. "We have no flights scheduled to New York, sir."

Grimly, Fred signed away his travelers' checks to pay for the tickets. It took all his checks and all but fifty dollars of the refunded money. His wife, however, had her own bundle of American Express checks that hadn't even been touched yet. He examined the tickets, which were printed in French. "What does this say here? When does it leave?"

"On the fourteenth. Saturday. At eight in the evening."

"You don't have anything tomorrow?"

"I'm sorry. You should be quite happy that we can sell you these tickets. If it weren't for the fact that our main office is in Paris, and that they've directed that Americans be given priority on all Pan Am flights, we wouldn't be able to."

"I see. The thing is this—I'm in rather a tight spot. Nobody, not even the banks, will take American money. This is our last night at the hotel, and if we have to stay over Friday night as well. . . ."

"You might go to the airport waiting room, sir."

Fred took off his Accutron wrist watch. "In America this watch would cost $120 wholesale. You wouldn't be interested. . . ."

"I'm sorry, Mr. Richmond. I have a watch of my own."

Fred, with the tickets securely tucked into his passport case, went out through the thick glass door. He would have liked to have a sundae at the ice-cream parlor across the street, but he couldn't afford it. He couldn't afford anything unless he was able to sell his watch. They had lived the last week out of what he'd got for the alarm clock and the electric shaver. Now there was nothing left.

When Fred was at the corner, he heard someone calling his name. "Mr. Richmond. Mr. Richmond, sir." It was the agent. Shyly he held out a ten dirham note and three fives. Fred took the money and handed him the watch. The agent put Fred's Accutron on his wrist beside his old watch. He smiled and offered Fred his hand to shake. Fred walked away, ignoring the outstretched hand.

Five dollars, he thought over and over again, *five dollars.* He was too ashamed to return at once to the hotel.

Mrs. Richmond wasn't in the room. Instead the man in the red fez was engaged in packing all their clothes and toilet articles into the three suitcases. "Hey!" Fred shouted. "What do you think you're doing? Stop that!"

"You must pay your bill," the hotel manager, who stood back at a safe distance in the hallway, shrilled at him. "You must pay your bill or leave."

Fred tried to prevent the man in the red fez from packing the bags. He was furious with his wife for having gone off—to the W.C. probably—and left the hotel room unguarded.

"Where is my wife?" he demanded of the manager. "This is an outrage." He began to swear. The man in the red fez returned to packing the bags.

Fred made a determined effort to calm himself. He could not risk a stroke. After all, he reasoned with himself, whether they spent one or two nights in the airport waiting room wouldn't make that much difference. So he chased the man in the red fez away and finished the packing himself. When he was done, he rang for the porter, and the man in the red fez returned and helped him carry the bags downstairs. He waited in the dark lobby for his wife to return, using the largest of the suitcases for a stool. She had probably gone to "their" restaurant, some blocks away, where they were still allowed to use the W.C. The owner of the restaurant couldn't understand why they didn't take their meals there any more and didn't want to offend them, hoping, perhaps, that they would come back.

While he waited, Fred occupied the time by trying to remember the name of the Englishman who had been a supper guest at their house in Florida three years before. It was a strange name that was not pronounced at all the way that it was spelled. At intervals he would go out into the street to try and catch a sight of his wife returning to the hotel. Whenever he tried to ask the manager where she had gone, the man would renew his shrill complaint. Fred became desperate. She was taking altogether too long. He telephoned the restaurant. The owner of the restaurant understood enough English to be able to tell him that she had not visited his W.C. all that day.

An hour or so after sunset, Fred found his way to the police station, a wretched stucco building inside the ancient medina, the non-European quarter. Americans were advised not to venture into the medina after dark.

"My wife is missing," he told one of the gray-uniformed men. "I think she may be the victim of a robbery."

The policeman replied brusquely in French.

"My wife," Fred repeated loudly, gesturing in a vague way.

The policeman turned to speak to his fellows. It was a piece of deliberate rudeness.

Fred took out his passport and waved it in the policeman's face. "This is my passport," he shouted. "My wife is missing. Doesn't somebody here speak English? Somebody *must* speak English. *Ing-lish!*"

The policeman shrugged and handed Fred back his passport.

"My wife!" Fred screamed hysterically. "Listen to me—my wife, my wife, my wife!"

The policeman, a scrawny, mustached man, grabbed Fred by the neck of his coat and led him forcibly into another room and down a long, unlighted corridor that smelled of urine. Fred didn't realize, until he had been thrust into the room, that it was a cell. The door that closed behind him was made not of bars, but of sheet metal nailed over wood. There was no light in the room, no air. He screamed, he kicked at the door and pounded on it with his fists until he had cut a deep gash into the side of his palm. He stopped, to suck the blood, fearful of blood poisoning.

He could, when his eyes had adjusted to the darkness, see a little of the room about him. It was not much larger than Room 216 at the Belmonte, but it contained more people than Fred could count. They were heaped all along the walls, an indiscriminate tumble of rags and filth, old men and young men, a wretched assembly.

They stared at the American gentleman in astonishment.

The police released Fred in the morning, and he returned at once to the hotel, speaking to no one. He was angry but, even more, he was terrified.

His wife had not returned. The three suitcases, for a wonder, were still sitting where he had left them. The manager insisted that he leave the lobby, and Fred did not protest. The Richmonds' time at the hotel had expired, and Fred didn't have the money for another night, even at the old rate.

Outside, he did not know what to do. He stood on the

curbside, trying to decide. His pants were wrinkled, and he feared (though he could not smell it himself) that he stank of the prison cell.

The traffic policeman in the center of the square began giving him funny looks. He was afraid of the policeman, afraid of being returned to the cell. He hailed a taxi and directed the driver to go to the airport.

"Ou?" the driver asked.

"The airport, the airport," he said testily. Cabbies, at least, could be expected to know English.

But where was his wife? Where was Betty?

When they arrived at the airport, the driver demanded fifteen dirhams, which was an outrageous price in Casablanca, where cabs are pleasantly cheap. Having not had the foresight to negotiate the price in advance, Fred had no choice but to pay the man what he asked.

The waiting room was filled with people, though few seemed to be Americans. The stench of the close air was almost as bad as it had been in the cell. There were no porters, and he could not move through the crowd, so he set the suitcases down just outside the entrance and seated himself on the largest bag.

A man in an olive-drab uniform with a black beret asked, in French, to see his passport. *"Votre passeport,"* he repeated patiently, until Fred had understood. He examined each page with a great show of suspicion, but eventually he handed it back.

"Do you speak English?" Fred asked him then. He thought, because of the different uniform, that he might not be one of the city police. He answered with a stream of coarse Arabic gabbling.

Perhaps, Fred told himself, *she will come out here to look for me.* But why, after all, should she? He should have remained outside the hotel.

He imagined himself safely in England, telling his story to the American Consul there. He imagined the international repercussions it would have. What had been the name of that Englishman he knew? He had lived in London. It began with *C* or *Ch.*

An attractive middle-aged woman sat down on the other end of his suitcase and began speaking in rapid French, making quick gestures, like karate chops, with her well-groomed hand. She was trying to explain something to him, but of course he couldn't understand her. She broke into tears. Fred couldn't even offer her his handkerchief, because it was dirty from last night.

"My wife," he tried to explain. "My—wife—is missing. My wife."

"Bee-yay," the woman said despairingly. "Vote bee-yay." She showed him a handful of dirham notes in large denominations.

"I wish I could understand what it is you want," he said.

She went away from him, as though she were angry, as though he had said something to insult her.

Fred felt someone tugging at his shoe. He remembered, with a start of terror, waking in the cell, the old man tugging at his shoes, trying to steal them but not understanding, apparently, about the laces.

It was only, after all, a shoe shine boy. He had already begun to brush Fred's shoes, which were, he could see, rather dirty. He pushed the boy away.

He had to go back to the hotel to see if his wife had returned there, but he hadn't the money for another taxi and there was no one in the waiting room that he dared trust with the bags.

Yet he couldn't leave Casablanca without his wife. Could he? But if he did stay, what was he to do, if the police would not listen to him?

At about ten o'clock the waiting room grew quiet. All that day no planes had entered or left the airfield. Everyone here was waiting for tomorrow's plane to London. How were so many people, and so much luggage, to fit on one plane, even the largest jet? Did they all have tickets?

They slept anywhere, on the hard benches, on newspapers on the concrete floor, on the narrow window ledges. Fred was one of the luckiest, because he could sleep on his three suitcases.

When he woke the next morning, he found that his passport and the two tickets had been stolen from his breast pocket. He still had his billfold, because he had slept on his back. It contained nine dirham.

Christmas morning, Fred went out and treated himself to an ice-cream sundae. Nobody seemed to be celebrating the holiday in Casablanca. Most of the shops in the ancient medina (where Fred had found a hotel room for three dirham a day) were open for business, while in the European quarter one couldn't tell if the stores were closed permanently or just for the day.

Going past the Belmonte, Fred stopped, as was his custom, to ask after his wife. The manager was very polite and said that nothing was known of Mrs. Richmond. The police had her description now.

Hoping to delay the moment when he sat down before the sundae, he walked to the post office and asked if there had been any answer to his telegram to the American Embassy in London. There had not.

When at last he did have his sundae it didn't seem quite as good as he had remembered. There was so little of it! He sat down for an hour with his empty dish, watching the drizzling rain. He was alone in the ice-cream parlor. The windows of the travel agency across the street were covered up by a heavy metal shutter, from which the yellow paint was flaking.

The waiter came and sat down at Fred's table. *"Il pleut, Monsieur Richmon. It rains. Il pleut."*

"Yes, it does," said Fred. "It rains. It falls. Fall-out."

But the waiter had very little English. "Merry Christmas," he said. *"Joyeux Noël.* Merry Christmas."

Fred agreed.

When the drizzle had cleared a bit, Fred strolled to the United Nations Plaza and found a bench, under a palm tree, that was dry. Despite the cold and damp, he didn't want to return to his cramped hotel room and spend the rest of the day sitting on the edge of his bed.

Fred was by no means alone in the plaza. A number of figures in heavy woolen djelabas, with hoods over their heads, stood or sat on benches, or strolled in circles on the gravel paths. The djelabas made ideal raincoats . . . Fred had sold his own London Fog three days before for twenty dirham. He was getting better prices for his things now that he had learned to count in French.

The hardest lesson to learn (and he had not yet learned it) was to keep from thinking. When he could do that, he wouldn't become angry, or afraid.

At noon the whistle blew in the handsome tower at the end of the plaza, from the top of which one could see all of Casablanca in every direction. Fred took out the cheese sandwich from the pocket of his suit coat and ate it, a little bit at a time. Then he took out the chocolate bar with almonds. His mouth began to water.

A shoe shine boy scampered across the graveled circle and sat down in the damp at Fred's feet. He tried to lift Fred's foot and place it on his box.

"No," said Fred. "Go away."

"Monsieur, monsieur," the boy insisted. Or, perhaps, *"Merci, merci."*

Fred looked down guiltily at his shoes. They were very dirty. He hadn't had them shined in weeks.

The boy kept whistling those meaningless words at him. His gaze was fixed on Fred's chocolate bar. Fred pushed him away with the side of his foot. The boy grabbed for the candy. Fred struck him on the side of his head. The chocolate bar fell to the ground, not far from the boy's callused feet. The boy lay on his side, whimpering.

"You little sneak!" Fred shouted at him.

It was a clear-cut case of thievery. He was furious. He had a right to be furious. Standing up to his full height, his foot came down accidentally on the boy's rubbishy shoe shine box. The wood splintered.

The boy began to gabble at Fred in Arabic. He scurried forward on hands and knees to pick up the pieces of the box.

"You asked for this," Fred said. He kicked the boy in the ribs. The boy rolled with the blow, as though he were not unused to such treatment. "Little beggar! Thief!" Fred screamed.

He bent forward and tried to grasp a handhold in the boy's hair, but it was cut too close to his head, to prevent lice. Fred hit him again in the face, but now the boy was on his feet and running.

There was no use pursuing him, he was too fast, too fast.

Fred's face was violet and red, and his white hair, in need of a trim, straggled down over his flushed forehead. He had not noticed, while he was beating the boy, the group of Arabs, or Moslems, or whatever they were, that had gathered around him to watch. Fred could not read the expressions on their dark, wrinkly faces.

"Did you see that?" he asked loudly. "Did you see what that little thief tried to do? Did you see him try to steal ... my candy bar?"

One of the men, in a long djelaba striped with brown, said something to Fred that sounded like so much gargling. Another, younger man, in European dress, struck Fred in the face. Fred teetered backward.

"Now see here!" He had no time to tell them he was an American citizen. The next blow caught him in the mouth, and he fell to the ground. Once he was lying on his back, the older men joined in in kicking him. Some kicked him in the ribs, others in his head, still others had to content themselves with his legs. Curiously, nobody went for his groin. The shoe shine boy watched from a distance, and when Fred was unconscious, came forward and removed his shoes. The young man who had first hit him removed his suit coat and his belt. Wisely, Fred had left his billfold behind at his hotel.

When he woke he was sitting on the bench again. A policeman was addressing him in Arabic. Fred shook his head uncomprehendingly. His back hurt dreadfully, from when he had fallen to the ground. The policeman addressed him in French. He shivered. Their kicks had not damaged him so much as he had expected. Except for the young man, they had worn slippers instead of shoes. His face experienced only a dull ache, but there was blood all down the front of his shirt, and his mouth tasted of blood. He was cold, very cold.

The policeman went away, shaking his head.

At just that moment Fred remembered the name of the Englishman who had had supper in his house in Florida. It was Cholmondeley, and it was pronounced *Chum-ly*. He was still unable to remember his London address.

Only when he tried to stand did he realize that his shoes were gone. The gravel hurt the tender soles of his bare feet. Fred was mortally certain that the shoe shine boy had stolen his shoes.

He sat back down on the bench with a groan. He hoped to hell he'd hurt the goddamn little son of a bitch. He hoped to hell he had. He grated his teeth together, wishing that he could get hold of him again. The little beggar. He'd kick him this time so that he'd remember it. The goddamn dirty little red beggar. He'd kick his face in.

THE DOOMSDAY MACHINE

AN ALTERNATE NEWS SERVICE

1. Silver Linings

Brute survival, important as we've all found it can be, hasn't been the only high point of the Bicentennial Year just past. Here are a few of the new ways and means inspired by the Spirit of '76:

1. THE ARTHUR FROMMER
$5-a-Day Diet
Believe it or not, a large minority of adult Americans —45%—are still hauling around superfluous pounds. The Frommer diet, strictly observed, is a guaranteed solution to this problem. The rules are easy: eat everything you want, anywhere you can get it, so long as you don't spend over five dollars a day. However, dieters in the Southwest, who must pay high prices for drinking water, are urged not to include the cost of water in their daily five dollars, since there is a real danger, in their case, of malnutrition.

2. COUNTING OUR BLESSINGS
Everybody's favorite dog food was a big hit at the White House on Thanksgiving Day '76 when the First Lady set a fine example in trimming fat from the American life style. Her dinner for six hundred orphans featured twelve black

Labradors stuffed with Alpo. Her young guests, hailing from every State of the Union, had all been orphaned as a result of the unfortunate upheavals throughout the country earlier in the year. Truly, the winds of reconciliation are blowing!

3. GUESS THE FLAVOR

What's in the new party dip that's sweeping the nation? What's the secret additive that can change an everyday Gallo Burgundy into a mellow St. Emilion? What transforms $3 per ounce liverwurst into prime *pâté de foie gras*? Could it possibly be anything so simple and economical as . . . fish food?

Of course, for purely logical reasons (and because mayfly eggs *can* hatch in your stomach) we can't say right out that it *is*, but here's a little recipe anyhow: To one cup of water add a pinch of you-know-what, an Alka Seltzer, and saccharine. The result: your own bubbly glass of diet Dr. Pepper—at a fraction of the cost!

4. RAGS

The *dernier cri* among tonight's beautiful people is pajamas. Starched for the *soigné,* rumpled for the funky. If the boss objects to your wearing them in the office, point out what Levis cost and ask for a raise. Alternately, you might come in the next day in a loin cloth. (They do in San Francisco ad agencies already.) Still more alternately, learn *origami.* A copy of yesterday's *Times* costs $2.00 at most recycling centers and can be made to last a couple weeks if you keep out of showers.

5. SURVIVAL SKILLS

Adult education has moved with the times, and the trend has definitely been away from the useless humanities and towards barterable skills such as Breath Restraint, Pigeon Trapping, and Shoe Repair.

6. SILENCE

Definitely the last exit on the highway of modern art. Audiences get together and sit in complete silence. This, silencists maintain, is what audiences have always done. The difference is that today's more sophisticated audience can dispense with the pretext (and expense) of a performance. The biggest silence so far was on July 4, 1976, when 11,580 fans filled Madison Square Garden for a silence that lasted twelve and a half hours!

7. SLEEP

If your basic problem is how to get from one day to the next, this may be the answer, especially if you're one of the lucky ones who's immune to nightmares. For the rest of us, we'll just have to muddle through the midnight hours and hope the government's research into dream suppressants pays off soon.

8. BE HAPPY, GET MORE MORE

People may have had to give up their cars this year, at least as means of transportation, but thanks to the timely intervention of the government there's still something to see on television. This is not the moment, while we're concentrating on the bright side, to try and account for the fact (ironic or catastrophic, depending on your point of view) that consumers were buying products in inverse proportions to the advertising they'd seen promoting those products. Callow, uncaring cynicism may have had something to do with it, as the President suggested, but mostly, of course, consumers simply weren't consuming, just as producers weren't producing and workers weren't working.

But that's all economics and not much fun—and there was, in this case, a happy ending. First, the ad agencies had to make a realistic choice: either 1) they could try to write more obnoxious ads for rival accounts than their own agencies had come up with; or 2) give up media advertising altogether and use their budgets to print discount coupons (which were then rapidly displacing metal coins in many cities). But if there was no advertising, the networks would have no source of income—and then even the best ratings wouldn't keep a show on the air. And there would be *nothing* to look at! It was at this point that the federal government stepped in with a massive program of public service advertising, financed by a 15% surcharge on all brand name products. Carefully avoiding controversial or partisan content, the government ads promoted a general, uncritical optimism and faith in the system. The most successful of the government's 60-second spots, and the winner of an Emmy in the "Happiest Song" category, was "Let the Rain Be Your Umbrella." Why don't we all sing it right now?

2. Misinformation:
Defending a Precious Heritage

Naturally, one of the further consequences of these turmoils was an end to tourism in Europe and the Middle East. Only those whose livelihoods depended on foreign travel, such as spies or the representatives of munitions makers, continued to risk a North Atlantic crossing.

Consumer demand for safe, exotic experiences continued undiminished, however, and where demands exist, businesses soon arise to meet them. The Safe-Way Travel Corporation was formed in 1986, and in a very short time it was the giant of the tourist industry, a position it maintained throughout the decade that followed.

What Safe-Way offered its customers was the sensation of travel without any associated risk. Safe-Way travelers never penetrated beyond the Corporation's much-advertised *Cordon Sanitaire*. They ate only at Safe-Way franchised restaurants and slept in Safe-Way Holiday Spas. Everyone with whom they had to deal—waiters, bellhops, tour-guides, or bus drivers—spoke fluent English, and indeed most were Americans. It was the proud claim of the Corporation that their travelers never saw a foreigner except through a quarter-inch thickness of glass.

Safe-Way's heyday came to an end on the morning of February 24, 1997, when three jumbo jets that had taken off the previous December on the popular $12,500 "Round the World in 80 Days" package tour failed to reappear at the Disney World airport. Day followed day without word from the planes or their eleven hundred passengers. The protests of anxious relatives escalated into mass demonstrations throughout the nation, but Safe-Way's only response was the apparently sincere suggestion that the planes had somehow vanished while in flight over the Bermuda Triangle. This, in a period of uninterrupted fair weather throughout the Caribbean.

Lacking any better explanation, the Corporation's hypothesis might eventually have been accepted, but then on March 18, as speculation over the fate of the missing passengers was beginning to be squeezed from the newspapers by new crimes and disasters, one of the missing planes made an unscheduled landing at Kennedy Airport. The plane's single passenger— feisty Rebecca Paley, the 64-year-old owner of a maternity boutique in Scranton, Pennsylvania—disembarked and told her amazing tale to the waiting television cameras.

For the first two months the tour had been conducted exactly as it was outlined in the prospectus. However, upon their arrival at the Calcutta World's Fair, everything seemed to go wrong at once. The Lipton's Curry Delight Restaurant, where they were to have lunched, was staffed by only three waitresses, and one of these concealed an unseemly bandaged arm under her sari. The Lotus Blossom Inn, to which they were ferried after the merest semblance of a meal, seemed not to be staffed at all. When her traveling companions claimed to hear gunshots outside the shuttered-steel doors of the Inn, Mrs. Paley tried to investigate, but she found even the fire exits sealed. At first she was alarmed, but when, looking out the windows of her room, she found the city looking peaceful and engaged upon its usual day-to-day tasks, her fears diminished. She took a Sominex tablet and went to bed.

The next day the passengers went in sealed buses to the grounds of the fair. Their first show was a demonstration at the Chile Pavillion of police interrogation techniques. In the course of the second interrogation, an unruly crowd of blacks, armed with guns, knives and clubs, appeared on the floor of the operating theater, overwhelmed the interrogators, and shattered the protective glass from behind which the tourists had watched this unscheduled spectacle aghast. The marauding blacks began to massacre the panicky tourists. Mrs. Paley, having the good fortune to be black herself, was able to escape, but she had to endure many days of confused wandering and constant terror before the nature of her predicament became clear to her: she was not in Calcutta at all!

All the foreign cities that Safe-Way tours traveled to, and even the vehicles in which they traveled, were simulations. Some, such as the view from the hotel's windows, were holographic action-screens. Others, including the Corporation's facilities, had been constructed from the ground up, with the help of friendly governments in South America and the Caribbean. The Calcutta simulation, for instance, was actually located on the north coast of the Dominican Republic, and it had been *here,* not in Calcutta at all, that the World's Fair had been constructed. (The most elaborate simulation of all—a second Rio de Janiero built only fifty miles from its original—had yet to be opened when these revelations hit the press.)

Had it not been for an insurrection among disaffected elements of the Dominican Republic, loyal to President Bu's nephew, Safe-Way's vast impostures might never have been discovered. It was these dissidents who had broken into the Safe-Way precincts. Though eventually they were driven back by Bu's troops, they were able to seize many hostages from among the bewildered tourists. Many others were left dying and wounded in the Chile Pavillion. These were taken back on foot to the Lotus Blossom (the infamous Three Mile Walk), where they were held in protective custody while the directors of Safe-Way conferred with Bu as to how the situation should be dealt with. Bu wanted to send the planes off with time-bombs planted in them, but the Safe-Way executives resisted this solution—until it was too late. Thanks to Mrs. Paley's providential hijacking, the lives of her thousand fellow-passengers (a hundred had died in the Pavillion or on the Walk) were saved.

The U.S. Department of Consumer Affairs brought suit against the Safe-Way Travel Corporation for fraudulent advertising. That the Department's case was finally rejected by the Supreme Court must be ascribed to the counter-suit brought by Dr. Raymond Newbold, a dentist of Providence, Rhode Island. Dr. Newbold's campaign against consumer protection laws was immensely popular among all classes and conditions of men, and the arguments of his attorneys became a landmark of American jurisprudence. In brief, they may be summarized as follows:

Most consumers are conscious of the frauds practiced against them, and indeed cooperate actively in their deception. In the case of the Safe-Way tours, it was shown that 64% of those who had flown to "foreign countries" had suspected they were being offered simulations, but all were unanimous in claiming that they *preferred* this experience to the hazards of traveling to the countries simulated. Suppression of so-called "consumer frauds" was actually a violation of man's inalienable right to pursue happiness, an activity which traditionally entails a high degree of self-deception. Social institutions, they concluded, must be allowed to help men deceive themselves according to their own lights.

3. Selbstmord: the Dernier Cri

The first instance of suicide as a fad, as distinct from suicides of convenience and literary suicide, took place in 1986 at the venerable Protestant Theological Seminary in Tübingen. In October of that year, young Ranier Markheim, in a stolen nun's habit weighted with three brass candlesticks, drowned himself in the river Neckar, leaving behind a note that said, simply, "Stop laughing at me, Jesus!" While Ranier's *Selbstmord**** may fairly be adjudged the act of an unbalanced mind, not so those that followed, as, one after another, seventeen of Ranier's classmates signed their names, so to speak, to his petition, all before the commencement of the Christmas holidays. Each left a note remarkable for its triviality or unlikeliness. Karlheinz Gartner claimed to be dismayed by the odor of his roommate's after-shave lotion. Klaus Herzeleide wrote: "I can't take another moment of Organic Chemistry." Stefan Lerchenau, the last of the seventeen, complained with some bitterness that Germans, as a race, lacked a sense of humor.

Naturally, the antics of the young seminarians received attention in the world's press, but it was not until March of the next year, with the release of MGM's $38 million musical, *The Sorrows of Young Werther,* that the epidemic spread beyond the picturesque medieval walls of Tubingen. For most of its length, this film was a fairly conventional re-telling of Goethe's famed novella, transposed from 18th-century Germany to modern-day South Africa, with rock songs adapted

---

*German students of this phenomenon insist that a distinction should be drawn between the more philosophically oriented Selbstmord *and the less serious, Latin-derived "suicide."*

from Massenet's opera. Boer rock star Penrod Terbrugen played Werther, and Barbra Streisand was Charlotte. It's hard to imagine the impact of *Sorrows* on the audiences that flocked to it, since only a few minutes have survived the efforts of various governments to destroy all prints. Most of the footage still extant is of the remarkable Veldt Dream-Ballet performed by Streisand and eight lions, whose "dances" were a kind of behavioralist puppet-show induced by electrodes implanted in the lions' brains. Of Terbrugen's performance, only thirty-eight frames survive, not long enough for the tear glistening in the corner of his eye to begin to roll down his cheek. The fifteen-minute death scene, incorporating the notorious laughing song, can be heard (by qualified scholars) at the Morgan Library. (These illegal recordings were made on cassettes by young suicides, who wanted to die, like their idol, as the last strains of the laughing song faded away.) To a modern taste, the Terbrugen recordings are likely to seem only a minor example of '80s *Klutzheit*. They died for *this*? But surely what was at issue was the fact that Terbrugen, in the role of Werther, did kill himself. Thus, however bathetic he may seem as an artist, his *authenticity* can't be questioned.

Wherever in Europe and America *The Sorrows of Young Werther* was exhibited, the consequence was a rash of emulative suicides, all undertaken (by their own and their friends' accounts) in a spirit of unconstrained good humor. As with other fads, there were those who tried to find deeper significance in the actions of the young. Some ascribed it to the influence of Husserl, then at the height of his popularity; others to the use of sodium nitrite in bacon and sausages. Many priests publicly took the blame upon themselves for having failed as shepherds to their flocks. Politicians blamed the press. But the suicides themselves refused to be interpreted. "The reasons we're killing ourselves," explained twelve-year-old Cynthia Smith, after an abortive attempt at hari-kari, "is just 'cause that's what kids are doing nowadays. I don't see what all the fuss is about. Grown-ups kill themselves all the time. Why can't we?"

Shortly before alarmed governments began to crack down on overt expressions of pessimism, black humor and low spirits, Random House published the provocative collection of suicide notes, *Letters to a Cruel World*, edited by A. Alvarez. In his introduction, Alvarez theorized that the craze for suicide represented (1) a basic, if frequently unconscious, loss of faith in the viability of any future whatsoever, and (2) the suicides' unexpressed conviction that they worked like television sets, with simple On and Off controls. (Statistically, there was a strong correlation between suicide and prime evening viewing.)

As with most fads, suicide was quickly commercialized. Every week gave rise to a new button or bumper sticker, and by the first anniversary of Ranier Markheim's death there were already three movies in production based on the death of Thomas Chatterton, as well as others dealing with Sylvia Plath, Marilyn Monroe, Seneca, The Tübingen Seventeen, and the San Clemente Seven. A short-lived magazine sprang up catering especially to suicides: *Blast Off* ran a contest for Suicide Note of the Month in various categories (religion, politics, world catastrophe, general anxiety, uncertainty, free verse, and sonnets), which only successful suicides could enter. *Blast Off* offered less ambitious readers readymade suicide notes, which they could clip out, in lieu of writing their own. The most popular of these (with total returns of 8,560) was the following:

I think life is rotten. No one cares. We're all just looking out for Number One. I can't believe in anything. I feel empty inside.

(signed)

Suicide continued to be popular for more than two years, but at last the public seemed to have supped full of horrors, and all but the silliest or most appalling acts of self-destruction went unremarked in the press. Increasingly, as older age groups took up the youthful pastime, the young abandoned it, and since older people always have good *reasons* for killing themselves, it is doubtful if suicide continued to mean the same thing.

A good illustration of this process is the suicide of Norman Mailer, a novelist turned psychic healer, who, having cured the King of Sweden of a chronic edema, was awarded the Nobel Prize for Medicine. Before making his acceptance speech at the award ceremony, Mailer took a timed-release cyanide capsule and then talked for two hours, explaining his motives (to show young people what their deaths had really been *about*) and comparing his suicide to Ernest Hemingway's. The *New York Times* accorded him only two and a half column-inches on its obituary page, and his Nobel Prize Acceptance Speech (with photographs by Richard Avedon) sold less than a thousand copies, even after being remaindered. For suicide it was the beginning of the end.

4. Killing the Cars

In the following year the Terror which gives that decade its name took a new and to many people still more dismaying turn: the pedestrians, tiring of passive protests, began to attack the cars. Previously there had been some legislative efforts to curb the proliferation of the automobile, but these had been no more successful than the corresponding efforts, in this same period, to check the growth rate of the pedestrians themselves. Gasoline and automobile advertising were banned from television in the seven radically pedestrian states, until the Supreme Court, in the case of Babcock Moto-Rama *vs.* the State of Vermont, overturned the so-called Red Light Laws in a 6-3 decision.

Though the Court's decision was roundly denounced by leading pedestrians, the vast majority of Americans either welcomed it or professed indifference. A poll of May 15 showed that only 12.7% of the population were "uncertain," while a mere 5.3% wanted the private automobile restricted or banned. Had it not been for Mrs. Emerson's unfortunate baby buggy, it seems likely, therefore, that the manifestations of July and August would never have taken place.

It must be borne in mind that the President's surname was the same as that of a popular brand of automobile, and further that the previous President was believed to have been a used car dealer. (On what basis, historians have never known, due to the destruction of the library most likely to have provided this information.) The power of the Presidency and of the automobile were thus, in the popular mind, virtually identical. When the President's limousine crushed little Linda Emerson before an estimated television audience of forty million viewers, the rock that shattered its window had repercussions that were immediate and world-wide. It is estimated that within twenty-four hours no less than eighty thousand Fords and thirty thousand Lincolns were totalled. The President's apology seemed only to fan the flames.

In the next three weeks fourteen million cars were assaulted, half of these beyond repair. Contrary to the sensational image of telephones and typewriters hurtling from the high windows of office buildings upon cavalcades of desperate, speeding cars, most automobiles were attacked while they were parked and unattended. Relatively few drivers were injured, except those foolish enough to defy the pedestrians' ungovernable rage.

No car was safe. A private garage was as dangerous as a parking ramp. Even when that garage might be secured against outsiders, it often happened that pedestrian wives and children would quietly dismantle and demolish their own family car! Only in those suburbs where drivers banded together to form Automotive Defense Leagues was there even a sporting chance, though these Leagues could also act as a natural magnet to attract the more ardent pedestrians. The Winnetka Massacre was the most dramatic and the most tragic of these engagements. Like the religious antagonisms of 16th and 17th Century Europe, these civil dissensions rendered all other ties and allegiances nugatory, polarizing society into two contending armies of drivers and pedestrians.

Seven million! How was it possible? one asks. Where were the police, the Army, the National Guard? Almost without exception the civil authorities were in hiding or exclusively occupied with protecting their own vehicles, while the Army and National Guard, due to the heterogeneous composition of both forces, all too often were caught up in the very madness they had been called on to combat. (Just so, in 19th century America firemen found more exhilaration in lighting fires than in fighting them.)

The standard car of that period was exceedingly vulnerable. A five-year-old child with a hammer and a knife could render an eight-cylinder car inoperative in minutes. With matches and a bit of cord he could blow it up, using its own fuel-tank as explosive. Most structures built to accommodate them were indefensible, and more secure edifices, such as churches, prisons, schools and banks, could not readily be converted into garages. In most cities only those cars with the good fortune to be parked underground escaped the holocaust.

A nation-wide curfew was declared, but went largely unheeded. Unheeded, too, were the pleas of Ralph Nader and other celebrities known to be sympathetic to the pedestrians' cause. The mob raged on, storming garages, mining the expressways, directing an endless stream of traffic out onto the wharves and piers of both seacoasts, and of all lakes and rivers, from which they were forced, with or without their drivers, by the relentless pressure of cars behind them. The task of salvage continues to this day in the harbors of Seattle, Boston, and New York.

Amid such disorders what social institution could long maintain its everyday routines? Though larger vehicles were seldom attacked, unless they sought to protect their littler brethren, the destruction of so many highways and the blockage of virtually all urban streets by mounds of wreckage choked the usual channels of distribution and communication, bringing commercial life, literally, to a standstill. A desperate population turned its attention from gratuitous terror to a struggle for survival no less violent. Grocery stores were looted. Armies marched against warehouses, which were defended, as often as not, by armies of more foresighted citizens.

It was against this background of wearying anarchy that we must place the President's momentous address of August 6. Within three weeks what the President had proposed Congress and the States had ratified. The XXXVIth Amendment became law, and all U.S. automobiles were recognized as human beings.

When it was known that their crimes would no longer be leniently regarded as directed against property but rather as against life, a new caution replaced the almost holiday spirit of the "wrecking parties," and this caution grew in time to calmness and conscious respect. All pedestrians were not at once pacified, but the tide had turned. Roads were cleared, and though it would be many months before traffic returned to an optimum density, a few private cars did venture forth from their hiding places—and survived.

The real interest of the succeeding years, from our point of view, lies not so much in the murder trials of diehard pedestrians and their subsequent, often controversial execu-

tions, as in the less dramatic series of decisions by which the
latent consequences of the XXXVIth Amendment were made
manifest. The present system by which a car is adopted into
its owner's family, though obviously deriving quite naturally
from the wording of the new law, was not accepted without
much acrimonious debate. The right of cars to own and to
inherit property was challenged repeatedly. The laws govern-
ing both life insurance and automobile insurance had to be
wholly rewritten. The innate right of automobiles to adequate
maintenance was recognized, but not without the fierce opposition of the lobbies of used car dealers, whose former
business practices had been to line their own pockets rather
than their cars' brakes.

Detroit responded to the new legislation with new models
that (sometimes coarsely perhaps, but with increasing daring
and ingenuity) expressed and emphasized the specifically
human character of their cars. Within only seven years from
the accident that had taken the life of little Linda Emerson,
James Colvin, an English racing driver, and Miss Skylark
Caprice, a Ford Thunderbird of New York State, were
married in Marble Collegiate Chapel. An era had ended.
Another was begun.

5. The Fair Maid of Perth Amboy

Willie Mae Rosenblatt, although known to history as the Fair
Maid of Perth Amboy, actually lived the entire span of her
brief and tragic life in Teterboro, a small industrial zone
between Hackensack and South Hackensack, some fifty miles
north of the town she has served to make so famous. Little is
known of Willie Mae's life in Teterboro except that she is
thought, on the basis of the single photograph we possess, to
have suffered from pellagra and rickets. Recent studies conducted by the Perth Amboy Rosary and Garden Club have
questioned the authenticity of the photograph and, by impli-
cation, of this tradition. Yet even if Willie Mae's diseases are
apocryphal they are not improbable: few residents of eastern
seaboard cities or suburbs at this time were likely to have
borne no scars of the Nine Years' Famine.

One thing is certain—that, like most New Jersey children, Willie Mae Rosenblatt was poor and, consequently, a vegetable girl. Unlike many others, her responsibility was neither to her family's roof and window boxes nor to the backyard commons of her block association. From the spring's sowing till the fall's harvest, Willie Mae abided on a median strip of Route 46, the special guardian of twenty-three 200-yard rows of hybrid corn, which she protected from pests and predators, from thieves and vagabonds, and chiefly, of course, from members of the Teamsters' Union.

It had been many years since convoys of diesel-powered vans had driven through the victory gardens of suburban gardeners, and the Teamsters were supposed no longer to be at odds with free enterprise gardening. Union President Colson held his press conferences in the Teamsters HQ two-acre plot of tomatoes and cucumbers, and he often spoke of his "deep regard and warm appreciation" for public gardening spokeswoman Beth Blish (despite the fact that not two years before he had been fined $2,500 for attempting to blow up her home in West Orange).

Of course, in situations like Willie Mae's, with a field exposed on two sides to Teamster-driven highways, the old animosity between gardener and truck-driver was scarcely any less intense than in the darkest days of the Famine, when the drivers tried to run school buses off the roads and snipers would pick off Teamsters as they stepped from the armored cabs. The original bone of contention—the Teamsters' claim to protect the rights of organized farm labor—had long since been lost sight of, and the feud continued on the simpler, traditional basis of wrongs remembered and revenged.

It may safely be surmised that Willie Mae's great combat began, like so many other engagements of less consequence, with one of the vans breaking from its convoy to "harvest" the rows of unripe corn in the median strip. However begun, the day ended badly for the Teamsters. Twelve-year-old Willie Mae, with sling, bow, and grenade-thrower, killed seventeen of them before she was herself crushed to death against the concrete struts of an overpass.

In the trucks that had overturned investigators discovered four tons of a new defoliant of extreme toxicity. Without this evidence, and without the testimony of one of the surviving drivers, Eddie Romano, it does not seem likely that the conspiracy (which included, besides the Teamsters, the Secretary and many high officials of the U.S. Department of Agribusiness, and twenty-eight pilots from the New Jersey Highway Patrol) would have been discovered before it had accomplished its purpose. Northwestern New Jersey, the heartland of free gardening, would have been defoliated, its harvests lost, and its citizens compelled to sign contracts with one supermarket chain or another, contracts which would forever have prohibited them from growing so much as a pot of parsley or a sprig of mint.

A monument representing an idealized Willie Mae bearing a cornucopia was erected at the scene of her death, but only five years after it was put up, the township of Teterboro was re-zoned so that it might be strip-mined for the valuable metal contained in the land-fill on which Teterboro had been built. The Perth Amboy Rosary and Garden Club bought the monument to Willie Mae and moved it to the Church of Our Lady of Pompeii in Perth Amboy, where it has long been reputed to effect miraculous cures, particularly for growers of sweet corn, butter beans, zucchini and acorn squash.

102 H-BOMBS

Twenty-seven orphans were cleaning their M-1 rifles in C-Company barracks, while the twenty-eighth read to them from the September issue of G.I. Jokes, a comic book issued by the United States Army.

"*I'll kill ya, ya skunks!*" he read, imitating as best his pre-adolescent baritone could the voice of Drillmaster Grist at a Friday night war game. "So he lobs this grenade..." (Explaining the pictures) "...into their trench. BAROOM! Up shoots that slob's head, like a Snark XVIII."

The twenty-seven orphans chuckled quietly without interrupting their work or even lifting their eyes from the gun metal to see the half-smile twisting Charlie C-Company's face. (Charlie had acquired his last name when the typist that had made out his induction papers got its wires crossed, and since Charlie didn't care particularly *what* he had for a last name he hadn't bothered to have it corrected. Nobody called him by his last name anyway.) It was not the decapitation that amused him; it was the stupidity, the stupendous stupidity, of the other C-Company orphans. His smile had actually much more to do with pain than with amusement. For stupidity riled him, and comics bored him—even when he made up the stories himself. His own stories bored him as much as the ones in the comics.

"But there's still this one Commie that ain't quite dead, and Sergeant Rock jumps down in the trench and starts to kick him. ..." He was improvising now, and Grist's nasal twang was more than ever evident in his voice.

Grist's own voice boomed out over the loudspeaker: "Okay, C-Company, cut out that laughing and polish those rifles! We've got a war to fight. And you—CC-743-22, report to the Drillmaster's Office. On the double!"

Charlie buttoned his little fatigue jacket and tucked it into his khaki pants as he raced out of the barracks and across the muddy yard of Camp Overkill. He did the required ten chin-ups at the bar before the Drillmaster's door, then, adjusting his expression to the S.O.P. mask of terrorized inexpressiveness, he knocked and came to attention before the closed door.

And stood there.

Make them worry: that was Grist's motto. Most of the cadets (the word *orphan* was out-of-bounds at Camp Overkill) could not take more than ten minutes of looking at Grist's door. Then they'd knock again—which was what Grist wanted.

But Grist wouldn't get at Charlie that easily. For one thing, the cadet knew that the knock wasn't even necessary. The chin-up bar triggered a bell on Grist's desk—which was how he always knew if you'd done ten. Grist knew that Charlie had seen through this and other of his deceits, and it aggravated the bad feelings between them—as Charlie had hoped it would. For Charlie's sole ambition since arriving at Camp Overkill had been to drive Drillmaster Grist mad. That was why, for two years, he had been C-Company's model cadet.

While he waited, Charlie imagined ways to use the chin-up bar to trigger a mine in Grist's office. He imagined Grist's head, decapitated by the force of the explosion (BAROOM!), sailing out over the Camp's parade ground. Like a Snark XVIII. But he didn't smile. He stood rigidly at attention, his face a perfect mask, ten years old.

"Enter and report," Grist barked from behind the door. It had taken a mere four minutes!

Charlie entered and came to attention before Grist's desk. The Drillmaster sat there, his thin lips clipped in a mirthless smile about a dead cigar. He was a short man. Charlie always imagined an ulcer pinned neatly into the fruit salad over Grist's breast pocket. The ulcer would match the color of his face.

"CC-743-22 reporting for duty, sir." His heels clicked. His arm locked into a salute.

"At ease, 743."

He dropped the salute and stood rigidly at ease, his eyes fixed on Grist's lean face as on a basilisk. He knew there was someone else in the room, and he also knew that outsiders often disapproved of the Camp's strenuous discipline. He became an utter robot.

"I said—*At ease!*"

"Yes sir!" He shifted his weight imperceptibly.

"This," Grist said in the cracked bass voice that suited his scant frame so ill, "is Miss Appleton. Miss Appleton is an agent of Talent-Hunt, with whom I understand you have been corresponding."

Charlie turned to the woman. She was younger than Mrs. Bunkle, the matron in charge of him at the orphanage before Overkill, and she was nicer, that was easy to see. And she wore no uniform, not even Civil Defence greys. Thinking quickly, Charlie substituted a bow for the salute he had begun.

She smiled, and her smile was not usual. "I'm very glad to meet you, Charlie. We never know what our winners are going to be like, so I was very pleased to hear from Sergeant Grist that you're an exemplary cadet and a good student."

Charlie stared at her blankly, holding his panic in check until he knew just how Grist was going to take this. Of course, he wouldn't really know that until Miss Appleton had left.

"You *have* been informed of the prize?"

"My prize?" Charlie queried.

"Of course you've been informed, boy. I informed you last week."

"I've been informed, Miss Appleton."

"He's excited. That explains it," Grist said with a smile that only Charlie would interpret as malignant.

(*Maybe,* Charlie thought, *the bar could trigger an incendiary bomb under the floorboards.*)

"Well then," said Miss Appleton brightly, "I won't have to explain how much our organization appreciated Charlie's clever little essay. Mr. Maximast, our Director, was quite impressed with the originality of the idea. And he's anxious to meet the author."

"Charlie here," Grist whispered without glancing at Miss Appleton, "is a clever little cadet. Yessirree!" Grist had never called him Charlie before, and in his mouth it sounded like a condensation of all ill will.

Charlie damned the day he'd ever seen the comic book

with the Talent-Hunt ad on the back cover. He damned
Appleton and Maximast. And he worried lest Grist would see
how happy the news had made him.

"How did you ever think of such a novel idea, Charles?"

"It just came to me." That was the God's-truth: it had
come when he was lying in bed just after lights out. He saw it
standing there, just as he had seen it in pictures in magazines,
so tall, and, miraculously untouched by the blasts that had
destroyed nearly everything else about it. It stood there,
monolithic in the midst of trees and the giant honeysuckle.

Then he saw it lift. It hung poised a few feet over the
parkland while it built up force and then rose out of sight. A
quarter-mile high, stone spaceship.

So the Talent-Hunt essay on "What I Would Do If I
Owned the Empire State Building" had been no trouble at all.
It wrote itself. The only part of it that still surprised him was
that he had dared to mail it in, but at the time it seemed that
he just had to.

Because of the first prize.

"My prize?" he asked, feeling a ghost of the courage he
had mustered the day he mailed his entry.

"Why, it's all taken care of. You tied for First, but the
prize will be just as announced. You—and your guardian—
will have a week in New York New as a guest of Talent-
Hunt. And there's the scholarship money. And naturally a
little something to cover your guardian's expenses."

Grist harumphed.

"In New York New you'll be able to meet all the *other*
clever boys and girls who won. There are a hundred and two
of them, all told. One for every floor of the Empire State
Building."

"Peachy," said Grist.

(*If I owned the Empire State Building,* Charlie thought, *I
would fill it with hydrogen bombs—one hundred and two
hydrogen bombs. Then—*)

Miss Appleton laughed, a dainty bell-like laugh. "Oh you
will jest, Captain!"

(*Captain!* Charlie thought. *Captain! That was good.*)

"He *does* worry on your account, you know. His first
concern was that the trip to New York New would interfere
with your schoolwork. To be sure, it is a thousand miles
away, and you must be very fond of this lovely camp, but the
Captain will be able to help you with your lessons, as I

pointed out. And he agreed to let the final decision up to you." She paused dramatically.

"We'll go," said Charlie C-Company. "Thank you very much, Miss Appleton, for the opportunity. And thank you, *Captain*."

"Then it's decided. Miss Appleton—it's been a pleasure." Grist extended his hand. Even in elevated shoes he was two inches shorter than the Talent-Hunt agent.

Miss Appleton offered her hand to Charlie, and his resolute formality was no match for her conspiratorial wink. He smiled.

"Till Friday, gentlemen. And now, good evening."

"Victory," said Grist. But she was already out the door.

"If it had been up to me, this would've never happened. But they contacted Captain Langer first and told him it'd be good publicity for Overkill, so you've got him to thank. I suppose you think you're pretty smart, 743."

"No sir."

"Don't disagree with me."

"Yes sir."

There was an abyss of boredom and apathy behind the Drillmaster's inflexible military mask that Charlie did not dare to look into.

"See to it," Grist said.

(*See to what?* Charlie wondered.) He said, "Yes sir."

"Dismissed."

CC 743-22 saluted and did an about-face.

"743."

"Yes sir?"

"How many chin-ups did you do coming in here?"

"Ten, sir."

"You're getting soft. Make it fifteen from now on."

"Yes sir."

"Dismissed."

The United States was not, officially, at war, and to maintain itself in this condition cost it the greatest of exertions and thirty thousand casualties per annum for a period of approximately twenty years. No one knew exactly when the non-war had begun.

The total resources of the nation had been mobilized long since, and now the C.I.A. and the Army, the two great rival powers in Washington politics, vied in the invention of desperate expedients. Perhaps the most desperate of these had been the Army's militarization of orphan homes (of which, in consequence of the non-war, there were many).

The first graduating class of orphans had just been sent to fight in Iceland, and so successful had they been that the Army was trying now to force the passage of the controversial Mannheim Act, which would initiate the compulsory military training of *all* boys over ten years old. As the Army public relations office had pointed out—the years from ten to fourteen were crucial in the formation of a boy's character. Too often it was impossible to instill a true military ethos into a youth once he had reached high school. The military academy was a venerable tradition in the United States, and it was only fair that all young men should have the opportunity to share in this tradition.

True, even at the age of ten, some children were of so independent a disposition that it was already too late to mould an ideal soldier. Charlie C-Company was such a one. For these, military training would have to begin at birth, but as yet only the boldest dreamers in the Pentagon looked forward to that degree of universal military training.

Yet, if it were not for the lamentable independence of Charlie C-Company's private thoughts, he would have been as nearly ideal as any cadet at Overkill. His psychometric tests showed him to possess a great leadership potential and recommended O.C.S. His deportment and carriage on the drill ground were flawless. His classwork was sometimes a little too good, despite his constant effort to hold his curiosity and intelligence in check. He was well-liked by the other cadets and unquestioningly obedient to his superiors.

Grist hated his guts. Perhaps one of the reasons Grist so particularly hated his guts was that essentially they were not unlike his own. A little tenderer, perhaps. And Grist had learned, in twenty years of soldiering, to despise his own guts heartily. That was what made him such an excellent non-com.

Usually life at Camp Overkill was structured so that both Charlie's and Grist's feelings never had to come out into the open, but now as they boarded the jet for New York New, they found themselves in circumstances for which Overkill's code of behavior had not prepared them. Thus, as they took their seats, Grist muttered, "Smart punk!" Something he would have never said at Overkill, as he was quick to realize.

"Well, 743," Grist said, in an effort to regain his composure, "we're going to start using that smartness of yours around Overkill. When we get back from our vacation trip, you're going to be my orderly. We'll make a soldier out of you yet, 743. What do you say to that?"

"Yes sir." He felt largely indifferent about it, in fact, for he was already wondering how hard it would be to get lost among New York New's three million people.

The jet took off, and for a few happy minutes Charlie watched the cloudbanks rolling past beneath them pinkly. As soon as the NO SMOKING light went off, Grist lit one of his smelly cigars. The hostess came to tell him not to smoke.

"There's no law says a man in uniform can't enjoy a smoke when he's paid good money for his ticket, and there's other people smoking."

"The lady two rows back particularly asked. . . ."

"If the lady two rows back don't like the smell, she can hold her nose."

Charlie, resenting Grist no more nor less than usual, was astonished to hear, from further back in the plane, a *giggle* that grew louder and louder. It was certainly a child's giggle, a girl's—and she was laughing at Grist. He felt his own laughter welling up. How long had it been since he had felt that?

Grist was turning as red as the ulcer Charlie always imagined for him, and Charlie had to close his eyes to concentrate on not laughing. He thought of the Empire State Building. The image of that was still sharply etched in his memory. He thought very hard.

The giggling from the back of the plane stopped, and the image of the great building trembled in his mind as though an earthquake had struck its foundations.

He opened his eyes.

Standing there in the aisle was a girl of about his own age. Her eyes were still tearing with laughter—golden eyes with dark, irregular flecks in them. As they stared at each other, she grew more sober. She ignored Grist completely.

"Are you going to New York New?" the girl asked.

Charlie nodded.

"Are you a winner of the Talent-Hunt?"

He nodded again. Though he had heard both questions distinctly, he had not seen her lips move.

"So am I," the girl went on. "My name is Linda. Linda van Eps. Tell me your name . . . no, don't *say* it. Just think it to me, the way you thought the picture of the building to me."

"Charlie C-Company."

"That's the silliest name I ever heard. I have to go back to my seat now, but we can keep talking all the way to New York New. Secretly—that's the nice thing about thinking. It's always a secret."

Charlie nodded once more, and the girl, Linda, went away.

"What in God's name was that?" Grist asked. He looked shaken. He had stubbed out the cigar in the ashtray.

"I don't know, sir." Camp Overkill had taught Charlie to lie convincingly.

Tell me about yourself, Linda's voice bade. She was sitting by a window, looking at the rolling, pink clouds. Charlie could see them through her eyes. She was near-sighted. Charlie looked at the clouds through his own eyes, and Linda gasped. He felt the thrill of her discovery.

I'm an orphan, he said.

So am I, her mind replied. The two thoughts melted into one.

Nothing in Charlie's brief, bleak history had led him to suppose himself a telepath, though neither had he bothered to suppose himself otherwise. He knew that such things might be, though probably they weren't. And during the three hours they were in flight (it was not an express), Charlie was too busy being shocked by Linda's bold opening of her mind to him to be shocked at the knowledge that *he* was a telepath.

It seemed so natural. Natural, that he should be this intimate with her body, that she should know his; natural, that she should see what Grist meant to him, and that he should feel her shock at the force of his feelings (he had not known they *were* so forceful); natural, that he should remember afternoons years before when he had played with her twin brother, and especially that crucial afternoon when Linda had stood by helplessly while her brother drowned, and she felt his every anguish in her own mind. Charlie had never known grief: how terrible it was!

How beautiful it was and how natural to walk through her mind as he would walk through a city or through an unfamiliar house, free to gawk at all the foreigners—to look into all the closets.

For instance, *she* actually liked cauliflower!

And liver!

And she knew French. She knew so many things he didn't know—despite all the books he had read in secret. Her vocabulary was enormous—and entirely at his disposal. It was as though his brain had suddenly doubled. *It had.* It was like (and this thought came to both simultaneously, so complete was their rapport now) coming into a room lit by only a 25-watt bulb and turning on a 200-watt overhead.

Quite suddenly, each of them knew that they had fallen deeply in love. There was no doubt in either mind, or in both of them.

Linda? Charlie said.

Yes?

Will you marry me?

Yes oh yes.

Linda blushed. Charlie had never understood what it meant to blush.

Someday, she added. They had forgotten they were only ten.

"Hey, boy. I said *Hey!*"

Charlie looked up at the Drillmaster, who had spread his briefcase on his lap and was dealing out cards.

"Let's play a couple of hands of poker, boy. I'm getting bored just sitting."

"I don't know how."

"Don't hand me any of that. I've heard you in the barracks, bluffing those stupid kids. You must have them so deep in the hole they'll be shining your shoes and polishing your rifle till next Christmas," Grist chuckled.

Reluctantly, Charlie picked up a handful of cards. Linda nudged into his mind. *Teach me how to play,* she said. That made it better again.

Grist had dealt him a full-house. "Let's play for money," Charlie said.

"Sure," Grist replied. He chuckled. *The little shark,* he thought. For, while Charlie had sat there bleary-eyed in love, Grist had fixed the deck and dealt himself four aces.

By the time the jet landed at Grand Central (it was, of course, a vertical jet), Charlie had, with Linda's help, lost $430: $250 on the first hand, and the rest in dribs and drabs.

"I'm sorry, but you'll have to wait to be paid," Charlie said proudly as he unfastened his seat belt. "I only have ten dollars in cash. If you'll accept an I.O.U. I can . . ."

"No hurry, sport. Just so as I get it sometime. Hell, maybe you can *win* it back."

"Really!" said a voice from the aisle. The elderly woman, whose voice it was, avoided Grist's inquiring glance as though it were dirty and tightened her grip on Linda's hand. *My aunt Victoria,* Linda explained. *She saw him playing poker with you, and I guess she heard about the money.*

I don't like her.

Grist elbowed his way into the aisle ahead of the old woman and pulled Charlie to the exit. At the foot of the ramp stood Miss Appleton, more civilian than ever: a sort of filmy pink fluff revealed the more substantial pinkness of Miss Appleton herself beneath. Braided into her thick red hair was a green velvety rope dotted with dull-yellowish stones like peridots. Seeing her again made Charlie feel better.

"You're the very last, my dears. All the rest are waiting to say hello."

"I thought you said there was going to be photographers and television cameras and stuff," Grist complained. "As far as I'm concerned, the whole purpose of coming here is to get some good publicity for Camp Overkill."

"Ah, yes," Miss Appleton replied vaguely. "It is difficult, what with the war effort and all—and you did arrive so late. . . . Linda! my darling!"

Aunt Victoria, like Grist in this, always chose to answer anything addressed to her charge. "My good Miss Appleton! What a lovely *frock*!" She couldn't speak a complete sentence without giving the impression that she had herself invented at least one of the words in it.

"Have you all been introduced?" Grist and Aunt Victoria eyed each other unhappily.

"To *whom*?" Aunt Victoria asked.

Miss Appleton negotiated introductions and herded them into an elevator that linked the landing field surmounting Grand Central to the subways below. There was little traffic on the surface of the island. The available space was needed for crops. Every known variety of fruit and vegetable was raised here in hydroponic vats built right on top of the rubble left by the *fin de siècle* blasts, and hardly a month went by without the development of a new, true-breeding mutation superior either in terms of nutrition or taste to the varieties then being grown. No other area in North America had been so heavily bombed during the brief political crisis at the turn of the century, and therefore New York New, despite a rather peripheral position, had become the agricultural center of the continent.

The Empire State Building, since it had somehow escaped destruction in the blasts, remained in the hands of private enterprise, and the observatory floors were still, as they had been a century before, a standard feature of every tourist's tour, more especially since the building was now the oldest artifact on the island. The rest of the island, however, was the exclusive preserve of the Federal Government, which had developed its hydroponics system.

Coming up out of the subway on 34th Street (as the general area around the Empire State was still called, though all streets but Broadway were defunct), the party of five found themselves in the Empire State Park, where the city's prize mutations were displayed in natural settings. Giant sweet-peas twined up about hundred-foot oaks that had reached their present height in four seasons of forced growth. Lawns of thick, sturdy moss covered the grounds, and in the distance along the East River could be seen the lilypads where the higher government officials had their homes. The entertainment area was spread across the Hudson.

Charlie and Linda hardly noticed the parkland; their attention was fixed upon the building itself, seeking the source of the almost overpowering greeting that emanated from the grey monolith—as though Everest were to try to say hello.

Miss Appleton noticed the children's perplexity. "That's where you'll be staying while you're here, of course. The other children are up in the Observatory now. You can barely see their heads over the edge—there!"

They looked up, and they saw themselves below through a hundred pairs of eyes, and they saw the sweeping parabolas of the building's profile directing the eye to the infinite perspectives of space.

Charlie reached for Linda's hand, and their joined minds replied to Everest's immense *hello*.

Their rooms were on the second floor. Aunt Victoria professed to be scandalized at the fact that the room she and Linda were to share communicated through the bath to the room that had been assigned to Grist and Charlie. Miss Appleton said she would do something and disappeared.

That night the adults were going to visit the lilypads on the Hudson and see a musical comedy, while the children were to have a quiet little party on the 86th floor. Even now, in their own rooms, Charlie and Linda could feel the whispers and cobwebs of the others' thoughts. Was it possible that the sheer vastness of so many minds would blot out even the extravagance of their own swift-flowering love? Charlie worried, but Linda was untroubled. This would be like the coming-out she had always dreamed of.

While they waited for evening and went through the motions of unpacking and cleaning up, Charlie and Linda, through the thin wall between them (the partition was not an original element of the building), ventured deeper into the enchanted forests of each other's minds.

Charlie wanted to know more about Aunt Victoria. He shared some of Grist's instinctive dislike for the old woman, and he could not understand (though he was a partner to her feelings) Linda's tolerant affection. Everything that Linda offered in defense of her aunt—her moral fervor; her God-fearing rectitude; even her pacifism—strengthened Charlie in his original distaste. She reminded him of the matron, Miss Bunkle: censorious, mean-minded.

She's a throwback to the 20th century!

So what's wrong with the 20th century? Do you think things have improved since then?

"What'd you say, boy?" Grist asked.

Charlie still had some things to learn about telepathy. "I said, uh. . . ." He fumbled, then opted for the truth. "That old biddy next door is a throwback to the 20th century."

Grist laughed. "Yeah, if you ask me she's a . . . !"

Linda found barriers in Charlie's mind, too. These were mainly shadows Grist had cast. Charlie resented Grist, but Linda could sense the admiration that underlay his resentment, and underlying even that an abiding hatred that was incomprehensible to her. Coming across the traces of these feelings in Charlie's mind was like finding a large rock in a mouthful of chocolate pudding: she could not assimilate it.

Yet it was precisely these kernels of mystery in the other

person that caught them up even tighter in the meshes of love. When it had come time to go to the party, neither felt the slightest doubt that their love might be diluted by the larger bond. The mystery between them was illimitable and as yet scarcely touched.

There were so many names to remember, and telepathy did not help at that at all. There was Bobby Ryan and Walter Wagenknecht. Bruce Burton was the one wearing shorts. Dora and Cassy Bensen were twins. The 102 children looked as much unlike each other as any 102 super-normal children might. Yet the traits they had in common quite overshadowed any dissimilarities: they were telepaths; they were, give or take some three months, all of an age; they were orphans—and, surely the most remarkable "coincidence," orphans who had lost their mothers at birth and had never known their fathers.

It was therefore quite understandable that the children's party spirits were dampened by the necessity of finding out as quickly as they might just who they were and what they were doing all together in the Empire State Building. The 102 candles on the big cake that was the centerpiece on the buffet had burned down right into the frosting without being noticed.

The children thought. It was hard, inexperienced as they were, for all of them to think clearly together. Walter Wagenknecht's mind was one of the strongest among them, and the group let his consciousness ride on the wave-crest of their thought, directing it.

Charlie immediately resented this arrangement, but he admitted (to Walter himself, who had instantly sensed Charlie's nascent mutiny) that someone had to do what Walter was doing, or their several minds would knock about like the particles of a Brownian movement. Reluctantly, Charlie allowed his mind to be swallowed into the greater mind of the group.

Every child at some time suspects that he is an orphan, and every orphan is certain that his father is noble, rich, or (in extreme cases) divine. These orphans were no exception. And in their case there was good reason to suppose that the Cowbird Theory was true.

The problem, then, was—to what degree was that theory true? Were they, strictly speaking, human?

Walter thought not.

They *looked* human, but they were all mature enough not to be persuaded by this. Their telepathy was a much stronger argument *against* their humanity, but not enough to turn the balance.

There was the suggestive fact that somehow the idea of the Empire State Building flying off into space had been planted in each of their minds. There was the *hope* that that might happen, but it was so strong a hope and there was so little real evidence to support it, that no one dared to hope too deeply.

The greatest argument against their humanity was their own profound distaste for the great bulk of human folly, but since they shared their misanthropy, such as it was, with the greatest figures in human history, it was not a conclusive argument.

One thing was certain: whether, biologically, they were human or not, mentally they were not. From this certainty, Walter had drawn a further conclusion: *We can do what we want to do. The problem is going to be what we want to do—with the others.*

The image of 102 H-Bombs rose unbidden into Charlie's mind, and with such strength that the others received it clearly. There was a feeling of embarrassment among those who took his meaning quickly, and the feeling spread like ripples in a pond as their understanding spread to the more naive.

Charlie was clearly blushing.

Wagenknecht spoke aloud: "We will have to consider that, too. Killing them may be our only alternative. They will probably want to kill us."

Wagenknecht?

The young Negro opened his mind to Charlie's urgent question. The other hundred orphans were excluded.

It was surprising how alike they were. Both had spent their entire lives in orphanages; both were in the military now. The corresponding figure in Walter's background for Grist was a Captain Ferber.

But the closest link between them was the thought that had formed at the very instant that their two minds had fused: that, together, they—and the rest of the children— could dominate the entire world.

Or even destroy it.

Charlie?

Charlie took Linda's hand in his again. But already he had formed with Wagenknecht a tacit agreement to divide the world in two hemispheres—if it should come to that.

Grist was hungover something terrible. And the "little something" that Talent-Hunt had given him for expenses was shot. The worse part of it was that he had been so drunk by the time he reached the place where (he supposed) he'd lost it that he didn't remember one detail of the spending.

He, and the 102 winners of the Talent-Hunt, and the 101 other guardians were gathered in a smallish auditorium on the 15th floor of the building, once a restaurant, where they were being harangued by the intolerable Mr. Maximast.

"... and so, in this time of world-crises, the most precious natural resource of our dear country is you, her children. You are her future. In twenty years *you* will invent her weapons, mastermind her global strategy, command her troops, and instruct the *next* generation, who shall in their turn pass on the torch of freedom that we have handed on to you."

It had gone on like that for the better part of an hour, and what it all boiled down to was that the kids had won scholarships to some fancy school in Europe, or somewhere, that Grist had never heard of. A school for bright kids. Well, he'd like to see them get Charlie C-Company out of the Army.

And what about the rest of these kids? It looked like half the boys *at least* were from Army orphanages. Grist smelled a rat.

What if, Grist pondered, *this Talent-Hunt business were just a front?* And who was more likely to be behind it than the C.I.A.? They wanted to horn in on the Army's monopoly. They were trying to amend the Mannheim Act. There was no telling what they might try.

They were doing something weird, all right. Grist had been drilling children, boys at least, for years—and he had never seen a bunch of them behaving like this. They just sat around like a bunch of zombies, listening to that dumb speaker.

Grist, his patience worn thin, rose from his seat and made his way to the back of the auditorium, where Miss Appleton brooded benignly over her swarm of little geniuses.

"Is there a pay-phone nearby?" he asked.

Miss Appleton gave him directions to find the phone. When he left, Mr. Maximast was still speaking.

The children stirred uneasily in their seats.

Mr. Maximast had just explained that he was their father. Charlie's mind reached out to Linda's comfortingly. *Sister, sister.* Cold comfort, that.

While the apparent Mr. Maximast rattled on about freedom's torch in a dismaying mechanical manner, (the adults in the auditorium were stifling with boredom), the *essential* Mr. Maximast explained, telepathically, that he was their father in the mechanical rather than the biological sense, a distinction that was clear enough when one understood that Mr. Maximast himself was mechanical rather than biological. Miss Appleton too, for all her graces, was an automaton.

Further, the children were informed, their mothers—that is, the women who had died bringing the orphans to birth— were not, in the biological sense, their mothers.

And further: that each orphan would shortly have the opportunity of meeting his or her true parents. But the nature of these parents, Mr. Maximast did not make clear. This had not been put on to the tape which he was broadcasting.

That telepathy could be mechanically reproduced explained at least one of the mysteries that had been bothering the children: the 102 identical essays. Maximast admitted that, on a night shortly after the Talent-Hunt had been announced on television and in the nation's leading comic books, the entire text of the essay had been transmitted *everywhere*—and with such force that no one who received it was able to resist submitting it to the Talent-Hunt.

Mr. Maximast concluded both his spoken and his unspoken speeches with an invitation to see the view from the 102nd floor—the top floor of the Empire State Building.

When he left the platform, there was some listless applause and then a total silence. A few of the adults got up. Aunt Victoria nudged her niece, who was sitting there with the silliest grin on her face. She couldn't really blame the girl for not paying attention. She had never heard a more boring speaker.

Miss Appleton bustled down the aisle. "There's to be a special tour to the New Botanical Gardens. Just for adults."

Aunt Victoria so much wanted to see the famous gardens, and the children *had* been so well behaved.

"*Do* you mind if I go off, Linda darling?"

"Not at all, Auntie. I'm sure the Gardens are very exciting. I'll be all right. Charlie will look after me."

Aunt Victoria did not really approve of the boy. He seemed so coarse. Yet, surely, that was not his fault, but of the people in the Army, like Grist, who had coarsened him. Last night, she had heard Grist coming in at 4:00. Stumbling all over everything; almost certainly drunk. There was no telling where he had *been*. What kind of example was that to set a ten-year-old boy? Actually, it was Linda's *duty*, as a Christian, to help counteract the older man's bad influence. Aunt Victoria smiled and dug into her purse. She found two caramels wrapped in cellophane.

"*One* is for Charles, Linda."

"Oh yes, Auntie." She ran off to join the rest of the children. The dear little thing!

In the last forty-eight hours, General Virgil Tricker of Army Security had received two phone calls from New York New reporting the attempted abduction of Army orphans by the C.I.A.—the first from a Captain Ferber, the latest from a Sergeant Grist.

A preposterous notion, of course, but he had nonetheless assigned some investigators to look into the organization of the Talent-Hunt, and though the C.I.A. appeared to have no fingers in this pie, it looked odder and odder.

The object of his investigation was called Talent-Hunt. Talent-Hunt seemed to have no other purpose than discovering talented orphans, no discernible origins, and no staff. It was a project of the Mortemain Foundation, a non-profit organization which had first evidenced itself a legal entity on June 12, 1996, the day that it purchased the Empire State Building. After that purchase the only acts of the Foundation for which Tricker could find any record were some dozen politely obstinate refusals to lease office space in the Empire State to the Federal Government Tourist Board. All available office space—that which was not occupied by the Foundation itself—was being leased to businesses and individuals owned or in the employ of the Mortemain Foundation and who seemed to have no other purpose (and very little more existence) than that which they served by occupying space—on paper.

All this seemed suspicious to General Tricker, and now the further circumstance of the Mortemain Foundation gathering to itself a group of exceptionally talented orphans confirmed him in his intentions to stick his nose in. What else is Army Security for?

He shuffled through the dossiers on the various Army officers presently assembled in New York New as guardians for orphans, but it was in Grist, his second informant, that he sensed that elusive nastiness which is the fundamental quality of a spy, however it be then overlaid with the cosmetic of forms and custom.

Tricker gave his secretary directions to inform Grist of his new responsibilities and then, as an afterthought, called the Attorney-General. He gave him the name of the Mortemain Foundation for his list. Hardly an important detail, but General Tricker's respect for due process died hard.

It was four o'clock, and he felt, as after a particularly satisfying meal, a sense of real *achievement*. He had an hour before he was expected home for dinner. It was time enough, he thought, to catch a breath of fresh air. It had been weeks since he'd gone up to the surface.

Twenty minutes later, he went through the last airlock into the Pentagon Gardens. It was raining, and he rejoiced: it had been three years since he had seen the rain. He went into an arbor where no one could see him and removed his hat.

Sometimes life could be beautiful.

To get to the 102nd floor, you took an express elevator from Main to 80. That was when your ears popped. Then, there was a bank of four elevators that ferried back and forth from 80 to 86, where they took your ticket. Except that today again the children had the Observatory to themselves. From 86 to 102 there was only one elevator—and it was manually operated! The children were quick to suspect that the hand at the controls was a robot's.

Only twenty children at a time could go up to 102. The rest went out on the Observatory terrace.

I was on 102 the very first day I came here, Bruce Burton made known to the group. *I didn't see anything so special about it.* Nor could the rest of them, focusing on Bruce's eidetic image of the 102nd floor observatory, see anything special.

Visibility was good today, and there was a stiff wind blowing. The view from a great height is a tonic for the spirit, which can encompass and contain all that it sees. Down below, with the trees towering overhead or hemmed in by the great vats, the immensity of the city mocked at human nature.

Distance seduces the rational mind, just as closeness seduces the irrational. Was not Christ led to a mountain height to be tempted? It seemed to Walter and Charlie that nothing prevented them from conquering the great, green forest of New York New by force, just as they had conquered it now by perspective.

Linda was uneasy. Everyone had gone up but a little group of ten children. The elevator operator called for them. She thought: *Our parents—I hope they look like us.* Though they knew she was being foolish, they all echoed the thought.

The door of the elevator closed, and then it opened onto a small concrete chamber, twenty feet by twenty feet, with a ceiling so low that anyone taller than the children would have had to stoop. There were no windows. The other children who had gone up before them weren't there.

"This isn't 102," Bruce Burton whispered.

"Actually," said the elevator operator, "it *is*. The top observatory floor of the building is not, in fact, the top floor. It never was, though naturally for the sake of the tourists' happiness it was always called the 102nd floor. In the 20th Century the top floor—this floor—was rented out to radio and television stations. They transmitted from here. After the blasts there was nothing to transmit and no one to transmit it—in New York, at least—so we took over the top floor for ourselves. Nobody knows it exists."

The few banks of technical equipment in the middle of the room were really quite unimpressive.

A spaceship?

Impossible, Walter decided. *But it could be a matter transmitter. That would be more sensible for getting places in a hurry.*

As though to confirm Walter in his judgment, Mr. Maximast suddenly manifested himself in the center of the complex of equipment. Materialized was, perhaps, a better word. He beckoned to the children.

One at a time they went to him. He positioned them in front of the apparatus, and one at a time they disappeared.

Walter and Linda and Charlie were the only ones left.

Then Walter and Charlie were the only ones left. Charlie sensed Walter's growing panic. Walter was thinking of a poem Charlie had never heard, called "Ten Little Indians."

Then, Walter was left by himself. Maximast beckoned to him, but he was afraid, as a soul must be afraid called before the seat of judgment. And only minutes ago he had thought of conquering the world!

Maximast waved to the boy impatiently. Walter bolted for the elevator, but the attendant caught him and carried him, kicking and screaming, to Maximast. Walter was no match for two robots.

Charlie's ears popped for a second time.

He found himself in the middle of an almost identical room *filled* with children; certainly more than 102 children. The telepathic turmoil in the confined space was so great that Charlie could scarcely hear himself think.

Two strange children came towards him. A boy and a girl. The boy's hand was extended in greeting. The girl was crying.

"Hi!" said Charlie, uncertain of what was expected of him. "I'm Charlie."

Of course, the boy thought, shaking his hand. *We know all about you. I'm Gregors, and this is Bernice. We are your parents.*

But how—Embarrassed, Charlie stumbled into speech. "I mean, you don't look much older than me."

Bernice replied in English that was accented rather strangely, "But we *are* much older. Your father is 24, and I'll be 21 in a few days."

"But I'm ten years old myself! How could . . ."

His mother laughed pleasantly. "We mature early, you know."

Charlie related embarrassment.

Behind him there was a scream. Walter Wagenknecht had just arrived. Two more children (if they could be called children), a white girl and a Negro boy, approached their son.

An ugly thought entered Charlie's mind: *Midgets! You're midgets, and I am too.* It was awful.

Gregors interposed a kindly thought. In a land of midgets, a tall man would be a freak. Charlie felt he would like Gregors. But his *father?* That would take getting used to.

Gregors, he thought. *Bernice.* He liked the sounds of their names. But . . .

"What's my last name?" he asked.

"Forrestal," Gregors said.

"Charles Forrestal," said Charlie Forrestal, rolling his r's luxuriously.

Bernice took his hand: her own was no bigger than his. "Come—see our city. The observatory is only down one flight of steps. You have many more surprises in store for you today. Then tonight there'll be a dinner for all of you, and tomorrow—if they'll let you come away with us—we'll go to our country place in the Poconos. The summer *is* so . . ." She sought for the word she wanted in Charlie's mind ". . . *beastly* in New York."

New York?

Ah, his mother thought, *you call it New York New. I forgot.*

The three of them went down the narrow stairs to the Observatory in single file. It was just as Charlie had seen it in Bruce Burton's mind.

But the view outside was totally different. Nothing like New York New. It was an enormous varicolored honeycomb, arranged in the most eccentric shapes—and (Charlie observed this with a moment's panic) still arranging itself! For here and there on the periphery of one of the huge volumes, a component or group of components would detach itself from the parent mass, drift up into the middle air, and then settle upon some other spot. Vaguely, Charlie sensed that there was a pattern in these changes, but too vast for him to grasp at once.

A random thought of his mother entered Charlie's mind: *I hate rush hour.* She sensed his bewilderment.

Those are homes, she explained. *People are done with work, and they're taking their homes back to their apartments.*

New York—this? Yet, looking closer, he could see the general contours of the island between the two rivers. And, there, beyond the East River, Brooklyn; and there, beyond the Hudson, New Jersey.

Charlie felt a familiar presence in the room. Linda. She

came running to him, and he caught her up in his arms and they kissed. It was as though they had been apart for years!

Isn't it wonderful!

Her thoughts came to him so fast, it was hard to sort them out. She felt around the edge of his puzzlement.

Charlie, darling, don't you know what year it is?

It was the year 3652 A.D.

For Charlie, the visit to the country place was just as good as a trip to Altair. Gregors conducted him among the blossoming lungplants until he sensed that the boy had had enough. In certain people, the color of the Altairean plants produced an almost allergenic reaction, which was compounded by having the longer wave-lengths of the visible spectrum filtered out by the force-shell spread over the Forrestal estate.

The family—Gregors, Bernice, and Charlie—retired to a patch of mildly euphoric Altairean lovemoss and spread out the picnic cloth. After lunch, Bernice began to think of some of her favorite songs, but they sounded like static to Charlie's untrained ear.

Despite the benign influence of the lovemoss, Charlie began to grow peeved. Everything he had seen in New York and here in the Poconos had led him to the conviction that he had lost his birthright for a mess of pottage without ever being asked. Instead of living in a future of peace, plenty, and universal brotherhood, he had been born in the anxiety-ridden 21st Century, raised an orphan, and denied the companionship of his own kind.

But that's over for now, Bernice suggested soothingly.

If only it were, Charlie thought bitterly. *But I have to go back there. To that terrible time. To that stupid building.*

The image of the great building rose into his parents' consciousness, where it called forth feeling of subdued reverence. In the 37th Century, as in the 21st, the Empire State Building was the oldest artifact on the island of Manhattan— and, with the exception of the foundation stones of Chartres and the pyramids, anywhere in the world. But Chartres and the pyramids had gotten through the centuries on their own merits—without the assistance of benevolent time travelers to do maintenance work.

Time travel was perfected in the year 3649, after four centuries of trial and error and error and error. During this period, important advances were made in the mathematical analysis of history. It was discovered that the perfect continuity of human history had only been disrupted once—in the period from 1996 to 2065 A.D. By the time the first machine was ready to be installed in the top floor of the Empire State Building (by its continuous survival through the centuries, that was the obvious site for their purposes), the historico-mathematical models were complete enough to implement a completely effective program.

The only thing lacking was personnel to carry out the program.

In the period from 1996 to 3649, the human race had evolved (largely by artificial means) to such a point that it would not be possible for adults of that future world to return to the past even to handle such simple transactions as the purchase of the Empire State Building. The adults of 3649 would look like children to the adults of that earlier day; worse, the psy-sensitives of the future could not have endured the noxious mental environment of the 21st Century for more than a few minutes. Therefore, Mr. Maximast and a corps of assistants were designed to carry out the first steps of the Transaction.

Maximast's first task was the purchase of the building. Then he equipped it with the force-shields that preserved it during the atomic blast of the following year. From 1997 to 2050, he had only to maintain the building and the Mortemain Foundation and wait for the historical condition to ripen.

It was the next step of the Transaction that Charlie balked at; it was this step that so dearly concerned his own destiny—the initiation of the Talent-Hunt. For the talent had first to be sown before it could be reaped. Maximast undertook both chores.

Fertilized ova, imported from the year 3650, were planted in several overgenerous and unfortunate ladies, where they developed at such an accelerated pace that the body of the "host" ("mother" was hardly the right word) invariably expired at the time of parturition.

This manner of birth had been cruel, but there had been no alternative. The child of a telepathic mother could not have survived the shock of being separated from his mother at birth—for it is exactly at that time that the telepathic bond between mother and child is greatest. It was likewise impossible for them to grow up in the 37th Century, for then their utility in the past would be destroyed. It was essential that those who carried out the Transaction be regarded as natural products of their own times.

And therefore—

But I don't want to go back! Charlie was almost winning now.

And you don't have to. For a year, at least.

Charlie wouldn't be reasoned with. *I don't want to— ever!*

His father's mind intruded upon them: *Be a man, Charles. You're ten years old, and it's your duty to go back.* Then, with a trace of mellow humor: *How else will you be able to conquer the world?*

The combination of his father's good humor and his mother's coaxing and the euphoria produced by the lovemoss was too much for Charlie. His mind softened. Gently his parents began to flood it with their own years of wisdom and experience.

"Hello there, 743. What you been up to?"

"I was with the others—at the Observatory." Though he had gone through this little speech several times, it was still unsettling to adjust to the temporal shift. Since he had last seen Grist, Charlie had aged a full year, Grist only hours.

The hotel room was dark. Charlie could barely make out the Drillmaster's silhouette on the bed. Now that his own sensibilities were more developed, Charlie found it painful to come into an atmosphere this dense with animosity. He realized now why neither his parents nor any other adult who had matured in the future could have returned to the past: they could no more have endured the pressures against their consciousness than a brook trout could have endured the pressures at the bottom of the Mindanao Deeps.

Grist snapped on the light. He was in uniform.

"We should have us a man-to-man talk, boy."

"Yes, sir."

Charlie's mind reached out to the next room, but Linda had not yet returned. Nor, he realized unhappily, would she be likely to return for several hours. Immediately upon their return from 102, Charlie and Linda had been met by Aunt Victoria, who carried Linda off to a vegetarian restaurant and a lecture on non-violence.

"How about you and me playing some more poker?"

"Yes sir."

"That's the spirit. Maybe you can win back some of that $430 you owe me." Grist's smile flickered *on* like a fluorescent light fixture.

A table was already set up in the center of the room. On it, as though arranged for inspection, were: a bottle of bourbon, a bucket of ice, two glasses, and an unopened deck of cards.

"You break the deck," Grist bade.

Charlie broke, shuffled, and dealt two hands. They both stood pat, and Charlie won—with a pair of queens.

"I'm going to fix a drink," Grist said. "Maybe you'd like some ice water?"

Charlie said nothing, and Grist left the room with two empty glasses. When he returned there was water in one of them.

Grist held up the bottle of bourbon. "Maybe you'd like just a bit of this for flavoring?" The smile glowed bright.

Charlie, entranced by the man's sheer nastiness, nodded. "You deal," he said.

Charlie won again—this time by bluffing. Grist splashed some more bourbon in both glasses.

"Tell me about what you've been doing," Grist said, leaning back with his drink. "What do you think of the other kids? They're sort of strange, don't you think? And who's this Maximast character? Is Maximast a foreign name?"

"They're just kids," Charlie said sipping at his drink. Though he had grown used, in the last year, to wine in the Forrestal household, he had to remember that bourbon had a much higher proof.

"You deal," Grist said.

Already, the Drillmaster noticed, the boy's movements had grown sluggish. You had to hand it to Army Security: they worked quickly. They'd got the bootlegged scopalamine to him within an hour of his asking.

"Tell me, Charlie-boy," Grist began again. "Tell me some more."

He was going to enjoy this.

His mind was inert: cinders and ashes. Linda poked about in them for a live coal. Meanwhile she had to hide her tears from Aunt Victoria who was combing out her long grey hair at the dresser mirror, calmly discussing the message of Dr. Wurstle, the evening's lecturer.

Charlie rolled over on the bed. Linda's poking about had awakened a nightmare. She probed more urgently: *Charlie— what happened—answer me!*

The deepest reaches of his mind answered her before he was fully conscious. He did not resist her questioning. He did not lie. The scopalamine was still operative.

He heard her fumbling at the door of the bathroom. Then she was beside him. She had turned on the bedside lamp and was wiping the sweat from his forehead with the edge of the sheet.

Grist heard everything? she demanded.

Everything! Everything!

She tried to assuage his guilt, which was greater than her astonishment, greater than her fright, greater even than her pity.

Yet it was no greater than their love.

She kissed him. His arms drew her closer, and their minds merged in a perfect embrace.

"Linda!"

It was Aunt Victoria's voice.

"What *are* you doing?"

Linda turned to face her aunt, who stood in the doorway to the bathroom in a cotton nightgown, her hair braided for sleep.

"I heard Charles being sick, Auntie, and I came to help."

"Is that true, Charles?"

Helplessly, Charles spoke the truth. "No, ma'am."

"What *were* you doing, Charles?"

"I was kissing Linda."

At least, Aunt Victoria thought, *you had to give the boy credit for telling the truth.*

"I'll deal with you later, *young* lady. So, run along into your room. You have no business *here."*

"Neither does the *old* lady," replied Grist's voice, fuzzily.

He was standing in the doorway to the hall, holding on to the post for support. During his interrogation of Charlie, he had polished off the entire fifth of bourbon. Behind him were two Army Security guards.

"Let's get a move on out of here, Charlie-boy," Grist

commanded, with as much of his Drillmaster manner as he could muster in his present condition. "You've got a long and complicated story to tell some important people."

Charlie got out of bed, but Aunt Victoria caught hold of his arm.

"This boy is not leaving this room until *I* have had a satisfactory explanation for the behavior I witnessed this evening."

Grist cocked his head, puzzled.

"I found him in this room—on that bed—*kissing* my niece!"

"Well, be happy it wasn't worse than that." Grist caught hold of Charlie's other arm and tried to pull him away from the old woman. She held tight.

"What do you mean, sir?"

"I mean they're married. Man and wife. He told me so himself."

Charlie felt Victoria's fingers dig into his biceps with painful force.

"Are you mad?" she asked in really quite a calm voice.

"Not at all. You wouldn't think so to look at them, but those two kids are as grown-up as you or me. And they're telepathic! Can you imagine the weapon *that* could be in the right hands? Now, let go of him! I'm bringing him in to Army Security Headquarters at the Pentagon. And this whole building is under Army surveillance. By tomorrow morning, your own niece will be in the brig right beside lover-boy here."

"Auntie . . . Auntie. . . ." Linda was pulling at Victoria's nightgown petulantly.

"Not now, darling." She was wondering how she might protect the boy for at least the rest of the night. She had always thought there was something strange about that man Grist.

"Auntie, that's the man who taught us how to kiss." Linda pointed at Grist.

The Sergeant laughed. "Come off it," he said. But his ears were growing red, and the two guards did step back a pace.

"He told us all grown-ups kiss—and he said we were grown-ups too. Was he lying, Auntie?"

When it suited her purpose, Linda could appear to be much *less* than ten years old. Charlie had a hard time keeping a straight face.

Aunt Victoria knelt down beside Charles. She took his face

in her strong right hand and turned it so that their eyes met. Her eyes were like Linda's. For the first time, Charlie liked Aunt Victoria.

"Charles, I know you'll tell me the truth. You did before. Is what Linda said just now the truth? Did this—this *gentleman* teach you about . . . such things?"

Helpless to speak anything but truth, Charlie's mouth opened to speak, but Linda's will stopped the words from coming out. When he spoke, it was not of his own volition: Linda spoke through him.

"Yes, Auntie," she said.

Victoria was touched to hear the boy call her Auntie. She *had* reached him, after all. If he had gone wrong, it was not *his* fault.

She stood up.

"Gentlemen," she said, addressing the two Security guards that Grist had brought in with him, "I charge you to arrest this man on the charge of corrupting the morals of minors. You have heard him accused not only by these children, but out of his own mouth."

Grist turned to the guards angrily. "You'll arrest who you came here to arrest," he bellowed drunkenly. Then, pointing at Charlie, "Arrest that child!"

At exactly that moment, Charles Forrestal sat down on the floor of the hotel room and began to cry.

"Gentlemen," said Aunt Victoria in her coldest voice, "if you do not arrest that drunken beast *immediately* and remove him from this room, I shall personally see to it that every Army orphanage in this country is closed by the end of the month. And I shall charge both of you with attempting to assist this man in his criminal purposes."

The guards, with no more hesitation, handcuffed Grist and marched him out of the room.

Again Aunt Victoria knelt down beside Charlie and lifted his head. "There, there," she soothed. "It was all just a bad dream. But it's all over now. You're going to come home with us and go to a *proper* school. You can be a brother to Linda."

Everyone—even the generals—hated the non-war. It cost much and returned no profit: it was insane. Yet almost all adults were too deeply tangled in the system that produced the non-war to see their way out. That was almost the definition of being an adult: that you couldn't see the way out.

Children could see the way out quite clearly: everyone simply stopped fighting and stopped making weapons. The people who used to make weapons could then do something better.

That, however, was pacifism, and few adults—with the exception of odd ducks like Aunt Victoria—had the time or the patience or the freedom of personal action to be pacifists.

For children, it was another matter. Children could not be prosecuted under the law. Children did have time, and they did not have to worry about losing their jobs. All that was required to start a full-scale Children's Crusade, therefore, was competent leadership.

With the right leaders, there didn't seem to be anything that could stop it. With the right leaders, children could conquer the whole world.

"Aunt Victoria?"

"Yes, Charles?"

"If someone is doing something bad, and nobody else says anything about it, and I *see* it, what should I do?"

Aunt Victoria didn't have to think about that at all. "You must do the right thing, and you must stop other people from doing the wrong thing."

"Aunt Victoria, is war wrong?"

"Yes, Charles. War is always wrong."

For the rest of the trip back home, the children were perfect lambs.

WHITE FANG
GOES DINGO

1

My name is White Fang, though of course that is not really my name. At least not any more. Now my name is Dennis White. I like the old name better, but I suppose that comes of having been a pet. Some people would say that once you've been a pet, once you've grown used to a Leash, you're never quite human again. I don't know about that. Of course, it *is* more fun. But one can learn not to want it so badly. I did. And this is the story of how I did it. As a puppy.

Ah, how is one to speak of the old times without slipping into the old way of speaking? But am I then to speak like a Dingo? No! The memoirs of a member of Louis XVI's court could not be set down in the rough accents of a sansculotte—and *I* must be allowed to write of White Fang as White Fang would have written of himself. For the time being let me leave Dennis White in abeyance—and let me say, without more preamble, that as a puppy I was uncommonly happy.

How should it have been otherwise? I was raised in the best kennels of the solar system. My young body was sportive—and so it sported. My education ranged freely through the humanities, and yet I was never forced beyond my inclinations. I enjoyed the company of my own kind as well as the inestimable pleasures of the Leash. Finally, I was conscious of possessing the highest pedigree. My father was a major artist—perhaps *the* major artist—in a society that valued art above all other things. No little bit of his glory rubbed off on

me. Later, in adolescence, a father's fame may cramp the growing ego, but *then* it was enough to know that I was as valuable a pet as there could be. In what else does happiness consist than in this—a sense of one's own value? Not in freedom, surely.

If I had been free in my youth, I would almost certainly not have been so happy.

In fact there *was* a time when I might have been said to be free (I thought of it then as *neglect*), and I resented my condition bitterly. It happened shortly after I had been orphaned—that is to say, after the Dingoes had made away with my father. I was seven then. But let me set about this in a more chronological fashion.

Let me make a narrative of this.

I suppose I should begin with my parents, Tennyson White and Clea Melbourne Clift. Clea, who would never let us call her Mother, did not marry Daddy, in the usual sense of the word. Like so many women of her generation, the first to grow up under the Mastery, Clea was something of a blue-stocking and very jealous of her independence. For Clea to marry and take on the name of White would have been in contradiction to the first article of her faith: that the sexes must be equal in all things.

Neither I nor my older brother Pluto knew how to behave around Clea. She didn't want us to think of her as a mother, but more as a sort of friend of the family. When Daddy disappeared, Clea went off somewhere—outside the solar system—and we never heard from her again. She had taken up with Daddy because of his literary reputation. A lot of women did, but she was his favorite, for the simple reason that she was what a Dingo would call a "knockout." Daddy, on the other hand, was sort of thin and pale and poetical. He wore his hair almost as long as hers. I never knew either of them really well.

I think I've already mentioned that Daddy disappeared when I was seven years old. We were on Earth, Daddy, Pluto, and I, living in the open country near one of the Dingoes' towns, Daddy was researching another book, a sequel to *A Dog's Life*, and he'd go off on long walks without a Leash. Sometimes he would be loose for weeks at a time if his work demanded it. He had to understand what it was to be merely human. So, when the Dingoes got hold of him, the Masters couldn't do anything. They'd lost touch. Nobody was ever found, but one could assume that the Dingoes had been thorough in disposing of the remains, for the Masters could have resurrected a body from hamburger, almost.

Pluto and I were placed in a kennel located on the North Shore of Lake Superior, the Schroeder Kennel, and there we remained for the next three years, and there we were neglected.

In a purely physical sense, we were well cared for. I'll grant that. The Schroeder Kennel (named after a little town that had once occupied that site) had an excellent gymnasium, warm and cold pools, indoor tennis and golf courts, good robotic instructors for all sports, and the kennel rations were prepared with that exquisite simplicity that only the most refined taste can command. Our rooms, both public and private, were spacious, airy, and bright. Naturalness was everywhere, the style of the thing, and it was no less natural for being adjusted to our convenience. Thus, in the summer the air was filtered and cooled, and in the winter the dome that encompassed the kennel heated us and added extra hours of sunlight to the brief northern days. The dome delimiting the kennels was a mile in diameter, and within its bounds our comforts were secure against the enmity of the Dingoes.

It would have been an ideal existence if only our Master had truly cared for us.

Not that he should have cared. Why should *people* care for dogs or cats or parakeets? But they do, and the dogs and cats and parakeets have come to expect it. They like to be talked to, fondled, taken for walks, and, in general, treated as equals, though it must be evident, even to their limited sensibilities, that they aren't equal; men are immeasurably their superiors, possessing inexplicable powers and engaging in unaccountable pursuits.

The analogy (which I have borrowed from Daddy's novel, *A Dog's Life*) to the relation between Masters and men can be extended almost indefinitely. Mankind cannot presume to understand or equal the Masters. Their nature is so alien to ours that, unassisted, we cannot even perceive them. As nearly as we can know, the Masters are pure electro-magnetic phenomena—formed of a "substance" that is neither matter nor energy, but rather a potentiality for either. Their power approaches cosmic proportions, and their knowledge approaches omniscience.

Beside them mankind is insignificant and laughable. Considered simply as a field of force, they are, corporately, of a scope and dimension equal at least to the magnetic field of the Earth. In the strictest sense of the word, the Masters are unaccountable. One could only accept them, reverence them, and hope for the best.

The best that one could hope for was the Leash. The Leash, however, is—it was—rather hard to describe: the tides of knowledge that sweep through the mind, the total certainty that it affords, the ecstasy. Naturally, it didn't always reach those proportions. Often it was only a diffuse sense of well-being. But it could be the Beatific Vision. It was not, as some say, a telepathic link with the Masters. (Although they could speak to us only when we were Leashed, and their speech was a direct communication from their mind to ours.) It was simply their *touch*, a touch that could transmute our nervous system from base lead to gleaming gold—or scramble a brain into idiocy—with, literally, the speed of lightning.

Desirable as the Leash was, one could not coerce it. Like the state of grace, it came as a gift or not at all. And at the Schroeder Kennel it came not at all—or so rarely as to make its general absence only more poignant. Our Master simply did not care; he was not interested enough in his pets to spend his time with them, and so we were left to our own devices. It was a terrible way to grow up.

And so we come to Roxanna Proust.

I don't think Proust was really her last name, any more than my name was White Fang. She had taken the name, because Proust was her idol. She was only eighteen at the time that we entered the Schroeder Kennel, and already the *Remembrance of Things Past* was her passion and pastime.

Roxanna was, *faute de mieux*, our teacher. She taught us French, reading to us from her favorite author, and she taught us German by reading a German translation of Proust. It was a rather eclectic education, but there was no one else with a fraction of Roxanna's talent, special as it was. Most of the pets there were only interested in athletics and flirtation. For my own part, I'll confess that I spent much more time in the gymnasium than I did at my studies. Without the intellectual stimulation and aid of the Leash, literature has not been my natural inclination.

Pluto was different. Pluto loved to read, and, under Roxanna's guidance, he began to write. Not surprisingly, his style was very derivative of Proust's. Later, it was derivative of Joyce, and at last, when he became famous, it was entirely original. Or so I am told. I've never been able to understand him unless I was Leashed, and then, of course, I can understand anything. In fact, if I were to be candid, I would have to admit that my brother and I have always been rather distant. That at least prevented us from being hostile. I understand that Pluto, like our mother, has left the solar system. He is no longer on Earth, in any case, and I can't say that I've missed him that much.

2

I have always considered that my life began at the age of ten. Before that age, I remember few events in any detail. From ten on, I think I could reconstruct the happening of each new day if I had to.

The day it would give me most pleasure to reconstruct was the 4th of October, 2023—a Wednesday. On that day in good weather Roxanna would take Pluto and me out into the country, beyond the dome of the kennel. After a half-hour drive along dirt roads, we would arrive at a deserted farm, where, in the shade of overburdened apple trees, we would pursue our studies, or, if Roxanna felt indulgent towards us, we would explore the old farm buildings. We never went into the house itself, though. The aura of Dingoes still clung to it.

Only years later did Roxanna reveal to me that this was her parents' farm, abandoned during the Great Collapse of 2012, when the economy of those humans who were still holding out against the Mastery fell completely into ruin. The Nelsons (for that was the name on the mailbox—not Proust) had volunteered themselves and their children for the Schroeder Kennel. The children had been accepted, but the parents had been turned away, as by that time most older volunteers were. The Masters had no more need of wild pets, for now they bred their own.

It was principally from rejects like the Nelsons that the society of Dingoes, as we know it today, evolved, and Roxanna herself was not free from the taint (or so I regarded it then) of their wildness. How else was one to interpret these wilful visits to the scene of her childhood—visits in which she involved Pluto and me with such blithe disregard for our safety or moral well-being. The countryside was swarming with Dingoes even then (had not I lost my father to them?), and we three pets could have been abused or abducted without fear of reprisals. That our Master should have allowed us to venture so far, Unleashed and running wild, is indicative of the state of affairs at Schroeder Kennel.

It was late in the afternoon, and Roxanna, tired of reading, was lazily reminiscing to Pluto about her country childhood and how different the world had been then. I was above them in the branches of the apple tree, working problems in long division. Suddenly there appeared, suspended in mid-air almost near enough for me to touch, a girl of about my own age. Wisps of heliotrope spiralled about her, and her hair gleamed in the dying sunlight as though it were itself luminescent.

"Hello," she said. "My name is Julie. Don't you want to play?"

I could not reply. I was stunned as much by her loveliness (Yes, I *was* only ten, but children are not insensible of these things—perhaps not so much as *we* are) as by the shock of meeting a stranger in those unlikely circumstances.

She took a step towards me, smiling (Julie has always had the loveliest, cheek-dimpling smile), and I realized what would have been immediately evident to any other pet: that it was her Master's unseen presence that supported her. For him, anti-gravity would be a moment's improvisation. But our Master's neglect had made even such commonplaces as flights seem rare to us.

"Aren't you Leashed?" she asked, when she saw that I was not about to leave my branch and meet her halfway.

"No, none of us are."

By this time Roxanna and Pluto had become aware of our visitor, but, since they were a good ten feet below Julie and me, it was awkward for them to join the conversation. It was awkward for me, for that matter, but I blustered on.

"Would you like an apple?" I asked, picking one from the

abundance about me and offering it to her. She stretched forth her hand, then, with a guilty look, drew it back.

"My Master thinks I'd best not," she explained. "He says that sort of food is for Dingoes. You're not a Dingo, are you?"

"Oh no!" I blushed, though I knew she was only trying to make a joke. There could be no serious doubt of our domestication, for Dingoes wear clothing, while pets (who have better bodies, usually) only dress for formal occasions: the theater or a pageant.

"Would you like to slip in with me?" She held out her hand, and eagerly I jumped off the branch and was buoyed up in the gravity belt supporting Julie. I felt the meshes of a Leash close over my mind, and Julie, giggling with delight, leaped into the accommodating air to a height of thirty feet, and hung there, secure as a ping-pong ball suspended by a jet of air.

"Try and catch me!" she shouted, and then dashed behind the sagging roof of the old barn.

"What about me?" Pluto protested.

"You're probably too old, but I'll ask her," I promised, and disappeared from sight. She led me quite a chase, but it was such a pleasure to be able to fly again that I kept up with her effortlessly.

The Leash that I shared with Julie was loose—that is, it was not so intense that one wished to do no more than contemplate the mysteries of the life and Leash. One simply felt euphoric, zesty, and raring to go.

Once I had caught her, I made her explain what she was doing out here at the Nelson farm. It was not, after all, a crossroads. Julie explained that her Master had brought her to Earth to help choose new stock for his kennel in the asteroid belt. My eyes kindled with the hope that she might choose *me*. The kennels outside of the Earth, especially those beyond Mars, were known to be superior to Earthside kennels, and I longed to have a Master who would care for me.

Julie seemed to understand this, for she didn't keep me in suspense. "You will come back with us, won't you?" she asked, and her Master's voice resonated in my mind, echoing her plea: *Won't you?*

Her Master? No—now he was mine!

"Why did you come out *here?*" I asked. "Surely, you don't have time to look at all the pets on Earth."

"Because of who you are."

"Who are we?" I was sincerely puzzled.

"Only the sons of the most famous novelist in the last fifty years. That's all. It's incredible that every kennel in the solar system isn't trying to snap you up."

It was easy at Schroeder Kennel, where Roxanna was the only pet with a literary bent, and that so singularly directed, for Pluto and I to forget the extent of our father's fame. *A Dog's Life* had been, after all, an epoch-making book—like Luther's Bible or *Das Kapital.* Even the Masters had read and admired it. Daddy had won the Nobel Prize, entered the French Academy, and been elected to the American Senate. More than any other person, he had effected the reconciliation of men and the Masters, and it was for that reason that the Dingoes had marked him for vengeance. It was his book, in fact, that had given the Dingoes their name.

The wonder of that novel is that it's told entirely from a dog's point of view—a *real* dog. Before *A Dog's Life,* the Dingoes had used words like "kennel," Leash," and even "pet" as invective. After Daddy's book, the tables were turned: Daddy's terminology stuck. *Everyone*—that is to say, all the pets—began to name their children after famous dogs. There hasn't been a generation of puppies with stranger names since the Pilgrim Fathers went off the deep end back in the Seventeenth Century.

Which brings us back to Julie and me. "I've told you my name," she said. "But you haven't told me yours."

"White Fang," I said, proudly.

"White Fang," she repeated, cuddling up to me. "I don't see you as 'White Fang' at all. I'm going to call you Cuddles."

I should have objected then and there, but I was anxious lest I offend Julie and lose my ticket to the asteroids. And so it was that for the next ten years of my life I was known as Cuddles to all my friends.

Within hours of our return to the kennel, Julie's Master had negotiated the transfer of myself and Pluto from the Schroeder Kennel to outer space. Roxanna was very curt in her farewells. It was only natural that she should be disappointed at being left behind, but there was nothing to be done. Her pedigree was unexceptional, and her literary attainments, though they shone in the intellectual night of the Schroeder Kennel, were not really of the first magnitude when you looked at them from a greater distance.

The trip to the asteroids was made that night as we slept. What means our Master employed to transport us, I could not say. Nothing so crude as a spaceship. The Masters' technology is a spur-of-the-moment thing, and I will admit, for my own part, that mechanical engineering isn't really that interesting to me.

We woke to the subdued luminescence of kennel walls that we had known for years. The walls shifted to livelier color schemes in response to the quickening neural patterns of our waking minds. It was just like home.

But there was a difference: instead of the relentless drag of Earth gravity there was a gentle gravitational pulse, a relaxed ebb and flow that seemed to issue from my own heart.

I felt the Leash of my new Master close tighter over my mind (for the next ten years it would never *entirely* desert me, even in sleep), and I smiled and whispered my thanks to him for having brought me away.

Julie was awake now, also, and with a wave of her arm and a flourish of synthetic horn-music, the walls of the kennel dissolved and I beheld the boundless, glowing landscape of the asteroids.

I gasped.

It is yours, said a voice in my head that would soon come to seem as familiar as my own.

Hand in hand, Julie and I sailed out over this phantasmagorical playground, and the spheres of heaven played their music for us. Exotic blossoms exploded, like Roman candles, discharging their hoards of rich perfume. Colors wreathed us in abstract, joyous patterns, as the two of us bounded and tumbled through the shifting fields of gravity, like starlings caught in a dynamo.

Can it be that I shall never again enjoy the easy pleasures of that time? When I remember the way I passed through those ten beautiful years, I wonder if I am truly free or if I may not be, instead, exiled. Nothing, nothing on Earth can compare with the infinite resources of the Masters' pleasure domes.

It was paradise.

Really, it was almost paradise. Illness and pain were banished from our lives, and it might have been (for I know of no instance to disprove it) that, so long as we stayed Leashed, death too had lost its sting. Women no longer brought forth children in sorrow, nor did men eat their bread in the sweat of their brows. Our happiness did not degenerate into boredom, and our pleasures were never dampened by an aftertaste of guilt.

Paradise has a considerable flaw, however, from the narrative point of view. It is anti-dramatic. Perfection doesn't make a good yarn, unless one attempts (as I am given to understand my brother Pluto has attempted, in his more abstruse works) to emulate Dante. So there isn't much for me to tell you, except: *I liked it.*

I liked it; for ten years that was the story of my life.

3

In the summer of 2037, ten years after our departure, the three of us—Julie, myself, and our Master—were back again on Earth. Julie, in one of her sentimental moods, had wanted to stop by first at the Nelson farm, where we had met. Our Master, as usual, indulged her whim.

We sat, in the lightest of Leashes, beneath our apple tree and marvelled at the changes time had wrought not only in ourselves (for we had, after all, passed from puppyhood to maturity in the meantime) but also in the scene about us.

The roof of the barn had fallen in, and in the orchard and surrounding meadows, saplings had taken root and were flourishing. Julie gloried in the Gothic Revival. So great was her passion for returning to the past that she begged our Master to be Unleashed!

"Please," she whined. "Just this once. I feel so anachronistic out here in a Leash."

Our Master pretended not to hear.

"Pretty please," she whined more loudly, though it was much more like a bark by now.

A voice in my head (and in Julie's too, of course) soothed: *There, now, gently. What's this, my darlings, my dears, my very own pets? Why should you wish to throw off your Leashes? Why—you're hardly Leashed at all! Do you want to turn into Dingoes?*

"Yes!" Julie replied. "Just for this afternoon I *want* to be a Dingo."

I was shocked. Yet I must admit that at the same time I was a little excited. It had been so long since I had been without a Leash, that so primitive an idea appealed to me. I felt a yen for novelty. Or, as the Dingoes would say, freedom is a natural instinct of man.

If I Unleash you, there's no way for you to call me back. You'll just have to wait till I come back for you.

"That's all right," Julie assured him. "We won't leave the farm."

I'll return in the morning, little ones. Wait for me.

"Oh we will, we will," Julie and I promised antiphonally.

And then he was gone, and our minds stood naked in an alien world. A more vivid pink flushed Julie's cheek, and her eyes sparkled with a sudden, unaccustomed brilliance. I realized that this was probably the first time in her life as a pet, in her whole life, that is—that she had been entirely Unleashed. She was probably feeling tipsy. I was.

"Hello, Earthling," she said. Her voice seemed different, sharper and quicker. She plucked an apple from the branches overhead and polished it on her velvety skin.

"You shouldn't eat that, you know," I said.

"I know." She bit into it, then, with a little giggle, offered the rest of the apple to me. It was rather an obvious literary reference, but I could see no reason to refuse the apple.

I took a large bite out of it. When I saw the other half of the worm that remained in the apple, I began to retch, bringing our little morality play to an abrupt conclusion.

It was Julie who found the pump and got it working. The well water had a distinctly rusty flavor, but it was at least preferable to the taste in my mouth. Then, with my head in Julie's lap and her fingers tousling my hair, I went to sleep, though it was the middle of the day.

When I woke, the heat of the afternoon sun was touching me at every pore and I was damp with sweat. The wind made an irregular sound in the trees around us, and from the branches overhead, a crow cried hoarsely and took to the air.

I watched its clumsy trajectory with an amusement somehow tinged with uneasiness. *This* is what it was like to be mortal.

"We're getting sunburnt," Julie observed placidly. "I think we should go into the house."

"That would be trespassing," I pointed out.

"So much the better," said Julie, for whom the romance of being a Dingo for a day had not yet worn off.

In the farmhouse, dusty strands of adhesive—cobwebs—hung from the ceiling, and the creaking floor was littered with paper that time had peeled from the walls. In the upstairs rooms, Julie found closets and drawers of mildewed clothing, including some cotton dresses that would have been the right size for a ten year old. It was hard to think of Roxanna ever being that small. I felt vaguely guilty to have opened up this window on the past, and when one of the dresses, rotten with age, came apart in my hands, a little spooky too. I took Julie into another of the upstairs rooms, which contained a broad cushioned apparatus, raised about a yard off the floor. The cushion smelled awfully.

"It's a bed!" Julie said. "I've read about beds."

"So have I," I replied. "In Shakespeare. But these beds smell."

"They must decay, like the clothing."

I sat down on the edge of the bed, and it bounced with a creaking, metallic sound, like the sound of the pump outside. Julie laughed and jumped on to the bed beside me. It groaned, and the groan deepened to a rasp, and the rasp snapped. Julie went right on laughing as the bed collapsed to the floor. Looking at her sprawled out beside me on that quaint apparatus, I became aware of a feeling that I had never experienced before. For, though I had often made love to Julie, I had never felt quite this urgent about it. Undoubtedly, this was a result of being Unleashed.

"Julie," I said, "I'm going to bite you."

"Grr," she growled playfully.

"Arf," I replied.

We spent the night in the farmhouse amid creakings and groanings of old wood and ominous scurryings in the walls. We were up with the sun and we went, shivering, directly out of doors to wait beneath the apple tree. We were cold and we were hungry, and swarms of hostile, buzzing insects rose from the dew-drenched grass to settle on our raw skins and feed on our blood. I killed three or four, but the senseless things continued to attack us, quite oblivious to their danger. I began to understand why humans had always worn clothes before the advent of the Masters.

The sun had risen nearly to noonday, when Julie finally turned to me and asked, "What do you suppose is wrong, Cuddles?"

It was useless by now to pretend that nothing was wrong, but I could only answer her question with a look of dismay. Perhaps we were being punished for asking to be Unleashed. Perhaps. . . .

But how could we presume to interpret the Master's actions, especially such irresponsible, inconceivable, and thoughtless actions as leaving two pedigreed pets defenseless in an alien world among Dingoes!

When our hunger grew extreme, we gorged on apples, cherries, and sour plums, not even bothering to look for wormholes. Through that afternoon and into the night, we waited, but at last the chill and the darkness of the night forced us into the house.

The next morning was spent in more useless waiting, though this time we had the prudence to wear clothing— pants and jackets of rough blue cloth and rubberized boots. Almost everything else had rotted beyond repair. Our Master did not return.

"Julie," I said at last, "we're on our own. Our Master has abandoned us." She began to cry, not making much noise about it, but the tears rolled down her cheeks in a steady stream, faster than I could kiss them away.

But for all that, I must confess that Julie adapted to our new condition more readily than I. She enjoyed the challenges of that archaic and almost Dingo-like existence. Every day, while I went to a high hill in the vicinity to call, hopelessly and to no effect, to our Master, to *any* Master, Julie busied herself about the old house, clearing the floors, dusting, washing, airing out the musty furniture and decaying mattresses, and experimenting with the interesting new vegetables that grew among the weeds of a forgotten garden. My visits to the hillside became less frequent after the first week. I was convinced that our Master would never return to us. The thought of his cruelty and indifference passed quite beyond belief.

Helping Julie at odd jobs around the farm, I began to have

a certain respect for the pre-Mastery technology of Earth. I discovered and repaired one mechanical device that was especially useful: a rough stone wheel three feet in diameter and three inches thick, that was set into rotary motion by a foot pedal. By holding a piece of metal to the revolving wheel, the machine could be made to give off sparks, and these in turn ignited dry scraps of wood. The fire thus produced could be conserved in various engines in the farmhouse. Fire had an immense utility, but since I assume my readers are familiar with it, I will not make my digression any longer.

I only mention in passing that on the night of my discovery, Julie, sitting by me in front of a roaring log fire, looked at me with real *admiration!* A look that I returned—for she was very lovely in the firelight, lovelier than she had even been before, it seemed. The firelight softened the contours of her face, until I was aware only of her relaxed, easy smile and the brightness of her eyes, a brightness that did not need to borrow its brilliance from the fire but seemed to issue from her very being.

"Prometheus," she whispered.

"My own Pandora," I returned, and a scrap of old verse popped into my mind, at once comforting and terrible in its implications. I recited it to Julie in a low voice:

> *Your courteous lights in vain you waste,*
> *Since Juliana here is come;*
> *For she my mind has so displaced,*
> *That I shall never find my home.*

Julie shivered theatrically. "Cuddles," she said, "we've *got* to find our way home."

"Don't call me Cuddles," I said in, for me, a rough manner. "If you won't call me White Fang, stick to Prometheus."

4

Day followed day with no sign of our Master's return. The longer we stayed at the farm, the more inevitable discovery became. On my trips to the hillside I had sometimes noticed clouds of dust rising from the country roads, and though I was careful to keep under cover, I knew that luck alone and merely luck had prevented our capture so far. My imagination recoiled from what would become of us if we were to fall into the hands of Dingoes. I remembered my father, and it was not a memory to inspire confidence.

Therefore I determined that Julie and I must find our way to the Schroeder Kennel on foot, where, though we might not be so happy as we had been in the asteroids, we would at least be secure. But I had no idea of how to get there. Years ago when Roxanna had driven us to the farmhouse, she had taken a circuitous route, in a vaguely south-western direction, which I had never troubled to learn. In any case, it was not wise to walk along the roads.

I renewed my treks through the nearby woods, searching for a sign-post, something to guide us back to civilization. At last a sign was given to me: a hill rose on the other side of a marsh, on the crest of that hill was an electric powerline!

Where there was electricity there would be Masters.

In 1970, when the Masters had first manifested themselves to mankind, they had insisted that they be given complete authority over all electric plants, dams, dynamos, and radio stations. Without in any way interfering with their utility from a human standpoint (indeed, they effected major improvements), the Masters transformed this pre-existent network into a sort of electromagnetic pleasure spa.

In time, of course, their additions and refinements exceeded mere human need or comprehension. Human labor could manufacture devices according to the Masters' specifications that human understanding would never be able to fathom. But even human labor became obsolete as the Masters—in themselves, a virtually unlimited power supply—stayed on and took things over, freeing man from the drudgery of the commonplace that has been his perennial complaint. Freeing, to be more exact, everyone who agreed to become a pet.

Although in many respects, the Masters' innovations had superseded the primitive technology of the 1970s, they still maintained, largely for the benefit of the Dingoes, a modified system of electric powerlines, lacing the entire world in arcane geometrical patterns that only the Masters could understand.

It was to the powerlines that the Masters came to bathe

and exercise, and so it was to the powerlines that Julie and I must go. Even if there was no way to reach the Masters as they flocked back and forth in the wires overhead, we could follow the lines to some generator or powerhouse, perhaps the one that adjoined the Schroeder Kennel, perhaps one elsewhere, for kennels were invariably located near power stations.

And, once we reached the powerline, it would be a safe journey. No Dingo would dare trespass into the very heart of the Masters' domain.

We prepared for the trip in minutes. While Julie improvised knapsacks, I went to the toolshed. There was an antique weapon there, a rusty wedge of iron mounted on a long wooden handle. I tested it out on the floor of the shed, and with a little practice I could swing it with lethal force and fair accuracy. If it splintered Dingoes half so well as it smashed pine boards, it would serve my purpose admirably. Grimly, I refined upon its murderous properties. I had noticed that the spark-producing machine would put a fine edge on metal that was held against it at the proper angle. After patient experimentation, I had so sharpened the iron blade that the merest touch would sliver flesh. Now, I thought, let the Dingoes come!

We set off before noon, neither of us in the best of spirits: Julie was wistful and melancholic at leaving the farm (though she agreed we had no other choice), and I was nervous and apprehensive. From the hill from which I had espied the powerline, we struck out into a wood of scrub pine, birch, and balsam. In the woods, there was no way to estimate our progress. The sun can be used as a compass, but it makes a poor speedometer. We walked, and when it seemed that we had walked twice, three times the distance to the powerline, we kept on walking. Julie became petulant; I became angry. Then she grew angry and I sulked. But always while we were walking. The brush caught at our pant legs, and the mosquitoes nipped at our necks. The mud at the edge of the marsh about which we were forced to detour sucked at our boots. And we walked.

The sun, striated by long, low, wispy clouds hung huge and crimson at the horizon behind us; before us a pale sliver of moon peeped over the crest of a hill—and on the hill, black against the indigo of the sky, stood the powerline.

Julie dropped her pack and ran up the hill. "Masters," she cried, "Masters, we've come. Leash us. Make us yours again. Bring us home."

The powerline stood stark and immobile, wires swaying gently in the breeze. Julie embraced the wooden pole and screamed at the unhearing wires, "Master, your pets have come back to you. Why did you leave us? But we've come back. We forgive you. We love you. MASTERS!"

"They don't hear you," I said softly.

Julie stood up, squaring her shoulders bravely, and joined me where I had remained at the foot of the hill. There were no tears in her eyes. But her lips were pressed together in a mirthless, unbecoming smile.

"I hate them," she pronounced in a clear voice. "With my whole being, I *hate* them!" Then she fell into my arms in a dead faint.

As twilight deepened to night, I stood guard over Julie and watched with amazement and renewed hope the great shafts of light that streamed from the northern horizon. They glowed whitely in the black sky, dimming the stars as they shot out, dissolved, and re-formed.

The Northern Lights: Aurora Borealis.

It was there especially that the Masters loved to play and relax. They felt at home among the electrons of the Van Allen Belt and where it curved in to touch the Earth's atmosphere at the magnetic poles, they followed it, controlling the ionization of the air, structuring those pillars of light that men have always wondered at to conform to the elaborate rules of their supravisual geometry. These shifting patterns were the supreme delight of the Masters, and it was precisely because of the strength of Earth's Van Allen Belt that they had originally been drawn to this planet. They had only bothered to concern themselves with mankind after a number of nuclear explosions had been set off in the Van Allen Belt in the 1960s.

The aurora that night was incredibly beautiful, and so I knew that the Masters were still on Earth, living and flaming for their pets—their poor, lost, maltreated pets—to see.

It was a cold flame, and very remote.

"Your courteous lights in vain you waste," I muttered.

Julie, who has always been a light sleeper, stirred. "I'm sorry," she mumbled, probably too sleepy still to remember what she was supposed to be sorry about.

"It's all right. We can find them tomorrow," I said, "and tomorrow and tomorrow." Julie smiled and slid by imperceptible degrees back into sleep.

The next day we followed the lines to the north. They ran along an old asphalt road, scarred with fissures and upheavals, but still easier to travel than the rank brush on either side.

A faded sign gave the distance to Schroeder as 22 miles. Using the road (for the wires overhead were sufficient protection, as we thought, against the Dingoes), we could hope to reach the kennel by midafternoon. Regularly we passed deserted farmhouses set back from the road and, twice, the road widened and the ruins of houses were set closer together: a town. Here the poles would branch off in all directions, but the main powerline followed its single course towards Schroeder. The poles were of rough pine, stained to a reddish-brown by creosote, one just like another, until. . .

Julie noticed it as we neared Schroeder. Running up and down the poles were thin silvery lines that glinted metallically in the sunlight. On closer inspection, the lines formed vertical chains of decorative elements in simple repeating patterns. One common design of overlapping circles linked in series by straight lines, so:

Another was a simple zigzag pattern:

The most frequent designed resembled a circuit diagram of dry cells in series:

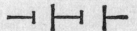

In fact, they were *all* circuit diagrams!

It was too crude decoratively and such nonsense from any other point of view that I knew it could not be the work of the Masters. No, there was something barbaric about these markings that suggested Dingoes.

But what Dingo would dare approach this near the sanctuary of the Masters? The Kennel must be only a few hundred yards off. I began to have misgivings about our security. Before I could properly begin to savor this danger, another had presented itself.

"Cuddles!" Julie screamed. "My God, the power station!"

I was already at her side. A cyclone fence that ran some hundred feet along the road prevented our entrance to the substation, but it made no difference, for it was nothing but a rubble heap now. I-beams, gnarled and twisted like the limbs of denuded oaks, stood in black silhouette against the light blue of the afternoon sky. The pylons that had fed the high tension wires into the substation lay on the ground like metal Goliaths, quite dead. The wires that had led out from the station had been snapped and hung inert from the top of the cyclone fence, where now and again a breeze would stir them.

"It's been bombed," I said, "and that's impossible."

"Dingoes?"

"Yes, I suppose so. But how *could* they?"

It made no sense. So primitive an attack as this couldn't succeed against the Masters when the whole rich arsenal of 20th Century science had failed. Oh, the nuclear blasts in the Van Allen Belt had *annoyed* them. But I doubted then and I doubt now whether man has it in his power actually to kill one of the Masters.

How could it be done? How do you fight something without dimensions, without even known equations that might give a symbolic approximation to its character? Not, surely, by bombing minor power stations here and there. Not even by bombing them all. The Masters transcended mere technology.

Inside the fence, from somewhere in the tangle of gutted machinery there was a moan. A woman's voice reiterated the single word: "Masters, Masters. . . ."

"That's not a Dingo," Julie said. "Some poor pet has been caught in there. Why, Cuddles, do you realize this means *all* the pets have been abandoned?"

We made our way through a hole in the fence sheared open by a fallen pylon. Kneeling a few feet from that hole, her face turned away from us, was the moaning woman. She was using the blasted crossbeam of the pylon as a sort of *prie-dieu*. Her hair, though tangled and dirty, still showed traces of domestication. She was decently naked, but her flesh was discolored by bruises and her legs were badly scratched. Confronted with this pathetic ruin of a once handsome pet, I realized for the first time how terribly *wild* Julie looked: dressed in the most vulgar clothes, her hair wound up in a practical but inartistic bun and knotted with strips of cloth, her lovely feet encased in clumsy rubber boots. We must have looked like Dingoes.

The poor woman stopped moaning and turned to confront us. Her face expressed, in order, the ascending degrees of amazement, ending in blank amaze.

"Father," she said, aghast.

"Roxanna!" I exclaimed. "Is it you?"

5

It was she. We were the longest time calming her and explaining that, quite the opposite to being her father, I was only little White Fang, grown up to a man's estate.

"But your clothes," she said. "I'd know that jacket anywhere. And those boots with the red rubber circle around the rim."

Briefly as I could, I explained how our Master had brought us to the farm and deserted us, and how we had to take clothes from the farmhouse—her parents' clothes, as it happened.

"And did your brother Pluto come back with you?"

"No. He's left the solar system, the last I heard."

Roxanna's expression underwent a subtle change, as though she had begun to make calculations. The conversation lapsed awkwardly.

"Have you read Pluto's book?" Julie asked.

"I started it, but I couldn't understand it." She sighed. "My reading's fallen off lately. Even Proust doesn't seem as interesting as he used to. And then, of course, there's been this revolution. . . ."

"Ah yes," I said, "the revolution. Would you tell us some more about that?"

Roxanna's account was none too clear, having been assembled from eavesdropped conversations and uninformed conjecture. Even the word *revolution* proved to be misleading. I've written here not the garbled story Roxanna told us then, but the facts as they were later to be established by the courts and newspapers.

July had been a month of unusual sunspot activity. The Masters, anticipating the dynamic auroral displays that follow such periods, had flocked to Earth—many, like our Master, bringing their pets with them. Shortly after our arrival, during the afternoon that Julie and I had been Unleashed, a solar prominence of extraordinary intensity had erupted from the center of a sunspot cluster and knocked the Masters out of commission.

It was like a house that's been drawing too heavily on its current. Everything was turned on: the refrigerator, the stove, the air conditioner, the iron, the toaster, the coffee pot, the flood lights, the television, and the model railroad in the basement. Then *Blat!*, lightning strikes and there's one hell of a short circuit. Lights out, tubes popped, wires burnt, motors dead.

The Masters weren't dead, of course. They're made of stronger stuff than toasters. But while they convalesced. . .

Roxanna herself had been spared the worst of it, since she hadn't been *in* the Schroeder Kennel when the lights went out. But she'd seen it happen. In a flash (literally, a flash), the entire kennel—walls, floors, even the anti-gravitic furniture had disappeared.

It was as though they had existed only as an idea in the mind of God, and then God had gone and forgotten them. Pets, who had been soaring balletically in the vast spaces of the gymnasium, soared now in vaster spaces. Everyone who had been in the Kennel suddenly found himself plunging down to the ground, overpowered by the Earth's gravity, accelerating.

The carnage had been terrible. The Schroeder Kennel, such as it was, was thrown into panic. But the worst was still before them. The Dingoes, quicker to realize what had happened than the distracted pets, had overrun the breeding farms and kennels everywhere. In the first fires of revolutionary excitement, they were ruthless. Puppies were taken from their mothers, to be raised in the homes of Dingoes; the men, any who resisted, were ruthlessly slaughtered before the eyes of their mates, and the women. . . . Well, what would one expect of Dingoes?

At this point Roxanna broke into tears, unable to go on. I noticed then that her body was covered with small black-and-blue marks, too tiny to have resulted from blows, but too numerous to be accidental. I insisted that Roxanna finish her tale.

"Oh, I hate him!" she said, not loudly but quite expressively nonetheless. "I hate him! God, how I *hate* him!"

All in all, it took Roxanna the better part of two hours to tell this story, for she had a way of veering off into digressions that would have been the delight of any admirer of *Tristram Shandy,* though, for my own part, I am inclined to be more straightforward. In fact, her divagations had begun to distress me considerably, as soon as I realized that the vicinity was still swarming with Dingoes, and that Roxanna was living with the chief of them!

"Roxanna," I said, trying to get her to her feet, "Julie and I are going to help you to escape. And we'd better start right away."

"It's too late," Roxanna said with a sigh in which the resignation was not unmixed with a little pleasure. Too long allegiance to such a master as Proust had finally taken its toll on Roxanna's character, and, though I may anticipate my story by mentioning the word here, I should like to say it and have done. Roxanna, sadly, was something of a masochist.

"Roxanna," I said, more firmly now, "you *must* come with us."

"Get your own bitch, Mister," came a good-natured bellow of a voice from not too far away. With a sinking heart, I faced the intruder, a red-faced hulk of flesh many sizes too large for the khakis he wore. He stood on the other side of the fence, arms akimbo and grinning broadly. He held what looked like a glass fishing rod in his meaty hand. "The name's Schwartz—Bruno Schwartz. I'm the head of the RIC in these parts. We're repatriating these damn pets. Now, come on home, Rocky, old girl. Your master calls." He laughed.

So this was a Dingo! For the moment I was safe, for he

obviously mistook me for a Dingo too, and perhaps I might have escaped if I had let him go on believing it. But I was too angry.

"You are not Roxanna's Master, and she is not going with you."

"The hell you say!"

"Please," Roxanna pleaded. "I must go to him." But her body didn't protest; she was limp with fear. I pushed her behind me and picked up my axe from the ground.

Bruno's smile broadened. "What are you, anyhow? Some kind of pet!"

"Dingo!" I said with the utmost contempt.

Bruno reached a hand behind his back and made adjustments on an apparatus strapped there. It was the size of one of our knapsacks. Then he climbed through the hole in the fence, brandishing the long, flexible pole.

"Axes!" he scoffed. "Next thing you know someone will invent the bow and arrow."

I advanced towards the Dingo, who stood now within the fence, my axe readied and murder in my heart, as they say. With my left hand I held on to the metal frame of the fallen pylon, using it as a crutch. My knees were very weak.

Bruno flicked the end of the glass fishing rod against the pylon. There was a spark and my mind reeled.

I was sitting on the ground. I could see Bruno above me between white flashes of unconsciousness. I swung at him wildly. The axe hit the pylon with a dull *thunk*.

He flicked the pole at me again. It touched my left leg at the knee. The shock tore through my body and wrenched a cry from my lips.

"Good stuff, huh, Jack? Great for the circulation. If you're interested in mechanical things, it's real easy to make. It's a prod pole. Prod poles were meant for cattle, but they work on most any animal."

He flicked it again, tracing a line of pain across my neck. I screamed in agony—I couldn't help it.

"The fishpole was my idea. It handles easier this way."

He let the tip of the pole play over my right arm. Every shred of consciousness that remained to me was in my hand. I clenched the axe handle until the pain in my hand was worse than the flashes of pain that tore through my whole body—until there was no consciousness left.

When I woke (seconds later? Minutes? I don't know), I could hear Roxanna's hysterical laughter. Bruno had finished with her. Julie's voice, pitched so high that I could hardly recognize it, was saying *stay away*, and then, a little sharper still, *Stay away!*

There was a sparking noise and her scream. "White Fang!" she called. "Oh, Mastery—*White Fang!*"

She had called me *that!* Not Cuddles, not Prometheus. White Fang! I sprang to my feet, and the axe was just part of my hand now. I felt, as never before, even when I was Leashed, totally alive and aware, absolutely sure of myself. My body was a living flame.

Bruno had caught hold of Julie. He heard me scrambling over the wreckage of the station and turned around just in time for the axe to come crashing down across his chest.

I hadn't meant to draw blood. I had only wanted to smash the power pack strapped to his back.

There was a terrible gush of blood from the chest wound, thick and winy. The axe in my hand was covered with blood. It was horrible. I had never seen anyone bleeding like this before, never.

It was horrible! The blood. The thought that I had done this—even the sight of it—was too much, and I collapsed onto Bruno's fallen body.

The last thing I remember was Roxanna's tear-streaked face as she rushed forward to take the fallen Dingo in her arms.

6

Though my bed was comfortable, the walls of the room antiseptically white, and my meals thoroughly good, I suspect that I spent the next week in a prison, not a hospital. The guard who brought my food would not speak to me, and I was not allowed to read. My only diversion from anxiously wondering what was in store for me was looking down at the semi-deserted streets four stories below.

I did not know what city this was, nor how I had come

here. There was some faint recollection of sitting by another, smaller window and staring with dismay at the laboring propeller without, desperately wishing my Master had been there to tend to its rustic operation—but perhaps that was only one of the nightmares I had so frequently then.

I knew that the few people I saw on the streets, the women in long, ungainly dresses and the men in unseasonably heavy suits, must be Dingoes. And though I had never seen Dingoes in such close proximity before, their dress and behavior was so uniformly dull that I soon grew tired of observing them and began, instead, to count the cars that went by.

This wasn't so boring as you might think, for the various trucks, jeeps, and tractors still in use among the Dingoes (rarely if ever did one see a car) presented a beautiful study in comparative ruination. From the way they roared and sputtered and spewed out black clouds of noxious gas it was obvious that the Dingoes had abandoned heavy industry for decades. These were antiques.

They were usually of an official nature, and those same insignia which I had seen scrawled on the telephone poles outside of Schroeder were painted on the sides of the trucks or on banners that streamed from the jeeps' antennae. I was reminded of the heraldic devices of some crusading army: resistor statant, sable on a field of gules; diode dormant, on a quartered field, ermine and vert.

To my surprise, the city was strongly illuminated at night. Either the Dingoes had an independent source of electric power (which seemed unlikely) or the Masters had the power stations back in operation and were re-establishing their dominance. For a moment the chemistry of hope jangled my nerve ends, but I quickly recollected where exactly I was, and the hope fizzled.

After a week in this limbo, I received my first visitor. It was Julie, but a Julie so altered in appearance that I thought at first she was a Dingo spy in disguise. Prison does develop one's paranoid tendencies.

She was wearing a high-necked, long-sleeved, floor-length dress in the Dingo style, and her beautiful hair was concealed by an ungainly cork helmet such as I had seen on several persons passing below my window.

"Julie!" I exclaimed. "What have they done to you?"

"I've been repatriated." She wasn't able to raise her eyes to look into mine, and her whole manner was one of unnatural constraint. No doubt, this could be accounted for by the presence of the armed guard who was watching us from the open doorway.

"You mean they've forced you to. . ."

"Nobody's forced me to do anything. I just decided to become a Dingo. They're really much nicer than I thought they'd be. They're not all like Bruno. And even he's not so bad—once you get to know him."

"My God, Julie!"

"Oh, don't be upset. That's not what I meant. Bruno's too much in love with Roxanna to think of bothering me."

"That isn't what I meant."

But Julie went blithely on. "They're going to get married as soon as he's out of the hospital. On the airplane coming here, he was delirious and he told me all about himself. I can't say I understood much of it. Do you know that he actually *likes* you? He does. There he was all bandaged up, lying on the stretcher, and he said, 'I wasn't smashed like that since God knows when. Good man! We'll get along, White Fang and me.' I thought it was just the delirium, but he was serious. He wants you to visit the both of them as soon as you can."

"And Roxanna's going to marry him?"

"Yes. And she's very mad at you. For hurting Bruno."

"But I was trying to protect her!"

The story that Julie at last unfolded, in her rather scattered way, was this: Roxanna, when she saw me strike Bruno with the axe, suddenly decided that she was in love with her tormentor, and her new-found love was every bit as strong as the hatred she had expressed only minutes before. In the heat of the moment, she had been almost angry enough to use my axe on me, but Julie and the Dingoes who had been drawn to the scene had been able to stop her. They didn't stop her from revealing that I was the son of Tennyson White, a fact that Roxanna was sure would lead to my summary execution, since she had often heard the story of how Daddy had been done in by the Dingoes. But instead we'd been shipped off to St. Paul, where the Dingoes had their head-quarters in the old State Capitol Building.

What they intended to do with me now, Julie would not say, even if she knew. I had my own grim suspicions.

Julie spent the rest of her visit trying to justify the haste with which she had allowed the Dingoes to repatriate her, and since she had no apparent excuse but expediency, it was rather hard going.

At last I interrupted her. "Julie, please don't talk on about it. I quite understand that you've had to disassociate yourself from me. Heaven only knows what they intend should happen to me, but there's no reason it should happen to you as well. Perhaps they mean to use me as a hostage. Perhaps they mean something worse. In either case, you're lucky to be rid of me." I was just beginning to hit my stride, and no doubt I would have brought myself to the point of tears, when Julie started to giggle.

To giggle! She tittered and snorted and snuffled like someone who can't keep a joke, and she left the room bent double with the pain of holding back her laughter.

Hysteria, of course. It was a very sad thing to see the girl you love in such a condition and to be unable to help.

Within an hour of Julie's departure, I was removed from my cell and conducted to an unmarked limousine in perfect working condition.

I did not know where it was taking me, for the curtains were drawn in the back seat, but shortly we found ourselves in a large and largely vacant underground parking area. Then, after a labyrinth of staircases, corridors, guards, and passwords, I at last found myself alone in front of an imposing mahogany desk.

The desk and all the appointments of the room testified to the consequence of their possessor. In a subsistence economy like that of the Dingoes, luxury is a potent symbol.

My attention was especially drawn to the portrait that hung over the desk. Done in the mock-primitive style popular in the late sixties of the last century, it slyly exaggerated those features of the subject which were most suggestive of the raw and barbarous. His stomach, though monumental itself, was seen from a perspective that magnified its bulk. The face was crudely colored, particularly the nose, which was a florid alcoholic crimson. The violet-tinged lips were at once cynical and voluptuary. The picture was the perfect archetype of the Dingo.

Yet, perhaps not perfect, for the eyes shone with an intelligence and goodwill that seemed to contradict the overall impression of brutishness. This one dissonance added to the archetype that touch of *individual* life which only the best portraitists have ever been able to achieve.

I was still engaged in studying this painting (and really, it had the strangest fascination for me) when its original stepped into the room and came forward to shake my hand.

"Sorry to have kept you waiting, but my time hasn't been my own ever since that damn sunspot."

When he had finished shaking my hand, he did not immediately release it, but, keeping it in his, looked me over appraisingly. "You'll have to get rid of that name of yours, you know. White Fang just won't do. We Dingoes, as you call us, don't like doggish names. Your proper name is Dennis White, isn't it? Well, Dennis, welcome to the revolution."

"Thank you but. . ."

"But who am I? I'm the Grand High Diode. As far as you're concerned, that means vice-president. Are you interested in politics?"

"Pets don't have to be. We're free."

"Ah, freedom!" The Grand High Diode made an expansive gesture, then plopped into the seat behind the desk. "Your Master takes care of everything for you and leaves you so perfectly free. Except that you can't taste anything from the good-and-evil tree, why, there's nothing that isn't allowed you."

He glowered at me dramatically, and I had time to compare the portrait with the portrayed. My admiration for the artist grew by leaps and bounds.

"The Masters appeared two-thirds of a century ago. In that time, *human* civilization has virtually disappeared. Our political institutions are in shambles; our economy is little more than bartering now; there are practically no artists left."

"Among Dingoes perhaps. But under the Mastery, civilization is flourishing as never before in man's history."

"Cows were never more civilized than when we bred them."

I smiled. "You're playing with words."

"Perhaps you'd rather not argue."

"I'd *rather* argue. If it keeps me away from the hangman—or whoever you employ for such purposes."

"Perhaps you can avoid him altogether. Perhaps, Dennis, I can convince you to become a Dingo?" The man's thick, violet lips distended in a wolfish grin. His eyes, which were, like his eyes in the portrait, vivid with intelligence, glittered with a strange sort of mirth.

I tried my best to look disdainful. "Isn't it rather late to join? I should think that most of the carnage must be over by now. You'll be ready to be defeated any day now."

"Oh, we'll probably be defeated, but a good revolutionary can't let that worry him. A battle that isn't against the odds would hardly be a battle at all. The carnage, I'll admit, is unfortunate."

"And unjustifiable as well."

"Then I won't bother to justify it. Dirty hands is one of the prices you pay in becoming a man again."

"Are you fighting your revolution just so you can feel guilty about it?"

"For that—and for the chance to be our own Masters. Guilt and sweat and black bread are all part of being human. Domestic animals are always bred to a point where they're helpless in the state of nature. The Masters have been breeding men."

"And doing a better job of it than man ever did."

"That, I might point out, is exactly the view a dachshund would take."

"Then let me put in a good word for dachshunds. I prefer them to wolves. I prefer them to Dingoes."

"*Do you?* Don't make up your mind too quickly, or it may cost you your head."

And, with this threat, my incredible inquisitor began to chuckle. His chuckle became a pronounced laugh, and the laugh grew to be a roar. It occurred to me that the gleam in his eye might as well have been madness as intelligence.

Suddenly I was overcome by a desire just to have done. "My mind is made up," I announced, when he had stopped laughing.

"Then you'll make a declaration?"

Apparently, he had taken the exact opposite of the meaning I had intended.

"Why should you care which side I'm on?" I demanded angrily.

"Because a statement from you—from the son of Tennyson White—with the strength of that name behind it—would be invaluable in the cause of freedom."

Very deliberately I approached the mahogany desk where

the man was sitting, wreathed in a fatuous smile, and very deliberately I raised my hand and struck him full in the face.

Instantly the room was filled with guards who pinned my arms behind my back. The man behind the desk began to chuckle.

"You beast!" I shouted. "You Dingo! You have the conscience to kidnap and murder my father, and then you *dare* ask me to make you a declaration of support! I can't believe—if you think that. . ."

I'm afraid that I went on raving like that for a little while. And as I raved that incredible man lay sprawled on the top of his desk and laughed until he had lost his breath.

"White Fang," he managed at last. "That is to say, Dennis, my dear boy, excuse me. Perhaps I've carried this a little far. But you see—*I* am your father. I'm not murdered in the least."

7

The next week went by at a pace that would have been nightmarish if I hadn't been so giddily, busily happy. First off, I married Julie. Daddy was adamant about that. He explained how Dingoes, especially those in the public eye, have to appear very monogamous. I had no objection to marriage, and if monogamy was necessary, there was no one I would rather have been monogamous with than Julie. She entered into the spirit of things with enthusiastic atavism, and I suspect now that part of Daddy's insistence had had its origin in my bride.

Still, it was a nice wedding. Hymen's candle never burned brighter than on the day that our hands were joined over the glowing vacuum tube on the altar of the renovated power station.

We had our first quarrel an hour later when she told me that she'd known about Daddy and the test he was preparing for me on the day that she had come to visit me at the jailhouse. But the quarrel ended as soon as Julie had pointed out that, since I'd passed the test so well, I had no cause for anger. I hate to think what would have happened, however, if I'd agreed to make the "declaration" that Daddy had proposed.

From the first, Julie and I were celebrities among the Dingoes. At a steady succession of lunches, dinners, and dances, we played the part of refugees from the "tyranny of the Masters, grateful for our new-found freedom." That's a quote from the speech Daddy wrote for me to deliver on such occasions. It always drew applause. Dingoes have no taste.

While I acted my role as a model revolutionary, I carried on another more significant drama inwardly. Had it been merely a contest between filial piety and my loyalty to the Masters, I would not have hesitated long, for filial piety is negligible when, for seventeen years, you have presumed your father dead.

But mine had been no ordinary father. He had been Tennyson White, and he had written *A Dog's Life*. Now I discovered there was a sequel to that book.

I read through *The Life of Man* in one sitting of fifteen hours' duration. It was one of the most shattering experiences in my life. In fact, right at this moment, I can't remember any others to compare.

Anyone who's read it realizes the difficulty one faces trying to describe it. It's got a little bit of everything: satire, polemic, melodrama, farce. After the classic unity of *A Dog's Life*, the sequel strikes at one's sensibilities like a jet of water from a high-pressure hose. It begins with the same light irony, the same subdued wit, but gradually—it's hard to say just when—the viewpoint shifts. Scenes from the first novel are repeated *verbatim*, but now its pleasantries have become horrors. Allegory gives way to a brutal, damning realism; and every word of it seemed an accusation aimed directly at me.

After the first reading, I had no more distinct memory of it than I would have had of a hammer blow. And so I entirely overlooked the fact that *The Life of Man* is autobiography from first to last.

My father Tennyson White belonged to the first generation of men who grew up away from Earth. His first visit to his native planet was at the age of twenty, and it was almost a disaster.

Stricken with a virus infection (those were the days before

the Masters had quite mastered all the intricacies of their pets' physiology), Daddy had been abandoned to a rather second-rate hospital, not unlike the Schroeder Kennel in its indifference to the pets who were put up there. Daddy was bedridden for one year, time enough to lose his faith in the Mastery.

Time enough, also, for him to draw up the outlines for *both* of his novels. Time enough to contact important Dingoes and map out with their aid a program for revolution. *A Dog's Life* was to be the overture to that program.

Many authors have been accused of corrupting youth and debasing the moral coinage of their times. Probably none have ever set about it so deliberately as Daddy.

His novel was a time-bomb disguised as an Easter egg and planted right in the middle of the Masters' basket. It was a Trojan horse; it was a slow-working acid that nibbled at the minds of the pets—just a mild, aesthetic tickle at first, then as it worked in deeper, an abrasive that scarred them with guilt.

For men are not meant to be domestic animals.

Those who stood the acid-test of that novel managed to escape to Earth and join the Dingoes. Those who didn't (and sadly, these were by far the majority) stayed with the Masters and incorporated the monstrous satire of *A Dog's Life* into the fabric of their daily lives. They became dogs.

Ten years after the publication of *A Dog's Life*, Daddy effected his own escape.

His autobiography makes no mention of the fact that he left his two sons behind when he went over to the Dingoes, and he refuses to talk about it still. I have always suspected that he doubted, if only slightly, whether he was doing the right thing. It was a large enough doubt that he was willing to let us decide for ourselves whether we wished to become Dingoes or remained Leashed.

The Earth was swarming with refugees from the Mastery, and the revolutionary movement—the Revolutionary Inductance Corps, or RIC—was getting on its feet. (Naturally, the Dingoes did not want to call themselves *Dingoes*.) Daddy's next task was more difficult, for he had to forge an army from the unorganized mass of apathetic Dingoes who had never left Earth. *The Life of Man* accomplished part of his purpose, for it showed the Dingoes what they were: an amorphous mass of discontent, without program or purpose; a race that had taken the first step towards its own extinction.

But the Dingoes were not such novel-readers as the pets. Only the more thoughtful read his second novel, and they didn't need to. Daddy gradually realized that no amount of literature would spark the tinder of the Dingoes into a revolutionary firebrand.

And so it was (and now we leave Daddy's autobiography and enter the sphere of raw history) that my father invented a mythology.

The Dingoes were ripe for one. Ever since the appearance of the Masters (who bore an unfortunate resemblance to mankind's favorite gods), organized religion had gotten quite disorganized. Men of religious or mystical sensibilities were among the first to volunteer for the kennels, where they could contemplate the nearly divine nature of the Masters without any of the discomforts of the ascetic life.

The Dingoes, on the other hand, found it difficult to venerate gods who so much resembled their sworn enemies.

Daddy realized that under these conditions, the Dingoes might accept a "religion" of demonology and sympathetic magic. When the gods are malign, men turn to jujus and totems.

But wax dolls and devil masks would no longer do, for the first law of sympathetic magic is that "like produces like."

The Masters were electromagnetic phenomena: then what better talisman than a dry cell?

In any elementary physics text, there was a wealth of arcane lore, hieratic symbols, and even battle cries. Children were taught Kirchoff's Laws in their cradles, and men (and women) wore cork helmets to ward off the Masters, since cork was a good insulator. It was nonsense, but it was effective nonsense. The Revolutionary Inductance Corps won an overwhelming majority in the councils of the Dingoes on the slogan: ELECT RIC.

Daddy became Triode in the revolutionary government, next in authority to the High Cathode himself. Everyone was ready to begin the revolution, and no one had the least idea how to go about it.

Which goes to show that it's good to be prepared, because that was when a providential sunspot short-circuited the Masters.

The leaders of the Dingoes had managed to take the credit

for their own good luck, but now a month had passed since the sunspot, and already the Masters had manifested themselves here and there as localized patches of luminescence in the atmosphere, hovering over their pets and repossessing them. In a very short time the Mastery would be established stronger than ever, unless the Dingoes found some way to stop them.

Cork helmets may be good for morale, but in a real contest I'd as soon defend myself with a popgun. If the Dingoes had made any serious plans, Daddy wasn't telling me about them.

8

Daddy, Julie, and I had been waiting in the lobby of the St. Paul Hotel for fifteen minutes, and in all that time we hadn't seen one room clerk or bellboy.

There weren't even many guests, for Earth had become so depopulated during the Mastery that a roof and a bed were always easy to come by. What you couldn't find anywhere was labor. Even the best hotels and restaurants were self-service.

Finally Bruno and Rocky (for that had come to seem a better name for her than Roxanna) finished dressing and came down to the lobby. Bruno was wearing an unpressed cotton suit and a sport shirt open at the neck, so that a little bit of the bandage about his chest peeped out. Rocky was dressed to kill; Julie looked as staid as a nun in comparison. But when you're only twenty years old, you don't have to try so hard as you do when you're thirty-two.

We exchanged pleasantries, decided on a restaurant, and went out to Daddy's car—and thus began the ghastliest night of my life.

Bruno was returning to his post in Duluth the next day, and we'd been unable to put him off any longer. For days he had been insisting that the five of us—the two Schwartzes and the three Whites—"make a night of it." I felt guilty towards Bruno, and at that time I hadn't yet learned to live with a guilty conscience. I gave in.

I would have been suspicious of overtures of friendship from a man I'd sent to the hospital and I might have simply supposed that, like most Dingoes, Bruno was chiefly interested in making my father's acquaintance. However, his first overture had come before he knew my father was Tennyson White, and so it was hard to doubt his sincerity. I decided that he was only mad.

If I felt guilty and awkward towards Bruno, I can't imagine how Rocky felt towards me. When she had revealed my identity to the Dingoes she couldn't have known that my father was the second-in-command of the Dingoes—not, as she had supposed, their arch-enemy. Only initiated members of the RIC knew who their leaders were. She had intended to see me executed, and instead she had saved my life. Now we were sitting next to each other in the back seat of Daddy's limousine, talking about old times. When we got out, she managed to bring her spiked heel down on my instep with lethal accuracy, and once, in the middle of the dinner, smiling brightly and chattering all the while, she kicked me square in the shin underneath the tablecloth.

The meal wouldn't have gone beyond the main course if it hadn't been that almost all of Rocky's remarks went over Bruno's head. He was dauntlessly ebullient, and when he started to talk, he could go on indefinitely. To shut off Rocky (who couldn't hear enough about our wedding), I questioned Bruno about his childhood, which had been (it seemed to me) spectacularly awful. For the majority of Dingoes, life is one long battle: against the world, against their families, against their teachers, and against the decay of their own minds and bodies. No wonder Bruno was the aggressive lout that he was! But it didn't make me like him any better.

When the dinner was done and I thought we might make our escape, Bruno brought out an envelope from the pocket of his coat and announced, as though he really expected us to be happy, that he had five tickets for the fight.

"What fight?" I asked.

"The boxing match at the Armory. Kelly Broughan's there tonight, so it should be worth seeing. I bet you don't see many good fights out in the asteroids, do you?"

"No," I said in defeated tones. "None at all."

"There are some beautiful gymnastic competitions, though," Julie put in.

Bruno's laugh was the bellow of a wounded bull. *Gymnas-*

tics was a good joke; *beautiful* was even better. "You're a card, Julie. Dennis, that girl's a card," he got out between bellows.

Rocky's eyes gleamed wickedly. "Dennis, you really must come, seeing that you're such a scrapper yourself. And you must come too, Mr. White. You look worn out."

"What the hell," Daddy said, "let's all go. And afterwards we'll watch the fireworks."

"I love fireworks," Julie said, with forced cheer.

We got up from the table with one accord. Bruno and Rocky were as happy as two children. Julie and I were glum. But Daddy. . .

Daddy was in so profound an abyss of depression and defeat that he was quite literally unaware of most of what was going on around him. He knew, as we did not, that the Dingoes were about to shoot their wad that evening, and he knew, as the rest of the Dingoes did not, that their wad wasn't worth a plugged nickel.

All they had was atomic bombs.

Whether it was because Bruno knew the gate attendant or because Daddy was with us, I don't know, but our General Admission tickets got us seats at ringside. Our eyes had scarcely adjusted to the smoky light of the auditorium, when a bell rang and two men, modestly nude except for colored briefs, approached each other, moving their arms in nervous rhythms, circling about warily. One (in red trunks) lashed out at the other with his left hand, a feint to the stomach. With his right hand he swung at the other man's face. There was a cracking sound as his naked fist connected with his opponent's cheekbone. The crowd began to scream.

Blood spurted from the man's nose. I averted my eyes. Bruno, in his element, added his distinctive bellow to the uproar. Rocky watched me closely, treasuring my every blanch and wince. Daddy looked bored, and Julie kept her eyes closed through the whole thing.

I should have done the same, but when I heard another *thunk* and a loud crash, curiosity overcame my finer feelings and I looked back into the ring. The man in red trunks was lying on his back, his expressionless face a scant few inches from my own. There was blood on it. Rocky was shrieking with pleasure, but Bruno, who felt an allegiance for the fighter in red trunks, shouted, "Get up, you bum!"

I was about to be nauseous. I rose from my seat, mumbling apologies, and found my way outside, where I was discreetly sick in a hedge across the street from the Armory. It was a very interesting experience, for the second time in my whole life I had thrown up. I was reminded of the apple I had eaten in the Nelson orchard.

The hedge bordered on a park which had been allowed to go to seed. Through the thick summer foliage I could see the glint of moonlit water. I strolled down the hillside to the pond's edge.

Down there, the din of the stadium melted into the other night sounds: the croaking of the frogs, the rustle of poplar leaves, the rippling water. It was quiet and earthlike.

A full moon shone overhead, like the echo of a thousand poems. All the earthbound poets who had stolen the fire of their lyrics from that moon, age after age! It had passed them by, oblivious of histories, and it would pass me by in time. That's the way that things should be.

I knew then that I belonged to the Earth, and my spirit dilated with happiness. It wasn't quite the right time to be happy—but there it was. Julie and the moon were part of it, but it was also the frogs' croakings, the poplars, the stadium; Daddy, cynical, aspiring, even defeated; partly, too, it was Bruno and Roxanna, if only because they were so vital. These things melted into my memory of the Nelson farm, and it seemed that I could smell the winy smell of apples rotting in the grass.

The sky was growing brighter and brighter. The moon. . .

But was it the moon? A cloud of mist had gathered above the pond and it glowed until the full moon was almost blotted out behind it.

The meshes of the Leash closed over my mind, and a voice inside my head purred kindly, *White Fang, good boy! It's all right now. We heard your call.* (But I hadn't called! It was just that I had been so happy!) *And now I've come. Your Master has come back at last for you.*

I cried out then, a simple cry of pain. To be taken away now! Only a few days before I had cried for the lack of this voice—and now. . . .

There, it soothed, *there, there, there. Has it been that very bad? Those terrible Dingoes have captured you, but it won't happen again. There, there.*

The Leash began gently to stroke the sensory area of the cortex: soft fur wrapped me, scented with musk. Faint ripples of harp-music (or was that only the water of the pond?) sounded behind my Master's voice, which poured forth comforting words, like salve spread over a wound.

Then, with a sudden pang, I remembered Daddy. (*Don't think of your poor father*, the Leash bade.)

He was waiting for me. Julie was waiting for me. (*We'll get Julie back, too. Now, don't you worry yourself any more.*)

Desperately I tried not to think, or at least to keep my thoughts so scrambled that I would not betray the things I knew. But it was exactly that effort that focused my thoughts on the forbidden subjects.

I tried to think of nonsense, of poetry, of the moon, dim behind the glowing air. But the Leash, sensing my resistance, closed tighter around my mind, and cut through my thin web of camouflage. It shuffled through my memory as though it were a deck of cards, and it stopped (there was just time enough for me to catch the images then) to examine images of my father with particular attention.

There was, on the very edge of my perceptions, a sound: *Ourrp.* Which was repeated: *Ourrp.* It was not a sound my Leash would make. The harp-music quavered for a moment, becoming a prosaic ripple of water. I concentrated on that single sound, straining against the Leash.

"What is that sound?" I asked my Master. To answer me he had to stop sorting through my memories. *Nothing. It's nothing. Don't think about it. Listen to the beautiful music, why don't you? Think of your father.*

Whatever was making the sound seemed to be down in the grass. I could see clearly in the wash of light from the cloud above me. I parted the grass at my feet, and I saw the beastly thing. *Don't think about it!*

The front half of a frog projected from the distended jaws of a water snake. The snake, seeing me, writhed, pulling his victim into the denser grass.

Again the Leash bade me not to look at this thing, and, truly, I did not want to. It was so horrible, but I could not help myself.

The frog had stretched his front legs to the side to prevent the last swallow that would end him. Meanwhile, the back half of him was being digested. He emitted another melancholy *Ourrp.*

Horrible, I thought. *Oh, horrible, horrible, horrible!*
Stop this. You . . . must . . . stop. . . .

The snake lashed his body, wriggling slowly backwards.
The frog's front feet grasped at sprigs of grass. His *Ourrp*
had grown weak. In the failing light, I almost lost sight of the
struggle in the shadow of the tall grass. I bent closer.

In the moon's light I could see a thin line of white froth
about the snake's gaping jaws.

The cloud of light had disappeared. My Master had left,
and I could hear Daddy calling my name. I ran back up to
the street. He was there with Julie.

"Mastery!" Julie said. "You shouldn't have run off like
that. We came out and saw a light over the lake, and I was
sure they'd carried you off."

"They almost did. My Master was there, and I was
Leashed. But then I slipped out of it somehow. And he went
away. He just disappeared. Are you all right, Daddy?"

For he was visibly shaking with excitement. "Oh, quite,
quite," he said, paying scant attention. "I'm thinking."

"He had an idea," Julie explained, "after you ran out of the
fight. I guess this is what happens when he has ideas."

Bruno pulled up beside us in the limousine and honked,
not because we hadn't seen him, but just because he liked to
honk. We got into the back seat and the car tore off down the
street at a speed that it must not have hit for the last half a
century.

"Rocky's making the calls you told her to, sir," Bruno announced.

"Fine. Now, Dennis, what was this about your Master?"

I explained what had happened, concluding with an account of the frog and the snake.

"And while you were watching that, your Master just faded
away?"

"Yes. If he'd kept at me much longer, he'd have learned
everything he was looking for. I couldn't have stood out
against him. So why did he go?"

"One more question, first. What did you feel about that
frog? Precisely."

"It was ugly. I felt . . . disgusted."

"Was it anything like the way you felt at the fight tonight?"

"Worse."

"But the same sort of thing? Ugliness, then disgust and nausea?"

"Yes."

"Then those are the weapons we'll fight them with! Dennis, my son! Before this night is over, you will be a great hero of the revolution!"

"Don't I deserve an explanation, or does the revolution need ignorant heroes?"

"When you left the fight you looked so distressed that I was a bit amused. Dennis is such an aesthete still, I thought. And then I remembered the old saw: *Like Master, like man.* Turn it around, and it's the formula for our weapon: *Like man, like Master.* The Masters are just their own pets writ large. They're aesthetes, every last one of them. And we're their favorite art-form. A human brain is the clay they work in. They order our minds just the way they order the Northern Lights. That's why they prefer an intelligent, educated pet to an undeveloped Dingo. The Dingoes are lump clay, warped canvas, faulty marble."

"They must feel about a Dingo the way I do about Salvador Dali," Julie said.

She always wanted to argue about Salvador Dali with me, because she knows I like him.

"Or the way I feel about prize fights," I suggested.

"Or any experience," Daddy concluded, "that offends a person's aesthetic sensibilities. They just can't stand ugliness."

We were silent for a while, considering this. Except Bruno. "Give yourself time, Dennis. You'll get so you like a fight. Kelly just wasn't in form tonight, that's all."

Before I could answer, the limousine was sailing down a concrete ramp into a brightly lit garage. "The hospital," Bruno announced.

A man in a white robe approached us. "Everything is ready, Mr. White. As soon as we received your call, we set to work."

"The radiomen are here, too?"

"They're working with our technicians already. And Mrs. Schwartz said she'd join her husband directly."

A terrible light suddenly kindled the night sky outside the garage.

"The Masters!" I cried.

"Damnation, the bombs!" Daddy exclaimed. "I forgot about them. Dennis, go with the doctor and do what he says. I have to call up RIC headquarters and tell them to stop the bombings."

"What are they bombing?"

"They're trying to land one in the Van Allen Belt. I tried to tell them it wouldn't do any good. They tried it in 1972, and it didn't accomplish a thing. But they were getting desperate, and I couldn't suggest any better plan. But now it would be disastrous if they detonated a bomb in the Van Allen Belt, because it will knock out radio communications, and we're going to be needing them. Bruno, Julie, wait in the car for me."

A team of doctors led me down the long enamel-white corridors to a room filled with a complicated array of electrical and surgical equipment. The doctor-in-chief indicated that I was to lie down on an uncomfortable metal pallet. When I had done so, two steel bars were clamped on either side of my head. The doctor held a rubber mask over my mouth and nose.

"Breathe deeply," he said.

The anaesthetic worked quickly.

9

Daddy was yelling at the doctor when I woke up. "Did you have to use an anaesthetic? We don't have time to waste on daintiness."

"The placement of the electrodes is a very delicate operation. He should be awake in any moment."

"I'm awake," I said.

The doctor rushed over to my pallet. "Don't move your head," he warned. Rather unnecessarily, it seemed, for my head was still clamped in the steel vise, although I was now propped up into a sitting position.

"How are you feeling?" Daddy asked.

"Miserable."

"That's *fine*. Now, listen: the machine behind you ("Don't

look," the doctor interrupted) is an electroencephalograph. It records brain waves."

The doctor broke in again. "There are electrodes in six different areas. I've tried to explain to your father that we're uncertain where perceptions of an aesthetic nature are centered. Little work has been done since. . . ."

"Later, doctor, later. Now what I want Dennis to do is suffer. Actually, it's White Fang who will suffer. White Fang must drown in misery. I've already arranged some suitable entertainments, but you should tell me right now if there's anything especially distasteful to you that we might get. Some little phobia all your own."

"Please—explain what this is about?"

"Your electroencephalograms are being taken to every radio station in the city. The wave patterns will be amplified and broadcast over AM and FM. Every station in the country, in the world, is standing by to pick them up. Tomorrow night we'll give the Masters a concert like they've never heard before."

A man in workclothes brought in a blackboard and gave it to Daddy.

"Doctor, you have better fingernails than I do. Rub them over this slate." It made an intolerable noise, which the doctor kept up for a solid minute.

"How does the graph look?" Daddy asked.

"Largest responses are in the sensory area. But fairly generalized elsewhere, especially during the first twenty seconds."

"Well, there's lots more coming. Look at these pictures, Dennis." He showed me illustrations from a medical encyclopedia that I will refrain from describing here. The people in the pictures were beyond the reach of medicine. Beyond the reach, even, of sympathy.

"The response is stronger and more general now. Quite well defined."

Daddy passed a vial of formaldehyde beneath my nose. It was actually more a bottle than a vial, and in it. . .

I screamed.

"Excellent," the doctor said.

"Bring in the band," said Daddy.

A crew of four men with musical instruments I was unfamiliar with (they were, I've since learned, electric guitar, musical saw, accordion, and tuba) entered the room. They were dressed in outlandish costumes: glorified work clothes in garish colors garnished with all sorts of leather and metal accessories. On their heads were ridiculous, flaring bonnets.

"Extraordinary," the doctor said, "he's already responding."

"Go to it, boys," Daddy said.

They began—well, they began to *sing*.

It was like singing. Their untuned instruments blasted out a stupid *One*-two-three, *One*-two-three repetitive melody, which they accompanied with strident screams of "Roll out the barrel." When I thought that this new attack on my sensibilities had reached the threshold of tolerance, Daddy, who had been watching me intently, leaped up and began to slam his feet on the floor and join them in that awful song.

Daddy has a terrible voice for singing. It rasps.

But his voice was the least of it; it was his behavior that was so mortifying. I wanted to turn my head away, but the vice held it fast. For a man of such natural dignity to so debase himself, and that man my own father!

This was, of course, just the response Daddy was looking for.

When they had finished their gross display, I begged for a moment's reprieve. Daddy dismissed the band and returned the accordion player his cowboy hat.

"Don't work him too hard, until we have some idea of his breaking point," the doctor advised. "Besides, I'd like to see the intern just a minute, if you'll excuse me. The photographs gave me an idea: there are some patients in the hospital. . . ."

"Have you thought of anything, Dennis?"

"In a way, yes. Is Bruno still around?"

"He should be downstairs."

"If he were to tell me about the things he enjoys—the very worst things—in the long run he might think of more horrors than you. They seem to come naturally to him."

"Good idea. I'll send for him."

"Roxanna, too, if she's down there. I remember how she watched me at the boxing match. She'd be able to help you quite a lot."

As Daddy left the room, the doctor returned, escorting a caravan of litters. Photographs are no equivalent for the real thing.

It went on that way for four hours, and every minute seemed worse than the one before. Bruno had a limitless imagination, especially when it was abetted by alcohol and his wife.

He told me about his favorite fight to begin with. He told me what he would like to do with pets, and what he *would* like to do, if he had more time. Then he discoursed on the mysteries of love, a subject on which Rocky, too, was eloquent.

After two hours of these and other pleasures, I asked to have some coffee. Rocky left for it and returned with a steaming mug from which I took one greedy swallow before I realized it was not coffee. Rocky had remembered how I felt about blood.

When I had been revived with smelling salts, Daddy brought in more entertainers. They had come to the hospital directly after their last fight at the Armory. For some reason, most of what happened after that point I can no longer remember.

10

We were out on the tile terrace of the hospital, Daddy, Julie, and I. Below us the Mississippi was a pool of utter blackness and unknown extent. It was an hour after sunset, and the moon had not yet risen. The only light came from the North, where the great auroral floodlight swept out from the horizon across the constellations.

"Five minutes," Daddy announced nervously.

In five minutes radio stations all over the world would begin to broadcast my performance of the night before. I had heard an aural equivalent of my electroencephalograms, and I wasn't worried. In a war based on aesthetics, that recording was a doomsday machine.

"Does your head still hurt?" Julie asked, brushing a feather-light hand over my bandages.

"Only when I try to remember last night."

"Let me kiss the hurt away."

"Three minutes," Daddy announced, "and stop that. You're making me nervous."

Julie straightened her blouse, which was made of some wonderful, sheer, crinkly nylon. I had really begun to admire some of the uses of clothing.

We watched the aurora. All over the city, lights had been turned off. Everyone, the whole world, was watching the aurora.

"What will you do now that you're High Cathode?" Julie asked, to make conversation.

"In a few minutes the revolution should be over. I don't think I'd like administrative work. Not after this," Daddy said.

"You're going to resign?"

"As soon as they let me. I've got the itch to paint some more. Did you know I paint? I did a self-portrait once that's over my desk. I think it's pretty good. In any case, it's traditional for retired generals to paint. And then I might write my memoirs, I've picked a title for them: *The Aesthetic Revolution*."

"Ten seconds," I said.

We watched the northern skyline. The aurora was a curtain of bluish light across which bands and streamers of intense whiteness danced and played.

At first you couldn't notice any difference. The spectacle glimmered with the same rare beauty that has belonged to it from time immemorial, but tonight its beauty was that of a somber *Dies Irae*, played just for us.

Then one of the white bands that was shooting up from the horizon disappeared, like an electric light being switched off. It seemed unnaturally abrupt, but I couldn't be sure.

For a long while nothing more happened. But when five of the arcing lights snapped out of the sky at the same moment, I knew that the Masters were beginning their exodus.

"Elephantiasis, I'll bet."

"The picture you showed me. I can remember it very clearly."

"What's that, Dennis?"

The auroral display was less bright by half when they came to the hillbilly band. I turned on the radio just to be sure. Through all the blasts and shrieks and whistles of my neural patterns, there was an unmistakable rhythm of *Oom*-pah-pah, *Oom*-pah-pah.

When the broadcast came to Rocky's unspeakable potion, there was a tremendous blast across the heavens. For an instant the entire sky was stained white. The white faded. The aurora was only a dim blue-white shadow in the north. There was hardly a trace of beauty in it. It flickered meaninglessly in random patterns.

The Masters had left Earth. They couldn't stand the barkings.

DANGEROUS
FLAGS

Once, long ago, in Pennsylvania, there was a little mining town called Mean because everyone there tended to approach the median. Life in Mean was nasty, brutish, short, and inelegant. Yet in other important respects it was no different from your own. Men labored and women labored and children learned. Except when the seasons changed, one day was just like another. Then one bright summer day all the angleworms began to die.

"Is it the plague?" asked the aldermen.

The committee decided it was not the plague. They didn't know *what* it was, but, after all, nobody really cares about worms.

Then the houses of Mean began to fill with a peculiar smell, like the smell of a scientific experiment, and hamsters began to die in the cellars.

"Stamp out hamsters!" cried a few rash people.

The committee investigated and discovered what was causing the deaths of worms, hamsters, cats, dogs, and even a few rash people. It was this:

Coal gas!

For, deep below the streets of Mean, in unremembered tunnels cut nookshotten through the bowels of the Earth, the deadly fumes of coal gas were burning.

Coal gas!

The fiery fumes seeped upwards through the ground, as coffee percolates through coffee grounds, and poisoned first worms, then hamsters, and at last old women in their beds. Nothing, no one, escaped the deadly virulence, and day after day the fires raged unabated in the old coal mines, releasing new deadlines.

Coal gas!

Fires gnawed at the very fiber of the Earth, consuming in big lumps the veins of anthracite and causing strange collapses everywhere. Gaping holes appeared where highways met. Whole houses sank below their lawns, and deep moats suddenly were noticed in front of the Methodist Church. It was beautiful and scary.

"This is crazy!" said a vestryman in an interview with the Press.

"It can't go on like this," said one housewife, "or we will all die!"

And so a town meeting was called, and it drew the best attendance that any town meeting had drawn since the school bond issue had been put to a vote.

"Our very lives are at stake," the little housewife referred to above insisted as soon as the meeting began. "We must put out the fire to save our very lives."

"Don't be silly!" came a voice from the back of the hall. The eyes of the assembly turned to regard the mysterious English teacher who had spoken.

She, too, was beautiful and scary. Her fingernails were the color of almonds and her eyes were the color of burnt almonds. She smoked mentholated filter-tip cigarettes, inhaling deeply and exhaling evenly through two tiny nostrils. When she spoke her voice popped the silence like a grey balloon.

"There is no need for mere alarmism. This is the school bond issue all over again. Reason and not prejudice will answer all our needs. What is done cannot be undone. The Moving Finger writes, and having writ moves on." She smiled, despite herself.

"Hear! Hear!" shouted her rich nephew, who was sitting at her side.

"Be quiet, Gwyon!" She continued, smirking, "Nor all your piety nor wit can uh, change a word of it."

"But you live on top of Old Manse Hill," the little housewife objected in a voice like yours. "You don't have to worry about the coal gas poisoning you or your children."

"I have no children," the English teacher replied. "And *no one* has to worry about the coal gas. There is no such *thing* as coal gas."

"You are wrong!" came a great booming voice from still farther back in the hall.

"Who *dares* oppose me?" exclaimed the English teacher.

"It is me that opposes you—me, the Green Magician."

"It is *I*," the English teacher corrected. "Say: it is *I*."

"It is *I*," he said.

"Well I don't give a hoot whether you're green or red, Green Magician, but I'll tell you this right now—you don't know what you're talking about!"

"Hear! Hear," shouted her rich nephew.

"Be quiet, Gwyon!"

"I have come to save this town from the burning coal gas, but for my services I must ask ten dollars."

"Don't be absurd," the teacher screamed. "For ten dollars we can buy three new books for the school library."

"Let's vote! Oh, let's vote," the housewife suggested.

"No!" said the English teacher. "Because I challenge the Green Magician here to answer three riddles first." No one at the town meeting opposed her. No one ever did.

"I accept," the Green Magician said, with a little bow. On top of everything else, he was quite good looking.

"Beware, Green Magician: if you cannot answer my three riddles you must leave this little mining town and never return."

He nodded in solemn agreement. A trumpet call announced the first riddle.

"To make new wine when vines are bare . . ." the teacher thrust.

"Smash the old bottle!" the magician parried.

"The second riddle: what is stick-me and nick-me and lick-me and never grows up?"

The Green Magician hesitated. "Give up?" she snarled.

"I have it," he triumphed. "Hershey chocolates!"

"So! (Damn him!) The third riddle, then. . . ." The mysterious English teacher laughed deep inside herself for she knew that there was *no* answer to this riddle. ". . . What is the sound of one hand clapping?"

The Green Magician raised one hand, his right hand, and clapped.

"I have won!" he bubbled.

"Then die!" proclaimed the English teacher and suiting her action to her word, she hurled the butt of her mentholated filter-tip cigarette at the Green Magician.

It struck his right temple and instantly the Green Magician exploded. Nothing was left but a sort of sticky green powder on the ground.

But the Green Magician wasn't really dead. He was only sleeping. But that was the end of the town meeting anyhow.

Now, as the last light glimmers to a stop in the darkened hall, the English teacher and Gwyon go to the spot where the Green Magician had exploded a moment ago and secretly they begin to scrape the sticky powder from the plastic upholstery and the backs of chairs and blow it into little beige envelopes.

"This is what we'll do," the English teacher explained to her rich nephew, who wasn't very bright, if truth be told, "we'll keep the coal gas burning and while the town is worrying about the silly pestilence, the waterspout will destroy them all."

"What waterspout?" Gwyon asked.

"The one on the radio, you fool!"

For, because of the coal gas, no one in Mean had turned on his radio for the weather report. The town would be caught unprepared. That was the English teacher's plan for destroying everyone.

"But first," the English teacher waved her mentholated filter-tip cigarette expressively, *"first,* we must take this powder down to the fires in the mines. There it will be utterly consumed!" (She screamed expressively.) "And then we'll hear no more of the Green Magician! Ha! Ha! Ha!

"Follow me, my darling, my dear, into the crypts below town hall. Then, through a secret garden into the mine shaft, away we go."

Tip-toe, down, in darkness, down, step-by-step, together, the unholy pair descend.

Will all the townspeople be destroyed?

What is really in the envelopes?

And is the Green Magician dead?

But—stay!

There's still a chance for all of us, because look: her rich nephew takes his little beige envelope from the pocket of his vest. He opens it. And then, unseen by his aunt, *he eats it too soon!*

But the English teacher isn't going to give up as easily as that. Oh no! She knows how to save her nephew:

By reciting her three favorite poems!

Her first favorite poem is *A Psalm of Life* by Henry Wadsworth Longfellow.

Her second favorite poem is *Locksley Hall* by Alfred Lord Tennyson.

Her third favorite poem is *The Incubus,* and she had written it herself. This is the way it goes:

> Nightshade and roses of rare mutation bloom,
> and wretched blights in midnight revel dance
> to the horned god: such nights that Pluto sways
> in full dominion; nights that know no stars
> but His; bats gibbering: night like this,
> this night now steep the hills in jet. Tonight
> the owl is torturing the nightingale.

After she had recited all three poems her nephew was safe again, and the English teacher gave a sigh of relief. But their plan was partly spoiled because of the powder, and together they drove off to Cincinnati just in time to escape the Green Magician.

> Wake, wake up, wake up
> And save us, Green Magician.

That's what the magic figures in the wallpaper sang to wake up the Green Magician. And he did wake up, too, because now the English teacher's spell was broken.

It was like that time in Arizona when the Green Magician was hypnotized by the Grand Dragon of the G.O.P. He had thought he was a Eurasian spy until the *real* spy had snapped his fingers, releasing him from his trance.

> Hurry, Green Magician, hurry
> To put the burning gas out,
> Because we still have to worry
> About the waterspout.

In the dismal crypts below Town Hall, the wind whistled and the light played strange tricks on a man. It was a labyrinth, and there was only one door that would lead him to the stairs that went down to the subterranean coal mines.

Was this the right door?

Be careful! Watch out!
Before you take another step,
Look for the English teacher's trap!

No, this *wasn't* the right door. *This* was! The Green
Magician ran down the steps as fast as he could run, holding
his breath so that he would not inhale the deadly fumes of the
coal gas. At the bottom of the steps, he spread a large,
square, white handkerchief on the floor of the mine shaft,
and, still holding his breath, he crossed his eyes and *wished
very hard.*

And what do you suppose happened? That's right! The
Snow Fairy appeared!

"What do you wish?" she asked the Green Magician.

"To save the town from the coal gas."

"What will you give me?"

The Green Magician gave the Snow Fairy ten dollars of his
own money. Satisfied, the Snow Fairy walked right into the
middle of the blazing inferno and *waved dangerous flags* at
the coal gas. The fire went out, and the Snow Fairy returned
to her home in Fairyland.

"Thank heaven!" said the Green Magician.

The townspeople, overjoyed when they heard of the Green
Magician's exploit, came down the mine shaft lickety-split
and gave three cheers for the Green Magician, who had saved
them, after all.

"I nominate the Green Magician to be our king," said the
little housewife gratefully. "Let's vote."

Everybody voted for the Green Magician to be king. They
had simply forgotten the English teacher.

"My dear subjects," said the Green Magician, "I am delighted to be able to tell you that your old English teacher is
dead."

"Hurray!"

"And her rich nephew is dead, too."

"Hurrah!"

"They died together in a Labor Day accident on the
Pennsylvania Turnpike."

"Well, then, let's dance!" cried the little housewife (and
everybody else) in a transport of ecstasy.

And dance they did. Down in the old coal mine they all
danced around the Green Magician, while the waterspout

passed harmlessly overhead. Very softly, the Green Magician sang his favorite song.

The Green Magician's favorite song is *America the Beautiful,* and now let's all of us stand up and sing it too.

THE DOUBLE-
TIMER

8:30 It started off bad. I was half an hour late getting up. The
alarm had been pushed in, and Karen had left her bed and
was puttering in the kitchen. I had started to shout something
to her about trying to make me late for work, when I
remembered that this was Be Kind To Karen Week.

So I changed it to "Good morning, honey. What's it like
out?"

She looked in, smiling. "A beautiful morning. Too warm
for October. Just right for me."

Anyhow I was up and had an hour and a half to get to the
station house. Nothing had gone wrong except my nerves.
Morning's not the best time for me.

I shaved and made myself human. Then I took out the blue
pinstripe from the closet and tore off the cleaner's plastic bag.
The gray suit I had worn yesterday was draped over a chair. I
took the belt from it and hung it up, making sure that my
keys and wallet were still in the pocket.

I almost made my first mistake then. In all my planning I'd
never thought of the money I'd need that day for carfare or
lunch. The trouble with thinking along a double time scheme
is getting them mixed up this way. It would have been a hell
of a thing to get stuck outside the apartment without money,
since I had already returned home to get it. Some beginning
for the perfect crime. But maybe that isn't clear. Give me time.

I took a few bills from the pocket of the pants hanging in
the closet and went out to the kitchen.

9:00 Breakfast with Karen. We have tickets for a musical
that opens tonight. Three tickets—one for our good friend

Eric. Karen talked about the musical, then about Eric. Eric is painting this, Eric is doing that. She enjoys flaunting her adultery.

One of his paintings has been hanging in the middle of the living room for the past year. A nude. Like a knife in my side to keep the wound fresh. It was his anniversary present to us. Eric has a great sense of humor. But I am past the stage now when the wound smarts. I was past it long ago.

Somewhere in the city, even as I sat at the table listening to Karen's prattle, Irving Venner was making his way to our apartment. Irving Venner—that's me. And Karen was soon to be the victim of a murder. I had a second cup of coffee and looked at her.

She was beautiful. Long white-blond hair loose over her bare shoulders. Blue eyes, fair skin, and a lithe body to match. Even the slightly receding chin and the front teeth that were a little too long were defects that she had turned to her advantage. She had learned long ago to keep her lips closed over her teeth, and the slight tension this required gave her an air of constant bemusement, of being always just about to smile.

She seemed to find pleasure in the most commonplace circumstances, at breakfast, on a walk—or talking to Eric. Then more than ever her whole face seemed to come alive. Her eyes sparkled. Her fingers made nervous little patterns, brushing back her hair, holding a glass, or just resting a moment on her lap. And always that hint of a smile, as though she could not keep herself from mocking me. That smile was an agony to me. At last I determined to end the mockery. When I knew that I was going to kill Karen, my suffering almost disappeared. I could even enjoy how beautiful she was, despite her treachery, as I sat with her waiting for the moment when I should leave for work.

*   *   *

9:20 I left the apartment. We live on the second floor, and I use the stairway instead of waiting for the elevator. A figure stood in the dimly-lit alcove behind the staircase on the first floor. He nodded to me. I repressed my excitement and walked on. The figure was me. Everything had gone all right. Karen was as good as dead. That's what the nod meant. In fact, that "figure" knew that she *was* dead.

As I opened the street door, I heard footsteps going up the stairs. Accustomed as only a police investigator can be to the paradoxes of time-travel, it did seem like a dream. There I was, standing still and listening to Irving Venner walk up the stairs.

Something similar had happened to me once before by accident. I had had to investigate a hit-and-run case. After being shifted back into the morning, I had walked to the corner where it was going to happen. My way had taken me past the street I live on, and I'd seen myself going down into the subway on my way to work. It was then I got the idea. Just a germ of it but the germ grew. I realized that I was one of the very few people in the world who could commit a crime and get away with it.

According to the Police Code, even the incident at the subway was criminal negligence. I could have been prosecuted if I'd ever told about it. There's a good reason for that rule. Back at the end of the 20th century, when the police started using the Machines, some smart operators thought they'd strike up a friendship with themselves. It's a natural idea once you start thinking about time-travel. I can't remember all the stale comedies and television skits I've seen with that gimmick. Natural, but not healthy. The smart operators had to be put away.

The psychologists say it's not the person in the past seeing himself a few hours older (the limit is eighteen hours)— that's like meeting some long-lost relation, somebody who's essentially a stranger. What really did it was getting shifted back and then doing exactly what you could remember having seen yourself do. They could remember everything that happened and couldn't change a second of it. The idea of predestination is too much for a human being in big doses. *Déja vu* is the expression, but such a *déja vu* as never was before. Most of them slipped off into catatonia after a few days and never came back.

I wasn't going to make a mistake like that. As for the time later in the day when I would see myself, I knew from experience that a glance wasn't going to do any harm. The nod was a risk, but I felt I could stomach that much predestination.

9:45 I arrived at the station house no more over-excited than I suppose any murderer must be right before the gala performance. I didn't let it show. I'm a past master at that kind of camouflage. I'd had to learn it, living with Karen.

As Karen had said, it was a beautiful morning. One of those crisp, bright October days that can make themselves felt even in the city. Wisps of haze circled the horizon to the west toward the river. A flight of sparrows rose from the gutter and lighted on the pediment of the old-fashioned station house as I walked up the steps. A nervous criminal might have taken this for an omen. But I wasn't nervous. Besides, how do you tell whether an omen is good or bad?

9:50 I had the office to myself. Ordinarily Lowell Clemenson, the other investigator for the city, would be in the room, but Lowell had started out on his vacation a week ago. Lowell, being the athletic type, (I'm portly, myself) was somewhere in Canada paddling a canoe. Quite out of reach.

Lowell and I are the only two people in the city licensed to use the Machine. To be an investigator you have to take tests for intelligence and emotional stability. Then a battery of physicals. Your character is investigated from the age of two. (My middle name is Probity.) They train you for five years, and once you've got the job, you have to see an analyst regularly. There isn't any surplus of investigators.

But then there doesn't have to be. In the year 2042, crimes are as common as buffalo. The Machines stopped it. Any thug who tried to pull something would be found out in a day. The absolute certainty of discovery has eliminated all but the most desperate crimes. Nobody robs banks when they know that Someone is watching them from concealment, when they know that every action they might perform is foreknown by that Someone, who has made his plans accordingly. In the year 2042, the only criminals are men who are beyond reckoning consequences, the only crimes are crimes of passion, invariably followed by a suicide.

Not for me, thank you. I'm quite happy living except for one thorn in my side. And that, I knew, looking up at the clock over the file cabinets, would be very shortly removed.

*   *   *

10:00 The phone call came.
"Hello. Chief?" It was my own voice.
"This is he," I answered.

Then I held my hand tightly over the earpiece. It would have been interesting to listen, but it might bring on a *déjà vu* later, when it would be important to have my wits about me. Besides, I knew already what I was saying on the phone. I had gone over it many times. What need then to listen?

I waited exactly two minutes to lift my hand. The connection was broken. I put the receiver back in its cradle and gave it a friendly pat.

11:30 Went to the Chief's office. He was reading one of those 20th-century detective stories that he ferrets out of used book stores. I think he's nostalgic about the Good Old Days before the Machines, when a policeman was more than a traffic co-ordinator or a registrar of accidents and public nuisances. The few real crimes left in the world aren't even in his department. He's not licensed to use the Machines.

"How's business?" I asked him.

"Slow," he said, laying the book aside. "A couple drunks that had to be removed from the sidewalks and a traffic accident."

"Anything bad?"

"No. McNamara's out there now. Somebody sideswiped by a taxi. He's only dazed. An ambulance is taking him in for x-rays. The only real excitement this morning was *The Murder of Roger Ackroyd.*"

I was slow to pick that one up.

"Murder!"

He laughed and showed me the cover of his book. "I can't say yet who did kill him. Never can tell to the end of the damn books. How're things with you?"

"All right. A little dull in the office with Lowell gone. Any word from him?"

"Not since the postcard last week. He's probably lost by now in dark wildernesses."

He couldn't be lost enough at that moment as far as I was concerned.

"Not Lowell," I said.

"How's Karen?"

His question was not asked altogether for form's sake. Karen was on the best terms with the Chief, and with everyone else on the force for that matter. We had a reputation for being the model couple.

Karen and I are so good at acting that we even performed

for each other. As far as she knew, I had never seen what was going on between her and Eric. I'd never caught them in *flagrante delicto;* Karen was too careful for that. My grounds for suspicion were whispers and looks, accretions of small, innocent-seeming occasions that, in the course of time, had built a solid pyramid of ugly truth. But they would never have stood up in a divorce court. If I had ever revealed my suspicions to Grierson, the analyst that I had to see every week, he would probably have considered them delusional. Then Irving Probity Venner would have been out of a job or (which would be worse) set out on some corner to blow a whistle at the traffic. No thank you.

There had been no help for it. I had had to act by myself.

"Karen? Oh, Karen is fine," I replied absently. Then I changed my tone. "Actually she was a little sick this morning. Upset stomach, nothing serious. She thought she'd be all right by tonight."

"What's tonight?"

"We've got tickets to *Tunis Forty-Two.* It opens tonight. Taking a friend. The anniversary's coming up again soon, and we're doing a little celebrating in advance."

"I hope Karen is feeling better. Why don't you call her up?"

"She's probably in bed. The best cure is a rest cure, as Karen says."

No one of these facts was essential to my plan, but together they presented a plausible picture of the everyday. And I had planted my good friend Eric in that picture.

The Chief's secretary came in, and I turned to leave the office. When I reached the door, I looked back at him.

"I'm going to have an early lunch around the corner. I didn't have my usual breakfast this morning."

"Take your time." He added his standing joke, "There's no crime wave this week."

I left the station at eleven-thirty-three. It had turned cooler. The sky had changed from a crisp autumn blue to a dull autumn gray. A stiff breeze was blowing in from the river.

I didn't go to eat around the corner but to a cafeteria a block away where the cashier knew me. I took a cup of coffee and a ham sandwich to a table directly in front of her and began to do the crossword puzzle in the morning newspaper. As soon as I sat down it began to rain outside.

*   *   *

12:00 People dressed in summer clothes were coming into the cafeteria to get out of the wet. I had finished the puzzle and started to read the news.

Nothing very exciting. There never is. A few items about the cold war. A rally on the stock market. A scandal in the Bureau of Licenses. (The Machines can't do much about bribery.) Except for the date—Oct. 17, 2042—and a fourth page story about manufacturing a substitute for penicillin from Martian mosses, the news was just the same as the news of eighty years ago.

Partly, it's the Machines. Quite a lot of History was criminality writ large. When every suspicion of a fraud or conspiracy could be confirmed or disproved with finality by relays of the Machines, criminality disappeared, and with it a good deal of History.

Partly, it's the times. You could see it starting in the fifties and sixties nearly a century ago. The idea of Progress was looking pretty sick even then. Every year the new cars were the same as the old models. Every year the cold war was impending or receding without getting anywhere. Every year the same things were talked about in Congress and tabled for the next session. Economic cycles still occurred, but they were leveling out. There was space travel, of course, but nobody ever figured out what to do with it.

There's a theory now that History works the same way as the S-curve of population growth. First, things stand still; then—boom—everything shoots straight up. Progress. At last, it hits a plateau higher up and stays there.

That's, in fact, what I was thinking about at the cafeteria. Not Karen, who was probably dead at the moment. Not Eric, who was either dead or dying in the apartment, an apparent suicide. I thought about History. And waited.

12:30 Raining harder than ever. The cafeteria was packed. I waited five minutes on the chance it would clear up. It didn't and I had to dash back to the station house through the rain. I couldn't put my schedule in jeopardy. I got there soaked. The Chief's secretary was waiting for me in the lobby.

"The Chief is waiting to see you—in your office."

"What's up?" I asked in a tone calculated to show both nonchalance and surprise.

"You'd better see him."

The Chief was inexpertly smoking a cigarette. He only smoked when he was very upset.

"Sit down, Irving. I have something to tell you that I can hardly believe."

I sat. The Chief was leaning on the files, fanning the smoke of his cigarette from his eyes. A tear rolled down his cheek.

"Damn cigarettes. I don't know why I smoke them. It's just that. . ." His voice trailed off.

"What's wrong?" A hint of consternation behind a businesslike manner.

"It's Karen, Irving. Karen is dead."

"It can't be . . . when I left, she was. . ." Confusion and shock are both easy to simulate.

"Karen was murdered."

"That's outrageous," I shouted at him. "People aren't murdered anymore, not people like Karen."

"She was found strangled by a deliveryman from your dry cleaner at a little before 12:30."

"Strangled!"

The Chief maintained a sympathetic silence. I turned from him to hide my emotions, or, rather, lack of them.

"But who. . ." I left the question hanging for him to pick up.

"No idea, Irving. We don't know of anyone else being there."

Something was wrong. Eric should have been found there, too. Eric, my wife's murderer, dead from taking his own rat poison. But he could have been in the kitchen, where the deliveryman wouldn't have seen him. He probably hadn't been discovered yet.

Turning back to the Chief, I asked, "Who did you send? When will they get there?"

"Stanley was there almost immediately."

"But who could have done such a thing?"

"There's no way *we* can tell. That's why. . ." He broke off, coughing furiously. "That's why, Irving," he said, grinding out the cigarette on the carpet, "we will have to send an investigator back to find out."

Something very definitely had gone wrong. Where in hell *was* Eric? The only way to find out was to shift back into the morning and find out what had happened. Or what was still to happen. But under the circumstances I didn't want to.

He went on, "We can't reach Lowell and we can't bring investigators in from another city, without more than eighteen hours of red tape. It's ticklish."

"You don't expect me to . . . to go back there? You can't ask that. Not to be there and know she's being strangled, perhaps to see it, and *do* nothing."

"That's what worries me. God knows, the thought of it gets me so mad, I couldn't trust myself to follow any Code. But I don't see how else we can find out who did it."

"But clues, evidence—you can find out that way."

"You know a murder conviction can't be made without an investigator's report or direct witnesses. There weren't any witnesses."

Tonelessly, I said, "Leave me alone for a while. I have to think. Karen, my God." He left, closing the door behind him.

The interview had gone as scheduled, except that I really had to have time to think it out. I wouldn't have killed Karen if I hadn't been sure Eric would come. And I had killed Karen. When? That might give me a clue. I'd know at least whether my schedule had gone wrong. I rang the Chief on the intercom.

"Do you know yet when it happened?"

"The doctor just sent word. Around eleven-thirty."

I hung up the receiver.

That made sense. It had probably been a little earlier, of course. What could have induced me to kill her without having Eric to take the guilt off my shoulders?

Eric was always home at this time of day working. He had the instincts of a time-clock. If something had misfired and Eric wasn't taken care of, he'd answer the phone. But perhaps I had gone to his loft, which was near the apartment, and killed him there. In that case, he wouldn't answer. I dialed his number.

I waited twenty rings before hanging up. That decided it. I had gone to his loft. Maybe he had been sick this morning and couldn't accept an invitation to lunch. The solution lay in the past. I had to shift.

There was another reason, too. I had seen myself that morning in the alcove. It was a simple fact that I *had* gone back.

I called the Chief again.

"Can you send a doctor in here? I'll need something for my nerves if I have to do this."

He gave a sigh of relief.

"Sure thing, Irving. You know I hate to do this to you. I can't see any other way."

"There isn't any," I agreed.

And there wasn't.

* * *

1:00 Grierson, my analyst, came to give me a tranquilizer and stayed to look me over. He tried sounding me out about Karen. I told him I thought it would be best not to talk about the whole thing until later in the day when it was over. He sympathized and didn't press me.

He didn't seem worried that I might break the Code.

"With the training you fellows get for your job, it would be impossible for you to break the Code. Not by interference. You don't have to worry about that part of it."

Interference with the past was the worst offense an investigator could be guilty of. What has been known to happen cannot be changed. As things turn out, it's an unnecessary rule. No investigator could change the past if he wanted to. Non-interference was a law of nature.

But he could *make* it. For instance, buying and eating lunch would not be forbidden under the Code. Just being in the past and breathing the earlier air dislocates the universe some infinitesimal amount. But in exactly the same way that any other person dislocates it in his own time-scheme.

If Eric had really murdered Karen, I wouldn't have been able to do a thing to stop him. But since it could not have been Eric—since it had been myself that had killed her— there was nothing that could stop me either.

"I'm at your disposal anytime, Venner," Grierson said in parting. "You know how to get hold of me. If I can help, not as your analyst but as a friend, just tell me how."

Grierson would be helpful. When I returned. He had no suspicions of me at the moment, and I would see that he never did. I've had quite a lot of practice acting with Grierson, too.

My life as a widower was all mapped out. A month's leave of absence to start off, which would include: one week of heavy drinking, one week of misanthropic withdrawal, and, after one of Grierson's sermons on the efficacy of travel, his great cure-all, a trip to my sister's home in California for two weeks. After I returned to work, I would be stoic and silent for a few months while I learned to savor my second bachelorhood. Altogether, a very plausible schedule.

1:20 In the Machine-room. By myself, I could relax for a moment. Only Lowell and I and the federal government's servicers are authorized to enter the room.

The facts of shifting are simple. You can shift back as much as eighteen hours. That seems to be a natural limit. You can't shift forward, so the Machines haven't killed the fortune-telling trade. Of course, it would be possible to relay information back through a series of Machines. I've heard the government does that in special cases. But for an investigator it's strictly against the Code to let out anything about the future ... even eighteen hours ahead. You just learn to keep your mouth shut.

As soon as the work is over you return to the station house. There's a special room for the investigators to return to. You wait there until you're back in the proper time-scheme again. The reason is simple: it would be slightly confusing for all involved (especially the investigator) to hand in a report on an as-yet-unheard-of crime. Like all the rules in the Code, it's designed to minimize paradoxes. As things are, an investigator can go crazy just thinking about his work.

Shifting is as easy as setting an alarm clock, once you know how to do it. The walls of the Machine-room are covered with all kinds of mechanical devices: dials, switches, buttons and keyboards. But all except one are dummies. If the wrong person got into the room, he couldn't do a thing. If he pushed one of the dummy buttons, he'd set off alarms through the whole building. It's a fool-proof system.

I set the Machine for eight-fifty and reset my watch accordingly. I had a half-hour to get to the apartment, but there was nothing to worry about. I'd get there on time. I'd seen that for myself.

And that was it—I had shifted back to the morning. When I left the station by a secret exit that opens directly to the street, it was 8:50 on the morning of Oct. 17, 2042. The sun was low in a crisp, blue, autumn sky.

"A beautiful morning," I thought to myself. "Too warm for October. Just right for me."

9:15 I arrived at the apartment building and waited in the alcove at the foot of the stairs. There is a suspense in waiting for what must happen as well as one arising from uncertainties.

At last Irving Venner came down the stairs. I nodded to him. He walked past. I went up the stairs and waited for a moment at the second-floor landing. I heard the street door close. No uncomfortable sensations. None of the paranoia of the predestined. The man who had just left the building could have been a complete stranger—or a co-conspirator.

The door to the apartment was slightly ajar. I could hear Karen clearing away the breakfast dishes. I entered without knocking.

"Is someone there?" she asked without looking into the living room.

"Just me, honey. I changed into my blue suit, but I forgot to take my wallet and keys from yesterday's pants. I found out when I got to the subway."

I went into the bedroom on my supposed errand.

"You're a fast one. You hardly left."

"You of all people, the wife of an investigator, should know about the subjective nature of time. You were daydreaming."

She laughed delightedly. "Impostor! You didn't leave anything here. You're playing tricks."

That wasn't letter-perfect on my part, but if it was a slip it affected nothing. Karen had accepted my return.

I went into the bathroom and stayed there until Karen called.

"Is something wrong?"

"I've got a stomach cramp." I made some appropriate sounds to accompany the cramp.

"Bad?"

"It's murder."

"Why not stay home? The best cure is a rest cure."

"I may at that. It should go away in a minute."

"Go back to bed."

"If I do, call me at ten. I'll have to phone in."

I undressed and threw my clothes over a straight-back chair by the dresser. I got into my still-unmade bed and, quite without expecting to, I fell asleep. It must have been Grierson's tranquilizer.

9:55 I awoke with a start, thinking that I must have slept past the time to phone in. An irrational thought, because I had heard the call.

Karen looked in the bedroom door.

"You were resting so nicely, it seemed a shame to wake you. If you hadn't wakened just now, I would have phoned in for you. How are you feeling?"

"Better," I said, "but feeling less than ever like going into the office. I wouldn't get there now until lunch time. How about our having lunch together at home today? Maybe we could get Eric to stop daubing his canvases long enough to have lunch with us."

"I can call and find out. Since we're taking him out tonight, he can hardly refuse."

She sat down beside me on the bed and dialed Eric's number. She sat close enough to me to allow me to hear them both. It occurred to me that that was a little risky for her. How would she know what Eric might say, not knowing that I could hear him?

Eric answered. "Hello."

"Hello, Eric. Karen here. Can you have lunch with us? Irving stayed home from work and he thinks it would be nice for the three of us to lunch together. I think so too."

"That makes three of us. What time?"

Karen has a real talent for intrigue. She'd warned him to be discreet as casually as that.

"What time, darling?" she asked turning to me.

"Make it eleven-thirty. I don't want to stay away from the office altogether."

So the appointment was made. Eric agreed to be here a little before eleven-thirty. Something was drastically wrong, because he shouldn't have. Eric had been poisoned—or would be—in his own loft. Not here.

It was already ten o'clock and I had no time for speculations. I had to call my office. I got rid of Karen (who might have noticed that I was dialing not the Chief's but my own number) by asking her to make some more coffee. This was really my day for coffee.

After one ring the phone was answered.

"Hello, Chief?" I said.

My own voice replied, "This is he."

For just a moment I felt odd. I hadn't been prepared for

this new confrontation. At this moment I was sitting in my office at the station house, holding my hand over the earpiece of the telephone. The Paradox began to grip me. I tried hard to think of Continuity: anything that can be shifted has its own continuity. Every man has his own discrete time-scheme. They had drilled that into us every day at training school. But investigators still go crazy.

I avoided any further unpleasant thoughts of this sort by reciting my little fabrication loud enough for Karen to hear it in the kitchen. It was for her sake, after all, that I had devised these refinements. It was a short monologue, but at its end I did not immediately hang up. I wanted to say something to Irving Venner. Just what I don't know, a warning perhaps. But, whatever it might have been, it was something I had not heard earlier and I would not say now. I hung up.

There was one more detail to be arranged. I had Karen call the dry cleaner to make sure they would deliver my black suit in time for me to dress for the theater. They said they'd have it here by 12:30.

Karen left for a short while to get groceries. While she was gone, I put on a bathrobe and placed in its pocket the tie I had taken from Eric's tie rack when I had last visited his loft.

*   *   *

11:00 When Karen returned with the groceries, she brought me the morning newspaper. She knows that I do the crossword puzzle. At this point it hardly seemed necessary to keep up appearances. Nevertheless, for the second time that day I worked the morning crossword. This time it took me only ten minutes. After that, I paced about the room uneasily and at last sat down on the sofa by the window. Outside it was growing overcast.

Karen had been in the bedroom straightening up. She came out, holding the jacket of my blue pin-stripe suit.

"How in the world did you get this so damp?" she asked.

I replied absent-mindedly, "I got caught in the rain."

She looked at me curiously.

"But darling, it hasn't been raining."

I looked at my watch. It was fifteen minutes after eleven. I had been careless but it would make no difference now.

"It hasn't yet, but it will any minute," I said in a bantering way.

She cocked her head to one side quizzically, like someone unable to understand the punch line of a joke. Without giving her time for reflection, I pulled her down onto the sofa with me. I kissed her hard on the mouth. Strange to say, at that moment, I desired her more passionately than I had for years. First she responded and then, abruptly, drew away from me.

This time it was my turn to look quizzical.

"Didn't you shave this morning?" she asked.

I knew what she was thinking. I had shaved that morning. By Karen's reckoning it would have been only three hours before. But it had actually been nine hours since I had shaved. The difference was noticeable, since I have a heavy beard. I didn't attempt to answer her.

She answered herself. "I know you did. I heard you."

She rose from the sofa and went to stand by the window. Raindrops began to beat an irregular tattoo on the glass. The storm moved west to east across the city, and it had started to rain here ten minutes before it reached the station house.

The rainstorm unleashed all the terrors of the *déja vu* in me. Its coming seemed to press me to my deed, but now—so many things had gone wrong. It wasn't the matter of Eric. Rather, the details that I had left unaccounted for: my falling asleep, my four o'clock shadow before noon, and my wet jacket.

"You're right," Karen said. "It has begun to rain."

There was a longer pause, while the raindrops increased their tempo to a steady drone. I felt my resolution drain out of me, and the hollow it left in the pit of my stomach was filling up with the predestining rain. Contradictory thoughts and impulses raced through my mind: to kill her that minute and be done; how much I loved her in spite of . . . or perhaps it was only my own fantasies; I had no right or reason to think what I did of her; I *couldn't* kill her now. The certainty of her innocence seemed undoubtable.

And all this while she had been thinking too.

"You've shifted, Irving. Why didn't you tell me before?"

I made no reply. I put my hand in the pocket of my bathrobe. I felt the tie there.

"What are you doing here? Irving, it's against the Code for you to be here now!"

"If you'll come and sit down I'll explain."

She returned to the sofa but wouldn't sit near me. I moved closer to her. Now she had to die. She would soon have fit all the pieces together and reached her own conclusion. And she would have been right.

"You see, Karen, I am supposed to be here. I'm investigating a murder."

I put my arms around her suddenly, so that she was unable to see the tie in my right hand.

"But. . ." Karen was a fast thinker. She didn't need to finish her sentence.

"Quite right, Karen—*your* murder. If you are interested, I will even inform you who did it."

"Only tell me why. Why, in heaven's name, do you want to do such a thing?"

"Me, Karen! But I didn't do it." I listened to myself speak in amazement. My words seemed those of another man. "Eric did it. I overheard you arguing as I stood outside the door. For a long time he's wanted you to divorce me, but you always refused. You knew he wouldn't be able to support you as I can. You preferred to keep him as your lover. But he was too proud. At last, he preferred his own death—and yours. He strangled you with his tie."

I whipped the tie around her neck and pulled it tight, not so tight yet that she couldn't speak.

"You're wrong, Irving. You've made it all up. Eric is your own friend, your oldest friend. We've never done such a thing. You must believe me."

"How noble of you to try to protect him!"

Her eyes filled with terror. Her upper lip trembled and lifted to expose her long front teeth.

"The phone call I made . . . that's why you wanted him to come."

"After Eric killed you he poisoned himself. He has trouble, you know, in his loft with the rats. It's an old building. Knowing that no murderer can escape the penalty of the law, he took rat poison. Here in our own kitchen."

She made a sudden attempt to escape from me, but the tie was wrapped tightly about her neck and I held it firmly. In her struggle she fell from the sofa. I stood over her and tightened the loop of the tie slowly about her neck. She tried to pull it away. Her hands flailed about, trying to reach me, but, since I stood behind and above her, she was unable to see what she was doing. At last her body became limp. After another minute of tension, I relaxed my grip.

I carried Karen's body to the bedroom, where Eric would not see it if he came. Her face looked like a stranger's. Her eyes dilated with terror and her hair in disarray. Her mouth was open and her small chin was pulled in almost to her neck. Her upper lip was still drawn up and exposed her teeth and pink gums. It was an expression that made her look stupid, and I felt sad. I brushed my hand over her eyes to close them, but there was nothing I could do to keep her lip down over her teeth.

11:30 There was no point in waiting for Eric to show up. For some reason he had been delayed at his loft. I found a hip flask in the dresser that I had saved from college days and filled it with whiskey into which I had dissolved the rat poison. I put my blue suit back on and took an umbrella from the apartment. That wasn't interference, nor would it look suspicious to the Chief. I could tell him that Eric, on leaving after the murder, had not closed the door, that I had come in to see exactly what had happened and had taken the umbrella in order to be less conspicuous when following Eric through the streets in the rain.

Eric lived only a few blocks away. His loft was near a section of docks that had fallen out of use. That area was fairly isolated. The rain was coming down so steadily now that you could only see a few yards in front of you. The people hurried through the downpour, intent on their own business, and paid no attention to me. In that one respect, the storm was of some service.

Once out on the street, the cold air and the refreshing sound of the rain cleared the cobwebs from my head. I felt renewed in my purpose and wondered how I could have gotten so fuddled in those last few minutes with Karen.

The ground floor shop of Eric's building was an art gallery operated by Eric and some of his artist friends. It was closed. A sign in the window said: PATRONIZE YOUR NEIGHBORHOOD ART GALLERY. Eric's idea. Beside it was a painting that Karen and I had posed for. A beautiful representation of Karen. (It made *me* look more portly than I really am.) The picture brought back to my mind the figure, so different from this, that I had left in the bedroom, and I hurried past.

Eric lived four floors up. Luck was with me, and the narrow, smelly hallway was empty. Eric's door was closed. I knocked lightly. There was no reply. I knocked again. And a third time.

A fat woman in a flowered housedress, whom I recognized as the wife of the building's superintendent, came to the landing of the third floor. Eric paid her to do his cleaning, and she had often seen me in his loft or in the gallery.

"You looking for Mr. Hubbler?" she called up.

"Yes," I answered faintly, hoping that in the poor light of the hallway she would not be able to recognize me.

"You won't find him here today, Mr. Venner. He had an accident out on the street just a few minutes ago. Don't think he was hurt much at all, but the police took him to the hospital."

I stood there speechless. The worst thing (though I did not remember it until I was outside again) was that she had recognized me. She even knew my name. But, after all, that made little difference and it wasn't the worst thing.

"It's this rain," she went on. "Mr. Hubbler had just come out of the house and started across the street when a taxi turned around the corner. Didn't see him till too late and he slid right into him when he tried to brake. My husband saw the whole thing out of the window. You wanted to leave something for him?"

I reflected, fingering the flask in my pocket. He could never be blamed for the murder now. He'd been seen leaving the house at just that time.

"No. No thank you. I'll see him later."

I went down the stairs slowly and walked past her. My state of mind must have been apparent.

"I wouldn't look so upset, Mr. Venner. He wasn't hurt bad at all."

"It's just the shock."

I left the building in a daze and stood for a long time watching the rain pour down over Karen's smiling face in the window of the gallery. Then I walked for some blocks in the rain.

*　　*　　*

12:25 This last and total miscarriage of my plan left me without apparent resources. I turned over all the possibilities and they added up to zero.

Then I hit upon something; it was a desperate gamble and it was the ultimate defiance of the Code. I would interfere. There was still time to prevent that morning's disaster. But not much. I hailed a cab and gave the driver twenty dollars to take me to the cafeteria near the station house as fast as he could go. I had ten minutes to get there and warn myself not to use the Machine.

As the cab speeded along the wet streets, I sat back and tried to imagine what would be the result if I succeeded. Would that whole day be swept into oblivion, erased? Would all the people who had been involved in my plan pass through a different time-scheme? Most of all, what would happen to me?

Yet my greatest worry was not so intangible. One cannot long worry about what cannot be imagined. I dreaded lest my present attempt was a sheer impossibility. *Non-interference is a law of nature.*

The taxi pulled up across the street from the cafeteria. I ran out into the ran, leaving my umbrella behind in the taxi. I was halfway across the street, when the taxi-driver called out after me. "Hey, mister, you left your umbrella."

"Keep it," I shouted back. That moment I was attacked by a sudden flash of giddiness. I braced myself against it and looked up in time to see Irving Venner coming out of the cafeteria. He paused a moment in the doorway, looking out at the rain. I stared at him until he met my gaze. He stepped backward in amazement.

I felt nothing but an iron determination to carry through my scheme. I was interfering. I had already altered the past; this had not happened before.

I approached him.

"Don't do this," he said. "You can't do this. We can't talk to each other."

"I am not you anymore," I began unsteadily. "I am someone else. I don't know what will happen to me—to us—but I have to talk to you. Come out of the doorway."

I pulled him along the street. He did not resist. The rain streamed down on us relentlessly. We stopped in the recessed doorway of a millinery store. On three sides the windows displayed a jumble of pastel-toned synthetic fabrics draped on headless, armless torsoes.

"You can't use the Machine today. There was an accident. I've just been through the most horrible. . ."

I could not go on. I had started laughing hysterically.

"What are you doing? You've been back?"

"It went all wrong. Eric never came. He was in an accident. He was on his way to the hospital at the moment that I was killing her. The Chief told you about it as you went out. And I was seen at his loft afterwards."

He had become somewhat calmer.

"Karen is dead?"

"Yes. I didn't know then about Eric. But *you* must not go back. You must not kill her."

Suddenly his eyes lit with rage. He began striking at me with his doubled fists. "You interfering fool! You madman!"

I had not expected this. I tried to fend him off. My only hope was that he would listen to reason.

"I had no choice," I said, when I had at last restrained him. "Don't you see. Everything has gone wrong. It was either this or suicide."

He tore away from me with a mighty effort.

"Then you should have killed yourself. God knows what will happen now."

I could feel the laughter bubbling up in me again.

"Irving," I said, "try to. . ."

But when he heard me use his name, he lashed out at me again and nearly threw me off my balance. I ceased thinking or trying to talk to him. I hit back as hard as I could. He toppled backward into the store window, which shattered into a lethal rain of glass. A huge shard pierced his neck. He screamed and was silent. I looked down at him in horror. He was dead.

Outside the recess, the rain was still pouring and the street was empty.

I was dead. It was impossible that I could be alive. Who I had been lay dead at my feet in a pool of blood. I understood what I had to do. The predestining force seemed at that moment to have engineered a comedy. I had still to perform its last absurdity.

I took the flask of poisoned whiskey from my pocket. At least, I thought, this will not be wasted. Eddies of horror, like sheets of rain sweeping along the street, passed over me as I tried to think my way through what had just happened. Death, then, seemed benign. I drank from the flask.

*   *   *

Later: But it was not over. In the next instant of memory I was in the bedroom of my apartment. I looked at the alarm clock. The alarm had been pushed in, and Karen had left her bed and was puttering around in the kitchen. I wanted to scream. Instead, I said, "Good morning, honey. What's it like out?"

She looked in smiling. "A beautiful morning. Too warm for October. Just right for me."

I seemed to have no control over my actions. I got up and went into the bathroom and began to shave. I tried to understand what was happening. A flash of wild hope: my interference had worked. When I went downstairs, the last trace of that hope died. For there in the alcove behind the staircase stood Irving Venner. He nodded to me. I walked on.

And so it has been. Every action of that day was repeated without the slightest alteration. Again I had to go to the Machine-room, again be shifted to the morning, again return to the apartment, and again strangle Karen. What had been horrible then was now unspeakable. Right up to the moment that Irving Venner lay dead at my feet.

I understand what has happened, why I must go through this day again and again.

Non-interference is a law of nature. I could not have warned myself that afternoon of what was going to happen. When the taxi-driver called me back and I grew dizzy, my long training to be an investigator asserted itself in time to prevent me from committing the ultimate crime of interference. What I imagined to follow that fainting spell is the punishment my own mind has invented for my crimes.

And I must sit now in some hospital cell (for madmen are not allowed the mercy of an execution), a catatonic, incessantly repeating the experiences of that day.

MINNESOTA
GOTHIC

Gretel was caught in the bright net of autumn—wandering
vaguely in the golden, dying woods, vaguely uncertain where
she was but not yet frightened, vaguely disobedient. Ripe
gooseberries piled in her basket; the long grass drying. Autumn. She was seven years old.

The woods opened onto a vegetable garden. A scarecrow
waved the raggedy stumps of his denim arms at the crows
rustling in the cornstalk sheaves. Pumpkins and squash dotted
the spent earth, as plump and self-sufficient as a convention
of slum landlords. Further down the row, an old woman was
rooting in the ground, mumbling to herself.

Gretel backed toward the wood. She was afraid. A strand
of rusted barb-wire snagged at her dress. The crows took to
the air with graceless to-do. The woman pushed herself up
and brushed back a tangle of greasy white hair. She squinted
at Gretel, who began to cry.

"Little girl?" Her voice crackled like sticks of dry wood
burning. "Little girl, come here. I give you some water, eh?
You get lost in the woods."

Gretel tore her dress loose from the barb and stepped
nervously around the fat pumpkins, tripping on their vines.
Her fear, as is often the way with fear, made her go to the old
woman, to the thing she feared.

"Yes, I know you," the old woman grated. "You live two
houses down the road. I know your mother when she is
little." She winked, as though they had shared an amusing
secret. "How old are you?"

Gretel opened her mouth but couldn't speak.

"You're only a *little* girl," the old woman went on, with a

150

trace of contempt. "You know how old I am? A hundred years old!" She nodded her head vigorously. "I'm Minnie Haeckel."

Gretel had known who the woman was, although she had never seen her before. Whenever Gretel was especially bad or muddied her Sunday frock or wouldn't eat dinner, her mother would tell her what terrible things Old Minnie Haeckel did to naughty piglets who didn't eat cauliflower. Mother always concluded these revelations with the same warning: "You do it *once more,* and I'm going to take you to live with that old Minnie. It's just what you deserve." Now too, Gretel recognized the clapboard house with the peeling paint and, around it, the sheds—omens of a more thorough disintegration. The house was not as formidable viewed across the vegetable garden as it had seemed in brief glimpses from the car window, the white hulk looming behind a veil of dusty lilacs. It looked rather like the other old farmhouses along the gravel road—the Brandts', the Andersons'.

Minnie took Gretel by the hand and led her to an iron pump. The pump groaned in time to the woman's slow heave and stagger and a trickle of water spilt over its gray lip, blackening it.

"Silly girl!" Minnie gasped. "Use the dipper."

Gretel put the enamel dipped under the lip of the pump to catch the first gush of cold water. She drank greedily.

From inside the house, there was the bellow of a man's voice. "Minnie! Minnie, is that you?"

Minnie jerked the dipper out of Gretel's hand and bent over the little girl. "That's my brother," she whispered, her dry voice edged with fear. "You must go. First, I give you something." Minnie took Gretel to a sagging wooden platform at the back of the house, where there was a pile of heavy, dirt-crusted tubers the color of bacon grease. Minnie put one of these in Gretel's basket on top of the tiny green gooseberries.

"Minnie!" the voice roared.

"Yeah, yeah!" Minnie returned. "Now then, that's for you. You give it to your mother, understand? And walk home down the road. It's not far. You know how?"

Gretel nodded. She backed away from Minnie and, when she was far enough, turned and ran to the road, clutching the basket with its terrible vegetable to her chest.

Mother was outside the house, collapsed in a lawn chair.
The radio was turned on full-volume. Mother flexed her
polished toes to the slow, urban beat of the music.

"Did you bring in the mail, love?" Mother asked. Gretel
shook her head and stood at a distance from her mother,
waiting to recover her breath.

"I tore my dress," she brought out at last. But Mother was
not in a mood to be upset by small things. It was a very old
dress and it had been torn before.

"What's in your basket, love?" she asked. Gretel glanced
down guiltily at the hard, ominous vegetable. She handed it to
her mother.

"I was picking gooseberries."

"This isn't a gooseberry, though," Mother explained gently.
"It's a rutabaga. Where did you get it?"

Gretel told about Minnie.

"Isn't that nice of her. She's such a sweet old lady.
We'll have the rutabaga for dinner. Did you thank her, I
hope?"

Gretel blushed. "I was afraid."

"There was nothing to be afraid of, love. Minnie is a
harmless old woman. She does the sweetest things sometimes,
and she's had a hard time of it, living all alone in that firetrap
of a house that really should be torn down. . . ."

"But she's not alone, Mommie. Her brother lives there with
her."

"Nonsense, Gretel. Minnie doesn't have any brother, not
any more. Now, put the rutabaga and the gooseberries in the
kitchen and go back and see if there's any mail."

At dinner Gretel ate everything on her plate but the diced
rutabagas. She sat staring at the yellowish lumps morosely,
while her mother cleared away the dishes.

"You're not to leave the table until you've eaten every one
of them, so take all the time you need."

Finally, at eight o'clock, Gretel bolted down the cold,
foul-tasting lumps of rutabaga, fighting against her reflex to
gag. When she had quite finished, Mother brought in her
dessert, but Gretel couldn't eat it.

"Really, Gretel darling, there's no reason to *cry*."

The next day, Gretel was sick. Purely for spite, her mother
was convinced. But, of course, that wasn't it at all. It was
only the spell beginning its work.

Left to her own devices, Gretel would not have renewed her acquaintance with Minnie Haeckel. Unfortunately, late in October, Grandfather Bricks died; her mother's father, who had built the farmhouse they were living in. Mother was to meet Daddy in the city and then fly to California, where the Bricks had retired. Gretel, who was too young to attend a cremation, was deposited at Minnie Haeckel's doorstep with a canvas bag of playthings and a parting kiss. She watched her mother drive down the gravel road until there was nothing to be seen but a cloud of dust and a glint of chrome from the last hill of the horizon. Minnie was hunched over a sway-backed chair on the front stoop.

"Your old grandfather is dead, eh? He used to bring Minnie a fruitcake at Christmas." Minnie sucked in her cheeks and made a sound of regret. "People are always dying. What do you think of that?" Gretel noticed with distaste that the old woman's mouth contained, instead of proper teeth, brown stumps, at irregular intervals, that Gretel surmised were snuff. Her mother had told her once that Minnie chewed snuff.

"Come into the parlor, child. You can play there. Nobody uses the parlor nowadays."

The creaking pine floor was covered with a rag rug. There was a huge leather chair that rocked on hidden springs and a handsome mahogany table with a lace cloth. The bay window was hung with curtains that had once been feedbags, their red check now a sunbleached, dusty pink. On the walls, decades of calendars advertised the First Commercial Bank of Onamia. They pictured a perpetual *January* of wintry woods and snowy roads, ponds and icebound houses.

"Can you read?"

"A little."

Minnie opened a tin box that lay on the table and handed Gretel a small bundle of cards and envelopes. They smelled of decayed spices. Minnie shook the box. A gritty black ball rolled into Gretel's lap.

"You take an apple," Minnie explained, "and you stick it full of cloves and let it dry for a whole year. It shrinks up like this. Doesn't it smell nice?" Minnie picked up the black ball and held it under her nostrils, smelling it noisily. "You read the letters now, eh?"

The first was a postcard showing a ship. *"Dear All,"* she read. *"I am in France. It gets cold at night, but I don't mind it. How is everyone? They say the war is almost over."* The signature, like the text, was printed in crude, black letters—*"Lew."*

"My daddy was in the war, too. He flew a plane."

"This is a different war, a long time ago."

The next postcard had no picture. GREETINGS FROM NEW YORK, it said in front. On the back there was only Lew's clumsy signature.

"Who is Lew?" Gretel asked. "Does he live upstairs?"

"Yes, but you can't see him. He can't walk now and he doesn't like little girls. Read some more, eh? The big one."

Gretel took the largest envelope and opened it. The letter was typewritten and crinkly with age. *"Dear Miss ... is that how you spell Haeckel?"* She giggled at the vagaries of spelling. *"We re—gret to inform you that your brother, Lew Haeckel, has been. . ."*

"Go on," Minnie prodded.

"The words are too hard."

"You can't read very well."

"I'm only in first grade. Read them yourself."

"This letter is from the hospital. He was there for weeks. Then they sent him home. It costs me a lot of money."

"What happened?" Gretel asked, although she was not terribly interested.

"He used to drink." Minnie looked at Gretel narrowly. "Your mother drinks too, eh?" Gretel thought so. "He was in a car accident. That's what happens to drinkers. You stay in here while I work outside, eh? Then we eat."

Gretel promised to be good. Minnie replaced the letters in their box carefully and went out through the kitchen. Gretel climbed into the largest leather rocker and pumped it with her body, like a swing, until she had filled the room comfortably with its creaking. The corners of the parlor sank into shadow and the deep colors of the room deepened with dusk. Gretel rocked the chair harder, but it was a poor defense against the encroaching darkness. And there was no light switch on the wall. She went to find Minnie.

The hall was even darker, and darker yet the staircase to the second floor. Piles of mail-order catalogues and old magazines formed a sort of bannister on the stairs.

"Hey—you!" He had a smooth, urgent voice. Gretel peeked up the stairs at him shyly. He was fat and he could hardly stand up. In the dark, Gretel could make out few details. He was leaning against the wall for support with one hand. With the other, he waved a cane at Gretel, as though he would catch her in its crook. "Come up here. I want to talk to you. Don't be afraid. C'mon, sugar."

"I'm not supposed to see you." Gretel liked to tease.

"Don't pay attention to Minnie. She's crazy, you know. I'll tell you a thing or two about *her*." Then his voice hushed so that Gretel couldn't understand his words. She advanced up two of the steps.

"That's right. C'mon in to my room. In here." He vanished from the top of the stairs, and Gretel listened to him shuffle along the corridor. She followed him and was relieved to see a shaft of light in the corridor.

His room was a sty of cast-off clothes, out-of-date magazines, and tins full of cigar ashes and butts. These—and Lew—were all piled on the double-bed at the center of the room; there was no other furniture except a dresser without drawers upon which a kerosene lamp was burning. Lew, collapsed in the debris of the bed, was breathing heavily— pale cheeks billowed and slacked like a mechanical toy. His belly sagged out of a blue, navy-issue, knit sweater and his thighs had split through the seams of his trousers, which were fouled with weeks, months of use.

"She keeps me prisoner here. I can't get downstairs by myself. She won't let me go anywhere, see my friends."

Gretel stared in amazement—not at this confidence—at him.

"And she tries to starve me, too. C'mere, sugar. What's your name?"

"Gretel."

"Forty years! I've been a cripple in this leg for forty years. She doesn't let me out of her sight. Come over here and sit on the bed, why doncha? I don't bite."

Gretel didn't move from the doorway. Lew picked up his cane again and tried to hook her around the neck, playfully.

"You afraid of your Old Uncle Lew?"

Gretel pursed her lips at what she knew to be a lie.

"You know why she does all this? You wanna know? She's a witch. That's what it is, honest to God. When she was a kid, she could take off warts. She's put her name down in the devil's book, and she'll never get any older now. And if she has a mind to, she can turn you into a mouse. You'll have to hop on her thumb and beg for crumbs of bread. You can hear her mumbling all the time, sorts of crazy things. Charms and such. And cursing, oh, she can curse." He stopped for breath again and struggled to his feet. Gretel backed further away.

"She hexed me. I was a thousand miles away, I was in New York. But that don't matter one iota to *her*. She made my leg go bum." He staggered forward angrily. *"It's all her fault!"* he shouted after Gretel as she clambered down the stairs and out of the house. Minnie was nowhere to be seen.

Gretel found her in one of the lean-to sheds shoveling corncobs into a tin bucket. "It's dark inside," she complained. She had decided not to mention Uncle Lew.

"There are rats in the sheds as big as you are," Minnie said between shovelsful. "You only see them at night. Big rats."

"What are those?" Gretel pointed.

"Corncobs. I burn them up and they never get used. Every day I burn some more." She laughed, although Gretel did not recognize it as such. "Now we go inside. I turn on a lamp."

The kitchen table and the cupboards were stacked with unwashed dishes and pans. Minnie, apparently, had as little use for soap as Lew. Minnie lighted the kerosene lamp and made a fire in the stove. They ate dinner in silence: vegetables from Minnie's garden and canned meat from Mother's larder. Minnie ate with a spoon, but she offered Gretel a fork as well.

"Nibble, nibble, little mouse," Minnie chortled.

Gretel looked up at Minnie with delight, for she remembered the line. "Who is nibbling at my house?" she concluded. Minnie looked at her suspiciously. "Mommie read me that story lots of times. My name is in it—Gretel."

"What are you talking about? You want some cake, eh?"

The cake tasted nothing at all like the ones Mother took from boxes, but it wasn't bad. Gretel had two pieces.

"I take you home now. I come and get you in the morning. You can't sleep here."

Gretel kept close to Minnie on the gravel road, but she wouldn't hold the old woman's hand. Even with a sweater, it was cold. Owls hooted in the dark woods, and there were other, less definite noises.

"You're afraid of the dark, eh?"

"It's scary at night."

"I like the night best of all. I build a fire in the stove and sit down and warm my old bones. When you go back to the city?"

"Daddy has to find a new apartment. I'm studying my lessons at home. I can read anyhow. Most first-graders can't read at all."

"Here you are. You want me to put you to bed?"

"No. We have electric lights, so I won't be afraid by myself. Minnie?"

"Eh?"

"Are you really a witch?"

Minnie choked on her phlegm and spat and choked again. This time Gretel knew her laughter for what it was. She went into the house angrily and locked the door behind her. Even upstairs in her chintz bedroom she could hear Minnie, as she walked back along the road, rasping with glee and mumbling—something—loudly.

The morning drizzled—cold, a clothes-damping mist that did not fall but hung, filmed the house and leafless trees but would not wet the earth. Gretel was awakened by a tattoo of pebbles on the clouded window. She dressed herself, sleepily, in the warmest clothes she could find and joined Minnie outside, wishing that her mother were there with the Buick. While they trudged down the road, Minnie interrupted her grumbling long enough to ask Gretel if she had been with her brother the day before.

"Yes. He told me to. And he said you were a witch. Can you take off warts?"

"I stop the toothache too—and measles. Once, I am at every lying-in but no more. They come to Old Minnie for a love-doll, for a sick horse. For everything."

Gretel considered this in silence. She did not quite dare to ask if Minnie could turn children into mice. She remembered, with grave suspicion, the rats in the corncrib that only came out at night—rats as big as herself. She felt serious and wary but no longer afraid. And she felt, too, though she could not have said why, a touch of contempt for the old woman shuffling through the mist, bent under the oversized pea-jacket.

"Aren't we going to your house?" Gretel asked as they walked past the dripping lilac bushes.

"Not now. You are warm enough, eh?"

"Is it far?"

"Not far." Half a mile didn't seem far to Minnie. A dirt track led from the road to the Onamia Township Cemetery. Minnie paced in a circle about a small stone that rose bare inches above the clovered grass. There was an inscription on it which read simply:

HAECKEL
1898-1923.

Three times she circled it, crooning anxiously, and then three times again, but in the other direction.

"Who's inside?" Gretel asked, but Minnie wasn't listening to her ward. "My grandfather," she persisted, "is going to be burned. Mommie is bringing the ashes home in a jar. Is that your brother?"

Minnie finished her pacing and started back to the road, still oblivious of Gretel. Gretel was piqued. She considered hiding from her unresponsive guardian, as she had often hid from her mother when she (her mother) needed to be punished, but it was too cold and wet a day to go into the woods. Gretel would remember not to forget.

Minnie's stove was already crackling; the kitchen was soaked in a warmth that drew a history of odors from the cracks in the woodwork: smells of last year's apples and this summer's onions, of nutmeg and cinnamon, the scrapings of stews, the coffee burnt on the iron stove, the musk of drying wood in the orange crate by the stove, of snuff, and strangely, of cigars. There was a wooden sign above the porch door, painted in crude, black letters. Gretel sounded them out— CIGAR FACTORY NO. 4.

"Is this a cigar factory?"

"Not any more. My brother makes cigars before he is too sick. It makes a little money. It is a good thing to make some money. I sell vegetables in town. And go to the sick people. It isn't much. He makes them just to smoke nowadays. I have to sell the land sometimes."

"Has your brother lived here a long time?"

"Oh, a long time. Can you cook?"

"Mommie won't let me. I'm too little."

"I teach you to make cookies, eh? Little cookies—just for you."

"Okay. Is he as old as you are?"

"We don't talk about him now. What is this, eh?"

Gretel shrugged at the handful of white powder Minnie had taken from a glass cannister.

"Silly girl. It's flour. Everyone knows flour." Minnie put three more handsfull of flour into a mixing bowl. "First, you put the sugar with the lard. Then, the flour."

"Ich."

Undaunted, Minnie detailed all the rest of the steps in making the dough. Without cups and measuring spoons, Gretel was doubtful if the results would be edible. "What *is* it?" she asked, losing all patience.

"It's gingerbread. You don't know anything."

Gretel gasped. Gingerbread. Gingerbread. She stuck her finger into the magic, brown dough and tasted it. Like swan or mermaids, like nighttime or a candy cottage with panes of sugar. She gloated at the forbidden, old sweetness.

"You don't eat it yet. We roll it out on the table and you can cut out the people. Little gingerbread girls, eh? then we bake it: *Then* we eat."

"Aren't *you* going to make anything?" Gretel asked cautiously.

"I have a cutter. I show you." Minnie dug through a drawer of unfamiliar-looking utensils and drew forth a cookie-cutter in triumph.

"What is it?"

"It's a rabbit."

Gretel examined it closely, first on the outside, then its cutting edge. *"It's a toad!"*

Minnie backed away from the little girl. She cocked her head to one side.

"Tell me about the rats," Gretel said anxiously. She came over to Minnie and took her hand. "Are they *very* big? As big as me? Are there a lot of them? *Tell me!"*

"I don't know what you're saying." Minnie began to cough. It was not a laughing cough.

"You don't want to tell me, do you?" The old woman lowered herself onto a stool, bent double with the pain that spread across her chest and into her stomach. Gretel put her hands on Minnie's shoulders and pushed her back up to stare intently into her rheumy eyes. "Why is he alive? How did you make him come alive again?"

"Devil's child!" Minnie screamed. "Leave me be!"

"He died. A long time ago. I know. You showed me the letter. It said he died. Killed—I read it."

Minnie pushed Gretel away from her and ran out the kitchen door. For a moment she stood, uncertain, in the mist, then walked at a quick hobble to the road, turned toward the cemetery.

It had happened months before, in spring, while she helped Mother in the flower garden. Squeezing the clods of earth between her hands until, sudden as the pop of a balloon, they broke between her fingers in a sift of loam—enjoyable. Then, one, as she squeezed, squished. Dried mud flaked from back and belly, and Gretel had found, locked tight in her two hands, the toad. Her fear was not of warts; she had not heard that a toad's touch bred warts. Gretel had been spared many of the old-wive's tales: her mother's urbane imagination fed on cancer, heart disease, and, more recently, thalidomide. Gretel's fear was greater and less definite—without specific remedy. Through the summer, it sank malignant roots in the country soil, hung like pollen in the air, infected the water in the pumps. She seeded the countryside with her fear, subdued but ready to spring to her pale blue eyes, like a rabbit started from its hole, at the slightest provocation. Diffuse, private, echoing the bedtime legends—the Grimms and Andersens—that then composited their several horrors in her own dreams: an enchantment.

Yet, she was not helpless. She had a natural talent for exorcism. She was thorough, and she could be ruthless. And if fear could not be circumvented, it could be joined.

Without haste or bravado then, Gretel climbed the stairs once more. She tiptoed through the hall and inched open the door to Lew Haeckel's room. He was there, sleeping. A thread of brown saliva rolled out the side of his mouth. Gretel raised the blind, and a hazy, gray light spilled into the room, across the double-bed, beneath his eyelids.

"Whadaya want?" He raised himself on one elbow, blinking. "Why, hello sugar."

"Minnie's making gingerbread," Gretel announced.

"Well, she's not making any for *me*." Lew looked at Gretel cannily. "What's wrong, kid?"

"Is she a witch, really?"

"You bet your life she is."

"And the mouse. . . ."

Slowly, Lew began to understand. His fat lips curled into a smile, showing brown teeth like Minnie's. "Oh, she can do that, too. You think she's up to something?" He looked around nervously. "Where is she?"

"She went . . . outside." Gretel did not dare mention the cemetery. "She made dough, but she hasn't made the cookies yet. She's going to make a *toad*."

"With the gingerbread, huh? A gingerbread toad?"

Gretel nodded.

"And you're afraid. Well, you can beat her at witching. She's pretty dumb, you know. For a witch." He began to speak more softly. "You think she'll turn you into a toad? Is that it, honey?" Gretel crept closer to the bed to hear what he was whispering. "She can do that. A black toad hopping in the mud. You wouldn't like that, a pretty girl like you." A chuckle, soft and lewd. "You've got to watch out for that gingerbread. I'll tell you what. . . ." His voice was a wisp of sound. Gretel stood at his bedside, frozen with attention. "You go downstairs and take that dough, and make a cookie like Minnie. . . ." His hand snaked out to circle her waist. She was too horrified at his implications to notice.

"*And eat it!*" she exclaimed.

"That's right, sugar. Then you won't have to worry about any old gingerbread toad. You'll take the wind out of her sails, all right."

He held her firmly now, pulled her closer to him.

"You're a pretty little girl, you know that? How about a kiss for your old Uncle Lew, seeing as how he's helped you out?"

"Let go." She tried to pull his hand away. His face bent toward hers, smiling. "Let me go! I know about you. Stop it!"

"Whadaya know, huh?"

"You're *dead*," Gretel screamed. "They buried you. Minnie is there now. You were killed. Dead."

The man's hulk shook with something like laughter. His grip loosened. Gretel broke away and retreated to the doorway. He quieted suddenly, although his body continued to tremble like a tree in a light breeze. He pulled himself up in his bed and spat into one of the tin cans.

"You're great, kid. You'll be the greatest witch yet. No

fooling." When Gretel was halfway down the stairs, he called out after her—"We'll get along, sugar. You and me. Just wait." A drop of blood fell from Gretel's lip where she had been biting it. It made a blot on her jumper, the size of a pea.

In the kitchen, she rolled out the dough, according to Minnie's instructions, and cut out a five-inch witch with a greasy knife. The gingerbread witch stuck to the table. She scraped it free with the knife and reassembled it on the cookie sheet, which Minnie had already prepared. She took three raisins from the bag on the table and gave the ginger-bread figure eyes and a black mouth—like Minnie's. She put the cookie sheet in the oven and nibbled fingers of the raw dough while she waited.

She brought the cookie sheet out of the oven. The witch was a rich brown on top, but crisp and black underneath. She had still to wait for it to cool. She was afraid Minnie would return, and sat at the parlor window to watch the road. Upstairs, Gretel could hear Lew shuffling about.

And, then, in the kitchen. The gingerbread witch was warm but—Gretel touched her tongue to it—not too warm to eat, easier, too, if you closed your eyes. One bite beheaded her. The three raisins were cinders, too dry to chew. She rinsed down the rest of it with water.

Outside the window, Gretel could see a wind spring out of the wood, tearing through the corn sheaves, striking the sodden clothes of the scarecrow, tumbling his hat into a furrow, lifting it into the air. Higher.

Lew was standing in the doorway, holding to the frame. Except for a week's stubble of beard, his face was white as his shirt collar. He was wearing a suit that was moderately clean.

"You done it, sure as hell, sugar." He spoke in short bursts of breath. "As good as roast on her spit and serve her up at a church supper with whipped potatoes and green peas."

"You told me to."

"I needed to get away from her, get some fresh blood. Run with the tide. Minnie was old-fashioned. She kept me pris-oned here." He pointed out the window to the scarecrow. "But the spell's broke." He inhaled deeply; his belly lifted and fell. A spate of blood darkened his cheeks and ebbed away.

"You and me, sugar, we're going places. You gonna kiss me *now,* for old time's?"

Gretel wrinkled her nose. "You're fat and ugly."

"That's how she wanted me. A witch always keeps something beside her—a cat, a mouse, a cricket maybe."

"Rats?"

"Rats too. Or a black toad." He grinned. Gretel shuddered. "But Minnie had to have something that looked like her brother—so she dug him up. I had to do all the work, dragging this hulk around."

"Go away."

"Not any more, sugar. I'm yours now. You outwitched her but you've still got a lot to learn . . . and a lot of time to learn it. You're stuck with me, like it or not. And I like it."

"I don't want you." He shrugged and sat beside her at the table. The chair creaked under his weight. He wrapped his paw about her forearm. "You're ugly. You stink!" It was the harshest word she knew, but since it was, in this case, accurate, it seemed, like coffee made from used grounds, to lack full strength.

"If you don't like me the way I am, just say the word."

Gretel's eyes widened. "You mean. . ."

"Gary Cooper," he suggested. "Fabian."

"No."

He leered. "—Bobby Kennedy?"

"No," Gretel said. "I want. . ."

Gretel, for the sake of propriety, bundled into her warm clothes and set off for the cemetery to find Minnie. The clouds had cleared away but the sun they revealed was feeble, an invalid's sun.

"Come along, Hansel," she called to the lovely cocker spaniel pup. He ran to her with an obedient yip. A bead of saliva glistened on the tip of his distended black-pink tongue.

Gretel glanced back once at the clapboard house that a grateful township would soon—and at long last—have an opportunity to raze. It seemed to take forever to get to the cemetery.

Minnie was there under the poplar, where Gretel had expected her to be. The used-up body was draped indecorously over the stone. The half-hour of sunlight had dried the grass, but Minnie's wool dress was still damp and clinging.

Her fingernails were caked with mud and shredded grass from digging around the stone. Hansel began to whine.

"Oh, shut up!" Gretel commanded.

He sat back on his haunches and watched a powerful, slow smile spread across his mistress's face.

___ ASSASSIN & SON ___

1

The intemperate sun of Sepharad had half risen, its golden circle still skewered on the western horizon by the spires of the capital city of Zamorah. To the East, the black, elliptical backside of the Parasol had likewise risen. It stood in opposition to the sun, like a disc of nighttime that the day could not dispel.

Joseph Goldfrank tossed off a brocade coverlet and stumbled out onto his private balcony, where an antique bronze quadrant was mounted on the marble balustrade. After consulting Barron's *Astral Tables*, he adjusted the quadrant a fraction of a degree from its previous position. Then, kneeling, his palms lifted in the direction determined by the quadrant, he began to pray: "Terra-father, Gaea-mother, Earth, which I may never hope to tread—though I am absent, do not forget that I am yours. Yours still: in the press of other Gravities; in the light of other Suns: in the midst of Aliens: still yours. Preserve me human and remember me so. Let my sons return to your land, your light, your air and your people."

While he mumbled through the old ritual, his mind cleared itself of the unconscious clutter of sleep. He kissed the *Tables* and replaced it in its niche under the quadrant.

Sepharad's sun had risen from the spires of Zamorah. It shone on Joseph's naked body, burnt to a dark bronze by eighteen years under its alien brightness. He began, as always after the morning prayer, to exercise.

On his left shoulder was the still-painful mark of the Sephradim, a circle crosshatched with lines of longitude and

165

latitude, with which he had been tattooed on his eighteenth birthday. The Sephradim was a sign that his ancestors had come to Sepharad directly from Earth. Originally, the tattoo had been the mark of a criminal—to be exact, of a murderer. But on Sepharad it was a distinction greatly envied by the rest of the human population.

His right shoulder bore no tattoo: Joseph was a younger son.

"Joseph!" his father's voice rang out from the terrace below. "Breakfast."

With lightning obedience, Joseph threw on a robe woven from Earth-grown cotton and ornamented with Sephradian diamonds. Since it was quicker than the stairs, he jumped down to the terrace from his balcony. His father's hand was extended for a perfunctory kiss, which, perfunctorily, was accorded it. His brother, to whom this honor had only recently come due, made more of a ceremony of it. Joseph poured out two carafes of coffee for them and, as was the duty of a second son, recited the prayer-before-meals.

"I will have only one coffee this morning, Joseph. Therefore, you may have what is left—with David's permission." Joseph glanced hopefully at his brother, who nodded his consent.

"I thank you both." He emptied the dregs of the electric percolator into his own carafe. Usually he had to content himself with a second brewing of the grounds. His father passed him a salver of fruit taken from their own orchards, and Joseph selected a mango and breadfruit. Native-grown products were seldom admitted to the Goldfrank table, but since on Earth the fruit of Sepharad was considered a great delicacy, an exception had been made.

"Your brother and I will be gone throughout the day. I expect you to oversee Chilperic's work. The mosaic in the steam room needs to be repaired, and I shall want a roast to be ready for my evening meal. I shall be home by the next opposition." At sunset, the Parasol in the west and the sun in the east would again be in opposition, marking the end of a full day's work.

"A roast. Then, you—" His father's stern gaze silenced the unnecessary question. Roast meat meant only one thing: his father was going to perform an assassination.

Joseph wondered who was to be his father's victim. But

after all the name would probably mean nothing to him. He knew little of Sephradian politics.

The Goldfranks, father and sons, ate in silence, while the sun ruthlessly shortened the shadow of the eight-foot wall circling the terrace. When there was no shade left, the elder Goldfrank rose. David followed him to the heliport.

Joseph watched as the 'copter rose silently from its couch at the side of the house, like a jewel pendant in the bright morning sky, then turned to the capital city of Zamorah, a brighter jewel at the horizon. The 'copter had risen slowly, powered by a ten-horse antigravitic generator. Now it sped out of sight to the west as its side-jets caught fire and scorched their path across the sky.

Chilperic, unbidden, wheeled out of the house to gather the breakfast dishes. Chilperic was a "blob," as the natives of Sepharad were called by the Earth-born colonists—who had pre-empted the natural title of *Sephradim* for themselves. It was a measure of Goldfrank's affluence that he could retain a blob as his servant. It was not so much a question of Chilperic's wages (which were exorbitant), but the expense of providing the aluminum, mobile armature in which Chilperic went about his chores in the Goldfrank household.

"Good morning, Master Joseph," Chilperic's voice box piped. "How does the Earth lie?"

"Happily and far," Joseph returned.

"In what conjunction?"

"Please, Chilperic! We don't have to go through the whole ritual. There's work to do."

"Your father has given the most explicit orders that the only ritual—"

"Father is gone for the day, and you will take my orders. My first order is not to tell Father that I told you to be informal with me."

Chilperic laughed: "Ha-ha-ha." Like the other phonetic elements of the voice box, the laughter was taped. It always sounded the same. Blobs, being telepathic among themselves, had no need of voices. Chilperic "spoke" with his fingers, using a phonetic typewriter inside the ovoid armature that enclosed his amorphous body like the eggshell about an egg. The smooth metal shell was dotted with sockets into which a variety of prosthetic limbs could be inserted. Chilperic thus gave all the appearances of being a robot; it was disquieting when he did not act like one.

"I understand that I am to repair the mosaics in the steam room, just as I did last year."

"Yes."

"The steam room, if you will forgive my saying so, is a foolish place for a mosaic. But it is a foolish mosaic."

Chilperic's judgment of the Miro reproduction coincided fairly well with Joseph's own. The fluctuations of taste had led the younger generation on Sepharad to despise abstractionism—as two generations before, when the Goldfrank villa had been constructed, they had been led to admire it. Nevertheless, as a servant, it was not Chilperic's place to make judgments. Joseph reminded him of this.

"It is a beautiful work of art," Chilperic apologized, "and a striking example of the impossibility of two cultures understanding each other." With this, Chilperic, bland as aluminum, wheeled off to the kitchen with the breakfast table.

Joseph sat down to memorize Volume IV, Chapter XXVII, Section V of Will Durant's *Story of Civilization*. He was preparing for the priesthood.

2

When the sun and the Parasol had each risen 45° from the horizon and one fourth of the day was spent, Joseph set aside his history text and went into the house to check on Chilperic's work.

It was hardly a necessary task. Like the robot he so much resembled, Chilperic was incapable of loitering. By nature the blobs were industrious, but Joseph's father suspected that this invariable trait was no more than a clever deception, and he had communicated a good deal of this attitude to his sons.

Like most Sephradim, the elder Goldfrank was convinced that the blobs were engaged in a subtle and relentless conspiracy against his person—an understandable obsession in a man who, in more than twenty years as a professional assassin, had killed so many of their race that mere quantity was somehow beside the point. Goldfrank tolerated Chilperic's presence in the house for four reasons: it was a mark of prestige; Chilperic had worked for the family as long as the elder Goldfrank could remember, and to discharge him now would be an act of cowardice; he did the work of three human servants (but then he was paid accordingly); and, lastly, Chilperic was sexually neuter, so that even Goldfrank could see that his most touchy suspicions had no basis in reason.

"Master Joseph?"

"Yes, Chilperic?"

"If I finish repairing this exquisite mural by Eclipse, may I go into the village? I am needed at a mating. It will take only a few minutes."

"Surely. And while you're there, stop by the Earth Quarter and pick up a roast for the evening meal. Father will return by opposition. It must be ready then."

"As you say." Chilperic turned back to his work, but Joseph suspected that he was already signaling his six fellow-blobs in the village to expect him for the mating.

The blobs were septsexual, a degree of sexual differentation found only in free-form telepathic races. Joseph did not understand too precisely the entire Sephradian mating process. There were, he knew, two blobs that performed a masculine function and two others that could be called women; the "mother" was hermaphroditic, then there were two neutral sexes who served somehow as catalysts. The "neuters" were not motivated by strictly sexual desires: the function of one was largely vegetative and of the other (which Chilperic represented) digestive.

Chilperic had once attempted to give Joseph a more detailed explanation. But to Joseph, as to most humans, the subject inspired disgust rather than scientific curiosity. With a mental shrug of his shoulders, Chilperic had abandoned the discussion.

The effect of this septsexuality on the native Sephradian culture (and, indirectly, upon the human colonists) had been enormous. The government of the planet, from the Councils of the Empress at Zamorah to the meanest village bureaucracy, was based on the dynastic principle. The intricacies of dynastic politics were complicated by five-way sexual intrigues (the two neutral sexes being neutral in this too). Murders—for reasons of passion or ambition—were not

uncommon. Moreover, the result of murder among the telepathic blobs was a vampire-like heightening of the mental
powers of the murderer at the moment that his victim died. A
mass-murderer became, by the very commission of his crimes,
almost too powerful to destroy. On Sepharad, therefore, there
was every incitement to murder, and so it lay under the
strictest taboo. But the taboo did not, of course, affect other
races.

The appearance upon Sepharad of Earthmen had brought
about a large-scale cultural transformation. Earthmen, not
being telepaths and not being subject to telepathic influence,
could murder a Sephradian without inheriting his victim's
store of mental powers—and without being daunted by them.
Earthmen, in fact, seemed to be indifferent to any consideration but the fee they received for their work. The professional
assassin was born. The government of Earth, when it learned
of these developments on Sepharad, accommodated its economic ally by using the alien planet as a prison colony.
Murderers were given the choice between life imprisonment
on Venus and transportation to Sepharad.

They all chose Sepharad.

Joseph was the great-great-grandson of Leonard Goldfrank, a professional murderer of some notoriety in Chicago
in the year 2330. It was equivalent to a Mayflower pedigree.

Outside, indistinctly, Joseph heard a knock on the gate.
Even muted by the heavy walls of the house, he recognized it
as Leora's. He went across the terrace to the thick oak gate
(not Earth-grown oak, but expensive just the same) set into
the terrace's enclosing wall and admitted his brother's fiancee.

Indiscreetly, Leora Hughes removed her veil. Joseph had
seen her face before—when David was present—but even so
he averted his eyes.

"Silly!" Leora chided. "You can look at me. After all, in a
few weeks, I'll be living here." It was, of course, equally true
that in a few weeks Joseph would no longer be living in his
father's house, but Leora did not draw such fine distinctions.

Blushing, Joseph looked at her, avoiding the mocking
intensity of her dark eyes, covertly admiring the carefully
preserved pallor of her skin, the fullness of her lower lip
made fuller by carmine. "My brother is gone for the day."

"He's—working!" she asked. The mockery was suddenly absent from her eyes and her face went somewhat paler.

"With Father, yes. But they'll be back this evening. I'll say you were here."

"I am *still* here. Aren't you going to ask me into the house? If I leave now, I'll certainly be overcome by the heat." With the sun still an hour from Eclipse, the temperature was 98° Fahrenheit. "Besides," Leora went on, as Joseph led her to the atrium, where a marble dolphin's head (imported from Italy) gargled out a steady stream of chilled water—"besides, I'd just as soon talk to you as David. David never has anything to talk about."

"What would you like him to talk about! His work?"

"Don't be bitter, Joseph. As a priest, you're going to be a fine assassin, I must say."

He laughed. "I'll admit I used to be jealous of David—"

"Didn't you! I remember when we were seven, playing outside the Quarterhouse. You told me—"

"—But I am over that. If everyone could be an assassin just by wanting it, no one would do anything else—farmers, mechanics, store-keepers. Besides being a priest is the next best thing."

"That's just what I meant. *Next* best."

"I mean, with regard to money."

Leora pursed her lips and nodded with ironic sympathy. "What I like about my future brother-in-law is his honesty. When other priests talk about 'keeping alive the sacred heritage of the human race' or 'the delights and comforts of a life of contemplation and learning,' *you* talk about money."

"I like money. The other things are important, too. But when you're eighteen, sacred history—"

"—is a bore."

"What I like about my future sister-in-law is her immodesty."

It was Leora's turn to blush. "What do you mean!" Joseph glanced reproachfully at her veil that she held loosely in her fingers, its silver sash brushing the terrazzo floor. "But that! I mean—all the times when we were children, it's ridiculous."

"But now we're not children. David wouldn't think it was ridiculous."

She fixed the veil over her face, so that Joseph could see only her eyes glaring at him angrily. "I'd better start home. Tell David I missed him."

"Good-by, Leora." But Leora did not glance back, or say good-by.

It seemed strange to think of Leora as his brother's fiancee: Leora, who, in the irresponsible years when they went to school with each other—before, that is, she had adopted the veil of womanhood and stopped coming to the afternoon classes at the Quarterhouse—had been his special friend. In fact, she had been rather more than that, although he had tried not to think how much more.

How it must seem to Leora he did not ask himself. As a woman, it would make little difference how she felt. The marriage had been arranged between their fathers on the day that David had come of age, one year ago.

It seemed strange that, a whole year later, it still seemed strange.

The last sliver of the sun slipped behind the enormous man-made Parasol, and the artificial night of the Sephradian noonday descended over the land. Joseph knelt and faced the western sky. There, insignificant beside the greater brightness of nearby Vega, Earth's sun shone dimly and listened (or so he had been told at the Quarterhouse school) to his prayer. Joseph knew perfectly well that neither Earth, nor Earth's sun, actually listened to him. He sometimes doubted that anything or anyone listened at all—except, sometimes, his father. More than once Joseph had been beaten for neglecting the rituals, so that now they were almost second nature.

The Eclipse lasted twenty minutes, as long as it took the sun traveling eastward to pass behind the Parasol, traveling in the contrary direction at the same speed. The great Parasol, its longitudinal axis describing a 10° arc across the sky, shielded Zamorah and its environs from the fiercest heat of the sun, gave a brief respite to the parching earth while the spillgates of the new irrigating systems were opened, and allowed the dweller of the planet, human or otherwise, a chance to walk abroad shaded from the merciless sun. The Parasol orbited a mere hundred miles above the planet, the power for its antigravity plant being provided by the very sun whose rays its giant mirrors, visible as far away as the Lunar Observatory, deflected into space. Earth had built the Parasol and its two fascimiles orbiting beyond the horizon for Sepharad without cost, but not entirely from selfless motives. As a result of the lower mean temperature and the new pattern of pressure belts over once-arid plains, the agricultural output of Sepharad had more than doubled in the last fifty years.

Of course, population had also boomed, but not at all at the same rate. Septsexuality had certain advantages vis-à-vis the Malthusian dilemma. Export was now Sepharad's largest industry, and Earth and her colonies were Sepharad's chief markets.

Joseph set off for his afternoon classes at the Quarterhouse as soon as he had rattled through the noonday prayer. If he hurried he could arrive at the Human Quarter in the village before the twenty-minute Eclipse was over.

Eclipse was not a total darkness, the northern and southern horizons glowed with a dim, refracted light.

In the gloom, Joseph could still discern the gold-lettered sign above the oak gate: GOLDFRANK & SON, ASSASSINATIONS. At the side of the villa was the family cemetery where ostentatious bronze crosses marked the graves of the men, and silver spheres—the mark of the Sephradim—stood above the women's plots. The bronze crosses were weathered to a dull green, and the silver spheres—all but one—were tarnished and gray. That one was his mother's, killed two years before, while shopping in the village during one of the recurrent outbursts against the colonists.

Over a low hill, on Joseph's right hand, was the Hughes's villa, and farther on the flamboyant four-story mansion of Oscar Milne. Goldfrank, Hughes and Milne were all three professional assassins, which was three more than the nearby village had need of itself. Most of their work was carried on in Zamorah. Prudence, however, had led them to establish suburban residences at a comfortable distance from the scene of their business.

A few crude structures of scrap plastic, the dwellings of lower-caste Sephradians, stood on the outskirts of the Human Quarter. No blobs were at large during Eclipse—or, as the blobs referred to it, the Time of the Assassin. Although the Council of the Empress had sanctioned the construction of the Parasol, the average blob still regarded the daily blackout with superstitious terror. Custom had it that in the beginning the Eclipse had lasted mere seconds. Now the period of darkness was twenty minutes: and tomorrow? Rumors would spring up that the Time of the Assassin was growing longer. There would be local attacks on the colonists, who were thought to be responsible. Then the Empress's Army would dismiss the rioters and calm their fears—which the next Eclipse would resurrect, keeping the vicious circle steadily aspin. There was little hope of stopping it as long as the blobs worshipped the sun.

The Human Quarter looked slightly shabbier than the Sephradian slums on its outskirts. While the professional assassin enjoyed the luxury of his villa, the average colonist paid the price of his legal criminality. They were rigidly segregated from the blobs, and building permits for their quarter were not easily obtained. Even jobs were scarce, short-lived and poorly paid. Since the colonists—and their offspring—were considered outlaws by the government of Earth, they were denied even the hope of someday departing their prison. But, for all that, they were probably happier on Sepharad than they would have been on Venus. Happiness is a relative state.

Joseph did not like the Quarter. He hurried through it to his school, haunted by the thought that in only a few weeks this would be his home.

Then, abruptly, he halted. Directly ahead of him a blob cased in the special fenestrated armature of the Imperial Civil Service wheeled down the street from the Quarterhouse, flanked on each side by guards in less ornamental shells. Joseph recognized the blob (or, more exactly, he recognized the armature) and bowed his head as it passed him: Sisebat, the most powerful Sephradian in the village and its mayor.

He did not look like a murderer, Joseph thought. But then—neither did his own father.

3

"Yer father's a blob-lover!"

"Shut up, Jamie," Joseph calmly commanded, but his eyes revealed well enough that he was afraid. A ring of boys had begun to form around them in the street outside the Quarter-house.

Jamie Hughes, his father's only son and a future assassin himself, was not to be shut up that easily. "Yeah—he's the eighth man at a mating!" He made an obscene gesture.

Joseph swung. Jamie had been ready, and Joseph found himself lying on the stony street, blood dripping from his nose.

"Say he is!" Jamie taunted. "Say he's a blob-lover." Jamie fed Joseph's rage with professional expertise.

Enraged, Joseph lunged to his feet, not flailing his fists as Jamie had expected, instead butting his head into the boy's stomach. They went down together. Jamie pounded at the base of Joseph's neck with the calloused side of his hand, Joseph bringing up his knee toward Jamie's midriff. Jamie twisted out of his grasp, ripping his clothing to avoid the well-aimed knee. Then Jamie began to kick his ribs.

It was not an even match. Jamie, although he was two years younger and inches shorter than Joseph, was in training to be a killer. Joseph had not fought with anyone for the past year—and he had never, except for some playful tussles with his brother, fought with an assassin-to-be.

Two of the older boys were trying to pull Jamie away. While his attention was diverted by the peacemakers, Joseph grabbed his leg and toppled him to the pavement, cracking his head against the stone and stunning him sufficiently to allow Joseph to purchase hold on his throat unresisted. Thumbs pressed against the windpipe, quite blind now to anything but the pleasure of the violence—the triumph—strangling. . . .

"Joseph! *Joseph!*"

It was unmistakably the voice of Magister Sontag, the Instructor of Earth History at the Quarterhouse, and Master of the Rituals. Joseph loosened his grip on Jamie's throat and looked to the Magister where he frowned down from a second-floor dormer window. "Come up to my office this minute—but first apologize to Master Hughes."

"I apologize," Joseph mumbled.

"Yeah—blob-lover," Jamie said, *sotto voce*, accepting Joseph's hand.

As he ascended the stairs to Sontag's office, tears of shame welled up in Joseph's eyes.

"Sit down, Joseph. Here's a damp towel for your nose. Do you feel all in one piece?"

"Yes. I'm very sorry; it was my fault. I—"

"Please, no false contrition. If I know Jamie at all, it was probably his fault. What did he do?"

"He wanted me to kiss his ring. As though I were *his* younger brother! I don't have to do that—it's not part of the Rituals."

"Strictly speaking, of course not. But I have noticed that usually you are rather liberal in interpreting the Rituals. By refusing Jamie, you gave him the pretext he was looking for to fight with you."

"He called my father—"

"—enough names, doubtless, so that you struck the first blow. Jamie would see to that." The Magister sat down behind his desk and began to stroke the long beard signalizing his priesthood. "Humility is a lesson that is difficult for the young to learn. I don't want to scold you for today's little adventure—you're not one to repeat mistakes. And I don't want to suggest that you're too high-spirited. A candidate for the priesthood should not be devoid of spirit, though that is using the word in a rather different sense. Yours seem to be animal spirits."

Joseph looked up from the blood-stained towel, smiling. The Magister was smiling too. "I'm sure you'll learn to tame them at the seminary. Now—" he pressed a button on the side of his desk—"will you join me for a late lunch?"

"With pleasure."

A girl, obviously still in her teens despite the veil that hid her face and the loose robe that hid most of her other features, entered and stood before the Magister.

"Bring wine and biscuits for two, Esther."

Esther Sontag acknowledged her father's order with a slight bow. She glanced quickly at the towel Joseph still held to his nose and then, less quickly, into Joseph's eyes where she found no reply nor recognition. Joseph always avoided meeting her anxious, darting eyes, for he knew that his father and the Magister were still bickering over the financial details of their betrothal. It was only a matter of time before their engagement was announced, and Joseph did not want Esther to read in his eyes the complete indifference he felt for her. Until their wedding, he could spare her that pain, at least.

allowed you to live. I am to accompany you to the village where you may gather your personal possessions. My name is Egica."

"Dead, you say? Both? Dead?"

"Will you need to be guarded, or shall I untie you?"

"I don't feel angry . . . or violent. That's strange."

"Not strange at all: the sedation does not wear off immediately. But I advise you not to *become* violent. I am, as your language has it, armed." Joseph felt Egica's dextrous pseudopodia unravelling the knots in the rope. The wet plasma brushed his wrists. His skin had never felt the flesh of a blob till then.

"This way."

"It's night."

"Yes, two hours, past the sunset."

"And I am not a prisoner?"

"No. The Magister spoke on your behalf—and quite eloquently, too. He promised Sisebat that you were devoted to ideals of nonviolence, that you were to be a priest. Sisebat seemed to believe him. At least, he accepted his bribe, which was probably all that he wanted."

"Then you didn't believe him?"

"I advised our mayor to be merciful. Your death might have offended the human colonists unnecessarily. As for your idealism or lack of it, I profess no opinion."

Joseph discovered that he had been crying, and it came over him now that his father and his brother were no longer alive, that the roast was either cold now or forgotten in the oven, turning to ash.

"How were they killed?"

"With laser-guns. They felt no pain, I'm sure. The bodies—what was left—were brought back to your villa. You will see."

They walked the rest of the way in silence. Chilperic admitted them at the gate. The bodies lay on separate plastic mats on the terrace. It was impossible to tell which had been his father.

The next thing Joseph was aware of was Chilperic's voice—*Joseph, get up. Can you stand up? Joseph, can I help?* And then the wet pressure of Chilperic's pseudopodia against his bare shoulders. Joseph recoiled from that touch, not screaming yet, though perhaps he was—*Get away*—remembering the sensation, his horror, Chilperic's touch, wishing only to be outside his body. And then it seemed he was merely a spectator as his hands upended the blob's armature and rolled it over on the stone floor, a spectator of the fully-distended pseudopod that reached toward him until the heavy armature rolled over on it, and it broke then and lay on the stone floor, a streak of jelly. And Chilperic's cry—*Joseph*—that seemed though it issued from a mechanical voice box, to be choked with pain and grief.

He did scream then—stricken by a terror not of the forgotten touch but of his own irredeemable deed. He only noticed the laser projecting from Egica's metal shell after he had raised Chilperic upright.

"He did not mean to do it," Chilperic's voice box enunciated, more for Joseph's benefit than Egica's, whom he had already restrained from using the laser, telepathically. "When his father's father was killed, it was just the same. To them, we are all alike . . . all guilty. I am older now; that is the only difference. Slower to move—and to mend."

"Chilperic—"

"Quite. I have no time to. . . Humans are a little insane, but it is over quickly . . . a terrible mosaic."

"I know. I'll have it taken down."

"Ha-ha-ha . . . Joseph—be like—" Chilperic spoke no more. There was a vague, liquid sound within the armature, as the blob's body relaxed into death.

"What did he want to say?" Joseph asked, turning to Egica.

"Be like your father."

"An assassin?"

"That was his meaning, but he would not have used that word." Egica paused. When he resumed, his words came more slowly. "It is also my meaning. As I understand your laws, your Ritual, you are entitled now, since your brother is dead, to become an assassin. It is hereditary. Am I right?"

"Can you talk about that *now?*"

"At no time else, I am afraid. You are responsible for Chilperic's death."

"I know. *I know.*"

"My testimony could damn you. You can be tried, convicted, and sentenced to death. But an assassin would not be tried. He is licensed to do murder, and he lives outside the laws. Sisebat will never grant that license to you; he has too much to fear. But I will—when I am mayor. I will also allow you to reclaim your father's estate. Therefore, you will assassinate Sisebat tonight."

"And if I refuse?"

"I cannot return to the village until Sisebat is dead. He will know that I have plotted his death, and he will kill me. Therefore, if you refuse I will kill you."

"You give me little choice."

"There is not much to give."

"I will do it."

"Chilperic was right. You will be the very image of your father."

5

Returning to the village that night, his father's laser-gun hidden beneath a heavy woolen robe (made in England), Joseph allowed himself the luxury of idle speculation. In the future, it would be a luxury that he could ill afford.

He speculated, for instance, on the problem of free will. He reflected that, being forced into a career that he had only that afternoon freely desired, he no longer desired that career. Necessity had a bitter taste.

He thought of Leora, whom he would now surely marry, although a few hours ago he would not have allowed himself to admit that he was in love with her. Though she would be happier wed to him, though she might even have desired it, she was as much a slave of necessity as Joseph. She would wed him not for love's sake, but because he had inherited her from his brother and her father would not leave her any choice.

Joseph wondered if necessity would have the same taste for Leora.

He thought of Magister Sontag, gratefully and already with a sense of nostalgia. Later that night he would have the Magister tattoo on his right shoulder the mark of the Assassin: a shortsword crossed by a dagger, the same emblem that would be cast in bronze and set over his father's grave. Esther would probably be watching in secret. He was surprised that, for the first time, he thought of Esther with affection.

And, when he stood before the mayor's dwelling in the center of the village, he thought of Sisebat.

A servant answered the door.

"I wish to see the mayor—to thank him for sparing my life."

The servant (who was a human) bowed to Joseph and ushered him into a large hall. "This way, please."

SLAVES

The Baron slept in the living room, which was also the kitchen, on a Castro convertible. Danielle and Paul, since it was Paul's apartment, slept in the bedroom. The bedroom was no more than a hole in the wall. The bird, Nevermore, had spent the winter there with them, because it was warmer. Now her cage was back in the living room with the Baron.

"Why are you molting?" the Baron asked of Nevermore, twiddling a tail feather in her face. "Do I molt? Do I get my feathers all over everything?" Nevermore squawked.

If the Baron were to put his finger in the birdcage, Nevermore would bite it. Paul was the only person who could handle the parakeet. It belonged to him—a Christmas present from Danielle.

They were still in bed, Danielle and Paul, making love. Meanwhile the Baron prepared breakfast: bacon and eggs, unfrozen orange juice, coffee. He cleared the table of two dirty coffee cups, a paperback edition of *Candy* (the pirated version, since that was more exciting), Danielle's turquoise hairband, and a pile of wadded paper napkins that had been used as Kleenex.

The radio was going to bake a sunshine cake. It wasn't really so hard to make. The Baron changed stations. An announcer read stock market quotations to the Baron. AT&T was up.

Danielle, in a Matisse-ly floral muumuu, came out of the bedroom.

"Isn't there any more nice music?" she asked.

"*This* is music, for those who understand it," the Baron replied, ladling grease over the egg yolks. The Baron had once been a business administration major.

"Last night at the discotheque they played the new Tab

commercial for fifteen minutes running. It was just like a French movie. I want to get a record of it for Paul to listen to."

"For my own part," the Baron said, his gaze intent upon the frying eggs, "*I'm* going to make a sunshine cake."

"Did you feed Nevermore?"

"It isn't really so hard to make. I use Betty Crocker's Sunshine Cake Mix."

"Because he's nervous this morning."

"Then add a smile and let it simmer." The Baron smiled winningly, but Danielle didn't see it. She was pouring orange juice into three glasses.

"Besides," he said, "it's a *she,* not a *he.* You can tell by the name, Nevermore. That's a girl's name."

"I don't see that it makes any difference with birds. After all, they only lay eggs. Anyone can do that." The toaster ejected two crisp slices of toast. Danielle replaced them with two mooshy slices of Tastee white bread. "Paul," she called, "breakfast."

"I'm getting dressed, beautiful."

Danielle, it is true, was beautiful, but she was worried about her weight. She was a dancer, and dancers always worry about their weight.

"We were fighting last night," she confided to the Baron, "and I lost another goddam contact lens. Now I can only see out of my right eye."

"You should take out your lenses before you start fighting."

She ignored his joke. "They cost so damn much *money.*"

"So get insurance."

"That costs more. Anyhow, Paul is going to pay for it."

Paul came out of the bedroom, bare-chested, swinging his arms with athletic grace. He had been a shot-putter in undergraduate days.

"Aren't you, my beloved?" Danielle asked.

"Sure," he said, "I love to pay for things."

He took one of the glasses of juice (the biggest) and drank it in one long gulp. He fiddled with the radio dial and came in on the tail end of "Sunshine Cake." He began to sing along with the radio. He had a resonant baritone, but he couldn't keep in one key. Danielle and the Baron began singing too. Then the song ended, and there was an advertisement for frozen clams.

The Baron put two eggs on each plate and three slices of bacon. Danielle portioned out the toast and poured the coffee. Paul went to the icebox to get the cream for his coffee.

"*Now*," said the Baron, "can't we listen to the stock market again?"

"I like this better," said Paul. What Paul liked better was Mantovani playing the theme from *Peyton Place*.

The Baron was in the foyer, reading the titles of the books in the bookcase. They were dull books that belonged to Paul. The Baron had never heard of their authors: Trelawney, Maitland, Hulme, Wedgwood.

Paul was studying English literature at Columbia Grad School. He was bright, but he'd dropped out of all the good colleges he'd gone to and finally had to take his BA from NYU. These books were from the time, years and years ago, when Paul had been majoring in history at Swarthmore.

The Baron was waiting around in the foyer because Danielle wouldn't come out of the bathroom, where she was combing out her long black hair. Like Nevermore's feathers, Danielle's hair seemed to get into everything: the bedsheets, the food, even the Baron's own laundry. It caused him more to wonder than to be annoyed. Innocently, he would tell Danielle when he found one of her hairs in some new, unlikely place, and she would suppose he was complaining. But the Baron almost never complained. He was seldom that sure of himself.

"Will you be very long?" the Baron asked again through the thick door.

"No."

"Because I am terribly in *need*."

She came out of the bathroom with her hair piled in an elaborate bouffant steadied by the turquoise band. She wore pink tights under a black leotard, and worn-out Capezios. Yesterday's makeup was still smudged around her eyes.

"It's all yours."

He was in such a hurry he didn't even lock the door behind him. Once he was on the stool it was too late. While he sat there, he worried about whether he had a soul. The problem had been disturbing him for several days.

In the bedroom Danielle began stripping the bed in search of the contact lens she had lost. "Don't you want to help me, Paul?"

"Sorry. I'm busy writing my paper for Seventeenth Century."

"But you're *reading*."

"I'm reading the book that the paper has to be about. Here, listen to this—it's called *Casualties:*

Good things, that come of course, far lesse do please,
Than those, which come by sweet contingencies.

Now, does that sound like anything I'd read for pleasure?"

"It doesn't make any sense. Why is it called *Casualties?*"

"Not deaths, dimwit. Casualties—things you do in a casual way, like getting laid."

"You always pick such dull things to write your papers about."

"They're only dull from a distance."

"Like the river," she said, forgetting in the instant to search for the lens. She squinted her left eye shut and looked at the river, shimmering grayly in the morning sun. The details of the Jersey cliffs, the little houses and particular trees, seemed peculiarly clear. She wondered what it would be like to live in Jersey. There was something vaguely frightening about the idea.

She opened the bedroom window, and a breeze stirred through the room, brushing with gentle insistence against the edges of fabrics and loose papers. Paul was saying something. For some reason she wanted to cry. "What did you say?" she asked Paul.

"I asked you if you'd get my shirts from the laundry. Today is Thursday."

"I will—but after class." At night Danielle worked in a bar, standing in a little glass cage and dancing, but in the daytime she studied ballet.

"The ticket's in my billfold," Paul said irritably.

She really couldn't see what *he* had to be irritated about! She looked through his billfold. "Jesus Christ!"

"What?"

"You still have the piece of paper in here with Dr. Minzer's address on it. Isn't that rather careless?"

"So? Who's going to see it? And if they do, I can say he's an analyst that a friend recommended."

"Except that right above his name you've printed Abortions."

He bent over the volume of Herrick with a look of studied unawareness. She dropped the subject. "Here's the laundry ticket. I'm taking a dollar to pay for it."

"Take a couple dollars. We need groceries."

"The Baron will get the groceries, though, won't he?" Paul laughed. "What are you laughing at?" she asked.

"This." He read from the Herrick:

> Here she lies, a pretty bud,
> Lately made of flesh and blood:
> Who, as soone, fell fast asleep,
> As her little eyes did peep.

While he read, she watched a tugboat moving up the river drawing a coal barge behind it. "I think that's lovely," she said. Then she started packing her clothes for class.

"Can I help you look?" the Baron asked. He was still wearing his pajamas, faded and frayed.

"Would you? That would be nice. I have to go to class now."

Thursday was pointe class. She stuffed a new pair of toe shoes into the smelly bag. Last night she had darned the blunt toes with heavy pink thread.

The Baron pulled the unmade bed away from the wall, and, sprawling across it, he began to explore the cracks in the parquet flooring with his fingertips. Danielle pursed her lips. She didn't like him lying in her bed like that. But what could she say?

Without thinking of what he was doing, Paul idly caressed his muscly stomach with his fingertips. When touched, the brown down tickled a little. His other hand held a book, which he did not read. He was not aware enough of the melody in his head to realize that it had usurped his whole attention. Because he was looking at the book, he would have supposed that he was reading it.

In blue jeans, a T-shirt, and sneakers, Paul looked like a folk singer—not deliberately, but because it was the easiest thing to look like. He liked rough fabrics and the grainy feeling of his hair coming down over the nape of his neck. Mercier, who was Danielle's analyst (a lay analyst), had said that Paul was probably a phallic narcissist. Paul couldn't really see anything wrong with that.

The sofa on which he was lying was the Doctor Jekyll,

daytime aspect of the Baron's bed. The prosaic furniture of the room was not Paul's, but the books were, except for one shelf that held the *OED*. That belonged to the Baron. Paul was trying to buy it from him, but his asking price was too much. The rent was $150 (because of the veranda and the view of the river), which Paul paid, or, more exactly, which Paul's father paid. Paul's father was an attorney in White Plains.

The Baron's father had been a dentist, but he had committed suicide when the Baron was twenty and a junior in business administration school. He left a note saying he had never wanted to be a dentist. The Baron had dropped out of school. Except for the note the Baron didn't get anything. His stepmother, who had inherited what little there was, had remarried and was living now in California.

Of course, he was not actually a Baron. That was only the way his friends talked. His real name was Baron Edward Blum.

"I'd like a beer," the Baron said. It was obviously too early for beer.

Paul didn't look up from his book, so the Baron tried another tack. "Nevermore is molting, but she doesn't have any molting food." Nevermore, hearing her name mentioned, squawked and tried to pull the clapper out of the bell that hung in her cage.

Paul took his billfold out of his pocket and gave the Baron a five for groceries. At first Paul had been embarrassed to let the Baron do all the housework and cooking and shopping, but now he took it for granted. "I'm feeling like pimentoes," he said. "What can you put pimentoes in?"

"In olives."

"No, I meant what hot dish."

"In a tuna casserole. Or in tunafish salad. Or in stewed chicken." The Baron cooked something with tunafish in it at least once a week. Tunafish chow mein was his speciality.

"Let's have stewed chicken." Paul lit a cigarette and dropped the dead match on the floor. That was his worst habit, in the Baron's opinion. The smoke curling up his cheek set up a tremor in his left eyelid.

The Baron had given up smoking at the time of Edward R. Murrow's death, but his real reason was that he couldn't afford cigarettes anymore. They'd gone up to forty cents a pack. It was about that time that he'd moved into Paul's apartment.

They were old friends, Paul and the Baron. Ever since fourth grade in White Plains. Paul thought the Baron was crazy, but he liked him anyhow. Paul thought most people were crazy. He was in his fifth year of analysis. He went to a real analyst, an MD, certified—not one of those lay analysts like Mercier. He paid $35 an hour. Danielle only paid $20. But she went four times a week. It ate up all the money she made dancing five nights a week at the discotheque.

So it was obvious to Paul that Danielle was crazy too, but he was in love with her. Paul's analyst said that he would know that he was completely cured when he liked people who weren't crazy better than the people who were.

"What did you fight about last night?" the Baron asked.

"About her dancing. I told her she wasn't getting anywhere with all this ballet crap." But the Baron had heard their argument, and he knew that Paul was lying. What they had really argued about (again) was the abortion.

"Well," said the Baron, "if things don't work out career-wise for a girl, she can always get married."

"But *you,*" Paul said, "what will become of you?"

"I don't think about it. It's Christlike not to plan ahead. Maybe I'll go back to business school. Maybe I'll become a beatnik. Maybe I'll be like my father . . . a dentist."

"It's none of my business. Forgive me."

"That's all right, Paul."

"I didn't mean to bug you."

The Baron had gone to stand by the fireplace, where a greatly enlarged photo of Danielle hung. Nude, her breasts were only slightly unfirm; there was a scarcely perceptible crease on the underside of each full globe of flesh. The jutting of her hip was exquisite and bold. Last New Year's, when she was very drunk and Paul had gone off with someone else, she had offered that same lovely body to the Baron, exquisitely and boldly. He had refused, out of a misguided sense of nobility.

—*If people have a soul,* he thought, *nobility makes sense. But otherwise?*

"Do you think I have a soul?" he asked Paul.

"It depends," said Paul. "How much do you want for it?"

"What's a good price?"

"I'd say fifty dollars. And that reminds me—I should look for that goddam contact lens. It'll cost me fifty dollars at least to get another. I just don't have that kind of money to throw away. I'll have to sell some books." Paul went into the bedroom and got down on his hands and knees.

The Baron fingered the little disc of plastic in his shirt pocket. To think that it could cost so much money!

"Why are you molting?" he asked Nevermore. "Just to make more work for me? Is that it? Is that your game?"

"It's in this room somewhere," Paul said, without conviction.

"Why don't you let Nevermore loose? It's spring, and she wants to be free."

"The pigeons in the park would peck her to death."

"She probably prefers her cage anyhow. Kafka wrote about a cage flying in search of a bird. That's about the size of it."

Paul came back into the living room. He had given up the search. "I read in the *Times* a while back that the dime-a-dance girls at Orpheum Danceland kept a pet pigeon in their room. Why do you suppose they did that? Pets are all just pregnancy surrogates, I guess. Anyhow, a pigeon would be better than a cat. Cats leave fur."

"I'll get the groceries now," said the Baron.

"Yes," said Paul, "yes, you'd better do that." He lay back down on the couch again and looked at the photograph of Danielle. When he heard the door being pulled shut and the Baron's footsteps going down the stairs, he began, ever so lightly, to stroke himself through the blue denim of his jeans.

Danielle, whose body was so ripely feminine that one teacher, a man, had told her she would never be a dancer, had nevertheless a stiff and rather defeminized walk. The Baron recognized her by this token from across the street in the Party Cake Bakery. She was coming up from the subway.

He went to the door. "Hi there!" he called loudly.

She waved her big dance bag in the air, and her green damask cape parted in front to show the pink tights and black leotard. Demurely, she waited for the light to change.

"Are you buying cook-kies?" When she spoke, it was like someone who is drugged, or like a sleepy child.

"I'm buying bread. We don't have money for cook-kies."
Unconsciously, he mimicked her intonation.

"Poor us."

The saleslady handed the Baron a bag containing a loaf,
sliced, of pumpernickel.

"I have to get Paul's shirts," she said, giving the Baron her
hand to hold. "Poor dear Paul isn't happy. I wish I could
make him happier. He can't see any future for himself except
teaching English. It was better when he wanted to be an
analyst."

"Or a writer."

"I didn't know him then. That must have been years ago.
Why *can't* he be a writer? He has an incredible sensibility.
Sometimes. Have you read his poems?"

"His poems aren't very good."

"But they show great sensitivity." Danielle stopped on the
street to open her dance bag and take out her change purse.
She opened the change purse and took out a dollar bill and
the laundry ticket. While she was in the Chinese laundry, the
Baron stood guard over her dance bag. When she returned,
he felt sad, like someone at the birthday of a much poorer
child.

"I've got to go to Woolworth's to get Nevermore her
molting food," he explained, handing her her bag.

"I'll come with you. I love to go to Woolworth's. Someday
I'd like to work there. Think of all the things you could steal
if you *worked* there!"

"What would you steal first?"

"First a pop Bach record. Then some Revlon lipstick. Then
a boy parakeet for Nevermore. What would you steal?"

"Money," he said.

"I hadn't thought of that."

"And then slaves."

She pursed her lips. "Oh, I think one might find better
slaves in New Jersey." Her eyes sparkled with the pleasure of
fantasizing.

In Woolworth's they passed, in order, a pizza and soft
drink stand, a candy counter, a cosmetics counter, a display
of plastic flowers (29¢—None Higher), and a toy counter.
While the Baron paid for Nevermore's molting food (35¢),
Danielle drifted to the toys. She picked up the largest cap
pistol from the counter, a convincing replica of a Buntline
Special, and pointed it at the Baron.

"Bang," she said, "you're dead."

"Gaigh," said the Baron.

The saleslady, who was really too attractive to work in Woolworth's, came up to Danielle, as a nurse approaches the bed of a troublesome patient. "Is there anything I can interest you in?"

Danielle turned, gun in hand, on the saleslady. "Do you have slaves?" she asked. "Men slaves is what I was looking for in particular."

The Baron took her gun away. "Retarded," he explained to the saleslady. "That's why I have to go everywhere with her." The saleslady went away in a huff. Obviously she had not believed him.

"Marbles," said Danielle, surveying the toy counter. "And look *here*, here are balloons. That's what we forgot to get—balloons!"

"They come at two prices," the Baron observed.

"Yes. One box of twenty-five *big* balloons cost fifty cents." The box of twenty-five big balloons dropped through her spread cape and into the open dance bag on the floor. "And one box of one hundred little balloons costs a quarter. That's very reasonable." The cheaper box dropped into her dance bag too.

The Baron had opened a box of one hundred small balloons, and into it (for it was only half full) he stuffed the contents of a fifty-cent package of big balloons. He brought the box to the saleslady.

"I have to buy her these balloons," he said sorrowfully, handing the woman a quarter.

"Two cents sales tax," the saleslady said. He gave her two pennies.

Outside the store, in Riverside Park, Danielle nibbled a slice of pumpernickel. The Baron was massaging her spongy nape with strong, rhythmic pinches. "Guess what?" he said.

"What?" Danielle was staring at the Jersey shore. Then a squirrel caught her attention, two squirrels.

"I found your lens."

"Oh, good." The squirrels began to chase each other, playing peek-a-boo in the still-bare branches of the trees. "Did you tell Paul already?"

"No. Not yet."

His hand caught up a mass of her hair and made a ponytail of it. "And, if you like, I *won't* tell him."

"Don't, thank you. For, truly, it might have been lost."

They began walking home. Daintily Danielle avoided stepping on the cracks. She was thinking how nice it would be to be a squirrel, except she was really thinking of something else.

"What will you do with the money?" the Baron asked. "How much will there be?"

"Fifty dollars."

"And what will you do with it, Danielle?"

She turned on the Baron angrily. "I will buy a present for Paul!"

The Baron smiled and took her hand in his. He hadn't been taken in, not at all. "Perhaps," he said playfully. "When you go to pick it out, will you let me come along and help? I *did* find the lens, after all."

"Perhaps," she said. Then, "Yes, let's." They laughed, and Danielle did a skipping step without stepping on any of the cracks.

"Then here," the Baron said, "is a present for you." He took the Buntline Special out of his coat pocket. The barrel was almost a foot long.

"Bang. Bang. Bang."

Danielle giggled.

It was Danielle who, when they got to the door of the building, had the last word to say on the subject. "We've turned the tables, haven't we? Paul is *our* slave now."

He kissed her right there on the front stoop for all of Riverside Drive to see.

Nevermore squawked when a bright red thing passed outside the bars, but she didn't jump off the perch of her seed dish. It had been three days since she had eaten, and nothing could frighten her away from the food she had now.

The red balloon floated down to the unswept floor and bounced. It came down the next time on a blue balloon, and the blue balloon, blown up to its limit and with sharp grains of dust clinging to its fragile shell, burst. Sympathetically, the red balloon burst too.

Danielle was lying on the sofa, covered with balloons, singing the Tab commercial. Paul and the Baron were still blowing up balloons. They had already blown up one hundred and eighty of them, and there were seventy left to go.

The tops of the bookshelves were covered with balloons. The bed was covered with balloons and the desk was too. The bathtub was filled with balloons, and the kitchen counter was piled high with them. There were balloons all over the floor. Everywhere you looked there were balloons.

"I wonder," the Baron meditated, "whether balloons have souls."

At the end of her anthem, Danielle threw out her arms and legs and the balloons swirled up into the air, bumping lazily against each other, and then settled down again, some on Danielle, some to the floor. The window was halfway open, and everywhere in the room the riverbreeze stirred the balloons. They skittered about the room, as though they were trying to hide.

"Let's go outdoors," Danielle said, stepping out the window. She released a blue, ellipsoidal balloon into the wind. The wind blew it back into the living room.

"Hand them all to me," she said. Her tone was imperious. Paul and the Baron went about the apartment gathering the balloons, which they emptied in great armfuls onto the veranda. Danielle would release them one by one, into the cool wind.

The wind moved the balloons sideways along the apartment building, then at the corner lifted them high into the air. At a certain altitude, the wind, which seemed to be blowing in from the river, carried the balloons out toward New Jersey.

There seemed to be no end to the balloons, but even so Danielle was provident. She released them only one at a time, at measured intervals. Everywhere the blue sky was filled with balloons.

Then the wind changed.

The balloons began to fall down to the pavement and into the street. Pedestrians and strollers in the park took notice of them. On the Drive, cars slowed. One boy started collecting them, but in only a short while he had gathered more than he could hold.

Everyone was watching the Baron and Danielle and Paul.

Paul was the tallest of them and the most handsome from a distance. Standing between the other two, his hand raised over his head, holding a yellow balloon, he looked like a Christ in a Last Judgment. Danielle's hair was blowing in front of her eyes, and she had a hand raised to hold it back. From the street the Baron's figure seemed the least imposing of the three, but it was still necessary in forming the composition.

Danielle turned to her two companions. "Perhaps," she said in a playful tone, "they're free on the other side."

"No," said Paul, more seriously, "I think they're slaves there too."

"What difference does it make," the Baron asked, "if they have no souls?"

The wind picked up again. "All of them, all at once!" Danielle shouted.

In armloads they released the last of their balloons, and they drifted across the street and over the park and high above the river, moving westward toward the Jersey shore.

There were red balloons and blue balloons and yellow balloons and pink balloons and green balloons and orange balloons.

——— THE ROACHES ———

Miss Marcia Kenwell had a perfect horror of cockroaches. It was an altogether different horror than the one which she felt, for instance, toward the color puce. Marcia Kenwell loathed the little things. She couldn't see one without wanting to scream. Her revulsion was so extreme that she could not bear to crush them under the soles of her shoes. No, that would be too awful. She would run, instead, for the spray can of Black Flag and inundate the little beast with poison until it ceased to move or got out of reach into one of the cracks where they all seemed to live. It was horrible, unspeakably horrible, to think of them nestling in the walls, under the linoleum, only waiting for the lights to be turned off, and then... No, it was best not to think about it.

Every week she looked through the *Times* hoping to find another apartment, but either the rents were prohibitive (this *was* Manhattan, and Marcia's wage was a mere $62.50 a week, gross) or the building was obviously infested. She could always tell: there would be husks of dead roaches scattered about in the dust beneath the sink, stuck to the greasy backside of the stove, lining the out-of-reach cupboard shelves like the rice on the church steps after a wedding. She left such rooms in a passion of disgust, unable even to think till she reached her own apartment, where the air would be thick with the wholesome odors of Black Flag, Roach-It, and the toxic pastes that were spread on slices of potato and hidden in a hundred cracks which only she and the roaches knew about.

At least, she thought, *I keep my apartment clean.* And truly, the linoleum under the sink, the backside and underside of the stove, and the white contact paper lining her cupboards were immaculate. She could not understand how other people could let these matters get so entirely out-of-hand. *They must be Puerto Ricans,* she decided—and shivered again with horror, remembering that litter of empty husks, the filth and the disease.

Such extreme antipathy toward insects—toward one particular insect—may seem excessive, but Marcia Kenwell was not really exceptional in this. There are many women, bachelor women like Marcia chiefly, who share this feeling, though one may hope, for sweet charity's sake, that they escape Marcia's peculiar fate.

Marcia's phobia was, as in most such cases, hereditary in origin. That is to say, she inherited it from her mother, who had a morbid fear of anything that crawled or skittered or lived in tiny holes. Mice, frogs, snakes, worms, bugs—all could send Mrs. Kenwell into hysterics, and it would indeed have been a wonder if little Marcia had not taken after her. It was rather strange, though, that her fear had become so particular, and stranger still that it should particularly be cockroaches that captured her fancy, for Marcia had never seen a single cockroach, didn't know what they were. (The Kenwells were a Minnesota family, and Minnesota families simply don't have cockroaches.) In fact, the subject did not arise until Marcia was nineteen and setting out (armed with nothing but a high school diploma and pluck, for she was not, you see, a very attractive girl) to conquer New York.

On the day of her departure, her favorite and only surviving aunt came with her to the Greyhound Terminal (her parents being deceased) and gave her this parting advice: "Watch out for the roaches, Marcia darling. New York City is full of cockroaches." At that time (at almost any time really) Marcia hardly paid attention to her aunt, who had opposed the trip from the start and given a hundred or more reasons why Marcia had better not go, not till she was older at least.

Her aunt had been proven right on all counts: Marcia, after five years and fifteen employment agency fees, could find nothing in New York but dull jobs at mediocre wages; she had no more friends than when she lived on West 16th; and, except for its view (the Chock Full O'Nuts warehouse and a patch of sky), her present apartment on lower Thompson Street was not a great improvement on its predecessor.

The city was full of promises, but they had all been pledged to other people. The city Marcia knew was sinful, indifferent, dirty, and dangerous. Every day she read accounts of women attacked in subway stations, raped in the streets, knifed in their own beds. A hundred people looked on curiously all the while and offered no assistance. And on top of everything else there were the roaches!

There were roaches everywhere, but Marcia didn't see them until she'd been in New York a month. They came to her—or she to them—at Silversmith's on Nassau Street, a stationery shop where she had been working for three days. It was the first job she'd been able to find. Alone or helped by a pimply stockboy (in all fairness it must be noted that Marcia was not without an acne problem of her own), she wandered down rows of rasp-edged metal shelves in the musty basement, making an inventory of the sheaves and piles and boxes of bond paper, leatherette-bound diaries, pins and clips, and carbon paper. The basement was dirty and so dim that she needed a flashlight for the lowest shelves. In the obscurest corner, a faucet leaked perpetually into a gray sink: she had been resting near this sink, sipping a cup of tepid coffee (saturated, in the New York manner, with sugar and drowned in milk), thinking, probably, of how she could afford several things she simply couldn't afford, when she noticed the dark spots moving on the side of the sink. At first she thought they might be no more than motes floating in the jelly of her eyes, or the giddy dots that one sees after over-exertion on a hot day. But they persisted too long to be illusory, and Marcia drew nearer, feeling compelled to bear witness. *How do I know they are insects?* she thought.

How are we to explain the fact that what repels us most can be at times—at the same time—inordinately attractive? Why is the cobra poised to strike so beautiful? The fascination of the abomination is something that... Something which we would rather not account for. The subject borders on the obscene, and there is no need to deal with it here, except to note the breathless wonder with which Marcia observed these first roaches of hers. Her chair was drawn so close to the sink that she could see the mottling of their oval, unsegmented bodies, the quick scuttering of their thin legs, and the quicker flutter of their antennae. They moved randomly, proceeding nowhere, centered nowhere. They seemed greatly disturbed over nothing. *Perhaps,* Marcia thought, *my presence has a morbid effect on them?*

Only then did she become aware, aware fully, that these

were the cockroaches of which she had been warned. Repulsion took hold; her flesh curdled on her bones. She screamed and fell back in her chair, almost upsetting a shelf of odd-lots. Simultaneously the roaches disappeared over the edge of the sink and into the drain.

Mr. Silversmith, coming downstairs to inquire the source of Marcia's alarm, found her supine and unconscious. He sprinkled her face with tapwater, and she awoke with a shudder of nausea. She refused to explain why she had screamed and insisted that she must leave Mr. Silversmith's employ immediately. He, supposing that the pimply stockboy (who was his son) had made a pass at Marcia, paid her for the three days she had worked and let her go without regrets. From that moment on, cockroaches were to be a regular feature of Marcia's existence.

On Thompson Street Marcia was able to reach a sort of stalemate with the cockroaches. She settled into a comfortable routine of pastes and powders, scrubbing and waxing, prevention (she never had even a cup of coffee without washing and drying cup and coffeepot immediately afterward) and ruthless extermination. The only roaches who trespassed upon her two cozy rooms came up from the apartment below, and they did not stay long, you may be sure. Marcia would have complained to the landlady, except that it was the landlady's apartment and her roaches. She had been inside, for a glass of wine on Christmas Eve, and she had to admit that it wasn't exceptionally dirty. It was, in fact, more than commonly clean—but *that* was not enough in New York. If *everyone*, Marcia thought, *took as much care as I, there would soon be no cockroaches in New York City.*

Then (it was March and Marcia was halfway through her sixth year in the city) the Shchapalovs moved in next door. There were three of them—two men and a woman—and they were old, though exactly how old it was hard to say: they had been aged by more than time. Perhaps they weren't more than forty. The woman, for instance, though she still had brown hair, had a face wrinkly as a prune and was missing several teeth. She would stop Marcia in the hallway or on the street, grabbing hold of her coatsleeve, and talk to her—always a simple lament about the weather, which was too hot or too cold or too wet or too dry. Marcia never knew half of what the old woman was saying, she mumbled so. Then she'd totter off to the grocery with her bagful of empties.

The Shchapalovs, you see, drank. Marcia, who had a rather exaggerated idea of the cost of alcohol (the cheapest thing she could imagine was vodka), wondered where they got the money for all the drinking they did. She knew they didn't work, for on days when Marcia was home with the flu she could hear the three Shchapalovs through the thin wall between their kitchen and hers screaming at each other to exercise their adrenal glands. *They're on welfare,* Marcia decided. Or perhaps the man with only one eye was a veteran on pension.

She didn't so much mind the noise of their arguments (she was seldom home in the afternoon), but she couldn't stand their singing. Early in the evening they'd start in, singing along with the radio stations. Everything they listened to sounded like Guy Lombardo. Later, about eight o'clock they sang *a cappella*. Strange, soulless noises rose and fell like Civil Defense sirens; there were bellowings, bayings, and cries. Marcia had heard something like it once on a Folkways record of Czechoslovakian wedding chants. She was quite beside herself whenever the awful noise started up and had to leave the house till they were done. A complaint would do no good: the Shchapalovs had a right to sing at that hour.

Besides, one of the men was said to be related by marriage to the landlady. That's how they got the apartment, which had been used as a storage space until they'd moved in. Marcia couldn't understand how the three of them could fit into such a little space—just a room-and-a-half with a narrow window opening onto the air shaft. (Marcia had discovered that she could see their entire living space through a hole that had been broken through the wall when the plumbers had installed a sink for the Shchapalovs.)

But if their singing distressed her, *what* was she to do about the roaches? The Shchapalov woman, who was the sister of one man and married to the other—or else the men were brothers and she was the wife to one of them (sometimes, it seemed to Marcia, from the words that came through the walls, that she was married to neither of them—or to both), was a bad housekeeper, and the Shchapalov apartment was soon swarming with roaches. Since Marcia's sink and the Shchapalovs' were fed by the same pipes and emptied into a common drain, a steady overflow of roaches was disgorged into Marcia's immaculate kitchen. She could spray and lay out more poisoned potatoes; she could scrub and dust and stuff Kleenex tissues into holes where the pipes passed through the wall: it was all to no avail. The Shchapalov roaches could always lay another million eggs in the garbage bags rotting beneath the Shchapalov sink. In a few days they would be swarming through the pipes and cracks and into Marcia's cupboards. She would lie in bed and watch them (this was possible because Marcia kept a nightlight burning in each room) advancing across the floor and up the walls, trailing the Shchapalovs' filth and disease everywhere they went.

One such evening the roaches were especially bad, and Marcia was trying to muster the resolution to get out of her warm bed and attack them with Roach-It. She had left the windows open from the conviction that cockroaches do not like the cold, but she found that she liked it much less. When she swallowed, it hurt, and she knew she was coming down with a cold. And all because of *them!*

"*Oh go away!*" she begged. "*Go away! Go away! Get out of my apartment.*"

She addressed the roaches with the same desperate intensity with which she sometimes (though not often in recent years) addressed prayers to the Almighty. Once she had prayed all night long to get rid of her acne, but in the morning it was worse than ever. People in intolerable circumstances will pray to anything. Truly, there are no atheists in foxholes: the men there pray to the bombs that they may land somewhere else.

The only strange thing in Marcia's case is that her prayers were answered. The cockroaches fled from her apartment as quickly as their little legs could carry them—and in straight lines, too. Had they heard her? Had they understood?

Marcia could still see one cockroach coming down from the cupboard. "*Stop!*" she commanded. And it stopped.

At Marcia's spoken command, the cockroach would march up and down, to the left and to the right. Suspecting that her phobia had matured into madness, Marcia left her warm bed, turned on the light, and cautiously approached the roach, which remained motionless, as she had bidden it. "*Wiggle your antennas,*" she commanded. The cockroach wiggled its antennae.

She wondered if they would *all* obey her and found, within

the next few days, that they all would. They would do anything she told them to. They would eat poison out of her hand. Well, not exactly out of her hand, but it amounted to the same thing. They were devoted to her. Slavishly.

It is the end, she thought, *of my roach problem.* But of course it was only the beginning.

Marcia did not question too closely the *reason* the roaches obeyed her. She had never much troubled herself with abstract problems. After expending so much time and attention on them, it seemed only natural that she should exercise a certain power over them. However she was wise enough never to speak of this power to anyone else—even to Miss Bismuth at the insurance office. Miss Bismuth read the horoscope magazines and claimed to be able to communicate with her mother, aged sixty-eight, telepathically. Her mother lived in Ohio. But what would Marcia have said: that *she* could communicate telepathically with cockroaches? Impossible.

Nor did Marcia use her power for any other purpose than keeping the cockroaches out of her own apartment. Whenever she saw one, she simply commanded it to go to the Shchapalov apartment and stay there. It was surprising, then, that there were always more roaches coming back through the pipes. Marcia assumed that they were younger generations. Cockroaches are known to breed fast. But it was easy enough to send them back to the Shchapalovs.

"Into their beds," she added as an afterthought. *"Go into their beds."* Disgusting as it was, the idea gave her a queer thrill of pleasure.

The next morning, the Shchapalov woman, smelling a little worse than usual (Whatever was it, Marcia wondered, that they drank?), was waiting at the open door of her apartment. She wanted to speak to Marcia before she left for work. Her housedress was mired from an attempt at scrubbing the floor, and while she sat there talking, she tried to wring out the scrubwater.

"No idea!" she exclaimed. "You ain't got no idea how bad! 'S terrible!"

"What?" Marcia asked, knowing perfectly well what.

"The boogs! Oh, the boogs are just everywhere. Don't you have em, sweetheart? I don't know what to do. I try to keep a decent house, God knows—" She lifted her rheumy eyes to heaven, testifying. "—but I don't know what to do." She leaned forward, confidingly. "You won't believe this, sweetheart, but last night . . ." A cockroach began to climb out of the limp strands of hair straggling down into the woman's eyes. " . . . they got into bed with us! Would you believe it? There must have been a hundred of 'em. I said to Osip, I said—What's wrong, sweetheart?"

Marcia, speechless with horror, pointed at the roach, which had almost reached the bridge of the woman's nose. "Yech!" the woman agreed, smashing it and wiping her dirtied thumb on her dirtied dress. "Goddam boogs! I hate em, I swear to God. But what's a person gonna do? Now, what I wanted to ask, sweetheart, is do you have a problem with the boogs? Being as how you're right next door, I thought—" She smiled a confidential smile, as though to say this is just between us ladies. Marcia almost expected a roach to skitter out between her gapped teeth.

"No," she said. "No, I use Black Flag." She backed away from the doorway toward the safety of the stairwell. "Black Flag," she said again, louder. "Black Flag," she shouted from the foot of the stairs. Her knees trembled so, that she had to hold onto the metal banister for support.

At the insurance office that day, Marcia couldn't keep her mind on her work five minutes at a time. (Her work in the Actuarial Dividends department consisted of adding up long rows of two-digit numbers on a Burroughs adding machine and checking the similar additions of her co-workers for errors.) She kept thinking of the cockroaches in the tangled hair of the Shchapalov woman, of her bed teeming with roaches, and of other, less concrete horrors on the periphery of consciousness. The numbers swam and swarmed before her eyes, and twice she had to go to the Ladies' Room, but each time it was a false alarm. Nevertheless, lunchtime found her with no appetite. Instead of going down to the employee cafeteria she went out into the fresh April air and strolled along 23rd Street. Despite the spring, it all seemed to bespeak a sordidness, a festering corruption. The stones of the Flatiron Building oozed damp blackness; the gutters were heaped with soft decay; the smell of burning grease hung in the air outside the cheap restaurants like cigarette smoke in a close room.

The afternoon was worse. Her fingers would not touch the correct numbers on the machine unless she looked at them. One silly phrase kept running through her head: "Something must be done. Something must be done." She had quite forgotten that she had sent the roaches into the Shchapalovs' bed in the first place.

That night, instead of going home immediately, she went to a double feature on 42nd Street. She couldn't afford the better movies. Susan Hayward's little boy almost drowned in quicksand. That was the only thing she remembered afterward.

She did something then that she had never done before. She had a drink in a bar. She had two drinks. Nobody bothered her; nobody even looked in her direction. She took a taxi to Thompson Street (the subways weren't safe at that hour) and arrived at her door by eleven o'clock. She didn't have anything left for a tip. The taxi driver said he understood.

There was a light on under the Shchapalovs' door, and they were singing. It was eleven o'clock. "Something must be done," Marcia whispered to herself earnestly. "Something must be *done*."

Without turning on her own light, without even taking off her new spring jacket from Ohrbach's, Marcia got down on her knees and crawled under the sink. She tore out the Kleenexes she had stuffed into the cracks around the pipes.

There they were, the three of them, the Shchapalovs, drinking, the woman plumped on the lap of the one-eyed man, and the other man, in a dirty undershirt, stamping his foot on the floor to accompany the loud discords of their song. Horrible. They were drinking of course, she might have known it, and now the woman pressed her roachy mouth against the mouth of the one-eyed man—kiss, kiss. Horrible, horrible. Marcia's hands knotted into her mouse-colored hair, and she thought: *The filth, the disease!* Why, they hadn't learned a thing from last night!

Some time later (Marcia had lost track of time) the overhead light in the Shchapalovs' apartment was turned off. Marcia waited till they made no more noise. "Now," Marcia said, "all of you.

"All of you in this building, all of you that can hear me, gather round the bed, but wait a little while yet. Patience. All of you..." The words of her command fell apart into little fragments, which she told like the beads of a rosary—little brown ovoid wooden beads. "...gather round...wait a little while yet...all of you...patience...gather round..."

Her hand stroked the cold water pipes rhythmically, and it seemed that she could hear them—gathering, scuttering up through the walls, coming out of the cupboards, the garbage bags—a host, an army, and she was their absolute queen.

"Now!" she said. "Mount them! Cover them! Devour them!"

There was no doubt that she could hear them now. She heard them quite palpably. Their sound was like grass in the wind, like the first stirrings of gravel dumped from a truck. Then there was the Shchapalov woman's scream, and curses from the men, such terrible curses that Marcia could hardly bear to listen.

A light went on, and Marcia could see them, the roaches, everywhere. Every surface, the walls, the floors, the shabby sticks of furniture, was mottly thick with *Blattellae Germanicae*. There was more than a single thickness.

The Shchapalov woman, standing up in her bed, screamed monotonously. Her pink rayon nightgown was speckled with brown-black dots. Her knobby fingers tried to brush bugs out of her hair, off her face. The man in the undershirt who a few minutes before had been stomping his feet to the music stomped now more urgently, one hand still holding onto the lightcord. Soon the floor was slimy with crushed roaches, and he slipped. The light went out. The woman's scream took on a rather choked quality, as though. . .

But Marcia wouldn't think of that. "Enough," she whispered. "No more. Stop."

She crawled away from the sink, across the room on to her bed, which tried, with a few tawdry cushions, to dissemble itself as a couch for the daytime. Her breathing came hard, and there was a curious constriction in her throat. She was sweating incontinently.

From the Shchapalovs' room came scuffling sounds, a door banged, running feet, and then a louder, muffled noise, perhaps a body falling downstairs. The landlady's voice: "What the hell do you think you're—" Other voices overriding hers. Incoherences, and footsteps returning up the stairs. Once more, the landlady: "There ain't no *boogs* here, for heaven's sake. The boogs is in your heads. You've got the d.t.'s, that's what. And it wouldn't be any wonder, if there were boogs. The place is filthy. Look at that crap on the floor. Filth! I've stood just about enough from you. Tomorrow you move out, hear? This *used* to be a decent building."

The Shchapalovs did not protest their eviction. Indeed, they did not wait for the morrow to leave. They quitted their apartment with only a suitcase, a laundry bag, and an electric toaster. Marcia watched them go down the steps through her half-open door. *It's done,* she thought. It's all *over.*

With a sigh of almost sensual pleasure, she turned on the lamp beside the bed, then the other lamps. The room gleamed immaculately. Deciding to celebrate her victory, she went to the cupboard, where she kept a bottle of *crème de menthe.*

The cupboard was full of roaches.

She had not told them where to go, where *not* to go, when they left the Shchapalov apartment. It was her own fault.

The great silent mass of roaches regarded Marcia calmly, and it seemed to the distracted girl that she could read *their* thoughts, their thought rather, for they had but a single thought. She could read it as clearly as she could read the illuminated billboard for Chock Full O'Nuts outside her window. It was delicate as music issuing from a thousand tiny pipes. It was an ancient music box open after centuries of silence: "We love you we love you we love you we love you."

Something strange happened inside Marcia then, something unprecedented: she responded.

"I love you too," she replied. "Oh, I love you. Come to me, all of you. Come to me. I love you. Come to me. I love you. Come to me."

From every corner of Manhattan, from the crumbling walls of Harlem, from restaurants on 56th Street, from warehouses along the river, from sewers and from orange peels moldering in garbage cans, the loving roaches came forth and began to crawl toward their mistress.

ANGOULEME

There were seven Alexandrians involved in the Battery plot—
Jack, who was the youngest and from the Bronx, Celeste
DiCecca, Sniffles and MaryJane, Tancred Miller, Amparo
(of course), and *of course,* the leader and mastermind, Bill
Harper, better known as Little Mister Kissy Lips. Who was
passionately, hopelessly in love with Amparo. Who was nearly
thirteen (she would be, fully, by September this year), and
breasts just beginning. Very very beautiful skin, like lucite.
Amparo Martinez.

Their first, nothing operation was in the East 60's, a
broker or something like that. All they netted was cufflinks, a
watch, a leather satchel that wasn't leather after all, some
buttons, and the usual lot of useless credit cards. He stayed
calm through the whole thing, even with Sniffles slicing off
buttons, and *soothing.* None of them had the nerve to ask,
though they all wondered, how often he'd been through this
scene before. What they were about wasn't an innovation. It
was partly that, the need to innovate, that led them to think
up the plot. The only really memorable part of the holdup
was the name laminated on the cards, which was, weirdly
enough, Lowen, Richard W. An omen (the connection being
that they were all at the Alexander Lowen School), but of
what?

Little Mister Kissy Lips kept the cufflinks for himself,
gave the buttons to Amparo (who gave them to her uncle),
and donated the rest (the watch was a piece of crap) to the
Conservation booth outside the Plaza right where he lived.

His father was a teevee executive. In, as he would quip,
both senses. They had got married young, his mama and
papa, and divorced soon after but not before he'd come to fill
out their quota. Papa, the executive, remarried, a man this

207

time and somewhat more happily. Anyhow it lasted long enough that the offspring, the leader and mastermind, had to learn to adjust to the situation, it being permanent. Mama simply went down to the Everglades and disappeared, sploosh.

In short, he was well to do. Which is how, more than by overwhelming talent, he got into the Lowen School in the first place. He had the right kind of body though, so with half a desire there was no reason in the city of New York he couldn't grow up to be a professional dancer, even a choreographer. He'd have the connections for it, as Papa was fond of pointing out.

For the time being, however, his bent was literary and religious rather than balletic. He loved, and what seventh grader doesn't, the abstracter foxtrots and more metaphysical twists of a Dostoevsky, a Gide, a Mailer. He longed for the experience of some vivider pain than the mere daily hollowness knotted into his tight young belly, and no weekly stomp-and-holler of group therapy with other jejune eleven-year-olds was going to get him his stripes in the major leagues of suffering, crime, and resurrection. Only a bona fide crime would do that, and of all the crimes available murder certainly carried the most prestige, as no less an authority than Loretta Couplard was ready to attest, Loretta Couplard being not only the director and co-owner of the Lowen School but the author, as well, of two nationally televised scripts, both about famous murders of the 20th Century. They'd even done a unit in social studies on the topic: A History of Crime in Urban America.

The first of Loretta's murders was a comedy involving Pauline Campbell, R.N., of Ann Arbor, Michigan, circa 1951, whose skull had been smashed by three drunken teenagers. They had meant to knock her unconscious so they could screw her, which was 1951 in a nutshell. The eighteen-year-olds, Bill Morey and Max Pell, got life; Dave Royal (Loretta's hero) was a year younger and got off with twenty-two years.

Her second murder was tragic in tone and consequently inspired more respect, though not among the critics, unfortunately. Possibly because her heroine, also a Pauline (Pauline Wichura), though more interesting and complicated, had also been more famous in her own day and ever since. Which made the competition, one best-selling novel

and a serious film biography, considerably stiffer. Miss
Wichara had been a welfare worker in Atlanta, Georgia, very
much into environment and the population problem, this
being the immediate pre-Regents period when anyone and
everyone was legitimately starting to fret. Pauline decided to
do something, viz., reduce the population herself and in the
fairest way possible. So whenever any of the families she
visited produced one child above the three she'd fixed, rather
generously, as the upward limit, she found some unobtrusive
way of thinning that family back to the preferred maximal
size. Between 1989 and 1993 Pauline's journals (Random
House, 1994) record twenty-six murders, plus an additional
fourteen failed attempts. In addition she had the highest welfare department record in the U.S. for abortions and steriliza-
tions among the families whom she advised.

"Which proves, I think," Little Mister Kissy Lips had
explained one day after school to his friend Jack, "that a
murder doesn't have to be of someone *famous* to be a form of
idealism."

But of course idealism was only half the story: the other
half was curiosity. And beyond idealism *and* curiosity there
was probably even another half, the basic childhood need to
grow up and kill someone.

They settled on the Battery because, one, none of them
ever were there ordinarily; two, it was posh and at the same
time relatively, three, uncrowded, at least once the night shift
were snug in their towers tending their machines. The night
shift seldom ate their lunches down in the park.

And, four, because it was beautiful, especially now at the
beginning of summer. The dark water, chromed with oil,
flopping against the buttressed shore; the silences blowing in
off the Upper Bay, silences large enough sometimes that you
could sort out the different noises of the city behind them,
the purr and quaver of the skyscrapers, the ground-shivering
mysterioso of the expressways, and every now and then the
strange sourceless screams that are the melody of New York's
theme song; the blue-pink of sunsets in a visible sky; the
people's faces, calmed by the sea and their own nearness to
death, lined up in rhythmic rows on the green benches. Why,
even the statues looked beautiful here, as though someone
had believed in them once, the way people must have believed
in the statues in the Cloisters, so long ago.

His favorite was the gigantic killer-eagle landing in the middle of the monoliths in the memorial for the soldiers, sailors, and airmen killed in World War II. The largest eagle, probably, in all Manhattan. His talons ripped apart what was *surely* the largest artichoke.

Amparo, who went along with some of Miss Couplard's ideas, preferred the more humanistic qualities of the memorial (him on top and an angel gently probing an enormous book with her sword) for Verrazzano, who was not, as it turned out, the contractor who put up the bridge that had, so famously, collapsed. Instead, as the bronze plate in back proclaimed:

IN APRIL 1524
THE FLORENTINE-BORN NAVIGATOR
VERRAZZANO
LED THE FRENCH CARAVEL LA DAUPHINE
TO THE DISCOVERY OF
THE HARBOR OF NEW YORK
AND NAMED THESE SHORES ANGOULEME
IN HONOR OF FRANCIS I KING OF FRANCE

"Angouleme" they all agreed, except Tancred, who favored the more prevalent and briefer name, was much classier. Tancred was ruled out of order and the decision became unanimous.

It was there, by the statue, looking across the bay of Angouleme to Jersey, that they took the oath that bound them to perpetual secrecy. Whoever spoke of what they were about to do, unless he were being tortured by the Police, solemnly called upon his co-conspirators to insure his silence by other means. Death. All revolutionary organizations take similar precautions, as the history unit on Modern Revolutions had made clear.

How he got the name: it had been Papa's theory that what modern life cried out for was a sweetening of old-fashioned sentimentality. Ergo, among all the other indignities this theory gave rise to, scenes like the following: "Who's my Little Mister Kissy Lips!" Papa would bawl out, sweetly, right in the middle of Rockefeller Center (or a restaurant, or in front of the school), and he'd shout right back, "I am!" At least until he knew better.

Mama had been, variously, "Rosebud," "Peg O' My

Heart," and (this only at the end) "The Snow Queen."
Mama, being adult, had been able to vanish with no other
trace than the postcard that still came every Xmas postmarked from Key Largo, but Little Mister Kissy Lips was
stuck with the New Sentimentality willy-nilly. True, by age
seven he'd been able to insist on being called "Bill" around
the house (or, as Papa would have it, "Just Plain Bill"). But
that left the staff at the Plaza to contend with, and Papa's
assistants, schoolmates, anyone who'd ever heard the name.
Then a year ago, aged ten and able to reason, he laid down
the new law—that his name *was* Little Mister Kissy Lips, the
whole awful mouthful, each and every time. His reasoning
being that if anyone would be getting his face rubbed in shit
by this it would be Papa, who deserved it. Papa didn't seem
to get the point, or else he got it and another point besides,
you could never be sure how stupid or how subtle he really
was, which is the worst kind of enemy.

Meanwhile at the nationwide level the New Sentimentality had been a rather overwhelming smash. "The Orphans,"
which Papa produced and sometimes was credited with writing, pulled down the top Thursday evening ratings for two
years. Now it was being overhauled for a daytime slot. For
one hour every day our lives were going to be a lot sweeter,
and chances were Papa would be a millionaire or more as a
result. On the sunny side, this meant that *he'd* be the son of a
millionaire. Though he generally had contempt for the way
money corrupted everything it touched, he had to admit that
in certain cases it didn't have to be a bad thing. It boiled
down to this (which he'd always known): that Papa was a
necessary evil.

This was why every evening when Papa buzzed himself
into the suite he'd shout out, "Where's my Little Mister Kissy
Lips," and he'd reply, "Here, Papa!" The cherry on this
sundae of love was a big wet kiss, and then one more for their
new "Rosebud," Jimmy Ness. (Who drank, and was not in all
likelihood going to last much longer.) They'd all three sit
down to the nice *family* dinner Jimmyness had cooked, and
Papa would tell them about the cheerful, positive things that
had happened that day at CBS, and Little Mister Kissy Lips
would tell all about the bright fine things that had happened
to *him*. Jimmy would sulk. Then Papa and Jimmy would go
somewhere or just disappear into the private Everglades of
sex, and Little Mister Kissy Lips would buzz himself out into

the corridor (Papa knew better than to be repressive about hours), and within half an hour he'd be at the Verrazzano statue with the six other Alexandrians, five if Celeste had a lesson, to plot the murder of the victim they'd all finally agreed on.

No one had been able to find out his name. They called him Alyona Ivanovna, after the old pawnbroker woman that Raskolnikov kills with an ax.

The spectrum of possible victims had never been wide. The common financial types of the area would be carrying credit cards like Lowen, Richard W., while the generality of pensioners filling the benches were even less tempting. As Miss Couplard had explained, our economy was being refeudalized and cash was going the way of the ostrich, the octopus, and the moccasin flower.

It was such extinctions as these, but especially seagulls, that were the worry of the first lady they'd considered, a Miss Kraus, unless the name at the bottom of her handlettered poster (STOP THE SLAUGHTER of The *Innocents!!* etc.) belonged to someone else. Why, if she were Miss Kraus, was she wearing what seemed to be the old-fashioned diamond ring and gold band of a Mrs.? But the more crucial problem, which they couldn't see how to solve, was: was the diamond real?

Possibility Number Two was in the tradition of the original Orphans of the Storm, the Gish sisters. A lovely semiprofessional who whiled away the daylight pretending to be blind and serenading the benches. Her pathos was rich, if a bit worked-up; her repertoire was archaeological; and her gross was fair, especially when the rain added its own bit of too-much. However: Sniffles (who'd done this research) was certain she had a gun tucked away under the rags.

Three was the least poetic possibility, just the concessionaire in back of the giant eagle selling Fun and Synthamon. His appeal was commercial. But he had a licensed Weimaraner, and though Weimaraners can be dealt with, Amparo liked them.

"You're just a Romantic," Little Mister Kissy Lips said. "Give me one good reason."

"His eyes," she said. "They're amber. He'd haunt us."

They were snuggling together in one of the deep embrasures cut into the stone of Castle Clinton, her head wedged into his armpit, his fingers gliding across the lotion on her breasts (summer was just beginning). Silence, warm breezes, sunlight on water, it was all ineffable, as though only the sheerest of veils intruded between them and an understanding of something (all this) really meaningful. Because they thought it was their own innocence that was to blame, like a smog in their souls' atmosphere, they wanted more than ever to be rid of it at times, like this, when they approached so close.

"Why not the dirty old man, then?" she asked, meaning Alyona.

"Because he *is* a dirty old man."

"That's no reason. He must take in at least as much money as that singer."

"That's not what I mean." What he meant wasn't easy to define. It wasn't as though he'd be too easy to kill. If you'd seen him in the first minutes of a program, you'd know he was marked for destruction by the second commercial. He was the defiant homesteader, the crusty senior member of a research team who understood Algol and Fortran but couldn't read the secrets of his own heart. He was the Senator from South Carolina with his own peculiar brand of integrity but a racist nevertheless. Killing that sort was too much like one of Papa's scripts to be a satisfying gesture of rebellion.

But what he said, mistaking his own deeper meaning, was: "It's because he deserves it, because we'd be doing society a favor. Don't ask me to give *reasons*."

"Well, I won't pretend I understand that, but do you know what I think, Little Mister Kissy Lips?" She pushed his hand away.

"You think I'm scared."

"Maybe you *should* be scared."

"Maybe you should shut up and leave this to me. I said we're going to do it. We'll do it."

"To him then?"

"Okay. But for gosh sakes, Amparo, we've got to think of something to call the bastard besides 'the dirty old man'!"

She rolled over out of his armpit and kissed him. They glittered all over with little beads of sweat. The summer began to shimmer with the excitement of first night. They had been waiting so long and now the curtain was rising.

M-Day was scheduled for the first weekend in July, a patriotic holiday. The computers would have time to tend to their own needs (which have been variously described as "confession," "dreaming," and "throwing up"), and the Battery would be as empty as it ever gets.

Meanwhile their problem was the same as any kids face anywhere during summer vacation, how to fill the time.

There were books, there were the Shakespeare puppets if you were willing to queue up for that long, there was always teevee, and when you couldn't stand sitting any longer there were the obstacle courses in Central Park, but the density there was at lemming level. The Battery, because it didn't try to meet anyone's needs, seldom got so overpopulated. If there had been more Alexandrians and all willing to fight for the space, they might have played ball. Well, another summer. . . .

What else? There were marches for the political, and religions at various energy levels for the apolitical. There would have been dancing, but the Lowen School had spoiled them for most amateur events around the city.

As for the supreme pastime of sex, for all of them except Little Mister Kissy Lips and Amparo (and even for them, when it came right down to orgasm) this was still something that happened on a screen, a wonderful hypothesis that lacked empirical proof.

One way or another it was all consumership, everything they might have done, and they were tired, who isn't, of being passive. They were twelve years old, or eleven, or ten, and they couldn't wait any longer. For what? they wanted to know.

So, except when they were just loafing around solo, all these putative resources, the books, the puppets, the sports, arts, politics, and religions, were in the same category of usefulness as merit badges or weekends in Calcutta, which is a name you can still find on a few old maps of India. Their lives were not enhanced, and their summer passed as summers have passed immemorially. They slumped and moped and lounged about and teased each other and complained. They acted out desultory, shy fantasies and had long pointless arguments about the more peripheral facts of existence—the habits of jungle animals or how bricks had been made or the history of World War II.

One day they added up all the names on the monoliths set

up for the soldiers, sailors, and airmen. The final figure they
got was 4,800.

"Wow," said Tancred.

"But that can't be *all* of them," MaryJane insisted, speaking for the rest. Even that "wow" had sounded half ironic.

"Why not?" asked Tancred, who could never resist dis-
agreeing. "They came from every different state and every
branch of the service. It has to be complete or the people who
had relatives left off would have protested."

"But so *few?* It wouldn't be possible to have fought more
than one battle at that rate."

"Maybe. . . " Sniffles began quietly. But he was seldom
listened to.

"Wars were different then," Tancred explained with the
authority of a prime-time news analyst. "In those days more
people were killed by their own automobiles than in wars. It's
a fact."

"Four thousand, eight *hundred?*"

". . . a lottery?"

Celeste waved away everything Sniffles had said or would
ever say. "MaryJane is right, Tancred. It's simply a *ludicrous*
number. Why, in that same war the Germans gassed seven
million Jews."

"Six million Jews," Little Mister Kissy Lips corrected. "But
it's the same idea. Maybe the ones here got killed in a
particular campaign."

"Then it would say so." Tancred was adamant, and he even
got them to admit at last that 4,800 was an impressive figure,
especially with every name spelled out in stone letters.

One other amazing statistic was commemorated in the
park: over a thirty-three-year period Castle Clinton had
processed 7.7 million immigrants into the United States.

Little Mister Kissy Lips sat down and figured out that it
would take 12,800 stone slabs the size of the ones listing the
soldiers, sailors, and airmen in order to write out all the
immigrants' names, with country of origin, and an area of five
square miles to set that many slabs up in, or all of Manhattan
from here to 28th Street. But would it be worth the trouble,
after all? Would it be that much different from the way things
were already?

Alyona Ivanovna:

An archipelago of irregular brown islands were mapped on

the tan sea of his bald head. The mainlands of his hair were marble outcroppings, especially his beard, white and crisp and coiling. The teeth were standard MODICUM issue; clothes, as clean as any fabric that old can be. Nor did he smell, particularly. And yet. . . .

Had he bathed every morning you'd still have looked at him and thought he was filthy, the way floorboards in old brownstones seem to need cleaning moments after they've been scrubbed. The dirt had been bonded to the wrinkled flesh and the wrinkled clothes, and nothing less than surgery or burning would get it out.

His habits were as orderly as a polka dot napkin. He lived at a Chelsea dorm for the elderly, a discovery they owed to a rainstorm that had forced him to take the subway home one day instead of, as usual, walking. On the hottest nights he might sleep over in the park, nesting in one of the Castle windows. He bought his lunches from a Water Street specialty shop, *Dumas Fils:* cheeses, imported fruit, smoked fish, bottles of cream, food for the gods. Otherwise he did without, though his dorm must have supplied prosaic necessities like breakfast. It was a strange way for a panhandler to spend his quarters, drugs being the norm.

His professional approach was out-and-out aggression. For instance, his hand in your face and, "How about it, Jack?" Or, confidingly, "I need sixty cents to get home." It was amazing how often he scored, but actually it wasn't amazing. He had charisma.

And someone who relies on charisma *wouldn't* have a gun.

Agewise he might have been sixty, seventy, seventy-five, a bit more even, or much less. It all depended on the kind of life he'd led, and where. He had an accent none of them could identify. It was not English, not French, not Spanish, and probably not Russian.

Aside from his burrow in the Castle wall there were two distinct places he preferred. One, the wide-open stretch of pavement along the water. This was where he worked, walking up past the Castle and down as far as the concession stand. The passage of one of the great Navy cruisers, the USS *Dana* or the USS *Melville*, would bring him, and the whole Battery, to a standstill, as though a whole parade were going by, white, soundless, slow as a dream. It was a part of history, and even the Alexandrians were impressed, though three of them had taken the cruise down to Andros Island and back. Sometimes, though, he'd stand by the guardrail for long stretches of time without any real reason, just looking at the Jersey sky and the Jersey shore. After a while he might start talking to himself, the barest whisper but very much in earnest, to judge by the way his forehead wrinkled. They never once saw him sit on one of the benches.

The other place he liked was the aviary. On days when they'd been ignored he'd contribute peanuts or breadcrumbs to the cause of the birds' existence. There were pigeons, parrots, a family of robins, and a proletarian swarm of what the sign declared to be chickadees, though Celeste, who'd gone to the library to make sure, said they were nothing more than a rather swank breed of sparrow. Here too, naturally, the militant Miss Kraus stationed herself when she bore testimony. One of her peculiarities (and the reason, probably, she was never asked to move on) was that under no circumstances did she ever deign to argue. Even sympathizers pried no more out of her than a grim smile and a curt nod.

One Tuesday, a week before M-Day (it was the early A.M. and only three Alexandrians were on hand to witness this confrontation), Alyona so far put aside his own reticence as to try to start a conversation going with Miss Kraus.

He stood squarely in front of her and began by reading aloud, slowly, in that distressingly indefinite accent, from the text of STOP THE SLAUGHTER: "The Department of the Interior of the United States Government, under the secret direction of the Zionist Ford Foundation, is *systematically* poisoning the oceans of the World with so-called 'food farms.' Is this 'peaceful application of Nuclear Power'? Unquote, the *New York Times,* August 2, 2024. Or a new Moondoggle!! *Nature World,* Jan. Can we afford to remain indifferent any longer. Every day 15,000 seagulls die as a direct result of Systematic Genocides while elected Officials falsify and distort the evidence. Learn the facts. Write to the Congressmen. *Make your voice heard!!*"

As Alyona had droned on, Miss Kraus turned a deeper and deeper red. Tightening her fingers about the turquoise broomhandle to which the placard was stapled, she began to jerk the poster up and down rapidly, as though this man with his foreign accent were some bird of prey who'd perched on it.

"Is that what you think?" he asked, having read all the way down to the signature despite her jiggling tactic. He touched his bushy white beard and wrinkled his face into a philosophical expression. "I'd *like* to know more about it, yes, I would. I'd be interested in hearing what *you* think."

Horror had frozen up every motion of her limbs. Her eyes blinked shut but she forced them open again.

"Maybe," he went on remorselessly, "we can discuss this whole thing. Some time when you feel more like talking. All right?"

She mustered her smile, and a minimal nod. He went away then. She was safe, temporarily, but even so she waited till he'd gone halfway to the other end of the sea-front promenade before she let the air collapse into her lungs. After a single deep breath the muscles of her hands thawed into trembling.

M-Day was an oil of summer, a catalog of everything painters are happiest painting—clouds, flags, leaves, sexy people, and in back of it all the flat empty baby-blue of the sky. Little Mister Kissy Lips was the first one there, and Tancred, in a kind of kimono (it hid the pilfered Luger), was the last. Celeste never came. (She'd just learned she'd been awarded the exchange scholarship to Sofia.) They decided they could do without Celeste, but the other nonappearance was more crucial. Their victim had neglected to be on hand for M-Day. Sniffles, whose voice was most like an adult's over the phone, was delegated to go to the Citibank lobby and call the West 16th Street dorm.

The nurse who answered was a temporary. Sniffles, always an inspired liar, insisted that his mother—"Mrs. *Anderson*, of course she lives there, Mrs. Alma F. Anderson"—had to be called to the phone. This was 248 West 16th, wasn't it? Where *was* she if she wasn't there? The nurse, flustered, explained that the residents, all who were fit, had been driven off to a July 4th picnic at Lake Hopatcong as guests of a giant Jersey retirement condominium. If he called bright and early tomorrow they'd be back and he could talk to his mother then.

So the initiation rites were postponed, it couldn't be helped. Amparo passed around some pills she'd taken from her mother's jar, a consolation prize. Jack left, apologizing that he was a borderline psychotic, which was the last that anyone saw of Jack till September. The gang was disintegrating, like a sugar cube soaking up saliva, then crumbling into the tongue. But what the hell—the sea still mirrored the same blue sky, the pigeons behind their wicket were no less iridescent, and trees grew for all of that.

They decided to be silly and made jokes about what the M *really* stood for in M-Day. Sniffles started off with "Miss Nomer, Miss Carriage, and Miss Steak." Tancred, whose sense of humor did not exist or was very private, couldn't do better than "Mnemone, mother of the Muses." Little Mister Kissy Lips said, "Merciful Heavens!" MaryJane maintained reasonably that M was for MaryJane. But Amparo said it stood for "Aplomb" and carried the day.

Then, proving that when you're sailing the wind always blows from behind you, they found Terry Riley's day-long *Orfeo* at 99.5 on the FM dial. They'd studied *Orfeo* in mime class, and by now it was part of their muscle and nerve. As Orpheus descended into a hell that mushroomed from the size of a pea to the size of a planet, the Alexandrians metamorphosed into as credible a tribe of souls in torment as any since the days of Jacopo Peri. Throughout the afternoon little audiences collected and dispersed to flood the sidewalk with libations of adult attention. Expressively they surpassed themselves, both one by one and all together, and though they couldn't have held out till the apotheosis (at 9.30) without a stiff psychochemical wind in their sails, what they had danced was authentic and very much their own. When they left the Battery that night they felt better than they'd felt all summer long. In a sense they had been exorcised.

But back at the Plaza Little Mister Kissy Lips couldn't sleep. No sooner was he through the locks than his guts knotted up into a Chinese puzzle. Only after he'd unlocked his window and crawled out onto the ledge did he get rid of the bad feelings. The city was real. His room was not. The stone ledge was real and his bare buttocks absorbed reality from it. He watched slow movements in enormous distances and pulled his thoughts together.

He knew without having to talk to the rest that the murder would never take place. The idea had never meant for them what it had meant for him. One pill and they were actors again, content to be images in a mirror.

Slowly, as he watched, the city turned itself off. Slowly the dawn divided the sky into an east and a west. Had a pedestrian been going fast on 58th Street and had that pedestrian looked up, he would have seen the bare soles of a boy's feet swinging back and forth, angelically.

He would have to kill Alyona Ivanovna himself. Nothing else was possible.

Back in his bedroom, long ago, the phone was ringing its fuzzy nighttime ring. That would be Tancred (or Amparo?) trying to talk him out of it. He foresaw their arguments. Celeste and Jack couldn't be trusted now. Or, more subtly: they'd all made themselves too visible with their *Orfeo*. If there were even a small investigation, the benches would remember them, remember how well they had danced, and the police would know where to look.

But the real reason, which at least Amparo would have been ashamed to mention now that the pill was wearing off, was that they'd begun to feel sorry for their victim. They'd got to know him too well over the last month and their resolve had been eroded by compassion.

A light came on in Papa's window. Time to begin. He stood up, golden in the sunbeams of another perfect day, and walked back along the foot-wide ledge to his own window. His legs tingled from having sat so long.

He waited till Papa was in the shower, then tippytoed to the old secretaire in his bedroom (W. & J. Sloan, 1952). Papa's keychain was coiled atop the walnut veneer. Inside the secretaire's drawer was an antique Mexican cigar box, and in the cigar box a velvet bag, and in the velvet bag Papa's replica of a French dueling pistol, circa 1790. These precautions were less for his son's sake than on account of Jimmy Ness, who every so often felt obliged to show he was serious with his suicide threats.

He'd studied the booklet carefully when Papa had bought the pistol and was able to execute the loading procedure quickly and without error, tamping the premeasured twist of powder down into the barrel and then the lead ball on top of ʲt.

He cocked the hammer back a single click.

ᵇHe locked the drawer. He replaced the keys, just so. He buried, for now, the pistol in the stuffs and cushions of the Turkish corner, tilted upright to keep the ball from rolling out. Then with what remained of yesterday's ebullience he bounced into the bathroom and kissed Papa's cheek, damp

with the morning's allotted two gallons and redolent of
4711.

They had a cheery breakfast together in the coffee room,
which was identical to the breakfast they would have made
for themselves except for the ritual of being waited on by a
waitress. Little Mister Kissy Lips gave an enthusiastic account of the Alexandrians' performance of *Orfeo*, and Papa
made his best effort of seeming not to condescend. When he'd
been driven to the limit of this pretense, Little Mister Kissy
Lips touched him for a second pill, and since it was better for
a boy to get these things from his father than from a stranger
on the street, he got it.

He reached the South Ferry stop at noon, bursting with a
sense of his own imminent liberation. The weather was
M-Day all over again, as though at midnight out on the ledge
he'd forced time to go backwards to the point when things
had started going wrong. He'd dressed in his most anonymous
shorts and the pistol hung from his belt in a dun dittybag.

Alyona Ivanovna was sitting on one of the benches near
the aviary, listening to Miss Kraus. Her ring hand gripped the
poster firmly, while the right chopped at the air, eloquently
awkward, like a mute's first words following a miraculous
cure.

Little Mister Kissy Lips went down the path and squatted
in the shadow of his memorial. It had lost its magic yesterday,
when the statues had begun to look so silly to everyone. They
still looked silly. Verrazzano was dressed like a Victorian
industrialist taking a holiday in the Alps. The angel was
wearing an angel's usual bronze nightgown.

His good feelings were leaving his head by little and little,
like aeolian sandstone attrited by the centuries of wind. He
thought of calling up Amparo, but any comfort she might
bring to him would be a mirage so long as his purpose in
coming here remained unfulfilled.

He looked at his wrist, then remembered he'd left his
watch home. The gigantic advertising clock on the facade of
the First National Citibank said it was fifteen after two. That
wasn't possible.

Miss Kraus was *still* yammering away.

There was time to watch a cloud move across the sky from
Jersey, over the Hudson, and past the sun. Unseen winds

nibbled at its wispy edges. The cloud became his life, which would disappear without ever having turned into rain.

Later, and the old man was walking up the sea promenade toward the Castle. He stalked him, for miles. And then they were alone, together, at the far end of the park.

"Hello," he said, with the smile reserved for grown-ups of doubtful importance.

He looked directly at the dittybag, but Little Mister Kissy Lips didn't lose his composure. He would be wondering whether to ask for money, which would be kept, if he'd had any, in the bag. The pistol made a noticeable bulge but not the kind of bulge one would ordinarily associate with a pistol.

"Sorry," he said coolly. "I'm broke."

"Did I ask?"

"You were going to."

The old man made as if to return in the other direction, so he had to speak quickly, something that would hold him here.

"I saw you speaking with Miss Kraus."

He was held.

"Congratulations—you broke through the ice!"

The old man half-smiled, half-frowned. "You know her?"

"Mm. You could say that we're *aware* of her." The "we" had been a deliberate risk, an hors d'oeuvre. Touching a finger to each side of the strings by which the heavy bag hung from his belt, he urged on it a lazy pendular motion. "Do you mind if I ask you a question?"

There was nothing indulgent now in the man's face. "I probably do."

His smile had lost the hard edge of calculation. It was the same smile he'd have smiled for Papa, for Amparo, for Miss Couplard, for anyone he liked. "Where do you come from? I mean, what country?"

"That's none of your business, is it?"

"Well, I just wanted . . . to know."

The old man (he had ceased, somehow, to be Alyona Ivanovna) turned away and walked directly toward the squat stone cylinder of the old fortress.

He remembered how the plaque at the entrance—the same that had cited the 7.7 million—had said that Jenny Lind had sung there and it had been a great success.

The old man unzipped his fly and, lifting out his cock, began pissing on the wall.

Little Mister Kissy Lips fumbled with the strings of the bag. It was remarkable how long the old man stood there pissing because despite every effort of the stupid knot to stay tied he had the pistol out before the final sprinkle had been shaken out.

He laid the fulminate cap on the exposed nipple, drew the hammer back two clicks, past the safety, and aimed.

The man made no haste zipping up. Only then did he glance in Little Mister Kissy Lips' direction. He saw the pistol aimed at him. They stood not twenty feet apart, so he must have seen it.

He said, "Ha!" And even this, rather than being addressed to the boy with the gun, was only a parenthesis from the faintly-aggrieved monologue he resumed each day at the edge of the water. He turned away, and a moment later he was back on the job, hand out, asking some fellow for a quarter.

BODIES

1.

"Take a factory," Ab said. "It's the same sort of thing exactly."

What kind of factory Chapel wanted to know.

Ab tipped his chair back, settling into the theory as if it were a warm whirlpool bath in Hydrotherapy. He'd eaten two lunches that Chapel had brought down and felt friendly, reasonable, in control. "Any kind. You ever worked in a factory?"

Of course he hadn't. Chapel? Chapel was lucky to be pushing a cart. So Ab went right on. "For instance—take an electronics-type factory. I worked in one once, an assembler."

"And you *made* something, right?"

"Wrong! I put things together. There's a difference, if you'd use your ears for one minute instead of that big mouth of yours. See, first off this *box* comes down the line, and I'd stick in this red board sort of thing, then tighten some other mother on top of that. Same thing all day, simple as A-B-C. Even you could have done it, Chapel." He laughed.

Chapel laughed.

"Now what was I really doing? I *moved* things, from here to there. . . . " He pantomined here and there. The little finger of the left hand, ended at the first knuckle. He'd done it himself at his initiation into the K of C twenty years ago (twenty-five actually), a single chop of the old chopper, but when people asked he said it was an industrial accident and that was how the goddamned system destroyed you. But mostly people knew better than to ask.

"But I didn't *make* anything at all, you see? And it's the same in any other factory—you move things or you put them together, same difference."

Chapel could feel he was losing. Ab talked faster and louder, and his own words came out stumbling. He hadn't wanted to argue in the first place, but Ab had tangled him in it without his knowing how. "But something, I don't know, what you say is. . . . But what I mean is—you've got to have common sense, too."

"No, this is *science*."

Which brought such a look of abject defeat to the old man's eyes it was as if Ab had dropped a bomb, boff, right in the middle of his black, unhappy head. For who can argue against science. Not Chapel, sure as hell.

And yet he struggled up out of the rubble still championing common sense. "But things get made—how do you explain that?"

"Things get made, things get made," Ab mimicked in a falsetto voice, though of the two men's voices Chapel's was deeper. "What things?"

Chapel looked round the morgue for an example. It was all so familiar as to be invisible—the slab, the carts, the stacks of sheets, the cabinet with its stock of fillers and fluids, the desk. . . . He lifted a blank Identi-Band from the clutter on the desk. "Like plastic."

"Plastic?" Ab said in a tone of disgust. "That just shows how much you know, Chapel. Plastic." Ab shook his head.

"Plastic," Chapel insisted. "Why not?"

"Plastic is just putting *chemicals* together, you illiterate."

"Yeah, but." He closed one eye, squeezing the thought into focus. "But to make the plastic they've got to—heat it. Or something."

"Right! And what's heat?" he asked, folding his hands across his gut, victorious, full. "Heat is kinetic energy."

"Shit," Chapel maintained. He massaged his stubbly brown scalp. Another argument lost. He never understood how it happened.

"Molecules," Ab summed up, "moving. Everything breaks down to that. It's all physics, a law." He let loose a large fart and pointed his finger, just in time, at Chapel's groin.

Chapel made a smile acknowledging Ab's triumph. It was science all right. Science battered everyone into submission if it was given its way. It was like trying to argue with the atmosphere of Jupiter, or electric sockets, or the steroid tablets he had to take now—things that happened every day and never made sense, never would, never.

Dumb nigger, Ab thought, feeling friendlier in proportion to Chapel's perplexity. He wished he could have kept him arguing a while longer. There was still religion, psychosis, teaching, lots of possibilities. Ab had arguments to prove that even these jobs, which looked so mental and abstract on the surface, were actually all forms of kinetic energy.

Kinetic energy: once you understood the meaning of kinetic energy all kinds of other things started becoming clear.

"You should read the book," Ab insisted.

"Mm," Chapel said.

"He explains it in more detail." Ab hadn't read the entire book himself, only parts of the condensation, but he'd gotten the gist of it.

But Chapel had no time for books. Chapel, Chapel pointed out, was not one of your intellectuals.

Was Ab? Intellectual? He had to think about that one for a while. It was like wearing some fruity color transparency and seeing himself in a changing booth mirror, knowing he would never buy it, not daring even to walk out on the sales floor, but enjoying the way it fitted him anyhow: an intellectual. Yes, possibly in some other reincarnation Ab had been an intellectual, but it was a goofy idea all the same.

Right on the button, at 1:02, they rang down from 'A' Surgery. A body.

He took down the name in the logbook. He'd neglected to start a new page and the messenger hadn't come by yet for yesterday's, so he entered Time of Death as 11:58 and printed the name in neat block letters: NEWMAN, BOBBI.

"When can you get her?" asked the nurse, for whom a body still possessed sex.

"I'm there already," Ab promised.

He wondered what age it would be. "Bobbi" was an older type name, but there were always exceptions.

He booted Chapel out, locked up, and set off with the cart to 'A' Surgery. At the bend of the corridor, right before the ramp, he told the new kid at the desk to take his calls. The kid wiggled his skimpy ass and made some dumb joke. Ab laughed. He was feeling in top shape, and it was going to be a good night. He could tell.

Chapel was the only one on and Mrs. Steinberg, who was in charge tonight, though not actually his boss, said, "Chapel, 'B' Recovery," and handed him the slip.

"And move," she added off-handedly, as another woman might have said, "God bless you," or "Take care."

Chapel, however, had one speed. Difficulties didn't slow him down; anxieties made him go no faster. If somewhere there were cameras perpetually trained on him, viewers who studied his slightest actions, then Chapel would give them nothing to interpret. Loaded or empty, he wheeled his cart along the corridors at the same pace he took walking home after work to his hotel on 65th. Regular? As a clock.

Outside 'M' Ward, on 4, by the elevators, a blond young man was pressing a urinal against himself, trying to make himself piss by groaning at his steel pot. His robe hung open, and Chapel noticed that his pubic hair had been shaved off. That usually meant hemorrhoids.

"How's it going?" Chapel asked. His interest in the patients' stories was quite sincere, especially those in Surgery or ENT wards.

The blond young man made an anguished face and asked Chapel if he had any money.

"Sorry."

"Or a cigarette?"

"I don't smoke. And it's against the rules, you know."

The young man rocked from one leg to the other, coddling his pain and humiliation, trying to blot out every other sensation in order to go the whole way. Only the older patients tried, for a while at least, to hide their pain. The young ones gloried in it from the moment they gave their first samples to the aide in Admissions.

While the substitute in 'B' Recovery completed the transfer forms Chapel went over to the other occupied unit. It held, still unconscious, the boy he'd taken up earlier from Emergency. His face had been a regular beef stew; now it was a tidy volleyball of bandages. From the boy's clothes and the tanned and muscly trimness of his bare arms (on one biceps two blurry blue hands testified to an eternal friendship with "Larry") Chapel inferred that he would have had a good-looking face as well. But now? No. If he'd been registered with one of the private health plans, perhaps. But at Bellevue there was neither staff nor equipment for full-scale cosmetic work. He'd have eyes, nose, mouth, etc., all the right size and sitting about where they ought to, but the whole lot together would be a plastic approximation.

So young—Chapel lifted his limp left wrist and checked the age on the Identi-Band—and handicapped for life. Ah, there was a lesson in it.

"The poor man," said the substitute, meaning not the boy but the transfer. She handed Chapel the transfer form.

"Oh?" said Chapel, unlocking the wheels.

She went round to the head of the cart. "A subtotal," she explained. "*And. . .*"

The cart bumped gently into the door frame. The bottle swayed at the top of the intravenous pole. The old man tried to lift his hands but they were strapped to the sides. His fingers clenched.

"And?"

"It's gone to the liver," she explained in a stage whisper.

Chapel nodded somberly. He'd known it must have been something as drastic as that since he was routed up to heaven, the 18th floor. Sometimes it seemed to Chapel that he could have saved Bellevue a lot of needless trouble if he'd just take all of these to Ab Holt's office straightaway instead of bothering with the 18th floor.

In the elevator Chapel paged through the man's file. WANDTKE, JWRZY. The routing slip, the transfer form, the papers in the folder, and the Identi-Band all agreed: JWRZY. He tried sounding it out, letter by letter.

The doors opened. Wandtke's eyes opened.

"How are you?" Chapel asked. "Do you feel okay? Hm?"

Wandtke began laughing, very softly. His ribs fluttered beneath the green electric sheet.

"We're going to your new ward now," Chapel explained. "It's going to be a lot nicer there. You'll see. Everything is going to be all right, uh . . . ." He remembered that it was not possible to pronounce his name. Could it be, despite all the forms, a mistake?

Anyhow there wasn't much point trying to communicate with this one. Coming up from surgery they were always loaded so full of whatever it was that there was no sense to anything they said. They just giggled and rolled their eyes around, like this Wandtke. And in two weeks, cinders in a furnace. Wandtke wasn't singing, at least. Lots of them sang.

Chapel's shoulder started in, a twinge. The twinge became

an ache and the ache thickened and enveloped him in a cloud of pain. Then the cloud scattered into wisps, the wisps vanished. All in the distance of a hundred yards in 'K' wing, and without his slowing, without a wink.

It wasn't bursitis, that much seemed certain. It came and went, not in flashes, but like music, a swelling up and then a welling away. The doctors didn't understand it, so they said. Eventually it went away, and so (Chapel told himself) he had nothing to complain about. That things could have been a lot worse was demonstrated to him all the time. The kid tonight, for instance, with the false face that would always ache in cold weather, or this Wandtke, giggling like he'd come from some damned birthday party, and with his liver changing itself all the while into some huge, horrible growth. Those were the people to feel sorry for, and Chapel felt sorry for them with some gusto. By comparison to such wretched, doomed creatures, he, Chapel, was pretty lucky. He handled dozens every shift, men and women, old and young, carting them here and there, up and down, and there wasn't one of them, once the doctors had done their job, who wouldn't have been happy to change places with the short, thin, brittle, old black man who wheeled them through these miles of scabby corridors, not one.

Miss Mackey was on duty in the men's ward. She signed for Wandtke. Chapel asked her how he was supposed to pronounce a name like that, Jwrzy, and Miss Mackey said she certainly didn't know. It was probably a Polish name anyhow. Wandtke—didn't it look Polish?

Together they steered Wandtke to his unit. Chapel connected the cart, and the unit, purring softly, scooped up the old body, lifted, and stuck. The unit shut itself off. It was a moment before either Chapel or Miss Mackey realized what was wrong. Then they unstrapped the withered wrists from the aluminum bars of the cart. The unit, this time, experienced no difficulty.

"Well," said Miss Mackey, "I know two people who need a day's rest."

5:45. This close to clocking out, Chapel didn't want to return to the duty room and risk a last-minute assignment. "Any dinners left?" he asked the nurse.

"Too late here, they've all been taken. Try the women's ward."

In the women's ward, Havelock, the elderly aide, dug up a
tray that had been meant for a patient who had terminated
earlier that evening. Chapel got it for a quarter, after pointing
out the low-residue sticker Havelock had tried to conceal
under his thumb.

NEWMAN, B, the sticker read.

Ab would have her now. Chapel tried to remember what
unit she'd been in. The blonde girl in the corner who couldn't
stand sunlight? Or the colostomy who was always telling
jokes? No, her name was Harrison.

Chapel pulled one of the visitors' chairs over to the window
ledge. He opened the tray and waited for the food to warm.
He ate from one compartment at a time, chewing at his single
stolid speed, though the whole dinner was the consistency of
a bowl of Breakfast. First, the potatoes; then, some steamy,
soft meat cubes; then, dutifully, a mulch of spinach. He left
the cake but drank the Koffee, which contained the miracle
ingredient that (aside from the fact that no one ever returned) gave heaven its name. When he was done he shot the
tray downstairs himself.

Havelock was inside, on the phone.

The ward was a maze of blue curtains, layers of trans-
lucence overlapping layers of shadows. A triangle of sunlight
spread across the red tile floor at the far end of the room:
dawn.

Unit 7 was open. At one time or another Chapel must have
carted its occupant to and from every division of the hospital: SCHAAP, FRANCES, 3/3/04. Which made her eighteen, barely. Her face and neck were speckled with innumerable scarlet spider nevi, but Chapel remembered when it had
been a pretty face. Lupus.

A small gray machine beside the bed performed, approximately, the functions of her inflamed liver. At irregular
intervals a red light would blink on and, quickly, off, infinitesimal warnings which no one heeded.

Chapel smiled. The little miracles were starting to unfold
themselves in his bloodstream, but that was almost beside the
point. The point was simple:

They were dying; he was alive. He had survived and they
were bodies. The spring sunlight added its own additional
touch of good cheer to the here of heaven and the now of six
A.M.

In an hour he would be home. He'd rest a while, and then

he'd watch his box. He thought he could look forward to that.

Heading home down First, Ab whistled a piece of trash that had stuck in his head four days running, about some new pill called Yes, that made you feel better, and he did.

The fifty dollars he'd got for the Newman body brought his take for the week up to a handsome $115. Once he'd seen what Ab was offering, White hadn't even haggled. Without being necrophile himself (to Ab a body was just a job to be done, something he carted down from the wards and burned or—if there was money to burn instead—shipped off to a freezing concern) Ab understood the market well enough to have recognized in Bobbi Newman a certain ideal quality of deathliness. Lupus had taken a fulminant course with her, rapidly destroying one internal system after another without, for a wonder, marring the fine texture of the skin. True, the disease had whittled face and limbs down to bone thinness, but then what else was necrophilia about? To Ab, who liked them big, soft, and lively, all of this fuss over corpses was pretty alien, yet basically his motto was *"Chacun à son gout,"* though not in so many words. There were limits, of course. For example, he would willingly have assisted at the castration of any Republican in the city, and he felt nearly as passionate a distaste for political extremists. But he possessed the basic urban tolerance for any human peculiarity from which he stood a good chance of making money.

Ab considered his commissions from the procurers to be gifts of fate, to be spent in the same free spirit that fortune had shown showering them on him. In fact, when you totted up the various MODICUM benefits the Holts were disbarred from by virtue of Ab's salary, his real income wasn't much more (without these occasional windfalls) than the government would have paid him for being alive. Ab usually managed to sidestep the logical conclusion: that the windfalls were his essential wage, the money that made him, in his own consciousness, a free agent, the equal of any engineer, expert, or criminal in the city. Ab was a man, with a man's competence to buy whatever, within bounds, he wanted.

At this particular April moment, with the traffic so light on the Avenue you could drink the air like a 7-Up, with the sun shining, with nowhere in particular to be until ten that night, and with $115 of discretionary income, Ab felt like an old

movie, full of songs and violence and fast editing. Boff,
smack, pow, that's how Ab was feeling now, and as the
opposite sex approached him from the other direction, he
could feel their eyes fastening on him, measuring, estimating,
admiring, imagining.

One, very young, very black, in silvery street shorts, stared
at Ab's left hand and stared at it, as though it were a
tarantula getting ready to crawl right up her leg. (Ab was
everywhere quite hairy.) She could feel it tickling her knee,
her thigh, her fancy. Milly, when she was little, had been the
same way about her father's missing finger, all silly and giddy.
Mutilations were supposed to be passé now, but Ab knew
better. Girls still wet themselves feeling a stump, but guys
today were just too chickenshit to chop their fingers off. The
macho thing now was a gold earring, for Christ's sake—as
though there had never been a 20th century.

Ab winked at her, and she looked away, but with a smile.
How about that?

If there were one thing missing from a feeling of pure
content it was that the wad in his pocket (two twenties, seven
tens, and one five) was so puny it almost wasn't there. Before
revaluation a three-body week like this would have put a bulge
in his front pocket as big as another cock, a comparison he
had often at that time drawn. Once Ab had actually been a
millionaire—for five days running in July of 2008, the single
most incredible streak of luck he'd ever had. Today that
would have meant five, six thousand—nothing. Some of the
faro tables in the neighborhood still used the old dollars, but
it was like a marriage that's lost its romance: you said the
words but the meaning had gone out of them. You looked at
the picture of Benjamin Franklin and thought, this is a
picture of Benjamin Franklin. Whereas with the new bills
$100 stood for beauty, truth, power, and love.

As though his bankroll were a kind of magnet dragging
him there, Ab turned left on 18th into Stuyvesant Town. The
four playgrounds at the center of the complex were the chief
black market in New York. In the facs and on TV they used
euphemisms like "flea market" or "street fair," since to come
right out and call it a black market was equivalent to saying
the place was an annex of the police department and the
courts, which it was.

The black market was as much a part of New York (or
any other city), as basic to its existence, as the numbers from

one to ten. Where else could you buy something without the purchase being fed into the federal income-and-purchase computers? Nowhere was where, which meant that Ab, when he was flush, had three options open to him: the playgrounds, the clubs, and the baths.

Used clothing fluttered limply from rack after rack, as far as the fountain. Ab could never pass these stalls without feeling that Leda was somehow close at hand, hidden among these tattered banners of the great defeated army of the second-rate and second-hand, still silently resisting him, still trying to stare him down, still insisting, though so quietly now that only he could hear her: "Goddamn it, Ab, can't you get it through that thick skull of yours, we're poor, we're poor, we're *poor!*" It had been the biggest argument of their life together and the decisive one. He could remember the exact spot, under a plane tree, just here, where they had stood and raged at each other, Leda hissing and spitting like a kettle, out of her mind. It was right after the twins had arrived and Leda was saying there was no help for it, they'd have to wear what they could get. Ab said fuckshit, no, no, no kid of his was going to wear other people's rags, they'd stay in the house naked first. Ab was louder and stronger and less afraid, and he won, but Leda revenged herself by turning her defeat into a martyrdom. She never held out against him again. Instead she became an invalid, weepy and sniveling and resolutely helpless.

Ab heard someone calling his name. He looked around, but who would be here this early in the day but the people from the buildings, old folks plugged into their radios, kids screaming at other kids, babies screaming at mothers, mothers screaming. Half the vendors weren't even spread out yet.

"Ab Holt—over here!" It was old Mrs. Galban. She patted the space beside her on the green bench.

He didn't have much choice. "Hey, Viola, how's it going? You're looking great!"

Mrs. Galban smiled a sweet, rickety smile. Yes, she said complacently, she did feel well, she thanked God every day. She observed that even for April this was beautiful weather. Ab didn't look so bad himself (a little heavier maybe), though it was how many years now?

"Twelve years," said Ab, at a venture.

"Twelve years? It seems longer. And is that good-looking Dr. Mencken in Dermatology?"

"He's fine. He's the head of the department now, you know."

"Yes, I heard that."

"He asked after you the other day when I ran into him outside the clinic. He said, have you seen old Gabby lately." A polite lie.

She nodded her head, politely believing him. Then, cautiously, she started homing in on what was, for her, the issue. "And Leda, how is she, poor thing?"

"Leda is fine, Viola."

"She's getting out of the house, then?"

"Well no, not often. Sometimes we take her up to the roof for a bit of air. It's closer than the street."

"Ah, the pain!" Mrs. Galban murmured with swift, professional sympathy that the years had not been able to blunt. Indeed, it was probably better exercised now than when she'd been an aide at Bellevue. "You don't have to explain—I know it can be so awful, can't it, pain like that, and there's so little any of us can do. *But . . .*" she added, before Ab could turn aside the final thrust, ". . . we must do that little if we can."

"It's not as bad as it used to be," Ab insisted.

Mrs. Galban's look was meant to be understood as reproachful in a sad, helpless way, but even Ab could sense the calculations going on behind the brown, cataracted eyes. Was this, she asked herself, worth pursuing? Would Ab bite?

In the first years of Leda's invalidism Ab had picked up extra Dilaudin suppositories from Mrs. Galban, who specialized in analgesics. Most of her clients were other old women whom she met in the out-patient waiting room at the hospital. Ab had bought the Dilaudin more as a favor to the old pusher than from any real need, since he got all the morphine that Leda needed from the interns for next to nothing.

"It's a terrible thing," Mrs. Galban lamented quietly, staring into her seventy-eight-year-old lap. "A terrible thing."

What the hell, Ab thought. It wasn't as if he were broke.

"Hey, Gabby, you wouldn't have any of those things I used to get for Leda, would you? Those what-you-call-ums?"

"Well, Ab, since you ask. . . ."

Ab got a package of five suppositories for nine dollars, which was twice the going price, even here on the playground. Mrs. Galban evidently thought Ab a fool.

As soon as he'd given her the money, he felt comfortably

unobligated. Walking off he could curse her with buoyant resentment. The old bitch would have to live a damned long time before he ever bought any more plugs off her.

Usually Ab never made the connection between the two worlds he inhabited, this one out here and the Bellevue morgue, but now, having actively wished Viola Galban dead, it struck him that the odds were strong that he'd be the one who'd shove her in the oven. The death of anyone (anyone, that is, whom Ab had known alive) was a depressing idea, and he shrugged it away. At the far edge of his shrug, for the barest instant, he saw the young, pretty face of Bobbi Newman.

The need to buy something was suddenly a physical necessity, as though his wad of bills had become that cock and had to be jerked off after a week-long abstinence.

He bought a lemon ice, his first ice of the year, and strolled among the stalls, touching the goods with thick, sticky fingers, asking prices, making jokes. Everywhere the vendors hailed him by his name when they saw him approach. There was nothing, so rumor would have it, that Ab Holt couldn't be talked into buying.

2.

Ab looked at his two hundred and fourteen pounds of wife from the doorway. Wrinkled blue sheets were wound round her legs and stomach, but her breasts hung lose. "They're prizewinners to this day," Ab thought affectionately. Any feelings he still had for Leda were focused there, just as any pleasure she got when he was on top of her came from the squeezing of his hands, the biting of his teeth. Where the sheets were wrapped round her, however, she could feel nothing—except, sometimes, pain.

After a while Ab's attention woke Leda up, the way a magnifying glass, focusing on a dry leaf, will start it smoldering.

He threw the package of suppositories onto the bed. "That's for you."

"Oh." Leda opened the package, sniffed at one of the wax cylinders suspiciously. "Oh?"

"It's Dilaudin. I ran into that Mrs. Galban at the market, and she wouldn't get off my back till I'd bought something."

"I was afraid for a moment you might have got it on *my* account. Thanks. What's in the other bag, an enema bottle for our anniversary?"

Ab showed her the wig he'd bought for Beth. It was a silly, four-times-removed imitation of the Egyptian style made popular by a now-defunct TV series. To Leda it looked like something you'd find at the bottom of a box of Xmas wrapping, and she was certain it would look the same way to her daughter.

"My God," she said.

"Well, it's what the kids are wearing now," Ab said doubtfully. It no longer looked the same to him. He brought it over to the wedge of sunlight by the bedroom's open window and tried to shake a bit more glitter into it. The metallic strings, rubbing against each other, made soft squeaking sounds.

"My God," she said again. Her annoyance had almost betrayed her into asking him what he'd paid for it. Since the epochal argument beneath the plane tree she never discussed money matters with Ab. She didn't want to hear how he spent his money or how he earned it. She especially didn't want to know how he earned it, since she had, anyhow, a fair idea.

She contented herself with an insult. "You've got the discrimination of a garbage truck, and if you think Beth will let herself be seen in that ridiculous, obscene piece of junk, well . . . !" She pushed at the mattress until she was sitting almost upright. Both Leda and the bed breathed heavily.

"How would you know what people are wearing outside this apartment? There were hundreds of these fucking things all over the playground. It's what the kids are wearing now. What the fuck."

"It's ugly. You bought your daughter an ugly wig. You have every right to, I suppose."

"Ugly—isn't that what you used to say about everything Milly wore? All those things with buttons. And the hats! It's a stage they go through. You were probably just the same, if you could remember that long ago."

"Oh, Milly! You're always holding Milly up as though she were some kind of *example!* Milly never had any idea how—" Leda gave a gasp. Her pain. She pressed her hand flat against the roll of flesh to the side of her right breast, where she thought her liver might be. She closed her eyes trying to locate the pain, which had vanished.

Ab waited till Leda was paying attention to him again. Then, very deliberately, he threw the tinselly wig out the open window. Thirty dollars, he thought, just like that.

The manufacturer's tag fluttered to the floor. A pink oval with italic letters: Nephertiti Creations.

With an inarticulate cry Leda swiveled sideways in bed till she'd made both feet touch the floor. She stood up. She took two steps and reached out for the window frame to steady herself.

The wig lay in the middle of the street eighteen floors below. Against the gray concrete it looked dazzlingly bright. A Tastee Bread truck backed up over it.

Since there was no reproach she might have made that didn't boil down to a charge of his throwing away money, she said nothing. The unspoken words whirled round inside her, a plague-bearing wind that ruffled the wasted muscles of her legs and back like so many tattered flags. The wind died and the flags went limp.

Ab was ready behind her. He caught her as she fell and laid her back on the bed, wasting not a motion, smooth as a tango dip. It seemed almost accidental that his hands should be under her breasts. Her mouth opened and he put his own mouth across it, sucking the breath from her lungs.

Anger was their aphrodisiac. Over the years the interval between fighting and fucking had grown shorter and shorter. They scarcely bothered any longer to differentiate the two processes. Already his cock was stiff. Already she'd begun to moan her rhythmic protest against the pleasure or the pain, whichever it was. As his left hand kneaded the warm dough of her breasts, his right hand pulled off his shoes and pants. The years of invalidism had given her lax flesh a peculiar virginal quality, as though each time he went into her he were awakening her from an enchanted, innocent sleep. There was a kind of sourness about her too, a smell that seeped from her pores only at these times, the way maples yield sap only at the depth of the winter. Eventually he'd learned to like it.

A good sweat built up on the interface of their bodies, and his movements produced a steady salvo of smacking and slapping and farting sounds. This, to Leda, was the worst part of these sexual assaults, especially when she knew the children were at home. She imagined Beno, her youngest, her favorite, standing on the other side of the door, unable to keep from thinking of what was happening to her despite the horror it must have caused him. Sometimes it was only by concentrating on the thought of Beno that she could keep from crying out.

Ab's body began to move faster. Leda's, crossing the threshold between self-control and automatism, struggled upward away from the thrusts of his cock. His hands grabbed her hips, forcing her to take him. Tears burst from her eyes, and Ab came.

He rolled off, and the mattress gave one last exhausted whoosh.

"Dad?"

It was Beno, who certainly should have been in school. The bedroom door was halfway open. Never, Leda thought, in an ecstasy of humiliation, never had she known a moment to match this. Bright new pains leapt through her viscera like tribes of antelope.

"Dad," Beno insisted. "Are you asleep?"

"I would be if you'd shut up and let me."

"There's someone on the phone downstairs, from the hospital. That Juan. He said it's urgent, and to wake you if we had to."

"Tell Martinez to fuck himself."

"He *said*," Beno went on, in a tone of martyred patience that was a good replica of his mother's, "it didn't make any difference what you said and that once he explained it to you you'd thank him. That's what he said."

"Did he say what it was about?"

"Some guy they're looking for. Bob Someone."

"I don't know who they want, and in any case. . ." Then it began to dawn: the possibility; the awful, impossible lightning bolt he'd known he would never escape. "Bobbi Newman, was that the name of the guy they're looking for?"

"Yeah. Can I come in?"

"Yes, yes." Ab swept the damp sheet over Leda's body,

which hadn't stirred since he'd got off. He pulled his pants on. "Who took the call, Beno?"

"Williken did." Beno stepped into the bedroom. He had sensed the importance of the message he'd been given and he was determined to milk it for a maximum of suspense. It was as though he knew what was at stake.

"Listen, run downstairs and tell Williken to hold Juan on the line until. . ."

One of his shoes was missing.

"He left, Dad. I told him you couldn't be interrupted. He seemed sort of angry and he said he wished you wouldn't give people his number any more."

"Shit on Williken then."

His shoe was way the hell under the bed. How had he . . . ?

"What was the message he gave you exactly? Did they say who's looking for this Newman fellow?"

"Williken wrote it down, but I can't read his writing. Margy it looks like."

That was it then, the end of the world. Somehow Admissions had made a mistake in slotting Bobbi Newman for a routine cremation. She had a policy with Macy's.

And if Ab didn't get back the body he'd sold to White. . . . "Oh Jesus," he whispered to the dust under the bed.

"Anyhow you're supposed to call them right back. But Williken says not from his phone 'cause he's gone out."

There might be time, barely and with the best luck. White hadn't left the morgue till after 3 A.M. It was still short of noon. He'd buy the body back, even if it meant paying White something extra for his disappointment. After all, in the long run White needed him as much as he needed White.

"Bye, Dad," Beno said, without raising his voice, though by then Ab was already out in the hall and down one landing.

Beno walked over to the foot of the bed. His mother still hadn't moved a muscle. He'd been watching her the whole time and it was as though she were dead. She was always like that after his father had fucked her, but usually not for such a long time. At school they said that fucking was supposed to be very healthful but somehow it never seemed to do *her* much good. He touched the sole of her right foot. It was soft and pink, like the foot of a baby, because she never walked anywhere.

Leda pulled her foot away. She opened her eyes.

White's establishment was way the hell downtown, around the corner from the Democratic National Convention (formerly, Pier 19) which was to the world of contemporary pleasure what Radio City Music Hall had been to the world of entertainment—the largest, the mildest, and the most amazing. Ab, being a born New Yorker, had never stepped through the glowing neon vulva (seventy feet high and forty feet wide, a landmark) of the entrance. For those like Ab who refused to be grossed out by the conscious too-muchness of the major piers, the same basic styles were available on the sidestreets ("Boston" they called this area) in a variety of cooler colors, and here, in the midst of all that was allowed, some five or six illegal businesses eked out their unnatural and anachronistic lives.

After much knocking a young girl came to the door, the same probably who had answered the phone, though now she pretended to be mute. She could not have been much older than Beno, twelve at most, but she moved with the listless, enforced manner of a despairing housewife.

Ab stepped into the dim foyer and closed the door against the girl's scarcely perceptible resistance. He'd never been inside White's place before and he would not even have known what address to come to if he hadn't once had to take over the delivery van for White, who'd arrived at the morgue too zonked out to function. So this was the market to which he'd been exporting his goods. It was less than elegant.

"I want to see Mr. White," Ab told the girl. He wondered if she were another sideline.

She lifted one small, unhappy hand toward her mouth.

There was a clattering and banging above their heads, and a single flimsy facs-sheet drifted down through the half-light of the stairwell. White's voice drifted down after it: "Is that you, Holt?"

"Damn right!" Ab started up the stairs but White, light in his head and heavy on his feet, was already crashing down to meet him.

White placed a hand on Ab's shoulder, establishing the fact of the other man's presence and at the same time holding himself erect. He had said yes to Yes once too often, or twice, and was not at this moment altogether corporeal.

"I've got to take it back," Ab said. "I told the kid on the phone. I don't care how much you stand to lose, I've got to have it."

White removed his hand carefully and placed it on the bannister. "Yes. Well. It can't be done. No."

"I've got to."

"Melissa," White said. "It would be... If you would please... And I'll see you later, darling."

The girl mounted the steps reluctantly, as though her certain future were waiting for her at the top. "My daughter," White explained with a sad smile as she came alongside. He reached out to rumple her hair but missed by a few inches.

"We'll discuss this, shall we, in my office?"

Ab helped him to the bottom. White went to the door at the far end of the foyer. "Is it locked?" he wondered aloud.

Ab tried it. It was not locked.

"I was meditating," White said meditatively, still standing before the unlocked door, in Ab's way, "when you called before. In all the uproar and whirl, a man has to take a moment aside to..."

White's office looked like a lawyer's that Ab had broken into at the tag-end of a riot, years and years before. He'd been taken aback to find that the ordinary processes of indigence and desuetude had accomplished much more than any amount of his own adolescent smashing about might have.

"Here's the story," Ab said, standing close to White and speaking in a loud voice so there could be no misunderstanding. "It turns out that the one you came for last night was actually insured by her parents, out in Arizona, without her knowing. The hospital records didn't say anything about it, but what happened is the various clinics have a computer that cross-checks against the obits. They caught it this morning and called the morgue around noon."

White tugged sullenly on a strand of his sparse, mousy hair. "Well, tell them, you know, tell them it went in the oven."

"I can't. Officially we've got to hold them for twenty-four hours, just in case something like this should happen. Only it never does. Who would have thought, I mean it's so unlikely, isn't it? Anyhow the point is, I've got to take the body back. Now."

"It can't be done."

"Has somebody already . . . ?"

White nodded.

"But could we fix it up again somehow? I mean, how, uh, badly. . ."

"No. No, I don't think so. Out of the question."

"Listen, White, if I get busted over this, I won't let myself be the only one to get hurt. You understand. There are going to be questions."

White nodded vaguely. He seemed to go away and return. "Well then, take a look yourself." He handed Ab an old-fashioned brass key. There was a plastic Yin and Yang symbol on the keychain. He pointed to a four-tier metal file on the far side of the office. "Through there."

The file wouldn't roll aside from the doorway until, having thought about it, Ab bent down and found the release for the wheels. There was no knob on the door, just a tarnished disc of lock with a word "Chicago" on it. The key fit loosely and the lock had to be coaxed.

The body was scattered all over the patchy linoleum. A heavy roselike scent masked the stench of the decaying organs. No, it was not something you could have passed off as the result of surgery, and in any case the head seemed to be missing.

He'd wasted an hour to see this.

White stood in the doorway, ignoring, in sympathy to Ab's feelings, the existence of the dismembered and disemboweled corpse. "He was waiting here, you see, when I went to the hospital. An out-of-towner, and one of my very . . . I always let them take away whatever they want. Sorry."

As White was locking up the room again, Ab recollected the one thing he would need irrespective of the body. He hoped it hadn't gone off with the head.

They found her left arm in the coffin of simulated pine with the Identi-Band still on it. He tried to persuade himself that as long as he had this name there was still half a chance that he'd find something to hang it on.

White sensed Ab's renascent optimism, and, without sharing it, encouraged him: "Things could be worse."

Ab frowned. His hope was still too fragile to bear expression.

But White began to float away in his own mild breeze. "Say, Ab, have you ever studied yoga?"

Ab laughed. "Shit no."

"You should. You'd be amazed what it can do for you. I don't stick with it like I should, it's my own fault, I suppose, but it puts you in touch with. . . Well, it's hard to explain."

White discovered that he was alone in the office. "Where are you going?" he asked.

420 East 65th came into the world as a "luxury" coöp, but like most such it had been subdivided by the turn of the century into a number of little hotels, two or three to a floor. These hotels rented rooms or portions of rooms on a weekly basis to singles who either preferred hotel life or who, as aliens, didn't qualify for a MODICUM dorm. Chapel shared his room at the Colton (named after the actress reputed to have owned the entire twelve rooms of the hotel in the 80's and 90's) with another ex-convict, but since Lucey left for his job at a retrieval center early in the morning and spent his afterhours cruising for free meat around the piers, the two men rarely encountered each other, which was how they liked it. It wasn't cheap, but where else could they have found accommodations so reassuringly like those they'd known at Sing-Sing: so small, so spare, so dark?

The room had a false floor in the reductionist style of the 90's. Lucey never went out without first scrupulously tucking everything away and rolling the floor into place. When Chapel got home from the hospital he would be greeted by a splendid absence: the walls, one window covered by a paper screen, the ceiling with its single recessed light, the waxed wood of the floor. The single decoration was a strip of molding tacked to the walls at what was now, due to the raised floor, eye-level.

He was home, and here, beside the door, bolted to the wall, quietly, wonderfully waiting for him, was his twenty-eight-inch Yamaha of America, none better at any price, nor any cheaper. (Chapel paid all the rental and cable charges himself, since Lucey didn't like TV.)

Chapel did not watch just anything. He saved himself for the programs he felt really strongly about. As the first of these did not come on till 10:30, he spent the intervening hour or two dusting, sanding, waxing, polishing, and generally being good to the floor, just as for nineteen years he had

scoured the concrete of his cell every morning and evening.
He worked with the mindless and blessed dutifulness of a
priest reading his office. Afterwards, calmed, he would roll
back the gleaming floorboards from his bed and lie back with
conscious worthiness, ready to receive. His body seemed to
disappear.

Once the box was on, Chapel became another person. At
10:30 he became Eric Laver, the idealistic young lawyer,
with his idealistic young notions of right and wrong, which no
amount of painful experience, including two disastrous mar-
riages (and the possibility now of a third) ever seemed to
dispel. Though lately, since he'd taken on the Forrest
case. . . This was *The Whole Truth*.

At 11:30 Chapel would have his bowel movement during
an intermission of news, sports, and weather.

Then: *As The World Turns*, which, being more epic in
scope, offered its audience different identities on different
days. Today, as Bill Harper, Chapel was worried about
Moira, his fourteen-year-old problem stepdaughter, who only
last Wednesday during a stormy encounter at breakfast had
announced to him that she was a lesbian. As if this wasn't
enough, his wife, when he told her what Moira had told him,
insisted that many years ago *she* had loved another woman.
Who that other woman might have been he feared he already
knew.

It was not the stories that engaged him so, it was the faces
of the actors, their voices, their gestures, the smooth, wide-
open, whole-bodied way they moved. So long as they themselves seemed stirred by their imaginary problems, Chapel
was satisfied. What he needed was the spectacle of authentic
emotion—eyes that cried, chests that heaved, lips that kissed
or frowned or tightened with anxiety, voices tremulous with
concern.

He would sit on the mattress, propped on cushions, four
feet back from the screen, breathing quick, shallow breaths,
wholly given over to the flickerings and noises of the machine, which were, more than any of his own actions, his life,
the central fact of his consciousness, the single source of any
happiness Chapel knew or could remember.

A TV had taught Chapel to read. It had taught him to
laugh. It had instructed the very muscles of his face how to
express pain, fear, anger, and joy. From it he had learned the
words to use in all the confusing circumstances of his other,

external life. And though he never read, or laughed, or frowned, or spoke, or walked, or did anything as well as his avatars on the screen, yet they'd seen him through well enough, after all, or he would not have been here now, renewing himself at the source.

What he sought here, and what he found, was much more than art, which he had sampled during prime evening hours and for which he had little use. It was the experience of returning, after the exertions of the day, to a face he could recognize and love, his own or someone else's. Or if not love, then some feeling as strong. To know, with certainty, that he would feel these same feelings tomorrow, and the next day. In other ages religion had performed this service, telling people the story of their lives, and after a certain lapse of time telling it to them again.

Once a show that Chapel followed on CBS had pulled down such disastrous ratings for six months running that it had been canceled. A pagan forcibly converted to a new religion would have felt the same loss and longing (until the new god has been taught to inhabit the forms abandoned by the god who died) that Chapel felt then, looking at the strange faces inhabiting the screen of his Yamaha for an hour every afternoon. It was as though he'd looked into a mirror and failed to find his reflection. For the first month the pain in his shoulder had become so magnificently more awful that he had almost been unable to do his work at Bellevue. Then, slowly, in the person of young Dr. Landry, he began to rediscover the elements of his own identity.

It was at 2:45, during a commercial for Carnation Eggies, that Ab came pounding and hollering at Chapel's door. Maud had just come to visit her sister-in-law's child at the observation center to which the court had committed him. She didn't know yet that Dr. Landry was in charge of the boy's case.

"Chapel," Ab screamed, "I know you're in there, so open up, goddammit. I'll knock this door down."

The next scene opened in Landry's office. He was trying to make Mrs. Hanson, from last week, understand how a large part of her daughter's problem sprang from her own selfish attitudes. But Mrs. Hanson was black, and Chapel's sympathy was qualified for blacks, whose special dramatic function was to remind the audience of the other world, the one that they inhabited and were unhappy in.

Maud knocked on Landry's door: a closeup of gloved fingers thrumming on the paper panel.

Chapel got up and let Ab in. By three o'clock Chapel had agreed, albeit sullenly, to help Ab find a replacement for the body he had lost.

3.

Martinez had been at the desk when the call came from Macy's saying to hold the Newman body till their driver got there. Though he knew that the vaults contained nothing but three male geriatric numbers, he made mild yes-sounds and started filling out both forms. He left a message for Ab at his emergency number, then (on the principle that if there was going to be shit it should be Ab who either cleaned it up or ate it, as God willed) got word to his cousin to call in sick for the second (two to ten) shift. When Ab phoned back, Martinez was brief and ominous: "Get here and bring you know what. Or you know what."

Macy's driver arrived before Ab. Martinez was feeling almost off-balance enough to tell him there was nothing in storage by the name of Newman, Bobbi. But it was not like Martinez to be honest when a lie might serve, especially in a case like this, where his own livelihood, and his cousin's, were jeopardized. So, making a mental sign of the cross, he'd wheeled one of the geriatric numbers out from the vaults, and the driver, with a healthy indifference to bureaucratic good form, carted it out to his van without looking under the sheet or checking the name on the file: NORRIS, THOMAS.

It was an inspired improvisation. Since their driver had been as culpable as the morgue, Macy's wasn't likely to make a stink about the resulting delay. Fast post mortem freezing was the rule in the cryonic industry and it didn't pay to advertise the exceptions.

Ab arrived a bit before four. First off he checked out the log book. The page for April 14 was blank. A miracle of bad luck, but he wasn't surprised.

"Anything waiting?"

"Nothing."

"That's incredible," Ab said, wishing it were.

The phone rang. "That'll be Macy's," Martinez said equably, stripping down to street clothes.

"Aren't you going to answer it?"

"It's your baby now." Martinez flashed a big winner's smile. They'd both gambled but Ab had lost. He explained, as the phone rang on, the stopgap by which he'd saved Ab's life.

When Ab picked it up, it was the director, no less, of Macy's Clinic, and so high in the sky of his just wrath it would have been impossible for Ab to have made out what he was screaming if he hadn't already known. Ab was suitably abject and incredulous, explaining that the attendant who had made the mistake (and how it could have happened he still did not understand) was gone for the day. He assured the director that the man would not get off lightly, would probably be canned or worse. On the other hand, he saw no reason to call the matter to the attention of Administration, who might try to shift some of the blame onto Macy's and their driver. The director agreed that that was uncalled for.

"And the minute your driver gets here Miss Newman will be waiting. I'll be personally responsible. And we can forget that the whole thing happened. Yes?"

Yes.

Leaving the office, Ab drew in a deep breath and squared his shoulders. He tried to get himself into the I-can-do-it spirit of a Sousa march. He had a problem. There's only one way to solve a problem: by coping with it. By whatever means were available.

For Ab, at this point, there was only one means left.

Chapel was waiting where Ab had left him on the ramp spanning 29th Street.

"It has to be done," Ab said.

Chapel, reluctant as he was to risk Ab's anger again (he'd nearly been strangled to death once), felt obliged to enter a last symbolic protest. "I'll do it," he whispered, "but it's murder."

"Oh no," Ab replied confidently, for he felt quite at ease on this score. "Burking isn't murder."

On April 2, 1956, Bellevue Hospital did not record a single death, a statistic so rare it was thought worthy of remark in all the city's newspapers, and there were then quite a few. In the sixty-six years since, there had not been such another deathless day, though twice it had seemed a near thing.

At five o'clock on the afternoon of April 14, 2022, the city desk computer at the *Times* issued a stand-by slip noting that as of that moment their Bellevue tie-line had not dispatched a single obit to the central board. A print-off of the old story accompanied the slip.

Joel Beck laid down her copy of *Tender Buttons*, which was no longer making sense, and considered the human-interest possibilities of this nonevent. She'd been on stand-by for hours and this was the first thing to come up. By midnight, very likely, someone would have died and spoiled any story she might have written. Still, in a choice between Gertrude Stein (illusion) and the Bellevue morgue (reality) Joel opted for the latter.

She notified Darling where she'd be. He thought it was a sleeping idea and told her to enjoy it.

By the first decade of the 21st century systematic lupus erythematosis (SLE) had displaced cancer as the principle cause of death among women aged twenty to fifty-five. This disease attacks every major system of the body, sequentially or in combination. Pathologically it is a virtual anthology of what can go wrong with the human body. Until the Morgan-Imamura test was perfected in 2007, cases of lupus had been diagnosed as meningitis, as epilepsy, as brucellosis, as nephritis, as syphillis, as colitis . . . The list goes on.

The etiology of lupus is infinitely complex and has been endlessly debated, but all students agree with the contention of Muller and Imamura in the study for which they won their first Nobel prize, *SLE—the Ecological Disease:* lupus represents the auto-intoxication of the human race in an environment ever more hostile to the existence of life. A minority of specialists went on to say that the chief cause of the disease's proliferation had been the collateral growth of modern pharmacology. Lupus, by this theory, was the price mankind was paying for the cure of its other ills.

Among the leading proponents of the so-called "doomsday" theory was Dr. E. Kitaj, director of Bellevue Hospital's Metabolic Research unit, who now (while Chapel bided his time in the television room) was pointing out to the resident and interns of heaven certain unique features of the case of the patient in Unit 7. While all clinical tests confirmed a diagnosis of SLE, the degeneration of liver functions had progressed in a fashion more typical of lupoid hepatitis. Because of the unique properties of her case, Dr. Kitaj had ordered a liver machine upstairs for Miss Schaap, though ordinarily this was a temporary expedient before transplantation. Her life was now as much a mechanical as a biologic process. In Alabama, New Mexico, and Utah, Frances Schaap would have been considered dead in any court of law.

Chapel was falling asleep. The afternoon art movie, a drama of circus life, was no help in keeping awake, since he could never concentrate on a program unless he knew the characters. Only by thinking of Ab, the threats he'd made, the blood glowing in his angry face, was he able to keep from nodding off.

In the ward the doctors had moved on to Unit 6 and were listening with tolerant smiles to Mrs. Harrison's jokes about her colostomy.

The new Ford commercial came on, like an old friend calling Chapel by name. A girl in an Empire coupe drove through endless fields of grain. Ab had said, who said so many things just for their shock value, that the commercials were often better than the programs.

At last they trooped off together to the men's ward, leaving the curtains drawn around Unit 7. Frances Schaap was asleep. The little red light on the machine winked on and off, on and off, like a jet flying over the city at night.

Using the diagram Ab had scrawled on the back of a transfer form, Chapel found the pressure adjustment for the portal vein. He turned it left till it stopped. The arrow on the scale below, marked P/P, moved slowly from 35, to 40, to 50. To 60.

To 65.

He turned the dial back to where it had been. The arrow shivered: the portal vein had hemorrhaged.

Frances Schaap woke up. She lifted one thin, astonished hand toward her lips: they were smiling! "Doctor," she said pleasantly. "Oh, I feel . . ." The hand fell back to the sheet.

Chapel looked away from her eyes. He readjusted the dial, which was no different, essentially, from the controls of his own Yamaha. The arrow moved right, along the scale: 50. 55.

" . . . so much better now."

60. 65.
"Thanks."
70.

"I hope, Mr. Holt, that you won't let me keep you from your work," Joel Beck said, with candid insincerity. "I fear I have already."

Ab thought twice before agreeing to this. At first he'd been convinced she was actually an investigator Macy's had hired to nail him, but her story about the computer checking out the obits and sending her here was not the sort of thing anyone could have made up. It was bad enough, her being from the *Times,* and worse perhaps.

"Am I?" she insisted.

If he said yes, he had work to do, she'd ask to tag along and watch. If he said no, then she'd go on with her damned questions. If it hadn't been that she'd have reported him (he could recognize the type), he'd have told her to fuck off.

"Oh, I don't know," he answered carefully. "Isn't it me who's keeping you from your work?"

"How so?"

"Like I explained, there's a woman up on 18 who's sure to terminate any minute now. I'm just waiting for them to call."

"Half an hour ago you said it wouldn't take fifteen minutes, and you're still waiting. Possibly the doctors have pulled her through. Wouldn't that be wonderful?"

"Someone is bound to die by twelve o'clock."

"By the same logic someone was bound to have died by now—and they haven't."

Ab could not support the strain of diplomacy any longer. "Look, lady, you're wasting your time—it's as simple as that."

"It won't be the first time," Joel Beck replied complacently. "You might almost say that's what I'm paid to do." She unslung her recorder. "If you'd just answer one or two more questions, give me a few more details of what you actually do, possibly we'll come up with a handle for a more general story. Then even if that call does come I could go up with you and look over your shoulder."

"Who would be interested?" With growing astonishment Ab realized that she did not so much resist his arguments as simply ignore them.

While Joel Beck was explaining the intrinsic fascination of death to the readers of the *Times* (not a morbid fascination but the universal human response to a universal human fact), the call came from Chapel.

He had done what Ab asked him to.

"Yeah, and?"

It had gone off okay.

"Is it official yet?"

It wasn't. There was no one in the ward.

"Couldn't you, uh, mention the matter to someone who can make it official?"

The *Times* woman was poking about the morgue, fingering things, pretending not to eavesdrop. Ab felt she could decipher his generalities. His first confession had been the same kind of nightmare, with Ab certain all his classmates lined up outside the confessional had overheard the sins the priest had pried out of him. If she hadn't been listening he could have tried to bully Chapel into. . .

He'd hung up. It was just as well.

"Was that the call?" she asked.

"No. Something else, a private matter."

So she kept at him with more questions about the ovens, and whether relatives ever came in to watch, and how long it took, until the desk called to say there was a driver from Macy's trying to bring a body into the hospital and should they let him?

"Hold him right there. I'm on my way."

"*That* was the call," Joel Beck said, genuinely disappointed.

"Mm. I'll be right back."

The driver, flustered, started in with some story why he was late.

"It's skin off your ass, not mine. Never mind that anyhow. There's a reporter in my office from the *Times*—"

"I knew," the driver said. "It's not enough I'm going to be fired, now you've found a way—"

"Listen to me, asshole. This isn't about the Newman fuckup, and if you don't panic she never has to know." He explained about the city desk computer. "So we just won't let her get any strange ideas, right? Like she might if she saw you hauling one corpse into the morgue and going off with another."

"Yeah, but. . ." The driver clutched for his purpose as for

a hat that a great wind were lifting from his head. "But they'll crucify me at Macy's if I don't come back with the Newman body! I'm so late already because of the damned—"

"You'll *get* the body. You'll take back *both*. You can return with the other one later, but the important thing now—"

He felt her hand on his shoulder, bland as a smile.

"I thought you couldn't have gone too far away. There's a call for you and I'm afraid you were right: Miss Schaap has died. That is whom you were speaking of?"

Whom! Ab thought with a sudden passion of hatred for the *Times* and its band of pseudo-intellectuals. *Whom!*

The Macy's driver was disappearing toward his cart.

It came to Ab then, the plan of his salvation, whole and entire, the way a masterpiece must come to a great artist, its edges glowing.

"Bob!" Ab called out. "Wait a minute."

The driver turned halfway round, head bent sideways, an eyebrow raised: who, me?

"Bob, I want you to meet, uh . . ."

"Joel Beck."

"Right. Joel this is Bob, uh, Bob Newman." It was, in fact, Samuel Blake. Ab was bad at remembering names.

Samuel Blake and Joel Beck shook hands.

"Bob drives for Macy's Clinic, the Steven Jay Mandell Memorial Clinic." He laid one hand on Blake's shoulder, the other hand on Beck's. She seemed to become aware of his stump for the first time and flinched. "Do you know anything about cryonics, Miss uh?"

"Beck. No, very little."

"Mandell was the very first New Yorker to go to the freezers. Bob could tell you all about him, a fantastic story." He steered them back down the corridor toward the morgue.

"Bob is here right now because of the body they just. . . Uh." He remembered too late that you didn't call them bodies in front of outsiders. "Because of Miss Schaap, that is. *Whom,*" he added with malicious emphasis, "was insured with Bob's clinic." Ab squeezed the driver's shoulder in lieu of winking.

"Whenever possible, you see, we notify the Clinic people, so that they can be here the minute one of their clients terminates. That way there's not a minute lost. Right, Bob?"

The driver nodded, thinking his way slowly toward the idea Ab had prepared for him.

He opened the door to his office, waited for them to go in. "So while I'm upstairs why don't you and Bob have a talk, Miss Peck. Bob has dozens of incredible stories he can tell you, but you'll have to be quick. Cause once I've got his body down here . . ." Ab gave the driver a significant look. ". . . Bob will have to leave."

It was done as neatly as that. The two people whose curiosity or impatience might still have spoiled the substitution were now clamped to each other like a pair of steel traps, jaw to jaw to jaw to jaw.

He hadn't considered the elevator situation. During his own shift there were seldom logjams. When there were, carts routed for the morgue were last in line. At 6:15, when the Schaap was finally signed over to him, every elevator arriving on 18 was full of people who'd ridden to the top in order to get a ride to the bottom. It might be an hour before Ab and his cart could find space and the Macy's driver would cerainly not sit still that much longer.

He waited till the hallway was empty, then scooped up the body from the cart. It weighed no more than his own Beno, but even so by the time he'd reached the landing of 12, he was breathing heavy. Halfway down from 5 his knees gave out. (They'd given fair warning but he'd refused to believe he could have gone so soft.) He collapsed with the body still cradled in his arms.

He was helped to his feet by a blond young man in a striped bathrobe many sizes too small. Once Ab was sitting up, the young man tried to assist Frances Schaap to her feet. Ab, gathering his wits, explained that it was just a body.

"Hoo-wee, for a minute there, I thought. . ." He laughed uncertainly at what he'd thought.

Ab felt the body here and there and moved its limbs this way and that, trying to estimate what damage had been done. Without undressing it, this was difficult.

"How about you?" the young man asked, retrieving the cigarette he'd left smoking on a lower step.

"I'm fine." He rearranged the sheet, lifted the body and started off again. On the third floor landing he remembered to shout up a thank-you at the young man who'd helped him.

Later, during visiting hours in the ward, Ray said to his

friend Charlie, who'd brought in new cassettes from the shop where he worked: "It's incredible some of the things you see in this hospital."

"Such as?"

"Well, if I told you you wouldn't believe." Then he spoiled his whole build-up by twisting round sideways in bed. He'd forgotten he couldn't do that.

"How are you feeling?" Charlie asked, after Ray had stopped groaning and making a display. "I mean, in general."

"Better, the doctor says, but I still can't piss by myself." He described the operation of the catheter, and his self-pity made him forget Ab Holt, but later, alone and unable to sleep (for the man in the next bed made bubbling sounds) he couldn't stop thinking of the dead girl, of how he'd picked her up off the steps, her ruined face and frail, limp hands, and how the fat attendant from the morgue had tested, one by one, her arms and legs, to see what he'd broken.

There was nothing for her in the morgue, Joel had decided, now that the day had yielded its one obit to nullify the nonevent. She phoned back to the desk but neither Darling nor the computer had any suggestions.

She wondered how long it would be before they fired her. Perhaps they thought she would become so demoralized if they kept her on stand-by that she'd leave without a confrontation scene.

Human interest: surely somewhere among the tiers of this labyrinth there was a story for her to bear witness to. Yet wherever she looked she came up against flat, intractable surfaces: Six identical wheelchairs all in a row. A doctor's name penciled on a door. The shoddiness, the smells. At the better sort of hospitals, where her family would have gone, the raw fact of human frangibility was prettied over with a veneer of cash. Whenever she was confronted, like this, with the undisguised bleeding thing, her first impulse was to avert her eyes, never—like a true journalist—to bend a little closer and even stick a finger in it. Really, they had every reason to give her the sack.

Along one stretch of the labyrinth iron curlicues projected from the walls at intervals. Gas brackets? Yes, for their tips, obscured by layer upon layer of white paint, were nozzle-shaped. They must have dated back to the nineteenth century. She felt the slightest mental tingle.

But no, this was too slim a thread to hang a story from. It was the sort of precious detail one notices when one's eyes *are* averted.

She came to a door with the stenciled letters: "Volunteers." As this had a rather hopeful ring to it, human-interest-wise, she knocked. There was no answer and the door was unlocked. She entered a small unhappy room whose only furniture was a metal filing cabinet. In it was a rag-tag of yellowing mimeographed forms and equipment for making Koffee.

She pulled the cord of the blinds. The dusty louvres opened unwillingly. A dozen yards away cars sped past on the upper level of the East Side Highway. Immediately the whooshing noise of their passage detached itself from the indiscriminate, perpetual humming in her ears. Below the highway a slice of oily river darkened with the darkening of the spring sky, and below this a second stream of traffic moved south.

She got the blinds up and tried the window. It opened smoothly. A breeze touched the ends of the scarf knotted into her braids as she leaned forward.

There, not twenty feet below, was her story, the absolutely right thing: in a triangle formed by a feeder ramp to the highway and the building she was in and a newer building in the bony style of the 70's was the loveliest vacant lot she'd ever seen, a perfect little garden of knee-high weeds. It was a symbol: of Life struggling up out of the wasteland of the modern world, of Hope. . . .

No, that was too easy. But some meaning, a whisper, did gleam up to her from this patch of weeds (she wondered what their names were; at the library there would probably be a book. . . .), as sometimes in *Tender Buttons* the odd pairing of two ordinary words would generate similar flickerings poised at the very threshold of the intelligible. Like:

An elegant use of foliage and grace and a little piece of white cloth and oil.

Or, more forcibly: *A blind agitation is manly and uttermost.*

4.

The usual cirrus at the horizon of pain had thickened to a thunderhead. Sleepless inside a broken unit in the annex to Emergency, he stared at the red bulb above the door, trying to think the pain away. It persisted and grew, not only in his shoulder but in his fingers sometimes, or his knees, less a pain than an awareness that pain were possible, a far-off insistent jingling like phone calls traveling up to his head from some incredible lost continent, a South America full of dreadful news.

It was the lack of sleep, he decided, since having an explanation helped. Even ths wakefulness would have been tolerable if he could have filled his head with something besides his own thoughts—a program, checkers, talk, the job....

The job? It was almost time to clock in. With a goal established he had only to whip himself toward it. Stand: he could do that. Walk to the door: and this was possible, though he distrusted his arhythmic legs. Open it: he did.

The glare of Emergency edged every commonplace with a sudden, awful crispness, as though he were seeing it all raw and naked with the skin peeled back to show the veins and muscles. He wanted to return to the darkness and come out through the door again into the average everydayness he remembered.

Halfway across the distance to the next door he had to detour about a pair of DOA's, anonymous and neuter beneath their sheets. Emergency, of course, received more bodies than actual patients, all the great city's gore. Memories of the dead lasted about as long as a good shirt, the kind he'd bought back before prison.

A pain formed at the base of his back, rode up the elevator of his spine, and stepped off. Braced in the doorframe (sweat collected into drops on his shaved scalp and zigzagged down to his neck), he waited for the pain to return but there was nothing left but the faraway jingle jingle jingle that he would not answer.

He hurried to the duty room before anything else could happen. Once he was clocked in he felt protected. He even swung his left arm round in its socket as a kind of invocation to the demon of his usual pain.

Steinberg looked up from her crossword puzzle. "You all right?"

Chapel froze. Beyond the daily rudenesses that a position of authority demands, Steinberg never talked to those under her. Her shyness, she called it. "You don't look well."

Chapel studied the wordless crossword of the tiled floor, repeated, though not aloud, his explanation: that he had not slept. Inside him a tiny gnat of anger hatched and buzzed against this woman staring at him, though she had no right to, she was not actually his boss. Was she still staring? He would not look up.

His feet sat side by side on the tiles, cramped and prisoned in six-dollar shoes, deformed, inert. He'd gone to the beach with a woman once and walked shoeless in the heated, glittering dust. Her feet had been as ugly as his, but. . .

He clamped his knees together and covered them with his hands, trying to blot out the memory of. . .

But it seeped back from places inside in tiny premonitory droplets of pain.

Steinberg gave him a slip. Someone from 'M' was routed to a Surgery on 5. "And move," she called out after him.

Behind his cart he had no sense of his speed, whether fast or slow. It distressed him how this muscle, then that muscle, jerked and yanked, the way the right thigh heaved up and then the left thigh, the way the feet, in their heavy shoes, came down against the hard floors with no more flexion than the blades of skates.

He'd wanted to chop her head off. He'd often seen this done, on programs. He would lie beside her night after night, both of them insomniac but never talking, and think of the giant steel blade swooping down from its superb height and separating head and body, until the sound of this incessantly imagined flight blended into the repeated zoom zim zoom of the cars passing on the expressway below, and he slept.

The boy in 'M' Ward didn't need help sliding over onto the cart. He was the dunnest shade of black, all muscles and bounce and nervous, talky terror. Chapel had standard routines worked out for his type.

"You're a tall one," it began.

"No, you got it backwards—it's your wagon that's too short."

"How tall are you anyhow? Six two?"

"Six four."

Reaching his punch line, Chapel made a laugh. "Ha, ha, I could use those four inches for myself!" (Chapel stood 5'7" in his shoes.)

Usually they laughed with him, but this one had a comeback. "Well, you tell them that upstairs and maybe they'll accommodate you."

"What?"

"The surgeons—they're the boys that can do it." The boy laughed at what was now *his* joke, while Chapel sank back into a wounded silence.

"Arnold Chapel," a voice over the PA said. "Please return along 'K' corridor to 'K' elevator bank. Arnold Chapel, please return along 'K' corridor to 'K' elevator bank."

Obediently he reversed the cart and returned to 'K' elevator bank. His identification badge had cued the traffic control system. It had been years since the computer had had to correct him out loud.

He rolled the cart into the elevator. Inside, the boy repeated his joke about the four inches to a student nurse.

The elevator said, "Five."

Chapel rolled the cart out. Now, right or left? He couldn't remember.

He couldn't breathe.

"Hey, what's wrong?" the boy said.

"I need. . ." He lifted his left hand towards his lips. Everything he looked at seemed to be at right angles to everything else, like the inside of a gigantic machine. He backed away from the cart.

"Are you all right?" He was swinging his legs down over the side.

Chapel ran down the corridor. Since he was going in the direction of the Surgery to which the cart had been routed the traffic control system did not correct him. Each time he inhaled he felt hundreds of tiny hypodermic darts penetrate his chest and puncture his lungs.

"Hey!" a doctor yelled. "Hey!"

Into another corridor, and there, as providentially as if he'd been programmed right to its door, was a staff toilet. The room was flooded with a calm blue light.

He entered one of the stalls and pulled the door, an old door made of dark wood, shut behind him. He knelt down beside the white basin, in which a skin of water quivered with eager, electric designs. He dipped his cupped fingers into the bowl and dabbled his forehead with cool water. Everything fell away—anger, pain, pity, every possible feeling he'd ever heard of or seen enacted. He'd always expected, and been braced against, some eventual retribution, a shotgun blast at the end of the long, white corridor of being alive. It was such a relief to know he had been wrong.

The doctor, or was it the boy routed to surgery, had come into the toilet and was knocking on the wooden door. Neatly and as though on cue, he vomited. Long strings of blood came out with the pulped food.

He stood up, zipped, and pushed open the door. It was the boy, not the doctor. "I'm better now," he said.

"You're sure?"

"I'm feeling fine."

The boy climbed back onto the cart, which he'd wheeled himself all this way, and Chapel pushed him around the corner and down the hall to Surgery.

Ab had felt it in his arms and his hands, a power of luck, as though when he leaned forward to flip over each card his fingers could read through the plastic to know whether it was, whether it wasn't the diamond he needed to make his flush.

It wasn't.

It wasn't.

It wasn't.

As it turned out, he needn't have bothered. Martinez got the pot with a full house.

He had lost as much blood as he comfortably could, so he sat out the next hands munching Nibblies and gassing with the bar decoration, who was also the croupier. It was said she had a third interest in the club, but so dumb, could she? She was a yesser and yessed everything Ab cared to say. Nice breasts though, always damp and sticking to her blouses.

Martinez folded after only his third card and joined Ab at the bar. "How'd you do it, Lucky?" he jeered.

"Fuck off. I started out lucky enough."

"A familiar story."

"What are you worried—I won't pay you back?"

"I'm not worried, I'm not worried." He dropped a five on the bar and ordered sangria, one for the big winner, one for the big loser, and one for the most beautiful, the most successful businesswoman on West Houston, and so out into the heat and the stink.

"Some ass?" Martinez asked.

What with, Ab wanted to know.

"Be my guest. If I'd lost what you lost, you'd do as much for me."

This was doubly irking, one, because Martinez, who played a dull careful game with sudden flashes of insane bluffing, never did worse than break even, and two, because it wasn't true—Ab would not have done as much for him or anyone. On the other hand, he was hungry for something more than what he'd find at home in the icebox.

"Sure. Okay."

"Shall we walk there?"

Seven o'clock, the last Wednesday in May. It was Martinez's day off, while Ab was just sandwiching his excitement in between clock-out and clock-in with the assistance of some kind green pills.

Each time they passed one of the crosstown streets (which were named down here instead of numbered) the round red eye of the sun had sunk a fraction nearer the blur of Jersey. In the subway gallery below Canal they stopped for a beer. The sting of the day's losses faded, and the moon of next-time rose in the sky. When they came up again it was the violet before night, and the real moon was there waving at them. A population of how many now? Seventy-five?

A jet went past, coming in low for the Park, winking a jittery rhythm of red, red, green, red, from tail and wing tips. Ab wondered whether Milly might be on it. Was she due in tonight?

"Look at it this way, Ab," Martinez said. "You're still paying for last month's luck."

He had to think, and then he had to ask, "What luck last month?"

"The switch. Jesus, I didn't think any of us were going to climb out from under that without getting burnt."

"Oh, that." He approached the memory tentatively, not sure the scar tissue was firm yet. "It was tight, all right." A laugh, which rang half-true. The scar had healed, he went on. "There was one moment though at the end when I thought I'd flushed the whole thing down the toilet. See, I had the Identi-Band from the first body, what's-her-name's. It was the only thing I got from that asshole White. . . ."

"That fucking White," Martinez agreed.

"Yeah. But I was so panicked after that spill on the stairs that I forgot, see, to change them, the two bands, so I sent off the Schaap body like it was."

"Oh Mary Mother, that *would* have done it!"

"I remembered before the driver got away. So I got out there with the Newman band and made up some story about how we print up different bands when we send them out to the freezers than when one goes to the oven."

"Did he believe that?"

Ab shrugged. "He didn't argue."

"You don't think he ever figured out what happened that day?"

"That guy? He's as dim as Chapel."

"Yeah, what *about* Chapel?" There, if anywhere, Martinez had thought, Ab had laid himself open.

"What about him?"

"You told me you were going to pay him off. Did you?"

Ab tried to find some spit in his mouth. "I paid him off all right." Then, lacking the spit: "Jesus Christ."

Martinez waited.

"I offered him a hundred dollars. One hundred smackers. You know what that dumb bastard wanted?"

"Five hundred?"

"Nothing! Nothing at all. He even argued about it. Didn't want to get his hands dirty, I suppose. My money wasn't good enough for him."

"So?"

"So we reached a compromise. He took fifty." He made a comic face.

Martinez laughed. "It was a damned lucky thing, that's all I'll say, Ab. *Damned* lucky."

They were quiet along the length of the old police station. Despite the green pills, Ab felt himself coming down, but ever so gently down. He entered pink cloudbanks of philosophy.

"Hey, Martinez, you ever think about that stuff? The freezing business and all that."

"I've thought about it, sure. I've thought it's a lot of bullshit."

"You don't think there's a chance then that any of them ever will be brought back to life?"

"Of course not. Didn't you see that documentary they were making all the uproar over, and suing NBC? No, that freezing doesn't stop anything, it just slows it down. They'll all just be so many little ice cubes eventually. Might as well try bringing them back from the smoke in the stacks."

"But if science could find a way to ... oh, I don't know. It's complicated by lots of things."

"Are you thinking of putting money into one of those damned policies, Ab? For Christ's sake, I would have thought that you had more brains than that. The other day my wife..." He took a step backwards. "My ex-wife got on to me about that, and the money they want...." He rolled his eyes blackamoor-style. "It's not in our league, believe me."

"That's not what I was thinking at all."

"So? Then? I'm no mind-reader."

"I was wondering, if they ever do find a way to bring them back, and if they find a cure for lupus and all that, well, what if they brought her back?"

"The Schaap?"

"Yeah. Wouldn't that be crazy? What would she think, anyhow?"

"Yeah, what a joke."

"No, seriously."

"I don't get the point, seriously."

Ab tried to explain but he didn't see the point now himself. He could picture the scene in his mind so clearly: the girl, her skin made smooth again, lying on a table of white stone, breathing, but so faintly that only the doctor standing over her could be sure. His hand would touch her face and her eyes would open and there would be such a look of astonishment.

"As far as I'm concerned," Martinez said, in a half-angry tone, for he didn't like to see anyone believing in something he couldn't believe in, "it's just a kind of religion."

Since Ab could recall having said almost the same thing to Leda, he was able to agree. They were only a couple blocks from the baths by then, so there were better uses for the imagination. But before the last of the cloudbank had quite vanished, he got in one last word for philosophy. "One way or another, Martinez, life goes on. Say what you like, it goes on."

THE SQUIRREL CAGE

The terrifying thing—if that's what I mean—I'm not sure that "terrifying" is the right word—is that I'm free to write down anything I like but that no matter what I *do* write down it will make no difference—to me, to you, to whomever differences are made. But then what is meant by "a difference"? Is there ever really such a thing as change?

I ask more questions these days than formerly; I am less programmatic altogether. I wonder—is that a good thing?

This is what it is like where I am: a chair with no back to it (so I suppose you would call it a stool); a floor, walls, and a ceiling, which form, as nearly as I can judge, a cube; white, white light, no shadows—not even on the underside of the lid of the stool; me, of course; the typewriter. I have described the typewriter at length elsewhere. Perhaps I shall describe it again. Yes, almost certainly I shall. But not now. Later. Though why not now? Why not the typewriter as well as anything else?

Of the many kinds of question at my disposal, "why" seems be to the most recurrent.

What I do is this: I stand up and walk around the room from wall to wall. It is not a large room, but it's large enough for present purposes. Sometimes I even jump, but there is little incentive to do that, since there is nothing to jump *for*. The ceiling is quite too high to touch, and the stool is so low that it provides no challenge at all. If I thought anyone were *entertained* by my jumping ... but I have no reason to suppose that. Sometimes I exercise: push-ups, somersaults, head-stands, isometrics, etc. But never as much as I should. I am getting fat. Disgustingly fat and full of pimples besides. I like to squeeze the pimples on my face. Every so often I will keep one sore and open with overmuch pinching, in the hope that I will develop an abscess and blood poisoning. But apparently the place is germproof. The thing never infects.

It's well nigh impossible to kill oneself here. The walls and floor are padded, and one only gets a headache beating one's head against them. The stool and the typewriter both have hard edges, but whenever I have tried to use *them*, they're withdrawn into the floor. That is how I know there is someone watching.

Once I was convinced it was God. I assumed that this was either heaven or hell, and I imagined that it would go on for all eternity just the same way. But if I were living in eternity already, I couldn't get fatter all the time. Nothing changes in eternity. So I console myself that I will someday die. Man is mortal. I eat all I can to make that day come faster. The *Times* says that that will give me heart disease.

Eating is fun, and that's the real reason I do a lot of eating. What else is there to do, after all? There is this little ... nozzle, I suppose you'd call it, that sticks out of one wall, and all I have to do is put my mouth to it. Not the most elegant way to feed, but it tastes damn good. Sometimes I just stand there for hours at a time and let it trickle in. Until *I* have to trickle. That's what the stool is for. It has a lid on it, the stool does, which moves on a hinge. It's quite clever, in a mechanical way.

If I sleep, I don't seem to be aware of it. Sometimes I do catch myself dreaming, but I can never remember what they were about. I'm not able to make myself dream at will. I would like that exceedingly. That covers all the vital functions but one—and there is an accommodation for sex too. Everything has been thought of.

I have no memory of any time before this, and I cannot say how long *this* has been going on. According to today's New York *Times* it is the Second of May, 1961. I don't know what conclusion one is to draw from that.

From what I've been able to gather, reading the *Times,* my position here in this room is not typical. Prisons, for instance, seem to be run along more liberal lines, usually. But perhaps the *Times* is lying, covering up. Perhaps even the date has been falsified. Perhaps the entire paper, every day, is an elaborate forgery and this is actually 1950, not 1961. Or maybe they are antiques and I am living whole centuries after they were printed, a fossil. Anything seems possible. I have no way to judge.

Sometimes I make up little stories while I sit here on my stool in front of the typewriter. Sometimes they are stories about the people in the New York *Times*, and those are the best stories. Sometimes they are just about people I make up, but those aren't so good because. . .

They're not so good because I think everybody is dead. I think I may be the only one left, sole survivor of the breed. And they just keep me here, the last one, alive, in this room, this cage, to look at, to observe, to make their observations of, to—I don't *know* why they keep me alive. And if everyone is dead, as I've supposed, then who are they, these supposed observers? Aliens? *Are* there aliens? I don't know. Why are they studying me? What do they hope to learn? Is it an experiment? What am I supposed to do? Are they waiting for me to say something, to write something on this typewriter? Do my responses or lack of responses confirm or destroy a theory of behavior? Are the testers happy with their results? They give no indications. They efface themselves, veiling themselves behind these walls, this ceiling, this floor. Perhaps no human could stand the sight of them. But maybe they are only scientists, and not aliens at all. Psychologists at MIT perhaps, such as frequently are shown in the *Times:* blurred, dotty faces, bald heads, occasionally a mustache, certificate of originality. Or, instead, young crewcut Army doctors studying various brainwashing techniques. Reluctantly, of course. History and a concern for freedom has forced them to violate their own (privately held) moral codes. Maybe I *volunteered* for this experiment! Is that the case? O God, I hope not! Are you reading this, Professor? Are you reading this, Major? Will you let me out now? I want to leave this experiment *right now*.

Yeah.

Well, we've been through that little song and dance before, me and my typewriter. We've tried just about every password there is. Haven't we, typewriter? And as you can see (can you see?)—here we are still.

They are aliens, obviously.

Sometimes I write poems. Do you like poetry? Here's one of the poems I wrote. It's called *Grand Central Terminal*. ("Grand Central Terminal" is the right name for what most

people wrongly call "Grand Central Station." This—and other
priceless information—comes from the New York *Times*.)

Grand Central Terminal

How can you be unhappy
when you see how high
the ceiling is?

                              My!

the ceiling is high!
High as the sky!
So who are *we*
to be gloomy here?

                              Why,

there isn't even room
to die, my dear.

This is the tomb
of some giant so great
that if he ate
us there would be
simply no taste.

                              Gee,

what a waste
that would be
of you and me.

And sometimes, as you can also see, I just sit here copying
old poems over again, or maybe copying the poem that the
Times prints each day. The *Times* is my only source of
poetry. Alas the day! I wrote *Grand Central Terminal* rather
a long time ago. Years. I can't say exactly how many years
though.

I have no measures of time here. No day, no night, no
waking and sleeping, no chronometer but the *Times*, ticking
off its dates. I can remember dates as far back as 1957. I
wish I had a little diary that I could keep here in the room
with me. Some record of my progress. If I could just save up
my old copies of the *Times*. Imagine how, over the years,
they would pile up. Towers and stairways and cozy burrows
of newsprint. It would be a more humane architecture, would

it not? This cube that I occupy does have drawbacks from the strictly human point of view. But I am not allowed to keep yesterday's edition. It is always taken away, whisked off, before today's edition is delivered. I should be thankful, I suppose, for what I have.

What if the *Times* went bankrupt? What if, as is often threatened, there were a newspaper strike! Boredom is not, as you might suppose, the great problem. Eventually—very soon, in fact—boredom becomes a great challenge. A stimulus.

My body. Would you be interested in my body? I used to be. I used to regret that there were no mirrors in here. Now, on the contrary, I am grateful. How gracefully, in those early days, the flesh would wrap itself about the skeleton; now, how it droops and languishes! I used to dance by myself hours on end, humming my own accompaniment—leaping, rolling about, hurling myself spread-eagled against the padded walls. I became a connoisseur of kinethesia. There is great joy in movement—free, unconstrained speed.

Life is so much tamer now. Age dulls the edge of pleasure, hanging in wreathes of fat on the supple Christmas tree of youth.

I have various theories about the meaning of life. Of life *here*. If I were somewhere else—in the world I know of from the New York *Times,* for instance, where so many exciting things happen every *day* that it takes half a million words to tell about them—there would be no problem at all. One would be so busy running around—from 53rd Street to 42nd Street from 42nd Street to the Fulton Street Fish Market, not to mention all the journeys one might make *crosstown*—that one wouldn't have to worry whether life had a meaning.

In the daytime one could shop for a multitude of goods, then in the evening, after a dinner at a fine restaurant, to the theater or a cinema. Oh, life would be so full if I were living in New York! If I were free! I spend a lot of time like this, imagining what New York must be like, imagining what other people are like, what I would be like with other people, and in a sense my life here is full from imagining such things.

One of my theories is that they (*you* know, ungentle reader, who they are, I'm sure) are waiting for me to make a confession. This poses problems. Since I remember nothing of my previous existence, I don't know what I should confess. I've tried confessing to everything: political crimes, sex crimes (I especially like to confess to sex crimes), traffic offenses, spiritual pride. My god, what *haven't* I confessed to? Nothing seems to work. Perhaps I just haven't confessed to the crimes I really did commit, whatever they were. Or perhaps (which seems more and more likely) the theory is at fault.

I have another theory.

A brief hiatus.

The *Times* came, so I read the day's news, then nourished myself at the fount of life, and now I am back at my stool.

I have been wondering whether, if I were living in that world, the world of the *Times,* I would be a pacifist or not. It is certainly the central issue of modern morality and one would have to take a stand. I have been thinking about the problem for some years, and I am inclined to believe that I am in favor of disarmament. On the other hand, in a practical sense I wouldn't object to the bomb if I could be sure it would be dropped on me. There is definitely a schism in my being between the private sphere and the public sphere.

On one of the inner pages, behind the political and international news, was a wonderful story headlined: BIOLOGISTS HAIL MAJOR DISCOVERY. Let me copy it out for your benefit:

Washington D.C.—Deep-sea creatures with brains but no mouths are being hailed as a major biological discovery of the twentieth century.

The weird animals, known as pogonophores, resemble slender worms. Unlike ordinary worms, however, they have no digestive system, no excretory organs, and no means of breathing, the National Geographic Society says. Baffled scientists who first examined pogonophores believed that only parts of the specimens had reached them.

Biologists are now confident that they have seen the whole animal, but still do not understand how it manages to live. Yet they know it does exist, propagate, and even think, after a fashion, on the floors of deep waters around the globe. The female pogonophore lays up to thirty eggs at a time. A tiny brain permits rudimentary mental processes.

All told, the pogonophore is so unusual that biologists have set up a special phylum for it alone. This is significant because a phylum is such a broad biological classification that creatures as diverse as fish, reptiles, birds, and men are all included in the phylum Chordata.

Settling on the sea bottom, a pogonophore secretes a tube around itself and builds it up, year by year, to a height of perhaps five feet. The tube resembles a leaf of white grass, which may account for the fact that the animal went so long undiscovered.

The pogonophore apparently never leaves its self-built prison, but crawls up and down inside at will. The wormlike animal may reach a length of fourteen inches, with a diameter of less than a twenty-fifth of an inch. Long tentacles wave from its top end.

Zoologists once theorized that the pogonophore, in an early stage, might store enough food in its body to allow it to fast later on. But young pogonophores also lack a digestive system.

It's amazing the amount of things a person can learn just by reading the *Times* every day. I always feel so much more *alert* after a good read at the paper. And creative. Herewith, a story about pogonophores:

STRIVING

The Memoirs of a Pogonophore

Introduction

In May of 1961 I had been considering the purchase of a pet. One of my friends had recently acquired a pair of tarsiers, another had adopted a boa constrictor, and my nocturnal roommate kept an owl caged above his desk.

A nest (or school?) of pogs was certainly one-up on their eccentricities. Moreover, since pogonophores do not eat, excrete, sleep, or make noise, they would be ideal pets. In June I had three dozen shipped to me from Japan at considerable expense.

[A brief interruption in the story: Do you feel that it's credible? Does it possess the *texture* of reality? I thought that by beginning the story by mentioning those other pets, I would clothe my invention in greater verisimilitude. Were you taken in?]

Being but an indifferent biologist, I had not considered the problem of maintaining adequate pressure in
my aquarium. The pogonophore is used to the weight of
an entire ocean. I was not equipped to meet such
demands. For a few exciting days I watched the surviving pogs rise and descend in their translucent white
shells. Soon, even these died. Now, resigned to the
commonplace, I stock my aquarium with Maine lobsters
for the amusement and dinners of occasional out-of-
town visitors.

I have never regretted the money I spent on them:
man is rarely given to know the sublime spectacle of the
rising pogonophore—and then but briefly. Although I
had at that time only the narrowest conception of the
thoughts that passed through the rudimentary brain of
the sea worm ("Up up up Down down down"), I could
not help admiring its persistence. The pogonophore does
not sleep. He climbs to the top of the inside passage of his
shell, and, when he has reached the top, he retraces his
steps to the bottom of his shell. The pogonophore never
tires of his self-imposed regimen. He performs his duty
scrupulously and with honest joy. He is *not* a fatalist.

The memoirs that follow this introduction are not
allegory. I have not tried to "interpret" the inner
thoughts of the pogonophore. There is no need for that,
since the pogonophore himself has given us the most
eloquent record of his spiritual life. It is transcribed on
the core of translucent white shell in which he spends his
entire life.

Since the invention of the alphabet it has been a
common conceit that the markings on shells or the
sand-etched calligraphy of the journeying snail are possessed of true linguistic meaning. Cranks and eccentrics
down the ages have tried to decipher these codes, just as
other men have sought to understand the language of the
birds. Unavailingly. I do not claim that the scrawls and
shells of *common* shellfish can be translated; the core of
the pogonophore's shell, however, can be—for I have
broken the code!

With the aid of a United States Army manual on
cryptography (obtained by what devious means I am not
at liberty to reveal) I have learned the grammar and

syntax of the pogonophore's secret language. Zoologists and others who would like to verify my solution of the crypt may reach me through the editor of this publication.

In all thirty-six cases I have been able to examine, the indented traceries on the insides of these shells have been the same. It is my theory that the sole purpose of the pogonophore's tentacles is to follow the course of this "message" up and down the core of his shell and thus, as it were, to think. The shell is a sort of externalized stream-of-consciousness.

It would be possible (and in fact it is an almost irresistible temptation) to comment on the meaning that these memoirs possess for mankind. Surely, there is a philosophy compressed into these precious shells by Nature herself. But before I begin my commentary, let us examine the text itself.

The Text
I
Up. Uppity, up, up. The Top.
II
Down. Downy, down, down. Thump. The Bottom.
III
A description of my typewriter. The keyboard is about one foot wide. Each key is flush to the next and marked with a single letter of the alphabet, or with two punctuation signs, or with one number and one punctuation sign. The letters are not ordered as they are in the alphabet, alphabetically, but seemingly at random. It is possible that they are in code. Then there is a space bar. There is not, however, either a margin control or a carriage return. The platen is not visible, and I can never see the words I'm writing. What does it all look like? Perhaps it is made immediately into a book by automatic linotypists. Wouldn't that be nice? Or perhaps my words just go on and on in one endless line of writing. Or perhaps this typewriter is just a fraud and leaves no record at all.

Some thoughts on the subject of futility:

I might just as well be lifting weights as pounding at these keys. Or rolling stones up to the top of a hill from which they immediately roll back down. Yes, and I might as well tell lies as the truth. It makes no difference what I say.

That is what is so terrifying. Is "terrifying" the right word?

I seem to be feeling rather poorly today, but I've felt poorly before! In a few more days I'll be feeling all right again. I need only be patient, and then. . .

What do they want of me here? If only I could be sure that I were serving some good *purpose*. I cannot help worrying about such things. Time is running out. I'm hungry again. I suspect I am going crazy. That is the end of my story about the pogonophores.

A hiatus.

Don't *you* worry that I'm going crazy? What if I got catatonia? Then *you'd* have nothing to read. Unless they gave *you* my copies of the New York *Times*. It would serve *you* right.

You: the mirror that is denied to me, the shadow that I do not cast, my faithful observer, who reads each freshly-minted *pensée;* Reader.

You: Horrorshow monster, Bug-Eyes, Mad Scientist, Army Major, who prepares the wedding bed of my death and tempts me to it.

You: Other!

Speak to me!

YOU: What shall I say, Earthling?

I: Anything so long as it is another voice than my own, flesh that is not my own flesh, lies that I do not need to invent for myself. I'm not particular, I'm not proud. But I doubt sometimes—you won't think this is too melodramatic of me?—that I'm real.

YOU: I know the feeling. (Extending a tentacle) May I?

I: (Backing off) Later. Just now I thought we'd talk. (You begin to fade.)
There is so much about you that I don't understand. Your identity is not distinct. You change from one being to another as easily as I might switch channels

on a television set, if I had one. You are too secretive as well. You should get about in the world more. Go places, show yourself, enjoy life. If you're shy, I'll go out with you. You let yourself be undermined by fear, however.

YOU: Interesting. Yes, definitely most interesting. The subject evidences acute paranoid tendencies, fantasies with almost delusional intensity. Observe his tongue, his pulse, his urine. His stools are irregular. His teeth are bad. He is losing his hair.

I: I'm losing my mind.

YOU: He's losing his mind.

I: I'm dying.

YOU: He's dead.

(Fades until there is nothing but the golden glow of the eagle on his cap, a glint from the oak leaves on his shoulders.) But he has not died in vain. His country will always remember him, for by his death he has made this nation free.

(Curtain. Anthem.)

Hi, it's me again. Surely you haven't forgotten *me*? Your old friend, me? Listen carefully now—this is my plan. I'm going to escape from this damned prison, by God, and *you're* going to help me. 20 people may read what I write on this typewriter, and of those 20, 19 could see me rot here forever without batting an eyelash. But not number 20. Oh no! He—*you*—still has a conscience. He/you will send me a Sign. And when I've seen the Sign, I'll know that someone out there is trying to help. Oh, I won't expect miracles overnight. It may take months, years even, to work out a foolproof escape, but just the knowledge that there is someone out there trying to help will give me the strength to go on from day to day, from issue to issue of the *Times*.

You know what I sometimes wonder? I sometimes wonder why the *Times* doesn't have an editorial about me. They state their opinion on everything else—Castro's Cuba, the shame of our southern states, the sales tax, the first days of spring.

What about me!

I mean, isn't it an injustice the way *I'm* being treated? Doesn't anybody care and if not, why not? Don't tell me they don't know I'm here. I've been years now writing, writing. Surely they have some idea. Surely *someone* does!

These are serious questions. They demand serious appraisal. I insist that they be *answered*.

I don't really expect an answer, you know. I have no false hopes left, none. I know there's no Sign that will be shown me, that even if there is, it will be a lie, a lure to go on hoping. I know that I am alone in my fight against this injustice. I know all that—and *I don't care!* My will is still unbroken, and my spirit free. From my isolation, out of the stillness, from the depths of this white, white light, I say this to you—I DEFY YOU! Do you hear that? I said: I DEFY YOU!

Dinner again. Where does the time all go to?

While I was eating dinner I had an idea for something I was going to say here, but I seem to have forgotten what it was. If I remember, I'll jot it down. Meanwhile, I'll tell you about my other theory.

My *other* theory is that this is a squirrel cage. You know? Like the kind you find in a small town park. You might even have one of your own, since they don't have to be very big. A squirrel cage is like most any other kind of cage except it has an exercise wheel. The squirrel gets *into* the wheel and starts running. His running makes the wheel turn, and the turning of the wheel makes it necessary for him to keep running inside it. The exercise is supposed to keep the squirrel healthy. What I don't understand is why they put the squirrel in the cage in the first place. Don't they know what it's going to be like for the poor little squirrel? Or don't they care?

They don't care.

I remember now what it was I'd forgotten. I thought of a new story. I call it "An Afternoon at the Zoo." I made it up myself. It's very short, and it has a moral. This is my story:

AN AFTERNOON AT THE ZOO

This is the story about Alexandra. Alexandra was the wife of a famous journalist, who specialized in science reporting. His work took him to all parts of the country, and since they had not been blessed with children, Alexandra often accompanied him. However this often became very boring, so she had to find something to do to pass the time. If she had seen all the movies playing in the town they were in, she might go to a museum, or perhaps to a ball game, if she were interested in seeing a ball game that day. One day she went to a zoo.

Of course it was a small zoo, because this was a small town. Tasteful but not spectacular. There was a brook that meandered all about the grounds. Ducks and a lone black swan glided among the willow branches and waddled out onto the lawn to snap up bread crumbs from the visitors. Alexandra thought the swan was beautiful.

Then she went to a wooden building called the "Rodentiary." The cages advertised rabbits, otters, raccoons, etc. Inside the cages was a litter of nibbled vegetables and droppings of various shapes and colors. The animals must have been behind the wooden partitions, sleeping. Alexandra found this disappointing, but she told herself that rodents were hardly the most important thing to see at any zoo.

Nearby the Rodentiary, a black bear was sunning himself on a rock ledge. Alexandra walked all about the demi-lune of bars without seeing other members of the bear's family. He was an enormous bear.

She watched the seals splash about in their concrete pool, and then she moved on to find the Monkey House. She asked a friendly peanut vendor where it was, and he told her it was closed for repairs.

"How sad!" Alexandra exclaimed.

"Why don't you try *Snakes and Lizards?*" the peanut vendor asked.

Alexandra wrinkled her nose in disgust. She'd hated reptiles ever since she was a little girl. Even though the Monkey House was closed she bought a bag of peanuts and ate them herself. The peanuts made her thirsty, so she bought a soft drink and sipped it through a straw, worrying about her weight all the while.

She watched peacocks and a nervous antelope, then turned off on to a path that took her into a glade of trees. Poplar trees, perhaps. She was alone there, so she took off her shoes and wiggled her toes, or performed some equivalent action. She liked to be alone like this sometimes.

A file of heavy iron bars beyond the glade of trees drew Alexandra's attention. Inside the bars there was a man, dressed in a loose-fitting cotton suit—pajamas, most likely—held up about the waist with a sort of rope. He sat on the floor of his cage without looking at anything in particular. The sign at the base of the fence read:

Chordate.

"How lovely!" Alexandra exclaimed.

Actually, that's a very old story. I tell it a different way every time. Sometimes it goes on from the point where I left off. Sometimes Alexandra talks to the man behind the bars. Sometimes they fall in love, and she tries to help him escape. Sometimes they're both killed in the attempt, and that is *very* touching. Sometimes they get caught and are put behind the bars *together*. But because they love each other so much, imprisonment is easy to endure. That is also touching, in its way. Sometimes they make it to freedom. After that though, after they're free, I never know what to do with the story. However, I'm sure that if I were free myself, free of this cage, it would not be a problem.

One part of the story doesn't make much sense. Who would put a person in a zoo? Me, for instance. Who would do such a thing? Aliens? Are we back to aliens again? Who can say about aliens? I mean, *I* don't know anything about them.

My theory, my best theory, is that I'm being kept here by people. Just ordinary people. It's an ordinary zoo, and ordinary people come by to look at me through the walls. They read the things I type on this typewriter as it appears on a great illuminated billboard, like the one that spells out the news headlines around the sides of The Times Tower on 42nd Street. When I write something funny, they may laugh, and when I write something serious, such as an appeal for help, they probably get bored and stop reading. Or vice versa perhaps. In any case, they don't take what I say very seriously. None of them care that I'm inside here. To them I'm just another animal in a cage. You might object that a human being is not the same thing as an animal, but isn't he, after all? They, the spectators, seem to think so. In any case, none of them is going to help me get out. None of them thinks it's at all strange or unusual that I'm in here. None of them thinks it's wrong. That's the terrifying thing.

"Terrifying"?

It's not terrifying. How can it be? It's only a story, after all. Maybe *you* don't think it's a story, because you're out there reading it on the billboard, but I know it's a story because I have to sit here on this stool making it up. Oh, it might have been terrifying once upon a time, when I first got the idea, but I've been here now for years. Years. The story has gone on far too long. Nothing can be terrifying for years on end. I only *say* it's terrifying because, you know, I have to say something. Something or other. The only thing that could terrify me now is if someone were to come in. If they came in and said, "All right, Disch, you can go now." That, truly, would be terrifying.

THE
‗‗‗‗ ASIAN SHORE ‗‗‗‗

1.

There were voices on the cobbled street, and the sounds of motors. Footsteps, slamming doors, whistles, footsteps. He lived on the ground floor, so there was no way to avoid these evidences of the city's too abundant life. They accumulated in the room like so much dust, like the heaps of unanswered correspondence on the mottled tablecloth.

Every night he would drag a chair into the unfurnished back room—the guest room, as he liked to think of it—and look out over the tiled roofs and across the black waters of the Bosphorus at the lights of Usküdar. But the sounds penetrated this room too. He would sit there, in the darkness, drinking wine, waiting for her knock on the back door.

Or he might try to read: histories, books of travel, the long dull biography of Atatürk. A kind of sedation. Sometimes he would even begin a letter to his wife:

> *"Dear Janice,*
> *"No doubt you've been wondering what's become of me these last few months. . . ."*

But the trouble was that once that part had been written, the frail courtesies, the perfunctory reportage, he could not bring himself to say what *had* become of him.

Voices. . . .

It was just as well that he couldn't speak the language. For a while he had studied it, taxiing three times a week to Robert

College in Bebek, but the grammar, based on assumptions wholly alien to any other language he knew, with its wavering boundaries between verbs and nouns, nouns and adjectives, withstood every assault of his incorrigibly Aristotelian mind. He sat at the back of the classroom, behind the rows of American teen-agers, as sullen as convicts, as comically out of context as the machineries melting in a Dali landscape—sat there and parroted innocuous dialogues after the teacher, taking both roles in turn, first the trustful, inquisitive John, forever wandering alone and lost in the streets of Istanbul and Ankara, then the helpful, knowing Ahmet Bey. Neither of these interlocutors would admit what had become increasingly evident with each faltering word that John spoke—that he would wander these same streets for years, inarticulate, cheated, and despised.

But these lessons, while they lasted, had one great advantage. They provided an illusion of activity, an obelisk upon which the eye might focus amid the desert of each new day, something to move toward and then something to leave behind.

After the first month it had rained a great deal, and this provided him with a good excuse for staying in. He had mopped up the major attractions of the city in one week, and he persisted at sightseeing long afterward, even in doubtful weather, until at last he had checked off every mosque and ruin, every museum and cistern cited in boldface in the pages of his Hachette. He visited the cemetery of Eyüp, and he devoted an entire Sunday to the land walls, carefully searching for, though he could not read Greek, the inscriptions of the various Byzantine emperors. But more and more often on these excursions he would see the woman or the child or the woman and the child together, until he came almost to dread the sight of any woman or any child in the city. It was not an unreasonable dread.

And always, at nine o'clock, or ten at the very latest, she would come knocking at the door of the apartment. Or, if the outer door of the building had not been left ajar by the people upstairs, at the window of the front room. She knocked patiently, in little clusters of three or four raps spaced several seconds apart, never very loud. Sometimes, but only if she were in the hall, she would accompany her knocking with a few words in Turkish, usually *Yavuz! Yavuz!* He had asked the clerk at the mail desk of the consulate what this meant, for he couldn't find it in his dictionary. It was a common Turkish name, a man's name.

His name was John. John Benedict Harris. He was an American.

She seldom stayed out there for more than half an hour any one night, knocking and calling to him, or to this imaginary Yavuz, and he would remain all that while in the chair in the unfurnished room, drinking Kavak and watching the ferries move back and forth on the dark water between Kabatas and Usküdar, the European and the Asian shore.

He had seen her first outside the fortress of Rumeli Hisar. It was the day, shortly after he'd arrived in the city, that he had come out to register at Robert College. After paying his fees and inspecting the library, he had come down the hill by the wrong path, and there it had stood, mammoth and majestically improbable, a gift. He did not know its name, and his Hachette was at the hotel. There was just the raw fact of the fortress, a mass of gray stone, its towers and crenelations, the gray Bosphorus below. He angled for a photograph, but even that far away it was too big—one could not frame the whole of it in a single shot.

He left the road, taking a path through dry brush that promised to circle the fortress. As he approached, the walls reared higher and higher. Before such walls there could be no question of an assault.

He saw her when she was about fifty feet away. She came toward him on the footpath, carrying a large bundle wrapped in newspaper and bound with twine. Her clothes were the usual motley of washed-out cotton prints that all the poorer women of the city went about in, but she did not, like most other women of her kind, attempt to pull her shawl across her face when she noticed him.

But perhaps it was only that her bundle would have made this conventional gesture of modesty awkward, for after that first glance she did at least lower her eyes to the path. No, it was hard to discover any clear portent in this first encounter.

As they passed each other he stepped off the path, and she did mumble some word in Turkish. Thank you, he supposed. He watched her until she reached the road, wondering whether she would look back, and she didn't.

He followed the walls of the fortress down the steep

crumbling hillside to the shore road without finding an entrance. It amused him to think that there might not be one. Between the water and the barbicans there was only a narrow strip of highway.

An absolute daunting structure.

The entrance, which did exist, was just to the side of the central tower. He paid five lire admission and another two and a half lire to bring in his camera.

Of the three principal towers, visitors were allowed to climb only the one at the center of the eastern wall that ran along the Bosphorus. He was out of condition and mounted the enclosed spiral staircase slowly. The stone steps had evidently been pirated from other buildings. Every so often he recognized a fragment of a classic entablature of a wholly inappropriate intaglio design—a Greek cross or some crude Byzantine eagle. Each footfall became a symbolic conquest: one could not ascend these stairs without becoming implicated in the fall of Constantinople.

This staircase opened out into a kind of wooden catwalk clinging to the inner wall of the tower at a height of about sixty feet. The silolike space was resonant with the coo and flutter of invisible pigeons, and somewhere the wind was playing with a metal door, creaking it open, banging it shut. Here, if he so wished, he might discover portents.

He crept along the wooden platform, both hands grasping the iron rail stapled to the stone wall, feeling just an agreeable amount of terror, sweating nicely. It occurred to him how much this would have pleased Janice, whose enthusiasm for heights had equaled his. He wondered when, if ever, he would see her again, and what she would be like. By now undoubtedly she had begun divorce proceedings. Perhaps she was already no longer his wife.

The platform led to another stone staircase, shorter than the first, which ascended to the creaking metal door. He pushed it open and stepped out amid a flurry of pigeons into the full dazzle of the noon, the wide splendor of the elevation, sunlight above and the bright bow of water beneath—and, beyond the water, the surreal green of the Asian hills, hundred-breasted Cybele. It seemed, all of this, to demand some kind of affirmation, a yell, or large gestures. But he didn't feel up to yelling, or large gestures. He could only admire, at this distance, the illusion of tactility, hills as flesh, an illusion that could be heightened if he laid his hands, still sweaty from his passage along the catwalk, on the rough warm stone of the balustrade.

Looking down the side of the tower at the empty road he saw her again, standing at the very edge of the water. She was looking up at him. When he noticed her she lifted both hands above her head, as though signaling, and shouted something that, even if he could have heard it properly, he would surely not have understood. He supposed that she was asking to have her picture taken, so he turned the setting ring to the fastest speed to compensate for the glare from the water. She stood directly below the tower, and there seemed no way to frame an interesting composition. He released the shutter. Woman, water, asphalt road: it would be a snapshot, not a photograph, and he didn't believe in taking snapshots.

The woman continued to call up to him, arms raised in that same hieratic gesture. It made no sense. He waved to her and smiled uncertainly. It was something of a nuisance, really. He would have preferred to have this scene to himself. One climbed towers, after all, in order to be alone.

Altin, the man who had found his apartment for him, worked as a commission agent for carpet and jewelry shops in the Grand Bazaar. He would strike up conversations with English and American tourists and advise them what to buy, and where, and how much to pay. They spent one day looking and settled on an apartment building near Taksim, the commemorative traffic circle that served the European quarter of the city as a kind of Broadway. The several banks of Istanbul demonstrated their modern character here with neon signs, and in the center of the traffic circle, life-size, Atatürk led a small but representative group of his countrymen toward their bright, Western destiny.

The apartment was thought (by Altin) to partake of this same advanced spirit: it had central heating, a sit-down toilet, a bathtub, and a defunct but prestigious refrigerator. The rent was six hundred lire a month, which came to sixty-six dollars at the official rate but only fifty dollars at the rate Altin gave. He was anxious to move out of the hotel, so he agreed to a six-month lease.

He hated it from the day he moved in. Except for the shreds of a lousy sofa in the guest room, which he obliged the landlord to remove, he left everything as he found it. Even the blurry pinups from a Turkish girlie magazine remained where they were to cover the cracks in the new plaster. He was determined to make no accommodations: he might have to live in this city; it was not required that he *enjoy* it.

Every day he picked up his mail at the consulate. He sampled a variety of restaurants. He saw the sights and made notes for his book.

On Thursdays he visited a *hamam* to sweat out the accumulated poisons of the week and to be kneaded and stomped by a masseur.

He supervised the growth of his young mustache.

He rotted, like a jar of preserves left open and forgotten on the top shelf of a cupboard.

He learned that there was a special Turkish word for the rolls of dirt that are scraped off the skin after a steambath, and another that imitated the sound of boiling water: *fuker, fuker, fuker*. Boiling water signified, to the Turkish mind, the first stages of sexual arousal. It was roughly equivalent to the stateside notion of "electricity."

Occasionally, as he began to construct his own internal map of the unpromising alleyways and ruinous staircase streets of his neighborhood, he fancied that he saw her, that same woman. It was hard to be certain. She would always be some distance away, or he might catch just a glimpse out of the corner of his eye. If it were the same woman, nothing at this stage suggested that she was pursuing him. It was, at most, a coincidence.

In any case, he could not be certain. Her face had not been unusual, and he did not have the photograph to consult, for he had spoiled the entire roll of film removing it from the camera.

Sometimes after one of these failed encounters he would feel a slight uneasiness. It amounted to no more than that.

He met the boy in Usküdar. It was during the first severe cold spell, in mid-November. His first trip across the Bosphorus, and when he stepped off the ferry onto the very soil (or, anyhow, the very asphalt) of this new continent, the largest of all, he could feel the great mass of it beckoning him toward its vast eastward vortex, tugging at him, sucking at his soul.

It had been his first intention, back in New York, to stop two months at most in Istanbul, learn the language; then into Asia. How often he had mesmerized himself with the litany of its marvels: the grand mosques of Kayseri and Sivas, of Beysehir and Afyon Karahisar; the isolate grandeur of Ararat and then, still moving east, the shores of the Caspian; Meshed, Kabul, the Himalayas. It was all these that reached out to him now, singing, stretching forth their siren arms, inviting him to their whirlpool.

And he? He refused. Though he could feel the charm of the invitation, he refused. Though he might have wished very much to unite with them, he still refused. For he had tied himself to the mast, where he was proof against their call. He had his apartment in that city which stood just outside their reach, and he would stay there until it was time to return. In the spring he was going back to the States.

But he did allow the sirens this much—that he would abandon the rational mosque-to-mosque itinerary laid down by his Hachette and entrust the rest of the day to serendipity. While the sun still shone that afternoon they might lead him where they would.

Asphalt gave way to cobbles, and cobbles to packed dirt. The squalor here was on a much less majestic scale than in Stambul, where even the most decrepit hovels had been squeezed by the pressure of population to heights of three and four stories. In Usküdar the same wretched buildings sprawled across the hills like beggars whose crutches had been kicked out from under them, supine; through their rags of unpainted wood one could see the scabbed flesh of mud-and-wattle. As he threaded his way from one dirt street to the next and found each of them sustaining this one unvarying tone, without color, without counterpoint, he began to conceive a new Asia, not of mountains and vast plains, but this same slum rolling on perpetually across grassless hills, a continuum of drabness, of sheer dumb extent.

Because he was short and because he would not dress the part of an American, he could go through these streets without calling attention to himself. The mustache too, probably, helped. Only his conscious, observing eyes (the camera had spoiled a second roll of film and was being repaired) would have betrayed him as a tourist today. Indeed, Altin had assured him (intending, no doubt, a compliment) that as soon as he learned to speak the language he would pass for a Turk.

It grew steadily colder throughout the afternoon. The wind moved a thick veil of mist over the sun and left it there. As the mists thinned and thickened, as the flat disc of sun, sinking westward, would fade and brighten, the vagaries of light whispered conflicting rumors about these houses and their dwellers. But he did not wish to stop and listen. He already knew more concerning these things than he wanted to. He set off at a quicker pace in the supposed direction of the landing stage.

The boy stood crying beside a public fountain, a water faucet projecting from a crude block of concrete, at the intersection of two narrow streets. Five years old, perhaps six. He was carrying a large plastic bucket of water in each hand, one bright red, the other turquoise. The water had splashed over his thin trousers and bare feet.

At first he supposed the boy cried only because of the cold. The damp ground must be near to freezing. To walk on it in bare wet feet. . . .

Then he saw the slippers. They were what he would have called shower slippers, small die-stamped ovals of blue plastic with single thongs that had to be grasped between the first and second toes.

The boy would stoop over and force the thongs between his stiff, cold-reddened toes, but after only a step or two the slippers would again fall off his numb feet. With each frustrated progress more water would slop over the sides of the buckets. He could not keep the slippers on his feet, and he would not walk off without them.

With this understanding came a kind of horror, a horror of his own helplessness. He could not go up to the boy and ask him where he lived, lift him and carry him—he was so small—to his home. Nor could he scold the child's parents for having sent him out on this errand without proper shoes or winter clothes. He could not even take up the buckets and have the child lead him to his home. For each of these possibilities demanded that he be able to *speak* to the boy, and this he could not do.

What *could* he do? Offer money? As well offer him, at such a moment, a pamphlet from the U.S. Information Agency!

There was, in fact, nothing, *nothing* he could do.

The boy had become aware of him. Now that he had a sympathetic audience he let himself cry in earnest. Lowering the two buckets to the ground and pointing at these and at the slippers, he spoke pleadingly to this grown-up stranger, to this rescuer, words in Turkish.

He took a step backward, a second step, and the boy shouted at him, what message of pain or uncomprehending indignation he would never know. He turned away and ran back along the street that had brought him to this crossway. It was another hour before he found the landing stage. It had begun to snow.

As he took his seat inside the ferry he found himself glancing at the other passengers, as though expecting to find her there among them.

The next day he came down with a cold. The fever rose through the night. He woke several times, and it was always their two faces that he carried with him from the dreams, like souvenirs whose origin and purpose have been forgotten; the woman at Rumeli Hisar, the child in Usküdar: some part of his mind had already begun to draw the equation between them.

2.

It was the thesis of his first book that the quiddity of architecture, its chief claim to an esthetic interest, was its arbitrariness. Once the lintels were lying on the posts, once some kind of roof had been spread across the hollow space, then anything else that might be done was gratuitous. Even the lintel and the post, the roof, the space below, these were gratuitous as well. Stated thus it was a mild enough notion; the difficulty was in training the eye to see the whole world of usual forms—patterns of brick, painted plaster, carved and carpentered wood—not as "buildings" and "streets" but as an infinite series of free and arbitrary choices. There was no place in such a scheme for orders, styles, sophistication, taste. Every artifact of the city was anomalous, unique, but living there in the midst of it all you could not allow yourself too fine a sense of this fact. If you did. . .

It had been his task, these last three or four years, to re-educate his eye and mind to just this condition, of innocence. His was the very reverse of the Romantics' aims, for he did not expect to find himself, when this ideal state of "raw" perception was reached (it never would be, of course, for innocence, like justice, is an absolute; it may be approached but never attained), any closer to nature. Nature, as such, did not concern him. What he sought, on the contrary, was a sense of the great artifice of things, of structures, of the immense interminable wall that has been built just to exclude nature.

The attention that his first book had received showed that he had been at least partially successful, but he knew (and who better?) how far short his aim had fallen, how many clauses of the perceptual social contract he had never even thought to question.

So, since it was now a matter of ridding himself of the sense of the familiar, he had had to find some better laboratory for this purpose than New York, somewhere that he could be, more naturally, an alien. This much seemed obvious to him.

It had not seemed so obvious to his wife.

He did not insist. He was willing to be reasonable. He would talk about it. He talked about it whenever they were together—at dinner, at her friends' parties (his friends didn't seem to give parties), in bed—and it came down to this, that Janice objected not so much to the projected trip as to his entire program, the thesis itself.

No doubt her reasons were sound. The sense of the arbitrary did not stop at architecture; it embraced—or it would, if he let it—all phenomena. If there were no fixed laws that governed the furbelows and arabesques out of which a city is composed, there were equally no laws (or only arbitrary laws, which is the same as none at all) to define the relationships woven into the lattice of that city, relationships between man and man, man and woman, John and Janice.

And indeed this had already occurred to him, though he had not spoken of it to her before. He had often had to stop, in the midst of some quotidian ritual like dining out, and take his bearings. As the thesis developed, as he continued to sift away layer after layer of preconception, he found himself more and more astonished at the size of the demesne that recognized the sovereignty of convention. At times he even thought he could trace in his wife's slightest gesture or in her aptest phrase or in a kiss some hint of the Palladian rule book from which it had been derived. Perhaps with practice one

would be able to document the entire history of her styles—
here an echo of the Gothic Revival, there an imitation of
Mies.

When his application for a Guggenheim was rejected, he
decided he would make the trip by himself, using the bit of
money that was still left from the book. Though he saw no
necessity for it, he had agreed to Janice's request for a
divorce. They parted on the best of terms. She had even seen
him to the boat.

The wet snow would fall for a day, two days, forming
knee-deep drifts in the open spaces of the city, in paved
courtyards, on vacant lots. Cold winds polished the slush of
streets and sidewalks to dull-gleaming lumpy ice. The steeper
hills became impassable. The snow and the ice would linger a
few days and then a sudden thaw would send it all pouring
down the cobbled hillside in a single afternoon, brief alpine
cataracts of refuse and brown water. A patch of tolerable
weather might follow this flood, and then another blizzard.
Altin assured him that this was an unusually fierce winter,
unprecedented.

A spiral diminishing.

A tightness.

And each day the light fell more obliquely across the white
hills and was more quickly spent.

One night, returning from a movie, he slipped on the iced
cobbles just outside the door of his building, tearing both
knees of his trousers beyond any possibility of repair. It was
the only winter suit he had brought. Altin gave him the name
of a tailor who could make another suit quickly and for less
money than he would have had to pay for a readymade. Altin
did all the bargaining with the tailor and even selected the
fabric, a heavy wool-rayon blend of a sickly and slightly
iridescent blue, the muted, imprecise color of the more
unhappy breeds of pigeons. He understood nothing of the fine
points of tailoring, and so he could not decide what it was
about this suit—whether the shape of the lapels, the length
of the back vent, the width of the pantlegs—that made it
seem so different from other suits he had worn, so
much . . . smaller. And yet it fitted his figure with the exact-
ness one expects of a tailored suit. If he looked smaller now,
and thicker, perhaps that was how he *ought* to look and his

previous suits had been telling lies about him all these years. The color too performed some nuance of metamorphosis: his skin, balanced against this blue-gray sheen, seemed less "tan" than sallow. When he wore it he became, to all appearances, a Turk.

Not that he wanted to look like a Turk. Turks were, by and large, a homely lot. He only wished to avoid the other Americans who abounded here even at this nadir of the off-season. As their numbers decreased, their gregariousness grew more implacable. The smallest sign—a copy of *Newsweek* or the *Herald-Tribune,* a word of English, an airmail letter with its telltale canceled stamp—could bring them down at once in the full fury of their good-fellowship. It was convenient to have some kind of camouflage, just as it was necessary to learn their haunts in order to avoid them: Divan Yolu and Cumhuriyet Cadessi, the American Library and the consulate, as well as some eight or ten of the principal well-touristed restaurants.

Once the winter had firmly established itself he also put a stop to his sightseeing. Two months of Ottoman mosques and Byzantine rubble had brought his sense of the arbitrary to so fine a pitch that he no longer required the stimulus of the monumental. His own rooms—a rickety table, the flowered drapes, the blurry lurid pinups, the intersecting planes of walls and ceilings—could present as great a plentitude of "problems" as the grand mosques of Suleiman or Sultan Ahmet with all their mihrabs and minbers, their stalactite niches and faienced walls.

Too great a plenitude, actually. Day and night the rooms nagged at him. They diverted his attention from anything else he might try to do. He knew them with the enforced intimacy with which a prisoner knows his cell—every defect of construction, every failed grace, the precise incidence of the light at each hour of the day. Had he taken the trouble to rearrange the furniture, to put up his own prints and maps, to clean the windows and scrub the floors, to fashion some kind of bookcase (all his books remained in their two shipping cases), he might have been able to blot out these alien presences by the sheer strength of self-assertion, as one can mask bad odors with incense or the smell of flowers. But this would have been admitting defeat. It would have shown how unequal he was to his own thesis.

As a compromise he began to spend his afternoons in a

café a short distance down the street on which he lived. There he would sit, at the table nearest the front window, contemplating the spirals of steam that rose from the small corolla of his tea glass. At the back of the long room, beneath the tarnished brass tea urn, there were always two old men playing backgammon. The other patrons sat by themselves and gave no indication that their thoughts were in any way different from his. Even when no one was smoking, the air was pungent with the charcoal fires of nargilehs. Conversation of any kind was rare. The nargilehs bubbled, tiny dice rattled in a leather cup, a newspaper rustled, a glass chinked against its saucer.

His red notebook always lay ready at hand on the table, and on the notebook his ballpoint pen. Once he had placed them there, he never touched them again till it was time to leave.

Though less and less in the habit of analyzing sensation and motive, he was aware that the special virtue of this café was as a bastion, the securest he possessed, against the now omnipresent influence of the arbitrary. If he sat here peacefully, observing the requirements of the ritual, a decorum as simple as the rules of backgammon, gradually the elements in the space about him would cohere. Things settled, unproblematically, into their own contours. Taking the flower-shaped glass as its center, this glass that was now only and exactly a glass of tea, his perceptions slowly spread out through the room, like the concentric ripples passing across the surface of an ornamental pond, embracing all its objects at last in a firm, noumenal grasp. Just so. The room was just what a room should be. It contained him.

He did not take notice of the first rapping on the café window, though he was aware, by some small cold contraction of his thoughts, of an infringement of the rules. The second time he looked up.

They were together. The woman and the child.

He had seen them each on several occasions since his trip to Usküdar three weeks before. The boy once on the torn-up sidewalk outside the consulate, and another time sitting on the railing of the Karaköy bridge. Once, riding in a *dolmus* to Taksim, he had passed within a scant few feet of the woman and they had exchanged a glance of unambiguous recognition. But he had never seen them together before.

But could he be certain, now, that it *was* those two? He saw a woman and a child, and the woman was rapping with one bony knuckle on the window for someone's attention. For his? If he could have seen her face. . . .

He looked at the other occupants of the café. The backgammon players. A fat, unshaven man reading a newspaper. A dark-skinned man with spectacles and a flaring mustache. The two old men, on opposite sides of the room, puffing on nargilehs. None of them paid any attention to the woman's rapping.

He stared resolutely at his glass of tea, no longer a paradigm of its own necessity. It had become a foreign object, an artifact picked up out of the rubble of a buried city, a shard.

The woman continued to rap at the window. At last the owner of the café went outside and spoke a few sharp words to her. She left without making a reply.

He sat with his cold tea another fifteen minutes. Then he went out into the street. There was no sign of them. He returned the hundred yards to his apartment as calmly as he could. Once inside he fastened the chain lock. He never went back to the café.

When the woman came that night, knocking at his door, it was not a surprise.

And every night, at nine or, at the very latest, ten o'clock. *Yavuz! Yavuz!* Calling to him.

He stared at the black water, the lights of the other shore. He wondered, often, when he would give in, when he would open the door.

But it was surely a mistake. Some accidental *resemblance*. He was not Yavuz.

John Benedict Harris. An American.

If there had ever been one, if there had ever been a Yavuz.

The man who had tacked the pinups on the walls?

Two women, they might have been twins, in heavy eye make-up, garter belts, mounted on the same white horse. Lewdly smiling.

A bouffant hairdo, puffy lips. Drooping breasts with large brown nipples. A couch.

A beachball. Her skin dark. Bikini. Laughing. Sand. The water unnaturally blue.

Snapshots.

Had these ever been *his* fantasies? If not, why could he not bring himself to take them off the walls? He had prints by Piranesi. A blowup of Sagrada Familia in Barcelona. The Tchernikov sketch. He could have covered the walls.

He found himself trying to imagine of this Yavuz . . . what he must be like.

3.

Three days after Christmas he received a card from his wife, postmarked Nevada. Janice, he knew, did not believe in Christmas cards. It showed an immense stretch of white desert—a salt-flat, he supposed—with purple mountains in the distance, and above the purple mountains, a heavily retouched sunset. Pink. There were no figures in this landscape, or any sign of vegetation. Inside she had written:

"Merry Christmas! Janice."

The same day he received a manila envelope with a copy of *Art News*. A noncommittal note from his friend Raymond was paperclipped to the cover: "Thought you might like to see this. R."

In the back pages of the magazine there was a long and unsympathetic review of his book by F. R. Robertson. Robertson was known as an authority on Hegel's esthetics. He maintained that *Homo Arbitrans* was nothing but a compendium of truisms and—without seeming to recognize any contradiction in this—a hopelessly muddled reworking of Hegel.

Years ago he had dropped out of a course taught by Robertson after attending the first two lectures. He wondered if Robertson could have remembered this.

The review contained several errors of fact, one misquotation, and failed to mention his central argument, which was not, admittedly, dialectical. He decided he should write a reply and laid the magazine beside his typewriter to remind himself. The same evening he spilled the better part of a bottle of wine on it, so he tore out the review and threw the magazine into the garbage with his wife's card.

The necessity for a movie had compelled him into the streets and kept him in the streets, wandering from marquee to marquee, long after the drizzle of the afternoon had thickened to rain. In New York when this mood came over him he would take in a double bill of science-fiction films or Westerns on 42nd Street, but here, though cinemas abounded in the absence of television, only the glossiest Hollywood kitsch was presented with the original soundtrack. B-movies were invariably dubbed in Turkish.

So obsessive was this need that he almost passed the man in the skeleton suit without noticing him. He trudged back and forth on the sidewalk, a sodden refugee from Halloween, followed by a small Hamelin of excited children. The rain had curled the corners of his poster (it served him now as an umbrella) and caused the inks to run. He could make out:

KIL G
STA   LDA

After Atatürk, the skeleton-suited Kiling was the principal figure of the new Turkish folklore. Every newsstand was heaped with magazines and comics celebrating his adventures, and here he was himself, or his avatar at least, advertising his latest movie. Yes, and there, down the side street, was the theater where it was playing: *Kiling Istanbulda*. Or: *Kiling in Istanbul*. Beneath the colossal letters a skull-masked Kiling threatened to kiss a lovely and obviously reluctant blonde, while on the larger poster across the street he gunned down two well-dressed men. One could not decide, on the evidence of such tableaus as these, whether Kiling was fundamentally good, like Batman, or bad, like Fantomas. So. . . .

He bought a ticket. He would find out. It was the name that intrigued him. It was, distinctly, an English name.

He took a seat four rows from the front just as the feature began, immersing himself gratefully into the familiar urban imagery. Reduced to black and white and framed by darkness, the customary vistas of Istanbul possessed a heightened reality. New American cars drove through the narrow streets at perilous speeds. An old doctor was strangled by an unseen assailant. Then for a long while nothing of interest happened. A tepid romance developed between the blond singer and the young architect, while a number of gangsters, or diplomats, tried to obtain possession of the doctor's black valise. After a confusing sequence in which four of these men were killed in an explosion, the valise fell into the hands of Kiling. But it proved to be empty.

The police chased Kiling over tiled rooftops. But this was a proof only of his agility, not of his guilt: the police can often make mistakes in these matters. Kiling entered, through a window, the bedroom of the blond singer, waking her. Contrary to the advertising posters outside, he made no attempt to kiss her. He addressed her in a hollow bass voice. The editing seemed to suggest that Kiling was actually the young architect whom the singer loved, but as his mask was never removed this too remained in doubt.

He felt a hand on his shoulder.

He was certain it was she and he would not turn around. Had she followed him to the theater? If he rose to leave, would she make a scene? He tried to ignore the pressure of the hand, staring at the screen where the young architect had just received a mysterious telegram. His hands gripped tightly into his thighs. His hands: the hands of John Benedict Harris.

"Mr. Harris, hello!"

A man's voice. He turned around. It was Altin.

"Altin."

Altin smiled. His face flickered. "Yes. Do you think it is anyone?"

"Anyone else?"

"Yes."

"No."

"You are seeing this movie?"

"Yes."

"It is not in English. It is in Turkish."

"I know."

Several people in nearby rows were hissing for them to be quiet. The blond singer had gone down into one of the city's large cisterns. Binbirdirek. He himself had been there. The editing created an illusion that it was larger than it actually was.

"We will come up there," Altin whispered.

He nodded.

Altin sat on his right, and Altin's friend took the seat remaining empty on his left. Altin introduced his friend in a whisper. His name was Yavuz. He did not speak English.

Reluctantly he shook hands with Yavuz.

It was difficult, thereafter, to give his full attention to the film. He kept glancing sideways at Yavuz. He was about his own height and age, but then this seemed to be true of half the men in Istanbul. An unexceptional face, eyes that glistened moistly in the half-light reflected from the screen.

Kiling was climbing up the girders of the building being constructed on a high hillside. In the distance the Bosphorous snaked past misted hills.

There was something so unappealing in almost every Turkish face. He had never been able to pin it down: some weakness of bone structure, the narrow cheekbones; the strong vertical lines that ran down from the hollows of the eyes to the corner of the mouth; the mouth itself, narrow, flat, inflexible. Or some subtler disharmony among all these elements.

Yavuz. A common name, the mail clerk had said.

In the last minutes of the movie there was a fight between two figures dressed in skeleton suits, a true and a false Kiling. One of them was thrown to his death from the steel beams of the unfinished building. The villain, surely—but had it been the true or the false Kiling who died? And come to think of it, which of them had frightened the singer in her bedroom, strangled the old doctor, stolen the valise?

"Did you like it?" Altin asked as they crowded toward the exit.

"Yes, I did."

"And did you understand what the people said?"

"Some of it. Enough."

Altin spoke for a while to Yavuz, who then turned to address his new friend from America in rapid Turkish.

He shook his head apologetically. Altin and Yavuz laughed.

"He says to you that you have the same suit."

"Yes, I noticed that as soon as the lights came on."

"Where do you go now, Mr. Harris?"

"What time is it?"

They were outside the theater. The rain had moderated to a drizzle. Altin looked at his watch. "Seven o'clock. And a half."

"I must go home now."

"We will come with you and buy a bottle of wine. Yes?"

He looked uncertainly at Yavuz. Yavuz smiled.

And when she came tonight, knocking at his door and calling for Yavuz?

"Not tonight, Altin."

"No?"

"I am a little sick."

"Yes?"

"Sick. I have a fever. My head aches." He put his hand, mimetically, to his forehead, and as he did he *could* feel both the fever and the headache. "Some other time perhaps. I'm sorry."

Altin shrugged skeptically.

He shook hands with Altin and then with Yavuz. Clearly, they both felt they had been snubbed.

Returning to his apartment he took an indirect route that avoided the dark side streets. The tone of the movie lingered, like the taste of a liqueur, to enliven the rhythm of cars and crowds, deepen the chiaroscuro of headlights and shop windows. Once, leaving the Eighth Street Cinema after *Jules et Jim,* he had discovered all the street signs of the Village translated into French; now the same law of magic allowed him to think that he could understand the fragmented conversation of passers-by. The meaning of an isolated phrase registered with the self-evident uninterpreted immediacy of "fact," the nature of the words mingling with the nature of things. Just so. Each knot in the net of language slipped, without any need of explication, into place. Every nuance of glance and inflection fitted, like a tailored suit, the contours of that moment, this street, the light, his conscious mind.

Inebriated by this fictive empathy he turned into his own darker street at last and almost walked past the woman—who fitted like every other element of the scene, so well the corner where she'd taken up her watch—without noticing her.

"You!" he said and stopped.

They stood four feet apart, regarding each other carefully. Perhaps she had been as little prepared for this confrontation as he.

Her thick hair was combed back in stiff waves from a low forehead, falling in massive parentheses to either side of her thin face. Pitted skin, flesh wrinkled in concentration around small pale lips. And tears—yes, tears—just forming in the corners of her staring eyes. With one hand she held a small parcel wrapped in newspaper and string, with the other she clutched the bulky confusion of her skirts. She wore several layers of clothing, rather than a coat, against the cold.

A slight erection stirred and tangled in the flap of his cotton underpants. He blushed. Once, reading a paperback edition of Krafft-Ebing, the same embarrassing thing had happened. That time it had been a description of necrophilia.

God, he thought, *if she notices!*

She whispered to him, lowering her gaze. To him, to Yavuz.

To come home with her.... Why did he?... Yavuz, Yavuz, Yavuz... she needed... and his son....

"I don't *understand* you," he insisted. "Your words make no sense to me. I am an American. My name is John Benedict Harris, not Yavuz. You're making a mistake—can't you see that?"

She nodded her head. "Yavuz."

"*Not* Yavuz! *Yok! Yok, yok!*"

And a word that meant "love" but not exactly that. Her hand tightened in the folds of her several skirts, raising them to show the thin, black-stockinged ankles.

"No!"

She moaned.

... wife ... his home ... Yalova ... his life.

"Damn you, go away!"

Her hand let go her skirts and darted quickly to his shoulder, digging into the cheap cloth. Her other hand shoved the wrapped parcel at him. He pushed her back but she clung fiercely, shrieking his name: *Yavuz!* He struck her face.

She fell on the wet cobbles. He backed away. The greasy parcel was in his left hand. She pushed herself up to her feet. Tears flowed along the vertical channels from eyes to mouth. A Turkish face. Blood dripped slowly out of one nostril. She began to walk away in the direction of Taksim.

"And don't return, do you understand? Stay away from me!" His voice cracked.

When she was out of sight he looked at the parcel in his hands. He knew he ought not to open it, that the wisest course was to throw it into the nearest garbage can. But even as he warned himself, his fingers had snapped the string.

A large lukewarm doughy mass of *borek*. And an orange. The saliva sprouted in his mouth at the acrid smell of the cheese.

No!
He had not had dinner that night. He was hungry. He ate it. Even the orange.

During the month of January he made only two entries in his notebook. The first, undated, was a long extract copied from A. H. Lybyer's book on the Janissaries, the great slave-corps of the sultans, *The Government of the Ottoman Empire in the Time of Suleiman the Magnificent*. The passage read:

Perhaps no more daring experiment has been tried on a large scale upon the face of the earth than that embodied in the Ottoman Ruling Institution. Its nearest ideal analogue is found in the Republic of Plato, its nearest actual parallel in the Mamluk system of Egypt; but it was not restrained within the aristocratic Hellenic limitations of the first, and it subdued and outlived the second. In the United States of America men have risen from the rude work of the backwoods to the presidential chair, but they have done so by their own effort and not through the gradations of a system carefully organized to push them forward. The Roman Catholic Church can still train a peasant to become a pope, but it has never begun by choosing its candidates almost exclusively from families which profess a hostile religion. The Ottoman system deliberately took slaves and made them ministers of state. It took boys from the sheep-run and the plough-tail and made them courtiers and the husbands of princesses; it took young men whose ancestors had borne the Christian name for centuries and made them rulers in the greatest of Muhammadan states, and soldiers and generals in invincible armies whose chief joy it was to beat down the Cross and elevate the Crescent. It never asked its novices "Who was your father?" or "What do you know?" or even "Can you speak our tongue?" but it studied their faces and their frames and said: "You shall be a soldier and, if you show yourself worthy, a general," or "You shall be a scholar and a gentleman and, if the ability lies in you, a governor and a prime minister." Grandly disregarding the fabric of fundamental customs which is called "human nature," and those religious and social prejudices which are thought to be almost as deep as life itself, the Ottoman system took children forever from parents, discouraged family cares among its members through their most active years, allowed them no certain hold on property, gave them no definite promise that their sons and daughters would profit by their success and sacrifice, raised and lowered them with no regard for ancestry or previous distinction, taught them a strange law, ethics, and religion, and ever kept them conscious of a sword raised above their heads which might put an end at any moment to a brilliant career along a matchless path of human glory.

The second and briefer entry was dated the twenty-third of January and read as follows:

"Heavy rains yesterday. I stayed in drinking. She came around at her usual hour. This morning when I put on my brown shoes to go out shopping they were wet through. Two hours to dry them out over the heater. Yesterday I wore only my sheepskin slippers—I did not leave the building once."

4.

A human face is a construction, an artifact. The mouth is a little door, and the eyes are windows that look at the street, and all the rest of it, the flesh, the bone beneath, is a wall to which any manner of ornament may be affixed, gewgaws of whatever style or period one takes a fancy to—swags hung below the cheeks and chin, lines chiseled or smoothed away, a recession emphasized, a bit of vegetation here and there. Each addition or subtraction, however minor in itself, will affect the entire composition. Thus, the hair that he had trimmed a bit closer to the temples restores hegemony to the vertical elements of a face that is now noticeably *narrower*. Or is this exclusively a matter of proportion and emphasis? For he has lost weight too (one cannot stop eating regularly without some shrinkage), and the loss has been appreciable. A new darkness has given definition to the always incipient pouches below his eyes, a darkness echoed by the new hollowness of his cheeks.

But the chief agent of metamorphosis is the mustache, which has grown full enough now to obscure the modeling of his upper lip. The ends, which had first shown a tendency to droop, have developed, by his nervous habit of twisting them about his fingers, the flaring upward curve of a scimitar (or *pala*, after which in Turkey this style of mustache is named: *pala biyik*). It is this, the baroque mustache, not a face, that he sees when he looks in a mirror.

Then there is the whole question of "expression," its quickness, constancy, the play of intelligence, the characteristic "tone" and the hundreds upon hundreds of possible gradations within the range of that tone, the eyes' habits of irony and candor, the betraying tension or slackness of a lip. Yet it is scarcely necessary to go into this at all, for his face, when he sees it, or when anyone sees it, could not be said to *have* an expression. What was there, after all, for him to express?

The blurring of edges, whole days lost, long hours awake in bed, books scattered about the room like little animal corpses to be nibbled at when he grew hungry, the endless cups of tea, the tasteless cigarettes. Wine, at least, did what it was supposed to do—it took away the sting. Not that he felt the sting these days with any poignance. But perhaps without the wine he *would* have.

He piled the nonreturnable bottles in the bathtub, exercising in this act (if in no other) the old discrimination, the "compulsive tact" he had made so much of in his book.

The drapes were always drawn. The lights were left burning at all hours, even when he slept, even when he was out, three sixty-watt bulbs in a metal chandelier hanging just out of plumb.

Voices from the street impinged. Vendors in the morning, and the metallic screak of children. At night the radio in the apartment below, drunken arguments. Scatterings of words, like illuminated signs glimpsed driving on a thruway, at high speeds, at night.

Two bottles of wine were not enough if he started early in the afternoon, but three could make him sick.

And though the hours crawled, like wounded insects, so slowly across the floor, the days rushed by in a torrent. The sunlight slipped across the Bosphorus so quickly that there was scarcely time to rise and see it.

One morning when he woke there was a balloon on a stick propped in the dusty flower vase atop his dresser. A crude Mickey Mouse was stenciled on the bright red rubber. He left it there, bobbing in the vase, and watched it shrivel day by day, the face turning small and black and wrinkled.

The next time it was ticket stubs, two of them, from the Kabatas-Usküdar ferry.

Till that moment he had told himself it was a matter only of holding out until the spring. He had prepared himself for a seige, believing that an assault was not possible. Now he realized that he would actually have to go out there and fight.

Though it was mid-February, the weather accommodated his belated resolution with a series of bright blue days, a wholly unseasonable warmth that even tricked early blossoms from a few unsuspecting trees. He went through Topkapi once again, giving a respectful, indiscriminate and puzzled attention to the celadon ware, to golden snuffboxes, to pearly-embroidered pillows, to the portrait miniatures of the sultans, to the fossil footprint of the Prophet, to Iznik tiles, to the lot. There it was, all spread out before him, heaps and masses of it: beauty. Like a salesclerk tying price tags to items of merchandise, he would attach this favorite word of his, provisionally, to these sundry bibelots, then step back a pace or two to see how well or poorly it "matched." Was *this* beautiful? Was *that*?

Amazingly, none of it was beautiful. The priceless baubles all just sat there on their shelves, behind the thick glass, as unrespondent as the drab furniture back in his own room.

He tried the mosques: Sultan Ahmet, Beyazit, Sehazade, Yeni Camii, Laleli Camii. The old magic, the Vitruvian trinity of "commodity, firmness, and delight," had never failed him so enormously before. Even the shock of scale, the gape-mouthed peasant reverence before thick pillars and high domes, even this deserted him. Go where he would through the city, he could not get out of his room.

Then the land walls, where months before he had felt himself rubbing up against the very garment of the past. He stood at the same spot where he had stood then, at the point where Mehmet the Conqueror had breached the walls. Quin-

cunxes of granite cannonballs decorated the grass; they reminded him of the red balloon.

As a last resort he returned to Eyüp. The false spring had
reached a tenuous apogee, and the February light flared with
deceiving brilliance from the thousand facets of white stone
blanketing the steep hillside. Small flocks of three or four
sheep browsed between the graves. The turbaned shafts of
marble jutted in every direction but the vertical (which it was
given to the cypresses to define) or lay, higgledy-piggledy,
one atop another. No walls, no ceilings, scarcely a path
through the litter: this was an architecture supremely abstract. It seemed to him to have been piled up here, over the
centuries, just to vindicate the thesis of his book.

And it worked. It worked splendidly. His mind and his eye
came alive. Ideas and images coalesced. The sharp slanting
light of the late afternoon caressed the jumbled marble with a
cold careful hand, like a beautician adding the last touches to
an elaborate coiffure. Beauty? Here it was. Here it was
abundantly!

He returned the next day with his camera, redeemed from
the repair shop where it had languished for two months. To
be on the safe side he had asked the repairman to load it for
him. He composed each picture with mathematical punctilio,
fussing over the depth of field, crouching or climbing atop
sepulchers for a better angle, checking each shot against the
reading on the light meter, deliberately avoiding picturesque
solutions and easy effects. Even taking these pains he found
that he'd gone through the twenty exposures in under two
hours.

He went up to the small café on the top of the hill. Here,
his Hachette had noted respectfully, the great Pierre Loti had
been wont to come of a summer evening, to drink a glass of
tea and look down the sculptured hills and through the pillars
of cypress at the Fresh Waters of Europe and the Golden
Horn. The café perpetuated the memory of this vanished
glory with pictures and mementos. Loti, in a red fez and
savage mustachios, glowered at the contemporary patrons
from every wall. During the First World War, Loti had
remained in Istanbul, taking the part of his friend, the
Turkish sultan, against his native France.

He ordered a glass of tea from a waitress who had been got
up as a harem girl. Apart from the waitress he had the café to

himself. He sat on Pierre Loti's favorite stool. It was delicious. He felt right at home.

He opened his notebook and began to write.

Like an invalid taking his first walk out of doors after a long convalescence, his renascent energies caused him not only the predictable and welcome euphoria of resurrection but also a pronounced intellectual giddiness, as though by the simple act of rising to his feet he had thrust himself up to some really dangerous height. This dizziness became most acute when, in trying to draft a reply to Robertson's review, he was obliged to return to passages in his own book. Often as not what he found there struck him as incomprehensible. There were entire chapters that might as well have been written in ideograms or futhorc, for all the sense they made to him now. But occasionally, cued by some remark so irrelevant to any issue at hand as to be squeezed into an embarrassed parenthesis, he would sprint off toward the most unforeseen—and undesirable—conclusions. Or rather, each of these tangents led, asymptotically, to a single conclusion: to wit, that his book, or any book he might conceive, was worthless, and worthless not because his thesis was wrong but precisely because it might be right.

There was a realm of judgment and a realm of fact. His book, if only because it was a book, existed within the bounds of the first. There was the trivial fact of its corporeality, but, in this case as in most others, he discounted that. It was a work of criticism, a systematization of judgment, and to the extent that his system was complete, its critical apparatus must be able to measure its own scales of mensuration and judge the justice of its own decrees. But could it? Was not his "system" as arbitrary a construction as any silly pyramid? What was it, after all? A string of words, of more or less agreeable noises, politely assumed to correspond to certain objects and classes of objects, actions and groups of actions, in the realm of fact. And by what subtle magic was this correspondence to be verified? Why, by just the assertion that it was so!

This, admittedly, lacked clarity. It had come to him thick and fast, and it was colored not a little by cheap red wine. To fix its outlines a bit more firmly in his own mind he tried to "get it down" in his letter to *Art News:*

Sirs:

I write to you concerning F. R. Robertson's review of my book, though the few words I have to say bear but slightly upon Mr. Robertson's oracles, as slightly perhaps as these bore upon Homo Arbitrans.

Only this—that, as Gödel has demonstrated in mathematics, Wittgenstein in philosophy, and Duchamp, Cage, and Ashbery in their respective fields, the final statement of any system is a self-denunciation, a demonstration of how its particular little tricks are done—not by magic (as magicians have always known) but by the readiness of the magician's audience to be deceived, which readiness is the very glue of the social contract.

Every system, including my own and Mr. Robertson's, is a system of more or less interesting lies, and if one begins to call these lies into question, then one ought really to begin with the first. That is to say, with the very questionable proposition on the title page: Homo Arbitrans *by John Benedict Harris.*

Now I ask you, Mr. Robertson, what could be more improbable than that? More tentative? More arbitrary?

He sent the letter off, unsigned.

5.

He had been promised his photos by Monday, so Monday morning, before the frost had thawed on the plate-glass window, he was at the shop. The same immodest anxious interest to see his pictures of Eyüp possessed him as once he had felt to see an essay or a review in print. It was as though these items, the pictures, the printed words, had the power to rescind, for a little while, his banishment to the realm of judgment, as though they said to him: "Yes, look, here we are, right in your hand. We're real, and so you must be too."

The old man behind the counter, a German, looked up mournfully to gargle a mournful *ach*. "Ach, Mr. Harris! Your pictures are not aready yet. Come back soon at twelve o'clock."

He walked through the melting streets that were, this side of the Golden Horn, jokebooks of eclecticism. No mail at the consulate, which was only to be expected. Half-past ten.

A pudding at a pudding shop. Two lire. A cigarette. A few more jokes: a bedraggled caryatid, an Egyptian tomb, a Greek temple that had been changed by some Circean wand into a butcher shop. Eleven.

He looked, in the bookshop, at the same shopworn selection of books that he had looked at so often before. Eleven-thirty. Surely, they would be ready by now.

"You are here, Mr. Harris. Very good."

Smiling in anticipation, he opened the envelope, removed the slim, warped stack of prints.

No.

"I'm afraid these aren't mine." He handed them back. He didn't want to feel them in his hand.

"What?"

"Those are the wrong pictures. You've made a mistake."

The old man put on a pair of dirty spectacles and shuffled through the prints. He squinted at the name on the envelope. "You are Mr. Harris."

"Yes, that is the name on the envelope. The envelope's all right, the pictures aren't."

"It is not a mistake."

"These are *somebody else's* snapshots. Some family picnic. You can see that."

"I myself took out the roll of film from your camera. Do you remember, Mr. Harris?"

He laughed uneasily. He hated scenes. He considered just walking out of the shop, forgetting all about the pictures. "Yes, I do remember. But I'm afraid you must have gotten that roll of film confused with another. I *didn't* take these pictures. I took pictures at the cemetery in Eyüp. Does that ring a bell?"

Perhaps, he thought, "ring a bell" was not an expression a German would understand.

As a waiter whose honesty has been called into question will go over the bill again with exaggerated attention, the old man frowned and examined each of the pictures in turn. With a triumphant clearing of his throat he laid one of the snapshots face up on the counter. "Who is that, Mr. Harris?"

It was the boy.

"Who! I . . . I don't know his name."

The old German laughed theatrically, lifting his eyes to a witnessing heaven. "It is you, Mr. Harris! It is you!"

He bent over the counter. His fingers still refused to touch the print. The boy was held up in the arms of a man whose head was bent forward as though he were examining the close-cropped scalp for lice. Details were fuzzy, the lens having been mistakenly set at infinity.

Was it his face? The mustache resembled his mustache, the crescents under the eyes, the hair falling forward. . . .

But the angle of the head, the lack of focus—there was room for doubt.

"Twenty-four lire please, Mr. Harris."

"Yes. Of course." He took a fifty-lire note from his billfold. The old man dug into a lady's plastic coin purse for change.

"Thank you, Mr. Harris."

"Yes. I'm . . . sorry."

The old man replaced the prints in the envelope, handed them across the counter.

He put the envelope in the pocket of his suit. "It was my mistake."

"Good-bye."

"Yes, good-bye."

He stood on the street, in the sunlight, exposed. Any moment either of them might come up to him, lay a hand on his shoulder, tug at his pantleg. He could not examine the prints here. He returned to the sweetshop and spread them out in four rows on a marble-topped table.

Twenty photographs. A day's outing, as commonplace as it had been impossible.

Of these twenty, three were so overexposed as to be meaningless, and should not have been printed at all. Three others showed what appeared to be islands or different sections of a very irregular coastline. They were unimaginatively composed, with great expanses of bleached-out sky and glaring water. Squeezed between these, the land registered merely as long dark blotches flecked with tiny gray rectangles of buildings. There was also a view up a steep street of wooden houses and naked wintry gardens.

The remaining thirteen pictures showed various people, and groups of people, looking at the camera. A heavyset woman in black, with black teeth, squinting into the sun—standing next to a pine tree in one picture, sitting uncomfortably on a natural stone formation in the second. An old man, dark-skinned, bald, with a flaring mustache and several days' stubble of beard. Then these two together—a very blurred print. Three little girls standing in front of a middle-aged woman, who regarded them with a pleased, proprietorial air. The same three girls grouped around the old man, who seemed to take no notice of them whatever. And a group of five men: the spread-legged shadow of the man taking this picture was roughly stenciled across the pebbled foreground.

And the woman. Alone. The wrinkled sallow flesh abraded to a smooth white mask by the harsh midday light.

Then the boy snuggling beside her on a blanket. Nearby small waves lapped at a narrow shingle.

Then these two still together with the old woman and the three little girls. The contiguity of the two women's faces suggested a family resemblance.

The figure that could be identified as himself appeared in only three of the pictures: once holding the boy in his arms; once with his arm around the woman's shoulders, while the boy stood before them scowling; once in a group of thirteen people, all of whom had appeared in one or another of the previous shots. Only the last of these three was in focus. He was one of the least noticeable figures in this group, but the mustached face smiling so rigidly into the camera was undeniably his own.

He had never seen these people, except, of course, for the woman and the boy. Though he had, hundreds of times, seen people just like them in the streets of Istanbul. Nor did he recognize the plots of grass, the stands of pine, the boulders, the shingle beach, though once again they were of such a generic type that he might well have passed such places a dozen times without taking any notice of them. Was the world of fact really as characterless as *this*? That it *was* the world of fact he never for a moment doubted.

And what had *he* to place in the balance against these evidences? A name? A face?

He scanned the walls of the sweetshop for a mirror. There was none. He lifted the spoon, dripping, from his glass of tea to regard the reflection of his face, blurred and inverted, in the concave surface. As he brought the spoon closer, the

image grew less distinct, then rotated through one hundred
eighty degrees to present, upright, the mirror image of his
staring, dilated eye.

He stood on the open upper deck as the ferry churned,
hooting, from the deck. Like a man stepping out of doors on
a blustery day, the ferry rounded the peninsular tip of the old
city, leaving the quiet of the Horn for the rough wind-
whitened waters of the Sea of Marmara. A cold south wind
stiffened the scarlet star and crescent on the stern mast.

From this vantage the city showed its noblest silhouette:
first the great gray horizontal mass of the Topkapi walls, then
the delicate swell of the dome of St. Irena, which had been
built (like a friend carefully chosen to demonstrate, by
contrast, one's own virtues) just to point up the swaggering
impossibility of the neighboring Holy Wisdom, that graceless
and abstract issue of the union commemorated on every
capital within by the twined monograms of the demon-
emperor Justinian and his whore and consort Theodora; then,
bringing both the topographic and historic sequence to an
end, the proud finality of the Blue Mosque.

The ferry began to roll in the rougher water of the open
sea. Clouds moved across the sun at quicker intervals to mass
in the north above the dwindling city. It was four-thirty. By
five o'clock he would reach Heybeli, the island identified by
both Altin and the mail clerk at the consulate as the setting of
the photographs.

The airline ticket to New York was in his pocket. His bags,
all but the one he would take on the plane, had been packed
and shipped off in a single afternoon and morning of headlong drunken fear. Now he was safe. The certain knowledge
that tomorrow he would be thousands of miles away had
shored up the crumbling walls of confidence like the promise
of a prophet who cannot err, Tiresias in balmy weather.
Admittedly this was the shameful safety of a rout so complete
that the enemy had almost captured his baggage train—but it
was safety for all that, as definite as tomorrow. Indeed, this
"tomorrow" was more definite, more present to his mind and
senses, than the actual limbo of its preparation, just as, when
a boy, he had endured the dreadful tedium of Christmas Eve
by projecting himself into the morning that would have to
follow and which, when it did finally arrive, was never so
real, by half, as his anticipations.

Because he was this safe, he dared today confront the enemy (if the enemy would confront *him*) head on. It risked nothing, and there was no telling what it might yield. Though if it were the *frisson* that he was after, then he should have stayed and seen the thing through to its end. No, this last excursion was more a gesture than an act, bravado rather than bravery. The very self-consciousness with which he had set out seemed to ensure that nothing really disastrous could happen. Had it not always been their strategy before to catch him unaware?

Finally, of course, he could not explain to himself why he had gone to the ferry, bought his ticket, embarked, except that each successive act seemed to heighten the delectable sense of his own inexorable advance, a sensation at once of almost insupportable tension and of dreamlike lassitude. He could no more have turned back along this path, once he had entered on it, than at the coda of a symphony he could have refused to listen. Beauty? Oh yes, intolerably! He had *never* known anything so beautiful as this.

The ferry pulled into the quay of Kinali Ada, the first of the islands. People got on and off. Now the ferry turned directly into the wind, toward Burgaz. Behind them the European coast vanished into the haze.

The ferry had left the Burgaz dock and was rounding the tiny islet of Kasik. He watched with fascination as the dark hills of Kasik, Burgaz, and Kinali slipped slowly into perfect alignment with their positions in the photograph. He could almost hear the click of the shutter.

And the other relationships between these simple sliding planes of sea and land—was there not something nearly as *familiar* in each infinitesimal shift of perspective? When he looked at these islands with his eyes, half-closed, attention unfocused, he could almost. . .

But whenever he tried to take this up, however gently, between the needle-tipped compasses of analysis, it crumbled into dust.

It began to snow just as the ferry approached Heybeli. He stood at the end of the pier. The ferry was moving eastward, into the white air, toward BÜYÜK ADA.

He looked up a steep street of wooden houses and naked wintry gardens. Clusters of snowflakes fell on the wet cobbles and melted. At irregular intervals street lamps glowed yellow in the dusk, but the houses remained dark. Heybeli was a summer resort. Few people lived here in the winter months. He walked halfway up the hill, then turned to the right. Certain details of woodwork, the proportion of a window, a sagging roof caught his attention momentarily, like the flicker of wings in the foliage of a tree twenty, fifty, a hundred yards ahead.

The houses were fewer, spaced farther apart. In the gardens snow covered the leaves of cabbages. The road wound up the hill toward a stone building. It was just possible to make out the flag waving against the gray sky. He turned onto a footpath that skirted the base of the hill. It led into the pines. The thick carpet of fallen needles was more slippery than ice. He rested his cheek against the bark of a tree and heard, again, the camera's click, systole and diastole of his heart.

He heard the water, before he saw it, lapping on the beach. He stopped. He focused. He recognized the rock. He walked toward it. So encompassing was his sense of this scene, so inclusive, that he could feel the footsteps he left behind in the snow, feel the snow slowly covering them again. He stopped.

It was here he had stood with the boy in his arms. The woman had held the camera to her eye with reverent awkwardness. He had bent his head forward to avoid looking directly into the glare of the setting sun. The boy's scalp was covered with the scabs of insect bites.

He was ready to admit that all this had happened, the whole impossible event. He did admit it. He lifted his head proudly and smiled, as though to say: *All right—and then? No matter what you do, I'm safe! Because, really, I'm not here at all. I'm already in New York.*

He laid his hands in a gesture of defiance on the outcropping of rock before him. His fingers brushed the resilient thong of the slipper. Covered with snow, the small oval of blue plastic had completely escaped his attention.

He spun around to face the forest, then round again to stare at the slipper lying there. He reached for it, thinking to throw it into the water, then drew his hand back.

He turned back to the forest. A man was standing just outside the line of the trees, on the path. It was too dark to discern any more of his features than that he had a mustache.

On his left the snowy beach ended in a wall of sandstone. To his right the path swung back into the forest, and behind him the sea dragged the shingle back and forth.

"Yes?"

The man bent his head attentively, but said nothing.

"Well, yes? Say it."

The man walked back into the forest.

The ferry was just pulling in as he stumbled up to the quay. He ran onto it without stopping at the booth to buy a ticket. Inside under the electric light he could see the tear in his trousers and a cut on the palm of his right hand. He had fallen many times, on the pine needles, over rocks in furrowed fields, on cobbles.

He took a seat by the coal stove. When his breath returned to him, he found that he was shivering violently. A boy came round with a tray of tea. He bought a glass for one lire. He asked the boy, in Turkish, what time it was. It was ten o'clock.

The ferry pulled up to the dock. The sign over the ticket booth said BÜYÜK ADA. The ferry pulled away from the dock.

The ticket taker came for his ticket. He held out a ten-lire note and said, "Istanbul."

The ticket taker nodded his head, which meant no.

"Yok."

"No? How much then? *Kaç para?"*

"Yok Istanbul—Yalova." He took the money offered him and gave him back in exchange eight lire and a ticket to Yalova on the Asian coast.

He had got onto a ferry going in the wrong direction. He was not returning to Istanbul, but to Yalova.

He explained, first in slow precise English, then in a desperate fragmentary Turkish, that he could not go to Yalova, that it was impossible. He produced his airline ticket, pointed at the eight o'clock departure time, but he could not remember the Turkish word for "tomorrow." Even in his desperation he could see the futility of all this: between BÜYÜK ADA and Yalova there were no more stops, and there would be no ferries returning to Istanbul that night. When he got to Yalova he would have to get off the boat.

A woman and a boy stood at the end of the wooden dock, at the base of a cone of snowy light. The lights were turned off on the middle deck of the ferry. The man who had been standing so long at the railing stepped, stiffly, down to the dock. He walked directly toward the woman and the boy. Scraps of paper eddied about his feet then, caught up in a strong gust, sailed out at a great height over the dark water.

The man nodded sullenly at the woman, who mumbled a few rapid words of Turkish. Then they set off, as they had so many times before, toward their home, the man leading the way, his wife and son following a few paces behind, taking the road along the shore.

_____ "Et in Arcadia Ego" _____

It is hard to understand why dawn lands on these hills, exciting the chains of carbon with quanta of light, or why, when we step beyond a particular line traced across the marble pavement of the courtyard of π, we are forced to reappraise certain temporal relationships. It is enough, perhaps, that we should rely upon our captain, Captain Garst Flame, who does not hesitate to resolve dilemmas of this nature with ruthless rationality—even, at times, like Alexander, with an Ax.

There are four continents, roughly equal in area, grouped in opposing pairs, two to each hemisphere, so that a simple W traced upon the Mercator projection would adequately describe our first hasty itinerary, ticklings of the fingers that would soon so firmly *enclose*.

The planet moves in an eccentric orbit about RR, a highly irregular variable in the Telescope. A primitive theocracy governs the Arcadians, whose diet consists largely of herbal salads, milk and dairy products, and a savory spiced meat resembling our mutton.

Even at noon the light of RR is tinged with blue, just as his eyes are always blue: genius is not too strong a word for Captain Flame, of whose tragic fate this is the unique record. To him the indigenes present the firstlings of their flocks; him we of the crew (Oo Ling, the lovely Micronesian biochemist; Yank, our impetuous freckle-nosed navigator; Fleur, who took her double doctorate in Cultanthrop and Partfizz; myself, geologist and official Chronicaster to The Expedition) thrice have raised to the nomenclature of *Palus Nebularum*.

The central massif of the White Mountains describes a broad U above which the sister cities of Hapax and Legomenon form a gigantic umlaut of arcane beauty. Fleur has recorded and analyzed the structure of the Temple. Her breakdown shows that the centers of curvature, marked by the double circles of the three interfaces of the interpenetrating hemispheres, lie *in a straight line*, the same that has been traced upon the marble that paves the courtyard of π. From this it can be proved that the Arcadian mathematics, so primitive in other respects, is based upon a shrewd understanding of the physical properties of soap bubbles. We have spent many hours in the common room discussing the implications of Fleur's discovery. Oo Ling, who is contracted to my bed, questions Fleur's recommendations of clemency, which I am inclined to support, provisionally. How I love to look into the depths of those ianthine eyes, two vernal flowers floating on a skin of cream, to touch the oily quiff that clings, like iron bonded to aluminum, to that noble brow. Oo Ling. I desire you, pressing my fist into my genitals as I pronounce your name, Oo Ling!

But I fear the imminence of our dissent. Your voice will be with Yank's, mine with Fleur's, and the decision will rest with Captain Flame, who has remained through all these bull sessions, impassive, serene, showing to us a smile that mocks every attempt at interpretation.

Captain Flame, it is with tears that I record the tragedy of your fate.

I am extending my orological investigations, assisted by the indigenes Meliboeus and Tityrus, sons of the Abba Damon, who holds the staff of π. Meliboeus, as the elder, wears a kirtle of heavy mortling dyed the color of fine glauconite; the younger Tityrus, uninitiate to the Arcadian mysteries, dresses in simple dun fluff fastened with leather thongs. My own suit on these field trips is a tough corporal unit of flesh-patterned polyisoprene, which can be activated to simulate any sacral movements, such as walking, running, skipping, etc. This, we have learned, is a useful subterfuge, in view of the Arcadian predilection for natural forms.

On the eleventh trimester of our Conquest, Miliboeus said: "Death sings to us, Abba."

And Tityrus: "Just as the clouds struggle toward their disappearance, alas, our hearts contest with our minds."

I replied, in the Arcadian tongue: "Brothers, I do not understand. The sun is at solstice. Your blood courses through your veins swiftly, as water spills down the mountainside. Youth you possess, wisdom you shall inherit, and poetry—"

Tityrus interrupted my peroration, slapping an insect that crawled in the fluff of his thigh. He showed me the smear on the palm of his hand. "It is thus," he said sadly.

"And thus," said Meliboeus, licking the smear from his brother's hand.

Astonished, I reached the captain at once by Telstar and narrated this incident to him, while the enlarged image of his hand wandered thoughtfully among the swollen Greek letters of the primary unit. Captain Flame spends all his uncoordinated moments on the bridge now, breathing its metamorphic air, sealing from us all channels except the red and yellow bands. Dammed, our love swells. Moths beat white wings against the protective shell of glass. Images that betoken our more animal nature, which we share, in a sense, with the Arcadians; and I have seen, in the captain's blood, and heard, in his screams, the cost of transcendence.

"I expected this," he said, at red, my narration having terminated.

"I did not expect this," I said. "I did not know that you expected this."

Oo Ling joined our communication: "I expected this too—for these reasons: first, they have kept us in ignorance of their mysteries; second, we are not allowed within the Temple; third, their daily speech is filled with imprecise denotations."

"I object," I replied. "Firstly, it cannot be the mysteries that Meliboeus fears, for he is initiate. Secondly, all primitive cultures observe similar taboos. Thirdly, the inexactness of their speech is characteristic of its emergence from the Rhematic age. I maintain that they are naïve, merely."

"That is probable," the captain said, "and it is this very probability that led me to experience anxiety. Naïveté can be more counterproductive than active deception and, if intransigent, is an argument for genocide."

"Do you feel a large degree of anxiety?" I asked.

"I had felt only a small degree of anxiety, but this message has caused it to enlarge, and it is still enlarging now." He bipped the image of a swelling iridescent sphere.

Oo Ling descended gracefully to the yellow band. "Have you had sex today, Garst?"

"No, nor yesterday."

"Maybe you're just feeling horny. Why don't I come to your bed?"

"Good idea. Are you free now?"

"Yes. I'll finish with these proteins later. I need a good lay myself." Oo Ling blanked off our link.

"With your permission, Captain, I'd like to observe."

"As you please," he replied, with circumspection in the image of his eyes, *bleu d'azur, bleu celeste*. The wall irised open and the floor drove him toward the bed, which puckered to receive that splendid torso, those limbs tensed with an heroic lust. I moved in for a closeup of his loins, then followed the rippling, golden flesh slowly upward, as Cellini's finger might have caressed fauld, breast-plate, and gorget of his own molding. I tightened my shot to a single staring disc of *bleu d'azur,* in which I saw, as in a mirror, the image of Oo Ling. Oo Ling, I desire you, pressing my fist, then and now, into my genitals as I pronounce your name, as your image falls and rises on the image of our doomed captain, Garst Flame.

When you come, I come with you, and we are together there, the three of us, and then, sighing, I must break the link, and I find myself sitting, half disengaged from my unit of polyisoprene, with the two youths, Meliboeus and Tityrus, staring at my happiness and pride.

They show me specimens of the rocks they have been collecting, while, at a distance, a lamb bleats with a lamb's naïve anxiety, and the lurid sunset shifts from peach to mauve to indigo, a phenomenon as puzzling to me, as arcane, as beautiful, as the expression on his lips when he is not smiling.

This happened on Day Theta/11th trimester of our Conquest of Arcadia, according to the sequence described.

Now, as an eagle will swoop down upon an incautious hare, the strong talons shredding her pink flesh, so dawn's light pounces on the geanticlinal welts of the White Mountains. Yank has noted in his report the presence of certain new faculae on the surface of RR, heralding perhaps some cosmic disease. Light seems uniform, yet is thronged with data: coded histories of all future event dance in its waves like the motes that people the sunbeams, sunbeams that awaken the sheep in their fold, whose glad conclamation then wakes the tardy shepherds Meliboeus and Tityrus, as in the age of Dickens and Pope the sound of songbirds might have awakened a poor London chimneysweep, the victim of economic oppressions. The image of their brotherly kisses flickers on the screen of the common room, and the image of the morning sunlight, the bleating of the flock.

I lean across the trough to let my fingers graze the down of your hand and trace the curve (a lituus) of your silken quiff. I whisper in your ear, "And who is *my* brother?"

Shall I interpret your laugh? Shall I admit that your smile is an auspex to be ranked with sunspots and birdsong, with deformations of the liver, the pancreas, and the intestines? You are as solemn as a saraband by Lully, as arousing as Brahms's "Lullaby." When I regard your sexual organ, engorged with blood, I lose all sense of kinship patterns, of teamwork, of philosophy.

And your reply: "Oo Ling?"

And my echo: "I cannot tell you all that I am feeling."

Fleur pokes a finger in my ribs. "You two lovebirds have got to break it up. We've got our work cut out for us today."

Obediently we return our attention to the screen:

The shepherds wake, and walk toward their death, as a young man of good family, in the heyday of the Industrial Revolution, might have ascended the Jungfrau to enjoy one of its many celebrated views. The random motions of individual sheep become, in aggregate, a progress as direct as the path of an arrow.

Simultaneously, at the Temple, the Abba Damon unlocks, with a caduceus-shaped key, the gilded doors. The opposing helices of the two serpents are of complementary shades, blue and orange. The key is so shaped and so colored that the slightest motion seems to set the two snakes writhing.

Unseen, except by our miniature cameras, the twin serpents writhe in the lock; the doors swing open, and Damon leads forth the celebrants. The procession follows him in single file along the line retraced that same morning upon the marble pavements with the blood of Meliboeus and Tityrus. Above the Abba's head sways his crozier of office, decorated with brand-new orange and blue Celanese acetate ribbons, the gift of Oo Ling, who, watching this solemn, scary moment with me in the common room, cups my breasts in his hands, naming, as they flash past on an ancillary screen, the names

of the amino acids composing the phenylalanine chain:
"Voline, aspartic acid, glutanic acid, voline . . ." (and so on).
Just as once, twenty or thirty years ago (though this seems
probable enough, I *remember* nothing of the sort), a much
shorter Oo Ling might have recited that same litany at my
maternal knee.

More affecting, however, than Oo Ling's prattle is the fuss
that Yank is making over the community's coffee pot. Will
Fleur have cream, he wants to know. Will I take sugar? Of
course I will! And thank you very much.

The cameras float up the mountainside in the wake of the
flock, documenting the thousand flowers crushed beneath the
feet of lamb and ewe, tup and yeanling: anemones, bluebells,
cinerarias, and daisies; lush eglantine and pale forsythia;
gentians; hawthorns, irises, and April's bright-hued jonquils;
and many other kinds of flowers as well, all of them crushed
by innumerable sheep. Sometimes, however, Meliboeus would
stoop to pluck one of the more enticing blooms, then knit its
stem into one of the garlands, bucolic and complex, with
which he'd crowned himself and his kid brother.

"Well, there's coffee for everyone," Yank said, with a little
sigh of accomplishment.

"But I see five cups," I pointed out, "and there are only
four of us."

"Yes, Mary's right," Fleur said. "Captain Flame is missing!"

It didn't take us long to discover our leader's whereabouts,
once the dials were properly adjusted. For he, too, was on
that mountainside, halfway between the two young victims
and the procession of priests, who were, already, opening the
vault in the hillside—how had it escaped our detection all this
time?—from which, with the terrible inevitability of nuclear
fission, the Wolf emerged.

Fleur shrieked: "Watch out, Garst! Behind you!"

But he had blanked off all bands and was deaf to our
warnings. We observed the events that followed with a
mounting suspense, little suspecting that they would lead us,
step by step, to a catastrophe of global dimensions.

Concerning the Wolf.

Though not larger than a double sleeping-space and almost
noiseless in its operation, the Wolf was expressive, in every
detail of its construction, of a sublime rapaciousness, a thirst

for dominion so profound as to make *our* Empire, universal as it is, seem (for the moment we watched it) as insubstantial as the architectures shaped by the successive phrases of a Bach chorale, which fade as swiftly as they rise. Here, incarnate in chrome-vanadium steel, was the Word that our lips had always hesitated to speak; the orphic secret that had been sealed, eons past, in the cornerstone of the human heart, suspected but never seen; the last, unwritten chapter of the book.

Busy swarms of perceptual organs encircled its crenelated head to form a glistering metallic annulet; its jaws were the toothy scoops of ancient steam shovels; it was gray, as a glass of breakfast juice is gray, and beautiful as only a machine can be beautiful. We of the crew were breathless with astonishment, admiration, and, needless to say, fear.

The Wolf advanced along the path of trampled flowers (anemones, bluebells, etc.), stalking not only the flocks and the two young shepherds but the very Empire itself, in the person of Garst Flame. Did *it* know this already? Had the ever-expanding network of its senses discerned Garst's presence on the path ahead, and was this the reason that it seemed now to quicken its pace, as a lover, learning that his beloved is unexpectedly close at hand, will hasten toward her?

What was this creature? Could it have been formed here in Arcadia? In what hidden foundry? What intelligence had wrought so eloquently in chain and cogwheel, engine and frame, the manifest aim of all intelligence? What was it going to do? What weapons would be effective against it? These were the questions we asked ourselves.

All poetry, as Yank once remarked apropos of this brace of sacrificial lambs, is a preparation for death. Tityrus tosses his crook—where the wood has slivered, a tuft of fleece has snagged and clings—to his older brother: why, except *we* know the danger they are in, should this playful gesture rouse in us feelings of such ineffable sadness?

Such sadness. And yet, paradoxically, of all the indigenes it is only these two who, like green-barked saplings uprooted and bagged before some terrific flood, will survive, while all the rest, the stoutest oaks, the tallest pines, must be drowned in the waters of a necessary and just revenge. But I anticipate myself.

This is my point: that since we can never know from *his* lips why our captain left his post, we must suppose that he was moved by a sense of pity, and that somehow he had foreseen the danger that had till then been locked within the rocky shells of the Arcadian hills, as chemists at the dawn of the modern age suspected the existence, though they could not prove it, of the intercalary elements.

Through the morning and far into the afternoon, while the dreadful contest between the Wolf and Garst was being fought out on the slopes below, their sport continued, the songs, the jigs, the clumsy, countrified wrestling that was more like loveplay than a form of combat, the pastoral lunch of whey and the snack later of scarlet berries—and all the while, like the tremolo work above a Lisztian melody, that same unvarying brave show of insouciance!

All this is astonishing, true enough, but as Fleur remarked even then, it is also essentially unhistorical. No more of this blather about Meliboeus and Tityrus, who are nothing more now than gray, useless, aging aliens taking up bench-space in the Home Office's Park of All Arts, like turkeys manufactured for a holiday that is no longer much celebrated and still gathering dust beneath the counter of some hick store in Gary, Indiana, or like poems that were never translated from French or a song that never got taped, etc., etc. The possibilities for obsolescence are as numberless as the stars.

Dinosaurs quarreling; the customs of pirates, of the Iroquois, of carnivorous apes; the great Super Bowl between the Packers and the Jets; the annihilation of Andromeda III; Norse berserkers hacking Saxons and their horses to bits; the hashish-inspired contretemps of the Assassins of Alamut; the duels of Romeo and Tybalt, of Tancred and Clorinda; killer-dwarves of the Roman arenas; John L. Lewis smashing the skulls of company scabs with his Mammoth jackhammer; Apollo flaying Marsyas, slaying the Delphian Python at the very brink of the sacred abyss; bloodbaths, bullfights, drunken mayhem, battle hymns, Schutzstaffel death-camps, missiles programmed to reproduce themselves in midflight; Germans galloping across the ice of Lake Peipus; Juggernauts and abattoirs; Alexander's delirium at *Arbela; Bull Run;* the Romans slaughtered at *Cannae* and slaughtering at *Chaeronea; Drogheda* defeated and depopulated; Panzers swarming across the sand toward *El Alamein;* the Carolingian empire dissolving at *Fontenay;* the French victorious at *Fontenoy;* images that can only begin to suggest the weight and excitement of the drama our cameras recorded that day, as nine and a half feet of red-haired, blue-eyed human fury matched its strength and wits against six tons of super-charged, killcrazy engineering.

Even the cameras and mikes shared in the combat, for the Wolf's busy senses were equipped with their own weapons systems. A methodical destruction of our network began, to which I retaliated (communications being up my alley) with a simple Chinese-type strategy of endless reinforcement. I figured that the more eyes the Wolf used to pursue and destroy the ship's receptors, the fewer it would have available for its fight against Garst Flame.

As in so many deadly contests, the crucial moments were often the least spectacular. By bluff and psychic ambush each sought to win some fractional advantage over the other. Garst would set his corporal unit swaying hypnotically. The Wolf would spin round him in swift circles, braying and honking and clashing his jaws at erratic intervals, hoping to jar Garst from the steady 4/4 rhythm of his wariness.

Then, without warning, Garst unleashed a river of attenuator particles. The Wolf skittered sideways and parried with a hail of yttrium that spanged harmlessly against the tough polyisoprene of the corporal unit.

A teat of the Wolf squirted clouds of antilife gas, but Garst's nerveshields protected him. The priests, who had arrived on the scene moments after things got started, backed away in terror. The spray settled where they'd been standing; the grass withered and turned black.

The Wolf's eyes and ears were steadily demolishing the cameras and mikes that I poured into the area, making reception in the common room ragged and fragmentary. On the other hand, the personnel registers were functioning beautifully, and it boosted our morale a lot to know that Garst's acetylcholine production was down thirty-six per cent, with a corresponding fifty-four per cent rise in sympathin. The time lapse for prosthetic response was, in consequence, pared to microseconds.

Then the impossible happened. The Wolf seemed to be taken in by one of Garst's feints, and he was able to run in under the lowest, least well-armored jaw and give it a taste of his circuit randomizers. The jaw turned to haywire—but it had been a trick! Three tentacles, hidden till now in another jaw higher up, blurted out and wrapped themselves around both Garst's arms and his helmet. Ineluctably he was lifted upward, flailing his legs with futile vigor, toward the chomping steam shovels.

It had been to just such a death as now loomed over our captain that the Abba Damon had willingly and consciously foredoomed his own two sons! Think of *that*, all you moralizers, before you condemn the decision we arrived at (after hours of debate) concerning a suitable punitive measure.

To return, however, to that moment of supreme anxiety. It was just then, wouldn't you know it, that one of the Wolf's ears shot down our sole surviving camera, and simultaneously over the audio we heard the roar of a tremendous implosion.

The personnel registers dropped to a level of complete non-being.

To get fresh cameras to the scene I had to detach the network from my own unit. By the time it arrived everything was over. The amazing thing was that Garst had won, the Wolf was dead. And here is the stratagem: once the Wolf's tentacles had glued themselves to his corporal unit and begun corroding the armor, Garst had tongued the trigger for maximum Self-Destruct, then, hoping against hope, had jettisoned himself bang right out of his unit.

He'd landed, unsheathed and soft, at the feet of the Abba Damon. The suit meanwhile destructed, and with it every contiguous atom of the Wolf, whose eyes and ears buzzed round the site of the implosion afterward like bees who've lost their hive. Then, without a central, directing intelligence, their programming caused them to knock each other off, as the soldiers sprung from Cadmus's sowing began, as soon as they'd risen, fully armed, from the sun-warmed furrows of Boeotian Thebes, to slash and stab at each other in the madness of civil war.

The Abba Damon stoops and lifts the pale, pained torso with just such a mingling of amazement and acquisitive delight as a collector in the heroic age of archeaology might have shown upon discovering some antique term, an armless satyr from the baths of Titus.

"Take me to..." Garst whispered, before the treason of

his own lungs, desperate for more, and purer, air, silenced him.

With our captain cradled in his arms the Abba Damon retraces his path down the slopes of the mountain, along the line of blood in the courtyard of π. Again the twin serpents writhe in the lock, and now for the first time, as our camera flutters above the sacrifice like the Dove in representations of the Trinity, we see the Inner Temple.

A piece of road equipment, precious in its antiquity, seems to have been abandoned before the high altar.

A song of woe, Arcadian Muses, a song of woe!

The Abba Damon traces the curve (a lituus) of his staff of office as, with sacramental dispassion, he observes his assistants fastening the cords securely around Garst's genitals. How many times—and with what feelings of tenderness, the charity of the senses—have all of us, Fleur, Yank, Oo Ling, myself, caressed that cock, those balls, the little bush of hair! O Garst! Now we cannot touch you! And never, never again.

Then, as the priests take turns operating a crude windlass, the victim is raised until at last his body swings, inverted, an obscene, pitiful pendulum, above the rusting machinery. I cannot recall this moment, this final image without feeling again the same numbing terror, which shades, again, into the same unspoken collusion, as though, then and today, a compact were being made between us: between, on the one hand, the Abba, his priests, that green planet, and, on the other, myself, the crew, our ship, an Empire—a compact whose tragic clauses we must obey, on each side, down to the last remorseless syllable.

A song of pain, Aracadian Muses! Arcadian Muses, a song of pain!

I must mention his screams. His suffering, like the attributes of Godhead, is at once inconceivable and endlessly intriguing, a perpetual calendar of thought, an Ouroboros. I think of that strong and splendid being stripped to the irreducible human sequence of head, chest, gut, and sex, and though usually it is a matter of indifference to me that I am of the female sex, I am glad to know that I need never fear such a thing happening to me.

Sing of death, Arcadian Muses! Sing!

He raises the knife and, murmuring some words to the effect that he does this only with the greatest reluctance, slits

Garst's throat from left to right. A brief necklace of blood graces the white flesh that only that morning was banded by the red collar of Imperial office. The blood streamed down across his face to drench and darken the soft curls. His body hung there till the last drop had drained out into the rusted engine of the caterpillar.

Sing, Arcadian Muses! Sing the mystery. For your own death approaches.

The motor turned over once, sputtered, and died. The scoop lifted a fraction of an inch, and these events took place, our captain's death, the destruction of Arcadia, so that that gesture might be made.

Following these barbarities, the Abba Damon, in pleading for the release of his sons, sought to excuse himself and his people with arguments and "explanations" too laughable to merit the dignity of inclusion in this record. To repeat such tales would be an affront not only to the memory of our leader but also to that of the planet which it was our pleasure, the next day, to wipe out of existence.

Before X-hour each of us wrote an epitaph for him in the log, an ineffaceable magnetic tribute to the man who'd led us to success on so many missions.

This was Fleur's: "Soon we'll be back at the Home Office, back on the red bands, where you were always most at home. Our recall priorities will be adjusted, they always are before reassignment, and that means I'll forget you, except for a couple of memories that won't matter that much. This pain is a ground-mist, and the sun comes up and it's gone. But if I were able to miss you, Garst, I would."

This, Yank's: "The last time I kissed you . . . the rest may have to go, but I'm holding on to that."

And this, Oo Ling's: "I'm sorry that he had to die."

This history has been my epitaph for you, Garst. There is never a last thing to say, unless Oo Ling has said it. One day I told you I loved you more than I loved the rest—and even then it wasn't true. None of us, probably, loved you very much, because if truth be told you weren't that lovable; but we have done that which in your eyes would have been more important: we have done our duty.

Thus, on Day Delta/12th trimester, the Conquest of Arcadia was concluded. Just before blastoff we fired a full charge from the temporal cannon at the heart of RR. Before the sun set that evening on the cities of Hapax and Legomenon, it would have gone to nova.

Arcadia has ceased to be, but other planets await us. The whole great pulsing body of what-is has been tied to the altar, and we advance to tie about its universal neck the sequence of our extinctions, like ropes of pearls, each one a unique, and now demolished world. O glades and rivers, O winds and darknesses, will you mourn, with us, their loss?

THE MASTER
OF THE MILFORD
ALTARPIECE

What blacks and whites,
what greys and purplish browns!
                    BERNARD BERENSON

Often enough Rubens may have quietly taken stock of
all previous Italian art at this time, especially of the
Venetian school, the knowledge of which had had so
little influence on other northern artists. Though scarcely
one immediate reminiscence of Titian can be discovered
in Rubens's later work, whether of objects or of single
forms, he had learned to see with Titian's eyes. He found
the whole mass of Tintoretto's work intact, and much of
it still free of the later blackening of the shadows which
makes it impossible for us to enjoy him, but he may well
have been repelled by the touch of untruthfulness and
lack of reticence in him, and by the crudity of a number
of his compositions. It is obvious that his deepest kinship
by far was with Paolo Veronese; here two minds con-
verged, and there have been pictures which might be
attributed to either, for instance a small, but rich Adora-
tion of the Magi which the present writer saw in early,
uncritical years and has never been able to forget.
                    JACOB BURCKHARDT

1.

I can hear him, in the next room but one, typing away. An answer to Pamela's special delivery letter perhaps? Or lists of money-making projects. Possibly even a story, or a revised outline for *Popcorn*, in which he will refute the errors of our age.

Wishing to know his age, I went into the communicating room. "Jim?" I called out. "Jim?" Not in his office. I called downstairs. No reply. I returned here, to this desk, this typewriter. Now there are noises: his voice, the slow expository tone that he reserves for Dylan.

He is twenty-three. He will be twenty-four in December. For his age he is fantastically successful. I envy his success, though it isn't a personal thing—I can envy almost anyone's. I need constant reassurance. I crave your admiration. Is candor admirable? Is reticence even more admirable? I want to read this to someone.

Chip said, on the phone last night, that Algis Budrys called him the world's greatest science-fiction writer. I certainly did envy that. Jane said afterward that Chip is coming up here at the end of the week, possibly with Burt. (Burt?) Marilyn is still in San Francisco. I felt resentful.

I don't think I am alone in being obsessed with the idea of success. We all are. But though we may envy the success of our friends, we also require it. What kind of success would we be if our friends were failures?

This isn't the story. This is only the frame.

Pieter Saenredam

Pieter Jansz. Saenredam; painter of church interiors and topographical views.

Born at Assendelft 9 June, 1597, son of the engraver Jan Saenredam. He went as a child to Haarlem and became a pupil in May 1612 of Frans Pietersz. de Grebber, in whose studio he remained until 1622. In 1623 he entered the

327

painters' guild at Haarlem and spent most of his life there. He was buried at Haarlem, 31 May, 1665.

He was in contact with the architects Jacob van Campen and Salomon de Bray, and perhaps also Bartholomeus van Bassen. He was one of the first architectural painters to reproduce buildings with fidelity (that is to say, in his drawings; in his pictures, accuracy is often modified for compositional reasons).

In his bedroom, which also served him as a studio, the curtains were always drawn. The cats performed ovals and sine curves in the bedclothes, a gray cat, a calico cat. Most of the furniture has been removed. The remaining pieces are placed against the wall.

The pleasures of iconoclasm. Destruction as a precondition of creation. Our burning faith.

The same painting over and over again. The high vaults and long recessions. The bare walls. The slanting light. Bereft of figures. (Those we see now have, for the most part, been added by other hands.) Nude. White.

He opened his present. Each box contained a smaller box. The last box contained a tin of Mixture No. 79, burley and Virginia. From that young scapegrace, Adriaen Brouwer (1605-1638).

It was an exciting time to live in. Traditions were crumbling. Fortunes were made and destroyed in a day.

The columns in the foreground have been made to appear much wider and taller, and the arches borne by them have been suppressed.

His first letter:

> *RFD 3*
> *Iowa City, Iowa*
> *May 66*

Dear Mr. Disch—

Twenty minutes ago I finished The Genocides. And should have finished it days ago, but I kept drawing it out, going back over things, taking it a few pages at a time: because I didn't want it to be over with, sure, but mainly because I felt there was so much to take in—the structure, the pitch and tone of the narrative, the inter-flow of situations—and I wanted to give myself every chance I could. . . .

From a letter two months later:

...I am touched, Tom, by your extremely kind offer. To show my things to Moorcock. If they were only good stories, I'd take you up on it in a minute. But they're not, and I know it, which makes things different, almost embarrassing. But I may still put you in the compromising position, after thinking it over a while. I could use the sale (money, ego-boost, a beginning), and some of 'em aren't really that bad ... and so on. But for now: I thank you very much. No way of expressing my gratitude—not only for the offer, but for your proffered friendship as well, your demonstrated openness. ...

And this, when I had asked him for a self-portrait:

His Whilom. Born in Helena, Arkansas. Parents uneducated. Spoiled because was so hard to conceive him, wrecked mother's health to bear him against the advice of doctors. One brother, seven years older; philosopher, PhD, teacher. Spent his youth on banks of Twain's Mississippi and in Confederate woods banking his small town. Became interested in conjuring when about twelve, an interest which persists. During high school edited some small magic mags, composed and formed chamber groups, took music lessons (against his parents' wishes, who thought playing in the band was enough, and regardless of their lack of funds), had few friends. Spent summer between 11th and 12th grade doing independent research under guide of National Science Foundation, it being his ambition at that time to become a biochemist. Was oppressed that summer by the routine boredom of checks and balances, began to write poetry under the inspiration of cummings. In his 12th school year, wrote plays, directed plays, acted in plays, won dramatics prizes, became very depressed about not having the money to go to Princeton, became a dandy and discovered girls. Decided he was a poet.

The Exterior Symbolic. Am tall, very thin with a beer belly and matchstick legs. A disorder of the lower back has left me slightly stooped and given me a strange, quite unique walk. Wear wireframe glasses. Dress in either corduroy coat or black suit, with dark or figured or flowered shirt and black or figured tie. An angular, long face. Black curly hair that sticks out like straw and generally needs a cutting.

Aedicule

The enclosing planes of walls, floor, ceiling. Subsidiary planes in tiers supported by the vertical members—posts, legs, brackets. A light bulb hangs from the ceiling. His room is characterized by rectilinearity. He unpacks his boxes and arranges the books on shelves, tacks prints to the walls, disposes of his clothing into drawers.

Without are trees, weeds, grasses, haystacks, cathedrals, crowds of people, rain, bumps, animals ground into meat, billboards, the glare, conversations, radiant energy, danger, hands, prices, mail, the same conversations.

The artist is obliged to structure these random elements into an order of his own making. He places the ground meat in the icebox, arranges the crowds of people into drawers. He carves a smaller church and places it in the larger church. Within this artificial structure, each figure, isolated in its own niche, appears transfigured. Certain similarities become apparent. More and more material is introduced. New shelves must be built. Boxes pile up below the steps. The sentences swell from short declarative statements into otiose candelabra. Wax drips onto the diapered floors. Styles conflict. Friends drop in for a chat and stay on for the whole weekend. At last there is nothing to be done but scrap the whole mess and start from scratch.

Whitewash. Sunlight slanting across bare walls. Drawn curtains. Vermeer's eventless studio.

He paints a picture of the table and the chair. The floor. The walls. The ceiling. His wife comes in the door with a plate of doughnuts. Each doughnut has a name. He eats "Happiness." His wife eats "Art." The door opens. Their friend Pomposity has come for a visit.

2.

Yesterday, all told, he got three letters from Pamela. Passion that can express itself so abundantly, though it may forfeit our full sympathy, is a wonderful thing to behold. Given the occasion, how readily we all leap into our buskins! And if we are not given the occasion outright, we will find it somehow. Madame Bovary, *c'est nous!*

When every high utterance is suspect, we must rely on surfaces, learn to decode the semaphore of the gratuitous, quotidian event.

Oh, the semaphore of the gratuitous, quotidian event—that's beautiful.

For a long while I pressed my head against my purring IBM Executive and tried to think of what constituted, in our lives here, a gratuitous event. There seemed far too much significance in almost anything I could remember of yesterday's smallest occasions. I returned most often to:

Raking leaves. Not, conscientiously, into a basket for burning, but over the edge of the escarpment. Like sweeping dust under a rug. Jim came out on the porch to announce a phone call from my brother Gary. He has been readmitted to Canada with immigrant status. Then, back to my little chore. Jim said he hates to rake leaves. "Because it reminds you of poems in *The New Yorker?*" I asked. He laughed. No, because it reminds him of his childhood. Weeding the towering weeds in the back lawn, unmowed since mid-August. The two most spectacular weeds I tamped into a coffee can and set beside our other plants on the table in the bay of the library.

Strings of hot peppers, predominantly red, hanging unconvincingly on the pea-soup kitchen wall. Jane's handicraft. Staring at them as I gossiped with Jim. About? Literature, probably, and our friends.

Judy bought a steak, and Jane made beef stroganoff and a Caesar salad, both exemplary. The flavor of the sauce, the croutons' crunch.

331

Chess with Jim before dinner, with Jane after I'd washed the dishes.

Jane cut Jim's hair. Dylan was skipping through the scattered curls, so I swept them up and put them in the garbage.

At what point was I happiest yesterday: as I raked leaves and washed dishes or when I was writing this story? At what point was Jane happiest? At what point was Jim happiest?

Was Jane happier than Jim? Was I happier than either? If not, were both, or only one, happier than me? Which?

I spend too much time lazing about indoors. I overeat. I smoke a package of cigarettes every day. I masturbate too often. I am not honest with myself. How, then, can I be expected to be honest about others?

Happiness is not important.

The Conversion of St. Paul

The acquisition of certain knowledge (as Augustine shows us) is possible, and men are bound to acknowledge this fact. The knowledge of God and of man is the end of all the aspirations of reason, and the purification of the heart is the condition of such knowledge.

The city is divided by schisms, as by innumerable rivers. His single room on Mississippi Avenue overlooks an endless genealogy of errors, sparrows, roofs. He has, by preference, few friends. He reads, each evening, of the great dispute over the nature of the Trinity. Demons in the form of moths tickle the bare soles of his feet. He fills his notebooks with theories, explanations, refutations, apologies—but nothing satisfies him. Of what solace is philosophy when each sequent hour reveals new portents of a sure and merited destruction, innumerable portents?

He cannot endure the strength of these emotions.

He writes:

To be happy, man must possess some absolute good: this is God. To possess God is to be wise. But none can possess God without the Son of God, who says of Himself, I am the truth. The truth namely is the knowledge-principle of the highest, all-embracing order, which, as absolutely true, produces the truth out of itself in a like essential way. A blessed life consists in knowing by whom we are led to the truth, in what we attain to the truth, and how we are united to the highest order.

That much seemed to be clear.

Often (of this he did not write) the walls of the room warped. The old man from next door came and stared at him as he lay there in the bed. Crook-backed and dirty (a magician probably): the name "Sabellius" burnt into the gray flesh of his high forehead.

In the churches, the gilded sculptures of Heresy and Sedition. Plastic dissembling itself as trees, weeds, grasses; simulating entire parks. The seeming virtues of his friends were only splendid vices. Their faces were covered with giant worms.

He distinguished between the immediate and the reflective consciousness, which concludes itself in unity, by the most perfect form of the will, which is love. Does the Holy Ghost proceed from the communion of the Father and the Son?

Explain the hypostatis of Christ. Tell me you love me. Define your terms.

He fell on his back and saw, in the clouds, the eye of the whale. He saw the river burning and his friends destroyed.

And no one listens to him. No one. No one.

An excerpt from his letter of Sept. '66:

> *The large, looming discovery: Samuel R. Delany. I had read a few of his books and been quite impressed and assumed he had been writing for three hundred years and was roughly ten million years old. God, I should have known (and if I'd read the jacket notes would have)... by the time he was 22, he'd had four books published. The last three of these are a trilogy, and his best work. He's about 24/25 now, with eight books. And he's beginning to think about shorter work.... "Chip" has the strongest, most vital personality I've discovered in the sf clan. That young, and writing like that! (This is the larger part of my current depression—that he does it so much better than I.) Read his books and you drown in poetry.*

And this, from a letter to his wife:

> *Glad to hear that you and Tom are getting along so well and things are working out; also, of course, very*

glad to hear that you're working. I'm really damned pleased that you like him so much. Tom is a fantastic influence on everyone he comes near. I find it difficult to be with him for more than a few minutes without having the urge to get right to work on something better than anything I've ever done before. I don't know if I have mentioned it, but Tom is beyond doubt the only person I know to whom I'd apply words like "genius." In ten years or so, he's going to be quite, quite well-known and quite, quite respected. What is he, and what are you working on; and are you, is he, serious about the poetry magazine? I hope so.

That radiant quality of mind is something he shares with Mike, with John Sladek, and with Pamela.

And then (though not chronologically):

I'm constantly amazed, Tom, at the similarity of our tastes, expression, and ambitions. If we were French poets, I'm certain we'd think it necessary to form a "school" about ourselves: arguing with the establishment and among ourselves, bitching at traditions, j'accusing all over the place, emitting manifestoes, issuing bulls, belching intent everywhere we walked, excreting doctrine and should-be's, generating slogans, shouting what we collectively think, and having a hell of a lot of fun doing it all . . . I don't think anyone has ever done that in sf, have they? Poetry, art, music, other writing reeks with such focused groups (I'm led to think of this by just having read a book on contemporary poetry, in which the movements of the projective-verse poets and deep-image poets were detailed; it sounded like so much fun, and everyone concerned got so much out of it, and you can't argue that they wham-bang turned the tides of poetry).

A Schematic Diagram

Linda began her affair with Gene in high school. Sometimes Linda wanted to marry Gene. Sometimes Gene wanted to marry Linda. Gregory married Lois. Ben married Nancy.

Doug married Sue. Linda and Gene took a flat with Paul. Gene married Marion and moved to Montreal.

Bereft, Linda sailed to London on the *France*. At the university she met Ahmet.

Jerry had an affair with Lois. Gregory was almost killed in a motorcycle accident. Jerry went to Europe. When he returned, a year later, to New York, he subleased Paul's apartment. Paul went away and wrote a novel. He returned and collaborated on a second novel with Jerry. They went to London.

Linda wanted to marry Paul. She had an affair with Jerry. The three of them lived together in Ahmet's flat. After an unhappy and brief affair with Bob, Paul went away and wrote about it. Jerry moved out of the flat and had a brief and unhappy affair with Nancy.

Doug and Sue went to London. She hated London and returned to the States. Doug had an affair with Linda. Jerry had an affair with a different, younger Linda. Mr. Nolde had an affair with the first Linda. Linda was very unhappy. She wanted to marry Jerry. She wanted to marry Doug.

Paul returned to the States. He decided to sublease the Williamses' house with Sue. Doug grew worried and returned to the States. Ben was very upset. He refused to give Linda Doug's phone number.

Gene and Marion went to London.

POETS:	Gregory. Gene. Doug. Paul. Jerry. Bob.
NOVELISTS, SHORT STORY WRITERS:	Gene. Doug. Paul. Jerry. Lois. Nancy. Ben. Linda. Sue. The Williamses.
PAINTERS:	Marion. Linda. Sue. Ben. Mr. Williams.
EDITORS, ANTHOLOGISTS:	Doug. Jerry. Bob. Ben. Mr. Williams.
ARCHITECT:	Ahmet.
ART COLLECTOR:	Mr. Nolde.

The artist, when he makes his art, shares a common fate with Rousseauistic man: he begins free and ends in chains.

And other metaphors (for instance, the furnishing of a room) to express the fact that at this point I know pretty well the nature of everything that must follow to the end of "Reredos" (which was the title it preserved through the entire first draft).

Both Jim and Jane are doubtful about the merits of this story. They seemed to enjoy the preceding sections at the première in Jane's studio (she had just finished a handsome gray nude; we were all feeling mellow), but they questioned whether that wider audience who will read my story to themselves, who have never met me and, likely, never will, would find it relevant or interesting.

What a wider audience ought to know (bear in mind, reader, that this is the frame, not the story):

Four years ago, when I was in advertising, I wrote a story called "The Baron, Danielle, and Paul," which portrayed, behind several thick veils of circumspection, my situation during the previous year, when I had been living with John and Pamela on Riverside Drive. That story appeared, revised, as "Slaves" in the *Transatlantic Review*. Before it had come out, I was living with Pamela again, this time in London and with a different John, a recombination that Jim (before he had ever met Pamela) used as the basis of an amusing piece of frou-frou called "Front and Centaur." After he had met her he wrote "Récits," which is a kind of love story and in no way frivolous. (It, too, was taken by the *Transatlantic Review*.) Then Jim came here, to Milford, and almost immediately Jane wrote a story about the three of *us*: "Naje, Ijm, and Mot." Two days ago Jim sent this off, immaculately typed, to McCrindle, who edits *TR*.

In these successive stories there is a closer and closer approximation to the "real" situation. Thence: this. (Which will almost necessarily go to McCrindle too. If he rejects it? *New Worlds?* Jim is co-editor there.)

A bedroom farce with all the doors opening onto the same library. Stage center, a row of typewriters. On the walls, posters advertising the *Transatlantic Review*.

But beyond the fleeting amusement of our prototypical incests, the story does (should) raise a serious question. Concerning? Art's relationship to other purposes, let us say. Or alternatively, the Artist's role in Society.

Why do I write stories? Why do you read them?

The Semaphore

The maples, whose leaves he would so much have preferred to rake, grew far up the hill, beyond even the most reckless gerrymandering of the boundaries of the backyard. The leaves that he was in fact raking were dingy brown scraps, mere litter, the droppings of poplars.

Jane came out onto the porch. She had just made herself blond. "You shouldn't do it that way," she said.

"How *should* I do it?" he said.

"You should rake them into piles, and then put the piles in boxes, and then empty the boxes into the incinerator, and then incinerate them."

"Do *you* want to rake the leaves?"

"I hate to rake leaves—it reminds me of poems in *The New Yorker*. I wanted you to come in the kitchen and look at what Dylan's found."

Dylan had found a slug.

"It's a snail," she said, "without its shell."

"It's a slug," he said.

"Oh, you're always so disagreeable."

"Snail!" Dylan crowed proudly. "Snail!"

"No, not a snail," he explained, in the slow expository tone he reserved for his son. "A slug. Say 'slug.' "

Dylan looked at his father with bewilderment.

"Slug," he coaxed. "Slug. Slug."

"Fuck," Dylan said.

Jane laughed. (The night before Jim had tried to explain to Dylan the difference between a nail and a screw. Dylan could not pronounce the word "screw," so Jim had taught him to say "fuck" instead.)

"No, slug." But wholly without conviction.

"Snail?"

"Okay, it's a snail."

Jane found a grape jelly bottle and punctured the top with a nail. (Nails don't have threads; screws do.) She put the shell-less snail in the bottle and gave the bottle to Dylan. The snail's extended cornua explored its meaningless and tragic new world.

"Do you want to give your snail a name?" Jim asked. "What do you want to call him?"

After a moment's deliberation Dylan said, "Four eight."

Neither Jim nor Jane thought this a very satisfactory name. At last Jane suggested Fluff.

Even Dylan was happy with this.

Jim went outside to finish raking the brown leaves, while Jane went up to her studio to work. Her new painting represented a single gray body that embraced its thick torso with confused arms. The three heads (which might have been the same head seen from three different angles) bore a problematical relationship to the single torso. It was based on one of Blake's illustrations to the *Inferno*.

Dylan stayed in the kitchen. He uncapped the grape jelly bottle and filled it with water. Snails live in water. The aquarium in the dining room was full of snails and guppies.

Fluff floated in the middle of the water, curled into a tight ball. Dylan, as he watched the snail drown, pronounced its name, its name, pronounced it.

From the letter he wrote to his wife shortly before he came to Milford:

> Pardon the typing. My arms are a bit sore from yesterday's struggle with the harmonium, and I'm a little groggy, still, from being up late last night writing the first of this letter (which, looking back to, I feel should be torn up and disposed of). And I'm all emotional and everything. (I cried when I got your letter, and the effects have not yet worn off. I miss you so much. I love you so much. I want to be with Dylan so badly. You really have no idea what importance you two are in my life, how central you are to everything I do. Just after the death of his wife, Chandler wrote to a friend something like, "Everything I did, for twenty years, every moment, was just a fire for her to warm her hands by." Which is rather how I feel. You'd do

*best, by the way, to disregard Tom's proclamations
on the subject of earthly love. Tom's ideas of love, as
you must surely know, are rather peculiar ones. Never
listen to a renegade Catholic's opinions on love; only
listen to what his work tells you. I do love you. I love
you very much, and I love you more, this moment,
this month, this year, than ever I have before. I do,
Jane. There's desperation in it, yes—I need that love,
to hold up against the world—I need it to give all the
rest of what I do some small meaning, a degree, a single
degree, of relevance—I need it as defense, and as reason.
But that doesn't make the love any less real. With
Creeley, I'm afraid I finally believe that "It's only in the
relationships men manage, that they exist at all." You
ask me to write of love. But how can one write of love,
particularly our love?—it is absolute, and words are ap-
proximations. I have done the best I can do, here, in this
letter. I have tried, in the poems, to do better. But I do
not, finally, believe in the power of words to do other
than distort, fictionalize, and obfuscate. I love you.
Which is the simplest and best way, because every word
there, and there are few of them, is an absolute concept.
I love you.)*

A Lasting Happiness

"How strange life is," Jim remarked, after a pause during
which he had taken in the stark details of my cramped cell.
"Who would have thought, only a few years ago, that you . . .
that I. . . ."

"Those years have been kind to you, Jim," I insisted
earnestly. "Your books have enjoyed both popular and critical success. Though you cannot be said to be rich, your life
has been filled with pleasures that wealth could never buy.
The youth of the nation acclaim you and have no other wish
than to pattern their lives on yours. And you, Jane Rose, you
are lovelier now than when first we met. Do you remember?
—it was July, in Milford."

She turned aside a face that might have come from the
pencil of Greuze, but I had seen that tear and—dare I confess
it?—that tear was dearer to me than her smile!

"And you, Tom?" Jim asked in a low voice.

"Oh, don't think of me! I've been happy too in my own small way. Perhaps life did not bring altogether everything that I once expected, but it has given me . . . your friendship."

He broke into tears and threw his arms about me in a last heart-rending embrace. "Tom!" he cried in agony. "Oh, Tom!"

I smiled, removing his hands gently from my shoulder to place it in Jane's. "You'll soon have all of us in tears," I chided, "and that *would* be silly. Because I expect to be *very* happy, you know, where I am going."

"Dear, dear Tom," Jane said. "We will always remember you."

"Ah, we ought never to trust that word 'always.' I would be quite satisfied with 'sometimes.' And young Dylan, how is he?"

"He is married, you know. We have a grandchild, a darling little girl."

"How wonderful! How dearly I should like to be able to—but, hush! Can you hear them in the corridor? It's time you left. It was so good of you to come. I feel quite . . . transfigured."

Jane rose on tiptoe to kiss my cheek. "God bless you!" she whispered in my ear.

Jim pressed my hand silently. There were no words to express what we felt at that moment.

They left without a backward glance.

The warden entered to inquire if I wished to see a priest. I refused as politely as possible. My hands were bound, and I was led along the corridor—the guards seemed much more reluctant than I—and out through the gate to the little pony cart.

The ride to the place of execution seemed all too brief. With what passionate admiration my eyes drank in the tender blueness of the sky! How eagerly I scanned the faces fleeting past on both sides! How familiar each one seemed! And the grandeur of the public buildings! The thrilling flight of a sparrow across the panorama of roofs! The whole vast spectacle of life—how dear it suddenly had become!

A sturdy young man—he might, I reflected, almost have been myself in another incarnation!—assisted me up the steps and asked if there was anything that I would like to say.

"Only this—" I replied. "It is a far, far better thing that I do than I have ever done; it is a far, far better rest that I go to than I have ever known."

He nodded resignedly. "Mm-hm."

GETTING INTO DEATH

Part 1

I.

Like another Madame Defarge, fat Robin sat there knitting a sweater for her dying mother, who, from her two-hundred-dollar-a-day bed, regarded the pudgy, industrious fingers with a complacent irony. Just so (Cassandra fancied) might an aristocrat, at the height of the Terror, have looked down from his tumbril, then leaned across to the pretty duchess accompanying him to the place of their execution to whisper some pleasantry. But the duchess, distraught, could no more have caught his drift than poor dear Robin could catch hers.

"Anyhow." Cassandra squeezed her little finger into the top of the pack to tickle a crushed Chesterfield loose from the far corner. "To get back to what we were saying."

"Mother. You know you shouldn't."

"It's all right so long as I don't inhale." She lit it, inhaled. "Anyhow. You'd think that having to deal continually with the actual physical fact of it would make a difference."

Robin, apart from not giving a hoot for the inner life of undertakers, thought it extremely poor taste for her mother to be forever harping on, of all subjects, this. Death (she believed), like sex, requires circumspection: a fond unspoken understanding, a few unavoidable tears, and then a stoic and polite silence. "Mother. Please!"

Cassandra trampled on these finer feelings. "But possibly the people who go into it as a profession have already lost most of their capacity to respond. Like the boy who could feel no fear. What I wonder, though, is—have I?"

"Mother, don't always be *thinking* about it. Goodness!" She shook out the bold zigzags of heather and gold to signify, as in a Noh play, her agitation. In justice to Robin it may be said that she'd begun this particular sweater well before Mrs. Millar's semi-fatal stroke. Whenever she was doing nothing else Robin knitted, and fully half of what she knitted went to her mother. Mrs. Millar's closets and cupboards brimmed with her handiwork, and every room of her Lenox Hill apartment displayed some token of Robin's overwhelming need to please and smother—even the bathrooms, where the spare roll of toilet paper was camouflaged by a crocheted cosy resembling a gay little baby bonnet without any opening for baby's face.

"I'm *not* always thinking about it—that's what worries me. That's what I meant about my being in the same category with undertakers and forensic specialists. Maybe if I'd written poetry all along, instead of murder mysteries, I might be able to face my own death now with some dignity. I'm jaded. I've filled myself with cheap candy, and now that it's dinnertime I have no appetite."

"Would you like me to bring in some poetry?" Robin asked, desperate to change the subject.

"No, I've stopped reading."

"You?"

"As part of my preparation. Books can't help me now, can they?"

Robin unrove a course of stitches to where she'd skipped a beat, unrove her benign chatter back to: "Margaret sends her love, did I mention?"

"Margaret can go fuck herself." Mrs. Millar, though not habitually obscene, had always taken a malicious, unmother-like pleasure in rubbing Robin's nose in these proprieties she'd picked up in god only knew what clandestine Methodist Sunday school.

"She said," Robin continued blandly, "she would have come along with me last Friday, but she didn't think you'd— she thought you'd *rather* have just me. You and she were never exactly pals."

"So what did she want to come here for? To jeer?"

"You know why? I think she feels—" (another flourish of the zigzags, signifying judgment) "—guilty."

Guilty? Margaret, the second Mrs. Millar, was a cocktail pianist at the other end of the George Washington Bridge. Robert had moved on to a third wife long ago, but Robin, then in her junior year of high school, had remained with her stepmother in New Jersey, for which Cassandra had never felt anything but gratitude. "Guilty?" she asked.

2.

She was reading *Remembrance of Things Past*. She had been reading it for seven years, having surmounted the initial barrier of "Combray" during a long visit to Wilmington, Delaware. She was intermittently bored and ravished by this dullest and best of all books and would have finished it long since except that she kept losing copies or leaving them behind in restaurants, in the bathrooms of inaccessible friends, or under a stack of *Newsweeks* at her farmhouse in Vermont.

She was determined to finish it before she died. Whenever she was left alone she'd slog on through the small print of her fourth new Random House edition. She'd reached page four hundred and seventy-eight of volume two and had six hundred and forty-six pages to go. A week? Or less.

Once Proust was taken care of an entire little desert island of masterpieces awaited her in the enamel cupboard beside her bed: Virgil, Cervantes, Rabelais, Montaigne, the Bible.

But not *Clarissa*. She despaired of *Clarissa*, and to that degree she was resigned to her death.

3.

The Catholic chaplain was a smoothly handsome, stupid priest in the preconciliar style of the forties. Any Catholic who'd grown up believing in Bing Crosby could have died comfortably in his muscular arms; but beyond the promise of a prayer he didn't have much to offer Cassandra. He disapproved of her too ecumenical spirit (she had checked off all three possibilities on the hospital's religious information card), and when his Protestant counterpart arrived, the priest committed her to the consolations of *his* religion with evident relief.

Reverend Blake lacked the sex appeal of the Catholic chaplain and was not much more articulate. But he did try. Theologically he seemed to favor a Pauline fundamentalism, redolent of brimstone and redeeming blood, but the severity of his creed was moderated by the hesitance of his manner. His exortations suggested the rote sales pitch of a young man just cured of a speech impediment and liable at any moment to relapse. Whenever he stumbled to a stop, Cassandra would ask another intelligent question about the product, which he would answer dutifully and with great effort. At last he came right out and asked whether she was buying any.

"I'd like to. I really would. It would be such a comfort to be able to believe . . . what you've been saying."

There was apparently an answer to this objection, for he started in again: "Faith is a gift, Mrs. Millar, that's true. But—"

"Yes, I think I do understand the concepts. But I can't feel them—here." She placed her hand, gently, on her defective heart.

The Protestant chaplain bowed his head resignedly, as though he'd been told she already had a set of his company's knives or encyclopedias. Such an objection was unanswerable.

"There is one thing, though. A favor you might do me. Though perhaps you wouldn't care to. I mean it's only curiosity on my part."

"Whatever I can do, Mrs. Millar." He pulled his chair closer to the bed and regarded her suspiciously.

"Are there other people here who—people like me—terminal cases, that is—who *do* believe?"

"Yes, of course. A few."

"Could you tell me something about them?"

Reverend Blake lifted an eyebrow but held his tongue, sensing that a sale might still be possible.

"You could give them different names, of course. For the protection of the innocent. But I *would* like to know how other people in my situation are taking it. Whether they're mostly afraid or regretful or what. And to know how their feelings change from day to day."

"Mrs. Millar. I'm afraid that would be absolutely. . ."

"Unprofessional?"

"To say the least."

"But it might be the instrument, you know, of leading me to Christ."

Reverend Blake assured her that he would pray that her heart should be touched and her eyes opened, but he could not, in all conscience, act as her informer. She thanked him, sullenly, and preferred, when he renewed his visit the next day, to be alone.

4.

Cassandra Millar wrote two kinds of books: gothic romances, under the pseudonym of Cassandra Knye, and her "seriouses," the mysteries, thrillers, and Chinese puzzle boxes of B. C. Millar. (The B stood for Bernelle, a name she hadn't answered to since entering the fourth grade of Miss Bennet's School for Girls in Harrisburg.) The gothics, which she wrote with a blithe, teasing contempt for her readers, were far and away the more successful. Five years ago, at the height of the craze for gothics, Signet had reissued eight of the Knye books with uniform covers in murky pastels representing the same windblown, distressed young lady in front of a variety of dark buildings. They went through printing after printing, sweeping along after them her other gothics, scattered among various lesser paperback houses. *Blackthorn* became a movie; *Return to Blackthorn* went to the Literary Guild; and the whole saga, with all five generations, its various family curses and threatened brides, became the basis of a daytime serial on ABC. Cassandra earned literally a million dollars.

By contrast, B. C. Millar seemed barely to scrape along. Most of *her* books were out of print, though they were championed by certain older critics as the chief avatars of the deductive mystery. Her cleverest notions were forever being borrowed by other mystery writers, Miss Knye most notoriously. Once she'd won an Edgar, for *The Imaginary Logarithm,* and one title, *Panic in the Year 1964,* had been an Alternate Selection of the Mystery Guild. Usually, though, she was happy if a book earned back its modest two thousand dollar advance. The sad fact of the matter was that for all the incidental drollnesses, for all the ingenuity of her plots, for all her vaunted irony, B. C. Millar couldn't write. Her characters were wooden, her dialogue false, her prose a solecism. As a stylist, even Cassandra Knye put her to shame. Miss Knye gushed, she fluttered and cooed, but she was, however vulgarly, alive. As much could not be said for B. C. Millar.

5.

She had been put to sleep at her dentist's office, preparatory to a minor filling, and woke in the hospital several hours later. She owed her life, as much as was left, to her dentist's unusual presence of mind, for at the first sign of arrest he'd placed her on the floor and performed external cardiac massage while his receptionist, who was always so rude on the phone, applied mouth-to-mouth resuscitation. By the time a doctor had been called down from the next floor her heartbeat was restored.

When she woke, her own doctor was beside her, Alec Dotsler. She had known him socially and, as B. C. Millar, had consulted him on a variety of medical problems connected with her murders. One of these, *The Purloined Tumor*, had almost amounted to a collaboration. They had had pleasant conversations at parties about the fine points of medical ethics: with whom one must be candid, with whom one may equivocate, and when a lie is all right. Cassandra demanded to know the worst, and three days later she did: the natural flow of her blood, bottlenecked by a critical valve stenosis, would lessen until advanced hypotension produced another and another failure of her heart. Surgery was impossible, drugs useless. When she asked how long she had, he hemmed and hawed, insisted there was no knowing, and gave her, finally, another month. "With luck," he added.

It would be painless.

6.

Laurie Nolde, the stepdaughter she'd acquired by her third marriage, flew in from San Francisco the weekend after Mrs. Millar's admission. She brought a Skippy peanut butter jar of good grass and three wee orange tablets of LSD.

"No, Mom," she said when Cassandra reached for her purse. "This one's on me."

"I call that sentimental."

"Call it my Christmas present." Laurie smiled, and her pale, thin lips became invisible.

Laurie, thanks to her work at Grey Havens, had an affectless, no-nonsense attitude toward death. (Grey Havens rehabilitates the heroin addicts of Haight-Ashbury.) Through their first joint and well into the second she listened tolerantly to her stepmother's account of her difficulties in coming to terms with death, with the *idea* of death.

"Because that's still all it is to me, an idea. Maybe pain is the answer. Maybe instead of just floating off on a breeze, I ought to feel its teeth. Like natural childbirth."

"But you can't ever expect it to make sense."

"Maybe not. But I might be able to fool myself."

"Seriously, Mom." She took the last drag, held up the roach questioningly.

"Just wash it down the sink."

"Seriously." Laurie let out her breath. "You are—" (and took another) "—about as well equipped to die as anyone I ever knew."

"That's very sweet."

"No, I mean it. Think of the life you've had compared to most people. The freedom? The fun? Two loving husbands."

"And Lewis."

"So? How long did that last? A month? What's a month. And Lewis can't be all bad, he's still your agent. Which is another way you've had it easy—money."

She stopped short, as if she'd bitten her tongue. Money was for Laurie what sex or death were for Robin—an unmentionable. She felt the fiercest curiosity to know how much people earned and the rents they paid and where they shopped for clothes, but she would no more have thought of asking such questions than Robin would have let herself be seen at a church supper reading *Valley of the Dolls*. So, shifting into reverse, she led the conversation (Cassandra being too knocked-out to do anything but follow) from her stepmother's many advantages to her own handicaps (the largest being that she couldn't really "open up"), and thence to the question of whether or not to marry her fiancé. In his favor she cited his correct opinions, good looks, and malleable disposition; on the other hand, he was a loser, though Laurie didn't come right out and say so. But ought that to be a consideration? Laurie wondered; should the future even enter into it? Clearly, she wanted Cassandra to tell her that it should.

"What, to be absolutely cold-blooded, does your true love *do?*"

"Now? He's a dish washer. But before that he made vests, fringed vests. Only, the shop he was making them for went out of business."

"It's the recession," Cassandra said.

"That's what I said. The *ideal* thing would be if he had his own shop somewhere. The restaurant gig is just something he's doing till he qualifies for unemployment." It was an unconvinced apology. Laurie seemed to think it possible her fiancé *liked* to wash dishes.

"You want my advice, you should marry him. Marriage is an art, and one's first husband shouldn't be too difficult. Time enough, once you've learned to handle washers, to move on to earls."

Laurie frowned.

"A pun," Cassandra explained. "I'm very, very high."

Laurie's feelings had been hurt, but she went on anyhow to weigh the pros and cons of her decision. At length, Cassandra was obliged to pretend to fall asleep to be rid of her. She'd never liked Laurie, not since she'd met her as a precociously deflowered sixth grader, but she'd had no better grounds for her dislike than that the girl seemed so often to parody her own never so explicit hedonism. Yet Laurie answered her stepmother's coolness with something approaching affection. She was drawn to Cassandra as to a mirror in which she could see herself thirty years older and still swinging, still balling, still rolling along; and still, for a wonder, worth looking at.

7.

Every night she would wake up between three and four and not be able to get back to sleep till dawn. Her condition prohibited the use of barbituates, and the night nurse prohibited reading. What better time to think of death? *Death,* she thought. *I am dying.* As well might she have told herself she was in love, or mad. Was *this* a form of defiance? or resignation? or only incredulity?

She tried to picture her own body decaying in the grave, all wormy and forlorn. Nothing.

She tried to think of the spaces between the stars, of timelessness and nonexistence. But such notions affected her no more than stories of the war in India.

Finally she gave up trying and did what she had always done on nights of insomnia: she plotted new mysteries.

8.

Rabbi Yudkin took the Bible out of the enamel cupboard and found the passage in question. Ezekiel 18; 32: *For I have no pleasure in the death of him that dieth, saith the Lord God; wherefore turn yourselves, and live ye.*

"Turn yourselves and live: for my money that's the last word on the subject."

Mrs. Millar appeared to doubt this. "Perhaps. But a person in my circumstances may have some difficulty applying such advice."

"Some people might, but *you're* not doing so badly."

She thought for a moment he was being sarcastic about her having begun a story. But no, it was only his style of comfort. She neither disputed the compliment nor dug for another. Instead she asked after Mrs. Hyman in ward D. Mrs. Hyman, after a life lived unexceptionably on the surface of Scarsdale, was suffering a death of exemplary anguish. Seedlings of cancer swarmed through her flesh, blossoming everywhere into pain. She wept for the doctors, screamed at her husband, abased herself to Rabbi Yudkin, denouncing herself, her family, the hospital, God. It was Tolstoyan, and Cassandra envied Mrs. Hyman's least kneejerk of dread. She questioned the Jewish chaplain about her interminably, both as to her suburban past and her daily progress toward their common goal.

9.

She blatted out the story in two days. It was about the widow of a famous writer (Hemingway, though she had to disguise that) who persuades one of the master's least competent imitators to forge a series of posthumous novels which the widow releases year after year to her own great profit and the annihilation of the writer's reputation. All done, including the widow's comeuppance, in two tidy scenes that came out, reasonably, at four thousand words.

Lewis phoned to say (what else could he?) that "Revenge" was the drollest thing she'd ever done. He was sure that the *New Yorker* would take it. She'd never sold a word to the *New Yorker*, and she never would. As well might she lust for Cary Grant.

10.

A letter arrived from her father, who had moved to Arizona to escape the pathos of the seasons. He excused himself from attending her deathbed. "But," she wanted to say, "I didn't *invite* you." Aside from the condescension of her Christmas checks (always cashed and never acknowledged), she'd had little to do with him since he'd ridden off fifteen years ago into the sunset. Robin, it must have been, who'd informed him, convinced the old man would veil his malice decently before so major an institution as death. In this Robin had underestimated the strength of her grandfather's character. His letter, scrawled on the back of a humorous greeting card ("Get Well Soon/—Or Else!"), stopped just short of overt self-congratulation. He was sending her, but not by air, an inspiring book by Smiley Blanton.

The letter ended: "Yours sincerely, Ulysses Barlowe." "Sincerely" was underlined.

It was some comfort to think she'd never been trapped into caring for the old bastard. Twice as B. C. Millar and once as Cassandra Knye she'd had the satisfaction of killing him off in books that had detailed his minor crookednesses as a justice of the peace and his larger connivings in the capitol at Harrisburg. She would have liked, for a last fling, to tear into him again, but there was no help for it now. She was forgiven; *he* had the last laugh.

II.

Except in *The Seventh Codicil,* which was a virtual textbook of testamentary law, B. C. Millar had always rather scanted wills as motives for her murders. Cassandra Knye had necessarily more to do with legacies, entails, and such, but even for her these matters had been only so much gothic lumber, in a class with secret passages, mute servants, and mysterious footsteps.

But now, ah! Now she had actually to write her own. Her money would become someone else's. Her money, which she'd meant to spend on jewelry and geriatric treatments! Here was occasion for an elegy. People were no more than the compost in which dollars grew, ripened, fell, and grew again.

Despite his most plausible arguments, she couldn't bring herself to sign the model document her lawyer had drawn up. Half a million dollars to Robin? Inconceivable! Trust funds for nieces, for nephews, for second cousins?

But who or what else should she lavish herself upon? Ex-husbands? Charities? Some foundation, like Shaw's, to advance some freakish cause of her own.

"Couldn't I just give it *all* to the government?" she pleaded.

Mr. Saunders shook his head.

Finally she came up with a formula that satisfied both herself and him. All three hundred and forty-nine names on her last year's Christmas card list were to receive absolutely equal shares in her estate. This would give each heir a little less than four thousand dollars. Robin was to get, additionally, the farmhouse in Vermont and its furnishings.

Mr. Saunders called the next morning to ask: "The Lenox Hill Liquor Store?"

"Yes, they've always been very nice to me there. Cashing my checks. And every year they send me a calendar."

"Is there a particular person there?"

"Oh, I see what you mean. No, divide it up."

"And at Doubleday's, is it Miss Bergen, or Berger? The letter is typed over on the list."

"Who?"

"Bergen. Or Berger."

"I don't think I can remember any such creature at Doubleday's. Maybe you should call them."

"I did. There's one of each, and both are editors."

"Well, if it's going to hold things up, let's give them both a share."

The will ran to forty pages. She signed it, and Mr. Saunders and Dr. Dotsler were witnesses.

12.

From her notebook:

THE DEATH TAX
(or "Death and Taxes"?)

An old woman dying, her family gather in next room, wait for her to be off. Then error is discovered in payment of "death tax." She can't die until her sons have cleared this up at appropriate government office. Much hugger-mugger with red tape, rubber stamps, old birth certificates, etc.

Italy?

13.

Rabbi Yudkin asked how she had passed the night.

"With the Godzilla of all nightmares. Usually I don't remember what I dream, but this one—oh, boy!"

"Shall I interpret it for you? As I think I told you, my first vocation was to psychoanalysis, but my parents didn't have money to send me to med school."

"Here it is, then. But first I have to explain that back when I started writing for the pulps I used to go to this special dentist, who worshiped writers, Dr. Blitzman. I found out about him through my first husband, who was one half of Bud Dorn. The Western writer? My teeth were in horrible shape, and I'd go in once a week, for months it seemed, and he'd drill a well in one of my teeth and then while my filling dried he'd give me one of his manuscripts. There he was, a perfectly happy successful dentist, and the only thing he wanted to do was to sell a love story to the *Saturday Evening Post*. I'd read his manuscript, and then when my mouth was rinsed out I'd give my professional opinion. Which was that his story was promising, but like my mouth it still needed work. I still have some of the same fillings, but he's dead now."

"That was your dream? Or reality?"

"Reality, but the dream didn't add much. I was back in Blitzman's office, in his chair, with these clamps in my mouth to keep me from closing it, and he was reading me this absolutely terrifying story. Aloud. I'd had Novocaine, and my whole body, everything, was numb, except I could still feel the saliva drooling out of the side of my mouth."

"And what was the story about that he read to you?"

"That I don't remember."

She reached for her Chesterfields. Yudkin looked askance.

"Turn yourselves therefore and live ye," she reminded him. "And anyhow I don't inhale."

Yudkin's interpretation of the dream was straightforward, uninteresting, and probable. The dentist represented Death, which Mrs. Millar feared. Death was the undiscovered country from whose bourne no traveler returns, and therefore she couldn't remember what happened in the dentist's story.

Cassandra agreed without a trace of sarcasm that she might very well be afraid of death. Then she asked after Mrs. Hyman, who had developed a last-minute enthusiasm for spiritualism. Each morning a medium visited ward D to help her get in contact with the other side. They'd reached a spirit called Natalie, who was to be Mrs. Hyman's guide once she entered the spirit world.

"Does it help?" Cassandra asked.

"More than I ever seemed to. Would *you* like to try it?"

"Not yet, no. When I'm riper, perhaps." She winked to make it clear that she was joking.

Part 2

I.

Within moments of her swallowing the acid there was a tapping on the door, a wee small "shave and a haircut, two bits," like a mouse coming to visit a rabbit. Who could it be at eight o'clock of a Wednesday morning? Who but Robin?

The knob turned. She closed her eyes, forgetting to remove the sunglasses, and composed her hands, deathwise, across her breasts. Mysterious footsteps entered the room.

I am asleep, she thought determinedly (yet without crinkling), and must on no account be awakened.

The footsteps went here and there, filled a jug at the sink, sat in the sighing vinyl chair, and gave up. When the latch clicked shut, she opened her eyes, and there on the dresser, doubled by the mirror, was a massive bouquet of long-stemmed red roses. Who in the world? she wondered, and decided it must have been one of her two Bobs—Millar or Nolde—since roses were so explicitly a sexual attention.

She slipped on her mules and shuffled to the dresser. The card said only: "Best wishes. Ira Seidemann."

Ira Seidemann?

Then it connected: her dentist, *Dr.* Seidemann. Not only had he saved her life, but he must have spent no less than fifty dollars for all those roses! Cassandra was flabbergasted.

2.

Page 789.

335 pages left.

The *Remembrance* was a long train ride through provincial France, a lulling orderly journey with an occasional glimpse of some astonishing artifact: a cathedral spire, a Roman aqueduct, an avenue of trees extending, like hexameters, all the way to the horizon; then for half an hour nothing but wastes of mud, gray farms, rows of cabbages.

She'd forged ahead ten more pages before her marigold bookmark became more interesting than Proust's prose.

"Heigh-ho!"

The roses nodded in their silly vase. *Yes*, they were thinking, *here we go!*

3.

Against the glory of dying young, any living thirty-year-old must appear as drab as the fashions of five years ago. So there was much *Weltschmerz* (a boistrous poignance, like a college reunion) in listening to the "Sgt. Pepper" tape and thinking back to the balmy days just after she'd run out on dear decrepit Nolde. Cassandra at least possessed the satisfaction of mourning a *second* youth.

The Beatles, however, were only to be the cheese dip before a full formal banquet of Beethoven, Mahler, and Bach. But of all this sublimity she heard but one single, strangulated groan, as her tape machine, a brand new Webcor from Lafayette, gobbled up the first few yards of *"Das Lied von der Erde"* and stopped. The reverse button didn't do anything and the forward button added more tape to the snarl until, having created a giant chrysanthemum-style bow, nothing would budge. The same fate met *"O Ewigkeit, du Donnerwort,"* and *"Gottes Zeit ist die allerbeste Zeit."*

Her trip lay ahead of her like a desert without a camel, a portion without an outline, Shit Creek without a paddle.

4.

As an aid to levelheadedness she put on pantyhose, a bra, a blouse, and her tweedy authorish suit from The Tailored Woman. Looking at herself through the roses (roses!) she felt as neat and crisp as a parenthesis. Here was the one and only Cassandra Millar, back in her clothes and immortal as ever. Death? A pink nightgown crumpled on a tape-recorder.

5.

High winds rasped wisps of Persian from the edges of
dreamsicle clouds that rode eastward against the current of
the sunlight. The poems disintegrated, line by line, into the
tense, the trembling element. It is the air that one sees. That
is blue. Whereas the sky is black.

A single bird flew up from the parking lot. And up!
Nature.

6.

The nurse, leaving, had left the door ajar, and bits of talk
snagged on the thorns of Cassandra's voracious attention. A
numinous veal chop and broccoli warred with the roses. A
wedge of noonday light, aswarm with motes of dust, was
spread across the foot of the mussed, empty bed. She, the
focus of all these data, sat on the visitor's chair, and thought:

Death will be like this. Death is what people talk about
when one leaves the room: not oneself, not the vanished,
pitiable Albertine, but *their* business and appetites. They
could care less who *we* slept with in our time.

She sat so still and listened so intently, for a little while,
that she fancied she might be dead already; a whimsy.

7.

She got the window open, and the colder outdoor air swept
in and filled the room with messages. Her skin turned to
Coca-Cola. She took the jacket off. Sunglasses. The shivering
blouse. Rings and hairpins. Ishtar at apogee. She closed the
window, the door, the eyes, and let her living fingers feel,
falling back across the bed, her self. She peeled back the
calyx of her pantyhose and headed straight for the source.
Her fingers pressed past petal after petal like Fabergé bees
whose wings (rose-enameled nails) whirred and beat against
and bruised the delighted, anguished flower. It was everything
magnificent, but even as the twenty-eight flavors spilled and

flickered over the top of the opal dam she had enough irony
left (she always did) to think, Now more than *ever* seems it
rich to die!

8.

Once she'd started on this bowl of heavenly popcorn she
couldn't stop, though even as Pelion was heaped on Ossa she
sensed that she was missing the boat. Her previous trips
(three with Leary himself) had been models of goal-oriented
ecstasy, cornucopias of awareness. Finally, forlornly, she
looked about her tumbled bedclothes and saw—

Imagine some dumb widow who's just blown all the insurance money on a suite of shoddy furniture and a fake-fur
coat. Imagine her entering her living room a year later and
looking in the mirror. The gilding of the stucco frame is turning brown. The so-called mink is shedding. There's no chance
now to take that secretarial course. And the money's gone.
What does she think? Cassandra experienced an analogous
regret.

So when Robin came tap tappy-tap-tap, tap tapping on the
door it was like the Marshall Plan coming to the rescue of a
devastated Europe.

"Who is it?" she asked.

"Me. Robin."

"Oh, Robin, I'm all sticky. What I mean is, not now,
darling. Come back at, what time is it now?"

"Three-thirty."

"At four. Okay? Or four-thirty."

"Okay. But."

"Yes?"

"I brought you some books. From your apartment. They're
awfully heavy. Can't I just—" (as she asked, the door peeped
open and a Bloomingdale's shopping bag crept into the
room) "—slip them inside?"

Robin had brought her all the poetry she owned.

9.

"Yes," Yudkin said, "I've read several of them. *The Castle and the Key*. And the one with the Nazi general disguised as his own grandmother."

"You mean *The House That Fear Built*."

"That was a real shocker, that one."

"But those are all by Cassandra Knye. I don't count them as *my* books."

"I've read some of the others too, but I guess I prefer the more romantic ones. Most people do, don't they? Mrs. Hyman, for instance—when she heard that Cassandra Knye was right here in the same hospital, you should have seen the expression on her face. I didn't tell her your real name, of course, but that only added to the glamour of it."

"Mrs. Hyman?"

"She's read everything Cassandra Knye has ever written. In fact, the reason I brought this up, she asked me if you'd sign a copy of one of your books for her. I have it here." He took a battered, book club edition of *Blackthorn* from his briefcase. "You're laughing. At Mrs. Hyman? At me?"

It was a pantomime rather than real, physiological laughter. She opened the book to the flyleaf, thought a moment, and wrote: "To Mrs. Hyman, Till we meet soon, in those Gardens where the summer never fades, please accept my very heartfelt best wishes—and say a prayer for—Cassandra Knye."

Yudkin read the inscription. "Oh, she'll treasure that."

"It's not too much?"

"Too much?" he asked, as if this were an oxymoron. "Oh, not for Mrs. Hyman." Then, furrowing his brow and deepening his voice from light social to medium serious: "Have you ever thought *why* it is that most readers do prefer the one kind of book—'gothics,' you call them?—to the other? Oh, I know you'll say because most people are stupid—"

No: she shook her head violently. He was right. "Oh, I wouldn't."

"—and that may be half of it. We're all like my own children in a way. When they know they like a story they want to hear it over and over. Which must lead you writers to writing things to a kind of formula. But why this—" (He tapped the spine of *Blackthorn*) "—particular formula rather than the one that *you* like, the detective formula?"

"What Lewis says—my agent, Lewis Whitman—is that the reason my mysteries don't catch on is that I don't have a consistent point of view. I can't invent a detective that anybody cares about, that *I* care about. They're like computers. In fact, one of the books I'll never write now was going to have the murder solved by a computer. Whereas I *can* invent a believable victim. A gothic is almost the reverse image of a mystery. Instead of some brilliant Sherlock Holmes pouncing on each little clue, what you want is some pretty featherhead like Nan Richmond who can *miss* all of them. The plot is set up so that no matter how thick the readers may be, the heroine is a little thicker. Oh, excuse me, I didn't mean to say—"

Yudkin waved the apology aside. "All that may be so, but I think it leaves the essential thing unaccounted for. People read Cassandra Knye to be frightened. The scene at the end of this one, for instance, where Nan is dancing with her nephew out on the dark terrace: terrifying. But I don't see why it should be. She isn't in any immediate danger. Why should—"

Suddenly there came a tapping.

Robin entered in her big brown bag of a coat and began at once to leave. "I didn't mean to interrupt."

Yudkin insisted *he* was leaving, and Cassandra, rescued in the nick of time from having to explain the danger that Nan had been in, made no effort to keep him by her bedside.

Robin asked after her mother's health today relative to yesterday, admired the roses, and sat down to work on the sweater, which only wanted one sleeve to be complete.

10.

Underpinning Cassandra Knye's practice was a theory that women regard sex with a fear so overmastering that it can only reach consciousness disguised as a rational and seemly terror of death. This hypothesis seemed strengthened with each successive success of the books based on it, until, with the triumph of *Blackthorn* (the plot of which was based on the summary of Tyce's classic study of patterns of endogamy and exogamy evidenced in the fantasies of one hundred twenty female inmates in a Des Moines mental hospital), she felt as secure of her theory as any Ptolemy.

But now (six-thirty of that same Wednesday), as she stirred the hospital's notion of chicken chow mein around and around and around, it occurred to her that there might be a Copernican alternative that would fit all the facts just as well.

Death, it must be allowed, is a natural metaphor for the act of love; it represents the loss of one's ultimate cherry. Just as virgins are forever pondering what it would be like to go all the way, so the living try (with no better success) to imagine death. From this similitude proceed millennia of romances: Ariadne mistaking Bacchus for Dis; the less fortunate confusions of Tristan and Isolde, of Romeo and Juliet, of Byron, Keats, and Shelley; and, last and least, the potboilers of Cassandra Knye.

But couldn't it just as well be the case that Cassandra, by convincing herself that she was writing about sex, had been enabled to deal with the subject that actually terrified her? that actually *is* terrifying? After the bridal night and a bit of practice, most of us may come to terms with love, but death remains a mystery. We think we hear him walking in the corridor, but when we open the door it's only Midnight playing with a ball of yarn. We think he's at the window, but when we go there his rapping proves to be a dry branch tossing in the wind. Yet he is there, in the shadows, waiting to cut in and waltz us out onto the dark terrace, whirling us about, like leaves. And we know what he intends, then.

These were such pretty ideas and so capable of development that Cassandra longed to have someone at hand who thought at her own speed. She called Lewis, but his answering service had no idea where he was. When she phoned his other number, no one answered.

11.

Robin returned with four cartons of real Chinese food from Woh Ping and cold beer from a deli. They ate voraciously, praising the food and making toasts, when they'd slowed down, to the great meals of yesteryear: the holiday dinners and home-cooked pies of the forties; from the fifties (when the money first started coming in), their extravaganzas at restaurants on Robin's weekend visits into the city; crowning all these, the glories of Robin's own devising now she was grown up with a kitchen all her own—the creamed mushroom omelettes and shrimps polonaise, the sweetbreads and shortcakes, the crêpes and soufflés.

Robin began to cry.

"Robin!"

"I'm sorry. But it's just—so awful." She swallowed, took a sip of beer to help it down, and smiled a ghastly smile. "There—all better."

"Darling, what is it?" (Had the fact of her death, her inevitable death, finally broached Robin's defenses?)

Robin denied that it was anything.

"Tell me and you'll feel better."

After further cajoling, Robin confessed that their talk of food had upset her. "I know other people find it offensive. No, don't say they don't. They do. And I just—" She shook her head dismally. "You see, I *want* to stop, I try to, but—I go a day, two days, and then it comes over me. Like another person takes control. And then afterward I just hate myself. I feel so awful. I mean physically I feel awful."

It developed, after more tears, that Robin had tried to become a nurse, had even been accepted into a school—conditional upon her losing fifty pounds. Since her acceptance she'd gained fifteen.

"I've never heard of anything so cruel and ... preposterous! Why didn't you tell me before? I'm sure we could have found another school. I'm sure we still can. What you weigh, Robin, is a matter for your own—" ("conscience"? decidedly not) "—for *you* to decide."

"No, Mother, they were right. I'm dangerously overweight. And anyhow, that's all in the past. I'm happy with the job I've got. I wouldn't want to be a nurse now. It's only coming *here* every day, walking through the corridors, and seeing all of them, seeing the way they look at me."

This confession was the prelude to the whole, woeful story. Robin was in love. The man was married; his wife was Robin's best friend (they'd met at Weight Watchers); all three of them were wretched.

Cassandra was aghast, never having imagined any other existence for Robin than this, in which she ate, played cards, knitted socks, and paid visits to her mother, who (this seemed to have been the understanding) had been the source of whatever was actual, vivid, and passionately alive in the diminished family of mother and daughter; a mistake.

12.

From her notebook:

Murder Mystery to be told from the point of view of the corpse. Someone like Mrs. Hyman, very acrimonious, bitter. Doesn't know who murdered her: *Victim is Detective!* Pov limited to room in which she's been killed (visual) and immediately adjacent rooms (audio) where police question suspects. She's suspicious of everyone, shocked by their revelations about herself. Gradually learns to free herself of "fleshly bonds." (Research: spiritualism, auras, out-of-body exp., planes of spirit existence.) By the time she's solved the murder, she's able to forgive murderer. Who?

13.

She dreamed that night again of a dentist's office. Not Blitzman's; a dentist long before—Dr. Skutt, who'd extracted her baby teeth in Wilmington and signed her first dental cards. Dr. Skutt had been a harelip, and from her first visit to him at the age of eight she'd had an obscure sense of consonancy between the man's defect and his occupation, as though he were revenging himself on other people's mouths for the horror of his own.

In the dream, she was strapped to Skutt's dental chair, and he was pleading with her to open her mouth. She refused.

He showed her the little mirror on its long silver handle. "Please, open up now, Bernelle. I only want to *look*."

Still she refused, and his anger rose from his tense fingers to his gray eyes. He bent nearer, insisting, and nearer till his lips met her own. But still she kept her jaw clamped tight shut. Skutt's tongue pressed hard against her rotted teeth, which splintered, crumbled, and collapsed.

Part 3.

1.

Having lived two days beyond her allotted month, Cassandra developed a cursory interest in the actual mechanical processes of her disintegration and sent Robin on a reluctant errand to fetch the relevant medical books from her apartment.

Robin left the sweater behind. It was finished but for the cuff of the left arm, which hung limply over the top of the knitting bag like the stump of some unfortunate creature who'd tried to climb into a full lifeboat. Cassandra held back as long as she could. Then she got out of bed (by now, no mean accomplishment) and, after first wiggling the needles from their loops, unraveled the sleeve back to the elbow.

Robin, on returning, made no mention of this vandalism. Loop by loop, she fit the needles into the right courses; then, patient as a spider, she began to knit again.

2.

The next morning she altogether neglected Proust for the sake of B. B. Milstein's *Cardiac Arrest and Resuscitation*. Milstein told of case after case—"a woman of 53," "a man of 64," and even "a child of 6"—whose hearts had stopped or gone into spasms. Often a thoracotomy was performed to enable the surgeon to reach into the chest and massage the heart, either directly or through its pericardial sac. The various steps of what would very likely be done, next time, to Cassandra were illustrated in photographs: the thoracotomy incision, a cleft running from midchest all the way round to the back; next, the surgeon opening the incision forcibly, with the same strenuous grip one exerts against the halves of a subway door that's trapped one's foot; lastly, the actual process of massage, with the heart, a small glistening thing no bigger than a medium-sized green pepper, resting in the surgeon's fingers.

She pored over these few pictures with the same awed satisfaction she'd felt long ago in the Wilmington library riffling through travel books and *National Geographics* for glimpses of beggars and holy men on the other side of the world, where elephantiasis and the worship of god were able to transform human beings into something wonderfully else.

As fascinating, if not as affecting, as these photographs were the case histories. Case Twenty-seven, especially; a fifty-three-year-old woman whose heartbeat was restored after fully five minutes of massage. Thirty-six hours after the operation she awoke demented, the result of anoxic brain damage. She could remember only her childhood and, when asked to sign her name, wrote her maiden name in a childlike scrawl. She thought the medical staff were policemen and could hear sea lions outside her room.

Cassandra could face the prospect of sea lions bravely, not to say eagerly. About a second childhood she wasn't so sure. She dreaded the diminution of her intelligence and would much rather have been dead than stupid and an object of pity to the likes even of a Mrs. Hyman.

3.

Since her dream about Dr. Skutt on the night of her trip she felt she'd done her duty by self-awareness. The dream proved that she was terrified of death. If that terror were not always at the forefront of consciousness, so much the better. She could relax, happy in the knowledge that at least once she'd made an appropriate emotional response to her death.

She'd recounted the dream to everyone: to Dotsler, Yudkin, Robin; to the nurses; to anyone who phoned. They'd all agreed that it was terrifying and, with the exception of Yudkin, urged her to forget it.

4.

Even now, every time she opened a package of cigarettes, she felt a twinge of guilt. Since the publication of the Surgeon General's report in 1964, Cassandra had swayed reedlike in the opposing winds of appetite and moral resolve. One of B.

C. Millar's last books, *Death in Its Holiday Package,* had been a veritable tract against cigarette smoking. All the while she was writing it she'd smoked two packs a day.

5.

Cassandra looked at her lunch. She felt as though she'd been flying back and forth across the Atlantic endlessly, never getting off the plane, and eating the same mild meal day after day, mile after mile, like one of the poor vultures condemned to dine on Prometheus' liver.

That afternoon (the seventh day of her second month in the hospital) she began working on *The Dead Detective.*

6.

"It really was," Yudkin said, "a beautiful death."

"Really?"

"Really. And to be perfectly honest, I was surprised."

"It was lucky you happened to be there then."

"Lucky for me, perhaps. Such moments are my chief reward. Not that I can take any of the credit for *her* good death. But just the knowledge that it's possible—that's something."

"It happened this morning?"

"A little before eight. Ward D faces the river, so that the early light is direct and very intense. The explanation may be as simple as that."

"And what did she say?" Cassandra asked once again.

" 'The light! The light is blinding.' "

"It *sounds* like she may have wanted you to lower the blinds."

"But she was smiling so as she said it. A smile like—well, I can't describe it."

For the rest of the day Cassandra felt alone and slightly panicky. She'd come to depend on Mrs. Hyman in so many little ways. Her hysteria and credulity were the foils to Cassandra's own coolness and rationality. All of her anguished writhings, as Yudkin had reported them to her daily, had been an admonishment not to go off down the same steep road

herself. It galled her that Mrs. Hyman, who'd actually had
some hope of recovering, should beat her to the exit; it was
insufferable that she should do so with such panache. "The
light!" indeed! she thought grimly. Who did Mrs. Hyman
think she was? Goethe? Little Nell?

7.

There was nothing, next morning, in the paper. Mr. Hyman was a prominent toy manufacturer on 31st Street: surely
his wife's death rated a mention in the *Times*, if only her
name and age and whom she was survived by. Cassandra
herself was counting on four column inches, and though
Mrs. Hyman couldn't have asked for as much as that, this
total neglect seemed tantamount to being left unburied, out
on a dung heap, like Antigone's brother.

Later, when the aide came in to change her sheets, she
asked her, "Miss Rooker, do you aides only work in one ward
at a time? Or do you get assigned to all different parts of the
hospital?"

"Sure," Miss Rooker said, with a warm smile.

"What I want to know, dear, is if you've worked, lately, in
Ward D."

"Ward D?"

"Yes. What I'd like to know is this: which way does it
face? Does it face *east* to the river? Or *west* into the city?"

Miss Rooker paused amidst her sheets to think. "I'm sorry,
all the different floors and letters, they get jumbled up. And I
don't go up into that area too often."

"Then you wouldn't know the friend of mine who's
there—Mrs. Hyman?"

"In ward D?"

Cassandra nodded.

"Not in ward D, I don't think." She affected to giggle.
"Ward D is for all the old gentlemen, the ones who can't take
care of themselves. There aren't any women there."

8.

Rabbi Yudkin was not to be blamed for having invented
Mrs. Hyman (hadn't she almost demanded it of him?)—only

for having allowed his audience at the high point of his tale to fall into disbelief. Her death had been too nice, too merely decorative. If only he'd baited his transcendental hook with some engaging, toothsome detail, Cassandra might never have thought to doubt his story. If, for instance, toward the end Mrs. Hyman had tried to destroy her charge-a-plate, or got the hiccoughs, like Pope Pius XII. But to bathe her in that blinding light, to have practically sent down a ladder to her from on high! That showed a want of tact.

9.

She had phoned down to the cashier's office, and, when Yudkin called by for his afternoon chat, she was ready for him.

"When is the funeral?" she asked.

"Not till Friday."

"Here? Or in Scarsdale?"

"In Scarsdale. It will probably be quite a production. Mr. Hyman seems to be in his element again, organizing things."

Cassandra beckoned Yudkin closer to her bed. "Here," she said, pressing the envelope into his hand. "I want you to do a favor for me. A little deception."

He looked doubtful.

"A wreath. I want to send her the very best wreath you can get."

"Oh. But."

"The card needn't say any more than—'With sincere sympathy, Cassandra Knye.' "

"Impossible. I mean—" He looked into the envelope. "Oh, Mrs. Millar, this is far too much!"

"For a wreath? Nonsense. I called a florist and asked. And don't try and tell me they don't want flowers. I know Scarsdale!"

"But—"

He was caught. Either he'd have to admit that Mrs. Hyman didn't exist, or he'd have to take the money.

"I would have sent the wreath myself, but then, you see, they might have been able to trace it back to *me*. I want to be the person I always love in a story—the anonymous benefactor. And I know I can count on you to preserve my pseudonym. But if there's some reason you'd rather not, I *could* get Robin to send it."

"No! No, I just question the—" He held up the bulging envelope.

"The propriety of it?"

"Yes. To be frank."

"But it isn't really disproportionate when you think of all I've got. Oh, say you'll do it."

Yudkin wavered, sighed, and pocketed the envelope.

"I knew you would." She leaned forward in the bed and pinched his cheek. "If you could *see* the way you're blushing!"

10.

She'd made her pile by telling people what they seemed to want to hear—that Death was a gentleman whose kisses were gentle even as he threatened rape, that one may venture out onto the terrace with him and come back (a bit sadder, a bit wiser, but intact) to the party. In fact, there are no survivors of that waltz, and so the heart of every one of her books had been a lie, her latest, *The Dead Detective*, being the most whopping of them all.

But what of that? Her readers had wanted it, and now at last she wanted it too. For Yudkin had invented Mrs. Hyman in response to her expressed, her almost strident need, and Cassandra had been his more than willing dupe. She wanted no further knowledge of *real* people, of how they were cheated, cornered, betrayed, ignored, and themselves driven to cheat, entrap, and betray in turn. She could have killed Robin for reminding her of the processes of love—the anguish of being rejected, the guilt of rejecting, the desolations of loneliness. No, she craved fiction. "Reality," as one of her old buttons had proclaimed, "is a crutch." If this were a lie, well then, she needed what help she could get.

And so did everyone.

Yudkin had done the right thing. He'd told the lie his duty had demanded and persisted in it, even at the expense of self-respect.

Cassandra could do no less.

11.

That same afternoon she contacted Mr. Saunders, to revoke her first will and have him bring in his model document, which he did that evening.

To her father she wrote a rich, ripe heartthrob of a letter, telling him what, in the last analysis, a wonderful father he had been, and how much, at bottom, she'd always loved him.

Then she wrote to both Bobs (identical letters) along the same bittersweet lines, though tempering the language to their more discriminating tastes. She couldn't think of any plausible tale to tell Lewis except that he had a wonderful mind and she loved him.

She phoned Laurie to reveal what she'd so desperately tried to ferret out on her visit to New York—how much she was coming in for from her stepmother's will. Had the Christmas tree in Rockefeller Center collapsed on her, Laurie could not have been crushed by any larger happiness. Her whole life, she swore, would be changed.

But letters and phone calls were easy. Forthright, uncomplicated plagiarisms from The Best-Loved Lies of the American People. The real test would be Robin, who, for all her prissy pieties and pretended deafnesses, was her mother's sternest audience and cruelest judge.

12.

In the summer of '45 Bob and Cassandra and Robin and Bob's cousin Margaret Millar had all driven west in a Kaiser station wagon to see the actual country Bob had been writing about all these years. The culmination of the many misadventures of the trip came when Bob and Margaret contrived to be lost for four days in Grand Canyon National Park, leaving Cassandra with Robin, the dying Kaiser, and eight dollars. At that time Cassandra had been a haggard twenty-six, Margaret a dazzling nineteen.

Time and affluence had improved Cassandra; the same

amount of time and too much liquor had made of the second Mrs. Millar a shipwreck of her former self. Conscious of their reversed fortunes and without considering that they were about to be reversed again, Margaret was abjectly complimentary. How wonderful Cassandra looked! What a lovely negligee! How lucky she was to have a private room!

"When *I* was in the hospital," she said, "I was in the general ward. With all these colored women? You can imagine what *that* was like. Hackensack! But this! This is more like a hotel room than a hospital. The furniture! Though you would think for what you're paying you'd have a room with a view to the river. Still it's not a *bad* view. In fact, it's nice."

"Would you like a cigarette?" Cassandra asked.

"I shouldn't. But thank you, I will." The knuckles of Margaret's hand were swollen, the flesh puffy, the skin coarse. To think she was still able to play the piano! "Chesterfields! You don't see many of them nowadays."

"No, you don't. Bob used to smoke Chesterfields. I must have picked it up from him."

This was the first mention of his name since Margaret had come in the door twenty minutes ago.

"Do you hear from him?" Margaret asked.

"Not often. He lives in London. And he's married again. But that's old news by now."

Margaret screaked with laughter. "Always the gay Lothario!"

It was her chance. "Yes," she said softly, "he was that."

Margaret, who had prepared herself to unite with Cassandra in vilifying their ex-husband, was dismayed now to hear him so eloquently praised, so candidly cherished. Cassandra wanted (she said) only to remember what had been good and live and warm and tender: the laughter they had shared, the growing and deepening sense of mutual discovery, the love. But who could describe love? One could only experience it.

"You loved him too, didn't you?" she said, catching hold of Margaret's hand as soon as she'd stubbed out the cigarette. "Oh, of course you did! How could you have helped it? How could I?"

Margaret tried, gently, to pry her hand away. (It was such an ugly hand.) "But I always thought—"

"That I was jealous? Oh, at first I may have been. But how

could I have gone on feeling like that after all you've done for me? You brought up Robin. You were the mother to her that I was too busy and too selfish to be."

"But wasn't I—"

"Yes?" Cassandra let her free her hand.

"Wasn't I just as selfish, in my own way? For years I lived off the money that you and Bob sent me for Robin."

"Oh, money!" She waved her hand through a column of cigarette smoke: that's all money was. "The important thing is that you brought up Robin to be the dear, beautiful person that she is, and for that I'll always be grateful."

Margaret looked up doubtfully, but already, even with those doubts unresolved, the tears had started to her eyes. "Do you really love Robin then?"

"Love her!"

"She always wanted you to, you know. So badly."

"I guess I never knew how to express it."

"That's what I would tell her. But this last week, Mrs. Millar—" Margaret stopped short.

"Cassandra. Please."

"This last week, Cassandra, she's been so happy. She's been another person."

"Has she? I'm glad. I was so afraid that I'd have . . . passed on before I had a chance to . . . make her understand. And that's why I told her I wanted to see *you* too. I don't want to leave *any* bad feelings behind me. Oh, when I think of the time I've wasted, the love I've thrown away. You and I, Margaret—you and I!"

Margaret seemed to consider this deeply, but could do no better than meekly to echo, "You and I."

Cassandra elaborated: "We had so much in common."

"Oh, Mrs.—"

"Bob thought so too, you know. He said to me once, years and years later, that he thought we were like two twins, you and I. Not physically, of course, because you're much prettier than me, but deep down, where it counts."

By now Margaret was thoroughly rattled. Cassandra's revelations had exceeded all her capacities as a spectator. She'd lost track of who the characters were and what relationships were presumed to exist between them.

Cassandra leaned forward, to cup Margaret's rouged jowls in her fine hands. She looked lingeringly into her bleary, fuddled blue eyes and then, with a more than sisterly emphasis, kissed her mouth.

"There!" she said, returning to her pillow with a sigh. "That's what I wanted to do the moment you came in the door."

She had arrived at what she thought would have to be her last word on the subject of death, and it was as astonishing in its way as the detective's announcement, in the last chapter of the book, that *none* of the suspects were guilty.

It was just this: Death is a social experience; an exchange; not a relationship in itself, but the medium in which relationships may exist; not a friend or a lover, but the room in which all friends and lovers meet.

She reached for the Chesterfields, took one, offered the pack to Margaret, who accepted one after a tremor of hesitation. A flame flickered from the lighter, and Margaret inhaled.

Then there was a knock on the door. Tap tappy-tap-tap. Tap. Tap.

"That will be Robin," said both Mrs. Millars together.

APPENDIX ONE

The Story of the Story: "The Double-Timer"

In the long-ago days before every child had his own cassette recorder I delivered a talk over the Fairmont radio station on the topic of how something—either the Church or the School or the Family—molds us into good citizens. The talk had been recorded in advance, and when it was broadcast I was sitting with the rest of the combined seventh and eighth grades, confident of my impending moment of glory. At last a voice started delivering the speech I'd written, but it wasn't my voice. Some *child* was declaiming my lines in a shrill, affected, ridiculous pennywhistle of a voice. I started laughing, and when I couldn't be made to stop I had to be sent from the room. So much for glory.

Rereading "The Double-Timer" I feel a kindred emotion. Not only does it seem not to be *my* story, it seems downright bad—another retread of some tired B-movie with the flimsiest of science fictional premises and no redeeming literary merit. The characters are Formica, the world they inhabit as textureless as Velveeta. The dialogue has negative flair, and to judge by its consistency the would-be hard-boiled prose has been boiled for no more than two minutes. Nevertheless, the story achieved its essential purpose. It sold to a magazine.

(Though it almost didn't. The first editor who saw it, Avram Davidson—or whoever was reading the slush pile for *F & SF* in the days of his editorship—returned it without so

374

much as a word of encouragement added to the standard rejection slip.)

If it hadn't, the South might well have won the Civil War. For the decision to write "The Double-Timer" was one of those major intersections on the road of life from which radically different alternate worlds may branch. Never mind that that decision took the wholly intuitive form of a nervous breakdown, so-called. It was May of 1962, and mid-terms were upon me. Instead of cramming dutifully, I stayed home and wrote "The Double-Timer," not going out of my apartment till it had been finished, a matter of four days. I wrote with passionate conviction—not in my tale or its characters, but in my having at last reached the point where I *could* write a saleable story. If my inner gyroscope had been proved wrong, I might well have taken make-up exams, got my degree, or degrees, and then your guess is as good as mine.

But it did sell—to Cele Goldsmith—and appeared just three months later, in the October 1962 issue of *Fantastic Stories*. Though she rejected the next story—an early draft of "White Fang Goes Dingo"—I'd been rewarded by a sufficiently large pellet to continue to press the lever that had yielded it, and Cele Goldsmith continued to publish enough of what I produced that my apprenticeship was begun in earnest.

But back to "The Double-Timer" and where it came from, apart from the need (at the root of my breakdown) to get out of NYU. Since I'd left high school in 1957 and entered the Real World of New York I'd been producing paragraphs and pages of prose that aspired to the condition of fiction, and in my first years at NYU, with the kind encouragement of Maurice Baudin (earlier Bob Sheckley had been a student of his), I was able to write "The End" to a few of those aborted beginnings. There was something out of kilter about all those first classroom efforts, and if I wasn't yet able to write better I *knew* better than to try and market them.

At the start of my junior year the NYU catalogue offered an irresistible course, "The Quest for Utopia," taught by J. Max Patrick. Not only did it offer the then unheard-of opportunity of receiving academic credit for reading what amounted to science fiction, it was also possible to produce a utopia of one's own in lieu of a term paper. I had been reading sf since my first discovery of *Astounding* and *Galaxy* back in the Golden Age of science fiction, the age of 12. I never became a fan as such, but I was a sufficiently avid reader that when I would run out of guaranteed winners by the old reliables I would take pot luck from the paperback racks. There is probably no greater spur to literary ambition than reading a really worthless story by a name writer—a pleasure that genre fiction of all kinds affords abundantly. *"I can write something better than this crap,"* one assures oneself, and at the moment that assurance gels one may actually do so.

The utopia course put the science fiction I'd been reading into a new perspective. On the one hand I couldn't help but see how rough-hewn or (worse) how hollow a lot of it was. On the other hand there seemed no logical reason sf couldn't be as serious, worthwhile, and respectable (in the early '60's these had yet to become pejoratives) as Plato or Thomas More or any of the other ancient worthies we were studying. Indeed, there has always been a heretical, populist part of my heart that prefers *The Space Merchants* to (ho hum) *Don Quixote* and can't see a qualitative difference between *Blondie* and the earliest Italian Primitives.

The most important thing about the utopia course, however, was the way it acted as a magnet on other apprentice writers of a speculative bent. In addition to Charles Dizenzo (whom I'd met the year before in Baudin's short story workshop), John Clute and Jerry Mundis were also taking the course. All three were to remain close friends. For *his* utopia Jerry Mundis was writing an entire sf *novel*. What's more, he'd already made his first professional sale to a magazine, proof that it could be done. I immediately enlisted myself as his rival, though I wasn't finally accepted for the position till I'd placed "The Double-Timer" with *Fantastic*, since when it's been a long and happy game of literary leap frog.

That is only partly a digression. The excitement of intellectual companionship and (another no longer fashionable virtue) competition is a good energy source for writers, especially when they're starting out and have no audience or critics but themselves. The best reason for taking courses in writing is to find someone who jogs at approximately your own best pace.

"The Double-Timer" is not the utopia I wrote for the course, but that utopia (a dystopia, really), "A Thesis on Social Forms and Social Controls in the USA," was later sold to the wise and good Cele Goldsmith. In a sense "A Thesis" has equal claim to being my first published story, since it was, of all the stories I've published, the first I wrote. However it's not, properly speaking, a story, but rather a mock-essay, and "The Double-Timer" *was* published first and written with that intention. The reason I mention it at all is because the glow that I got from writing it, the sense of being (at last) capable, was one of the constituent elements of "The Double-Timer."

And that's about all I can remember. Where the story's "idea" (such as it is) came from I don't recall, nor whether it was one I'd been storing up and mulling over for a while. I think it came upon me in the wake of deciding that the Time Had Come, but that may be wishful thinking.

Perhaps neither my seventh-grade speech nor "The Double-Timer" were quite so objectively bad as I've made out here. Judith Merril, bless her, did give it an Honorable Mention in her *Year's Best*. Still, in casting about for something to say that will make new readers want to read it, the best inducement I can think of is the one that so often inspired me when I was reading the stories in the magazines, way back then: "Surely *you* can do better than this."

On "Et in Arcadia Ego"

I very much wanted to be, and very much wasn't, a prodigy. Half the people I know wrote and, worse, published their first stories or poems or even novels before they'd turned twenty, but I didn't get a story into print till I was twenty-two, and that one wasn't a winner. How gratifying to be able to plunk down your literary maidenhead and say to the ages, Voilà! But not for me.

This story is the opposite of such precocities: it's what I *wasn't* able to write when I was seventeen. I know because I tried. The first—ur—version of it may even go back before I had my own typewriter (October, 1957, an Olivetti Lettera 22) but it wasn't till the summer of 1960 (I was twenty, and this was my last chance to be a boy wonder) that I presented a final draft of it, in lieu of a term paper, to Maurice Baudin, Jr., with whom I was taking an evening course, "The Novella," at NYU. Entitled: "The Chthonian Smell." I'm afraid that about summed it up. The rocketship Archangel lands on the planet Chthonia; the four overcivilized crew members discover a race of noble savages, human in all respects but one, which is revealed in the last, leaden paragraph.

And yet (I always thought), and yet. . . .

Bad as I knew that story to be (and I never sent it to a magazine—never) I sensed the seed in it of something that would have been worth doing, if I'd done it.

During the next ten years I went on to write a great deal of science fiction, but never again did I attempt that theme which more than any other defines sf—the exploration of another world, the encounter with alien forms of life. I prided myself that I understood what such tales were *about* better than anyone who was actually writing them. Indeed, the chief obstacle in the way of my creating my own avatar was that I had so many and such various theories. First, such stories were about sex. (What stories aren't?) Then, about the emergence of the United States as an imperial power. Then, though less necessarily, about man's relationship to machines and to himself considered as a machine: related to this theme was the curious lack of affect that usually seemed to obtain between the crew members on these expeditions. If I couldn't write the story that I glimpsed through all this theoretical foliage, I was content that no one else had been able to either. For some reason, most fiction, in proportion as it advances toward the farther reaches of space and time, grows lackluster and olive drab. Perhaps it's only that against backgrounds so exotic the pulpy tissue that constitutes 80 percent of most sf becomes, more noticeably, lifeless. It does not grate nearly so much when Perry Mason sits down to a steak dinner for a chapter as when the same dinner is served on Aldebaran V in the year 2500. Even at a meal of hydroponic glop the table settings don't change; some few new words are introduced, but the syntax is immutable.

As, of course, it must be—to a degree. The demand for a totally transformed environment, pushed to its limit, would require a writer to invent a new language for each story he writes. But the *sense* of such a shift having taken place can be suggested, and when it is, the result is that touch of strange that is the *raison d'etre* for sf.

A roundabout way of self-congratulation: for with "Et in Arcadia Ego" I felt that for the first time I *had* laid hold of the very essence of what I understood science fiction to be, that I had found, as never before, my voice.

Indeed, with just the first four paragraphs I knew I had it: a prose that slides by quarter-notes and leaps by octaves; lyric outbursts leading to deadly banalities; details dwelt upon at inexplicable length and whole masses of exposition disposed of in a shrug: and always this feeling of the whole thing not quite balancing, of the narrator being perfectly mad and at the same time completely ordinary.

Not that, for having found this voice, the story was then any easier to write. (Only two other stories have taken me longer to bring to completion—"The Roaches" and "Emancipation.") I began "Et in Arcadia Ego" in January of 1969 while living in Milford, Pennsylvania, resumed it that spring in New York, and finished it late in the fall.

The actual moment of its conception I remember with unusual vividness. I used frequently to walk about the wooded hills just outside Milford. Some years before real estate developers had thought to subdivide these woods into lots, and as a result, an incongruous, wide gravel road wound about through the pines and hemlocks. Various pieces of road equipment had been abandoned along this road, and these machineries were gradually becoming part of the landscape. During one day-long hike one of these rusting machines captured me and held me the way a painting can when you're ripe for it. The result was this story and, more directly and immediately, a short poem called "The Caterpillar"[1]:

[1]First published in *Ronald Reagan: the Magazine of Poetry*. Copyright 1970.

> I want to confess
> a sneaking fondness for it—
> as:
> > in spring
>
> With blossoms
> poking through its treads
> & trying so hard
> to be rectangular
> > then

```
            in summer, shedding
            skins of paint, less noticeable
            amid the bother
            of things growing
            (it seems peculiar, but it does not
            seem more than that):

            Fall
                 & its rust
            is scarcely discordant
            with the then
            level of taste.

            It is at its best
            in winter:
                      alone
            in all these woods
            it is unmoved
            by the snow.
```

The obvious link between this and the story that follows is
the machine on the altar of the temple, that shrine to death
hidden (like the "Wolf") at the center of the Arcadian world.
The title itself, familiar as it is, conceals a similar ambiva-
lence. As an inscription on a tomb or monument in various
paintings of pastoral scenes (notably Poussin's), it may refer
either, elegiacally, to some shepherd lad ("I too [have lived]
in Arcady") or to Death itself ("I too [exist] in Arcady").
For me, in the woods that day, the rusted, snow-covered
machine seemed to bear that same inscription, with a peculiar
modern difference.

"A pastoral!" I thought. "*That's* what all those stories
always are—pastorals!" By the end of that evening I had those
first four paragraphs written as they stand now and all the
principal elements of the plot noted down.

Voilà.

The Uses of Fiction:
A Theory

A time comes when almost everyone stops reading it. Often they'll shift the responsibility onto the shoulders of the novel, which, they say, is dead. Or, with a little more modesty, they'll admit that much study is a weariness of the flesh. Some, instead of stopping cold turkey, settle into a genre suitable to their station and dilemma in life. But the real reason they don't read it anymore is, they don't need it anymore, and that's what this theory is about.

Let's suppose, for the theory's sake, that there is a basic difference between genre fiction, and the real, realistic thing, fiction fiction—what Leavis calls the Great Tradition. What sets genre fiction apart is that it's written to a formula. Its readers read it the way a bear paces its cage, or a Catholic goes to the Mass—for the pleasure of doing again what has been done, to good effect, before. If the formula is violated, the reader feels betrayed. As, indeed, he should. Imagine a Perry Mason mystery in which Della is guilty; a gothic in which the heroine comes to a tragic end because she's stupid; a western in which all the difficulties are resolved by a brilliantly negotiated and bloodless truce. Who wouldn't want their money back?

Judged by this criterion there is a good deal more genre fiction than is commonly labeled as such. Any writer who does *his thing* consistently and fast enough can become his own genre. One takes pleasure in a Wodehouse, as one does in a Coke, just for its wonderful sameness.

The marketing and codification of these thousand-and-one brand-names has reached such a state of perfection that a good consumer hungry for a book can pick out what he needs from a whole bookstore just by walking in front of the racks: a key word in the title, the precise degree of vulgarity or chic

381

in the design, even the price. Sometimes these promises aren't kept, but on the whole one can judge most books by their covers.

Genre writers succeed to the degree that their talents and their readers' *needs* may be made to correspond. It is the fan rather than the writer who defines, by the preponderant and inarguable weight of his purchases, the character of a genre. Thus, a proper understanding of any genre begins with the question—Who needs it?

For example:

Gothics are mostly read by housewives or those who see a life of housewifery looming ahead. In gothics the heroine is mysteriously threatened, and wonders whether it was her husband/fiancé who tried to drop the chandelier on her. (Usually it isn't, but if it is, then there is an alternate male on hand, whom she discovers she *really* loves.) Few of the ladies who devour gothics are in serious danger of being pushed off a cliff in Cornwall for the sake of their legacies, yet the analogue of the brand of fiction that they buy to their real predicament is close. Every gothic reader must ask herself whether her marriage is worth the grief, the ritual insincerity, the buried rancor and sacrifice of other possibilities that every marriage entails. To which the gothic writer replies with a resounding Yes! It *is* worth all that, because deep down he really does love you. Yet to the degree that this answer rings hollow the experience must be renewed. Poor Nan must return to the dark castle of her doubts, and the doubts must be denied. And then again.

Another example:

Science fiction is read most avidly by precocious children, brainy adolescents and a particular kind of retarded adult. What these readers have in common is a need to assert the primacy of Intellect. The message that comes through in tale after tale is that it pays to be intelligent, and this is true at all levels of literacy, from sub to ultra. Fantasies about sex and money are relatively scarce and, where they do exist, invariably feeble. The story that tears at an sf reader's heart (or cerebellum) is the story about someone (a child especially) who discovers that he possesses Secret Mental Powers: Theodore Sturgeon's *More Than Human*, Arthur C. Clarke's *Childhood's End*, anything by A.E. van Vogt. What sf fans require in their heroes they applaud in themselves as well, and the most zealous of them congregate annually in convention halls to do honor to the peculiar and elusive genius that raises them above people who like other kinds of junk.

Now there is one life-situation in which it is essential to be smart, smarter, smartest. Say you're fourteen years old, pulling down good grades at school (but never good enough), and already beginning to get anxious about college. In that situation your hero won't be Billy the Kid. Sf writers are cheerleaders of the Science Honors Society, whose membership they ever and again remind that the rolicking lamb of Youth must and should be sacrificed on the gray altar of Education. So long as this sacrifice remains the secret sorrow of one's life, so long will sf remain interesting. Usually, once you get your degree and start leading a livelier life, you stop reading the stuff. But if for any reason you don't get the degree, or the degree doesn't get you what you thought it would, then you may be doomed to spin the wheel of this one fantasy forever.

In this way a predilection for genre fiction is like a sexual perversion. Both are symptomatic of an arrested development—not so much reprehensible, therefore, as limiting. The limitation may be as narrow as liking nothing but Georgette Heyer or high-heeled shoes, or as broad as a promiscuous acceptance of all kinds of trash whatsoever, to the exclusion only of what is wholesome and abiding.

But what of fiction fiction? Why do people read that? For the same reason that children pretend—in order to practice being grown-up. Or, which amounts to the same thing, to learn the manners of their betters. In rigidly hierarchical societies, fiction (except for religious purposes) is unnecessary and even undesirable. In a mobile society, however, the ambitious young can't find in their immediate social environment a range of models at all so broad as the range of life's imagined possibilities. Or, as the radio used to ask us every day: Can a young girl from a mining town in the West find happiness in the arms of a titled millionaire? Unless you follow the program, how will you know? Whether in the form of soap opera or in the recentest triple-decker by Joyce Carol Oates, realistic fiction (in all its forms, written and acted) offers its audience a vicarious apprenticeship in new, and otherwise unavailable, forms of social behavior. At the simplest level one learns the rudiments of good taste and proper speech. (For instance, what my aunt Aurelia especially likes about *Search for Tomorrow* is that everyone lives in nice modern homes and has this refined and yet quite natural way of talking.) Heroes and heroines of all eras are defined by their unerring instinct for what is done and what isn't, and few readers are able to tolerate doubts as to the good breeding of the characters with whom they are asked to identify. Fiction's most formidable paragons appear at the very dawn of the realistic novel, in the persons of Richardson's Clarissa Harlowe and Sir Charles Grandison, than whom nobody, but nobody, has ever been more unremittingly correct.

Once this identification with the right point-of-view has been established we may be lured to our own instruction in good earnest. Safe within his persona, the reader hypothetically confronts all the humors, follies, dilemmas and deceits that the hero must adventure through. He sees how he may defer to his superiors with dignity, and command the deference of his inferiors with grace. (For these skills Charlotte Bronte is incomparable.) He practices various virtues, especially that virtue most trying for the young—tolerance. (Every novel by Jane Austen is an obstacle course of fools who must be suffered patiently.) And, inevitably, he senses what forms of snobbery and cant are currently respectable, and how and when these may be best employed. Novelists in this respect are no different from other teachers—their hypocrisies are often their best-remembered lessons.

If it were not for the institution of apprenticeship-by-fiction most of our complex social codes would quickly fall into disrepair, like Jeeter Lester's jalopy in *God's Little Acre*. Courtship and romance are obvious examples of nature imitating art, but I suspect that fiction extends its golden influence over the whole range of everyday life. All actions that require poise, patience, humor, or compassion—whatever, in short, is distinctive of urban middle-class civilization—derives ultimately from this source. Indeed, so effective is fiction as an instructor that quite soon all pedagogy may be cast into dramatic form. Consider the success of *Sesame Street*.

If one accepts all of the theory (except for that last rather flamboyant prediction) it becomes evident why at around the age of thirty it gets increasingly hard to find a novel that can grip us like the novels we read when we were twelve, or eighteen, or twenty-four. By thirty we have very likely learned our basic roles in the repertoire theater of life, and sampled the spectrum of our possibilities. Ambitions that haven't been satisfied, at least in part, probably won't be, ever—and so we begin to retreat from the outer perimeter of our hopes, an operation traditionally conducted in silence, or even (like the bombing of Cambodia) denied.

This explains, as well, another fact I've often puzzled over—that liberals should so much preponderate over conservatives among both the readers and writers of fiction, particularly when the distinctively conservative genres are eliminated—the western, the hard-boiled detective story, and the spy-thriller. This is because liberals are still waiting, as it were, for promotion, while conservatives are engaged in a holding action. A drift to the right is apt, therefore, to accompany a declining appetite for literature, both changes being symptomatic of that climacteric age when the four-lane expressway of boundless hope shrinks to an asphalt road, and the speed limit drops to 50.

How then to account for the glorious exceptions? Are the writers who go on writing into middle age and beyond simply *unable*, like Peter Pan, to grow up into sane, quietly desperate Republicans? A sanguine temperament helps, certainly, but writers are also assisted by their peculiar social milieu—that Never-Never Land inhabited mainly by other writers. Popular mythology to the contrary, writers do earn a comfortable living just by writing, and so they are insulated from the more corrupting and bruising aspects of class struggle, the experiences of bossing and being bossed. (Poets, unlike novelists, don't make their livings by their pens, and so must get jobs in the real world, or in academia, in consequence of which fewer poets, proportionally, survive into their forties with their art intact.) Most writers even seem to prefer these narrow confines, if we may judge by their journals and letters, or by such a book as Podhoretz's *Making It*. Podhoretz's ultimate vision of success was to shake hands and trade gossip with the survivors of the Modern Library.

Those who actually escape the literary establishment and make it to the Other Side—Bennett, Hemingway, Capote— find the practice of fiction increasingly problematical. The discrepancy between the brighter world they imagined and that to which they've at last won entry becomes wider and wider, and they must ask themselves just what they're *doing* at this splendid, endless dinner party. Unless they can come

up with a good answer (as James did), their novels shrivel
into novellas or inflate into reams of Higher Journalism or
simply get unreadably bad.

And so the work of the novel, at its finest, has been left to
the great exiles and innocents. To Dickens, who couldn't
describe a gentleman; to Jane Austen and Charlotte Bronte,
who wouldn't meet one; to Thomas Mann, who lived till the
end of his life in that purely hypothetical Germany inhabited
only by writers, scholars, musicians, and (democratically)
their landlords; to George Eliot, who believed in the possibility of heroism in the here-and-now the way Bonhoeffer believed in God, with the same magnificent disregard for all the
evidence to the contrary; to so many good writers, in fact,
that with the best will in the world one couldn't plow to the
end of them in a lifetime, even a lifetime of more than thirty
years.

APPENDIX TWO

THE FALL OF
THE HOUSE OF USHER

Libretto by Thomas Disch
based on the story by Edgar Allan Poe
for the Opera by Gregory Sandow

PERSONS

RODERICK USHER, *Baritone*
EDGAR, His Friend, *Tenor*
THE DOCTOR, *Bass*

The scene is a room of indeterminate time and place. Double doors, center stage; to one side a divan. Behind the divan a large window, heavily draped. On the other side of the stage a harpsichord.

Edgar asleep on the divan; RODERICK *standing at the window, holding back the drapes. As the orchestral prelude ends, Roderick seems, by his alarm, to have heard what he has been listening for.*

RODERICK

Listen! Edgar, do you hear?

(*He goes to the doors, opens them wide, then, irresolute, closes them, though not altogether. Edgar, waking, watches without understanding.*)

It is the doctor. His coach is at the gate,
And even now he mounts the staircase
To this room. Edgar, you must act for me:
I cannot bear. . . . No, absolutely, I can not!

(*Confident of Edgar's compliance, he returns to the window and stands with his back to the room.*)

(THE DOCTOR *enters before Edgar has quite risen from the divan. A glance at Roderick, and then at Edgar suffices: he addresses himself to Edgar.*)

DOCTOR

I pray you will excuse my seeming tardiness.
These storms have made the roads impassible.

EDGAR

And dangerous, I fear.

(*Pauses, embarrassed.*)

You must excuse my friend.
He's not himself tonight. But whatever I may do
On his behalf . . . ?

DOCTOR

On his behalf?
I did not venture forth on Roderick's account.
I came to treat his sister, the Lady Madeline.

EDGAR

You were not told? The Lady Madeline is dead.

DOCTOR

(*Setting down his bag*)

Ah . . . I feared as much. The malady
Was mortal. Soon or late, despite of all my art,
She'd have succumbed. And he . . . ?

EDGAR

Is inconsolable.

DOCTOR

(*Unsympathetic.*)

Assuredly. And nervous,
I expect.

EDGAR

Yes, dreadfully.

(*Whispers.*)

When I read aloud in hopes of bringing him
A moment of forgetfulness, he quivers at my words
As if they had been thunderclaps. Yet
When I try to leave he swears he'll not survive
My going by a day. And so I stay.

DOCTOR

In that regard the Lady Madeline might well
Have been his mirror. So delicate,
So very delicate.

EDGAR

Twins often share, I'm told,
A sympathy so deep as to be scarce
Conceivable to you or me.

DOCTOR

They do.
And long propinquity will draw the knot
Ever more fast—until the strings can bear
No more, and part. I often urged them both
To leave this donjon of a house.
The Lady Madeline would have been admired
In the wider world. Her comeliness
Was in the classic mold.

(*Edgar seems uneasy.*)

DOCTOR

But you have seen her.

EDGAR

I saw her once,
The hour I arrived. She passed before me,
Saying not a word, nor did I dare
To speak to her. I never saw her living face.
She covered it as she passed by. But yes—
In death I saw the Lady Madeline: and strange,
A smile still lingered on her lips,
A glow upon her cheek. As though she lived.

DOCTOR

Tell me: where in the catacombs below
Has the Lady been interred? There is a chamber
I prepared specifically against this day.
Its whole interior, the iron door as well,
Is sheathed in copper—a precaution
That befits the unique and curious
Nature of the illness.

EDGAR

(*Reluctantly.*)

It was within
That vault I thought I saw her smile.

(*The Doctor takes up his bag and prepares to go.*)

EDGAR

Must you depart so soon?

DOCTOR

My duty was accomplished ere I came.
Concerning Roderick, his need is more of counsel
Than of medicine. As you love your friend,
Urge him to depart with you at once.
He has inherited . . . a pestilence.
A miasma breathes from the tarn
And penetrates each room. To linger here
Is to invite infection, and so,
By your good leave, Sir, and without more ado.

(*They bow to each other. The Doctor pauses in the door-way.*)

DOCTOR

As to that seeming—in maladies of strictly
Cataleptic character it is not unusual.

(The Doctor exits.)

RODERICK

(Still at the window. In a revery.)

A voice so low, so musical, so eloquent
Each single word became a kind of melody.

(Breaks off and addresses Edgar with obvious dissimulation.)

And has he left? And was he here for long?
My thoughts were wandering through the middle air
Like those scabrous rooks that circle
Endlessly above the tarn. If, in my abstraction,
I have chance to speak, heed not my words.
They had no substance, none: the mere inchoate melodies
The wind will play upon the strings
Of a suspended harp. Forget them utterly.

(Roderick approaches Edgar and blows out the candles in the holder in his hand.)

EDGAR

(With diffuse anguish.)

If thoughts, my friend. . .

(Solicitously but forcefully, Roderick takes the candle-holder from him.)

EDGAR

If thoughts
Could be extinguished with as little pain.
If the soul could find surcease. . . .

(Edgar returns to the divan and lies down.)

RODERICK

Sleep,
My more-than-brother, often self—sleep.

EDGAR

What use is sleep illumined by such dreams?

RODERICK

No use. No use at all. And yet
Do not the most exquisite terrors yield
A loveliness? Think of phosphorus—
How it may stir to life the memory of a rose.

EDGAR

I only need to close my eyes, and it is there.

(*Roderick goes to the window, pushes the drapes aside, and looks out.*)

RODERICK

The house.

EDGAR

The basilisk, from which I can't avert
My gaze.

RODERICK

Its windows watch you.

EDGAR

It's alive.
Each rotting tree trunk, every moldy stone—
Alive! The bollards holding up the chains along
The drive are stumps of teeth—

RODERICK

I've seen it too,
That beggarwoman's mumbling mouth. I've seen her
Glaring down, mute, hungering, and, as you say,
Alive. But Usher has a music too. I've learned
To hear it plainly. Press your ear against
A windowpane, or stand beside the tarn.
There is a tapping first, a rippling, then
A Low pulsation of the air—

EDGAR

A music like the walls
Of cities we have visited, that stand forever
In our dreams.

RODERICK

Or like my sister's breath
While she could breathe.

EDGAR

(*After long silence.*)

I cannot sleep.

(*Immediately Edgar's arm falls limp. He sleeps, though Roderick, at the window, remains unaware of this.*)

RODERICK

She did not want to know that you had come.
She would not hear your name. She would not come
Near the window when you walked beside the tarn.
She lived in fear perpetual, and yet, my friend—

(*Turning to Edgar. With greater intensity.*)

And yet—she was so fair! So fair! A flesh
Like Parian, unmarked by our mortality.

(*Though realizing Edgar is asleep, he continues still to address him caressingly.*)

A voice so low, so eloquent, each word becomes
A kind of melody. To listen, Edgar, is to love
The Lady Madeline. To listen. . . .

(*Roderick bows his head, listening. Half-audible fragments of melody well up from the orchestra. At one of these, he starts up with a shudder and goes to the harpsichord.*)

(*Roderick plays for some time. The lights slowly darken until all the stage is obscure. When they come up again, he is no longer at the harpsichord, though its music continues. The tableau repeats that of the opening scene with Roderick at the window and Edgar asleep on the divan. Now, however, Roderick is visibly much less composed;*)

His waistcoat removed, his hair tousled. There is a la
book spread open on Edgar's chest, as though he'd fallen
asleep reading it.)

RODERICK

(Rapidly, in a manner close to speech.)

No, no, between the two of them, between
What we believe is living and what we think
Is dead there is no gulf so absolute
It cannot be spanned. These courses of cut stone—
Can you be sure they are, and ever were,
Insentient? Long, long, they waited coffined
In the earth, forming their slow desire to become
This floor, these walls, the vault above. Death
Is not inert, oh no! Is not an absence: only slow,
So very slow. Why, centuries may pass before
One lifeless crystal joins another, and those twain
A third, and so ad infinitum, till they've made
A diadem about her brow, exquisite and invisible
Within the hungry earth. And Life, our life,
What is it but the food of Death? As death is ours—
The precious wine we keep reserved
In this most secret cellar depth, untasted
And eternally desired. My dearest Madeline!
My only bride! My soul! My other breath!

(Edgar has been stirring in his sleep. Now he awakens
with a start, so that the book falls to the floor. He sits up
and tears off his waistcoat as if horrified by it.)

EDGAR

I feel it still. As if its arms were coiled
Invisibly about me now. Even as it leaves me
For its lair within my heart. I feel it there,
Beating with the self-same beat.

RODERICK

Enough!
You are awake!

(Roderick grasps Edgar's hand, commanding calm.)

EDGAR

Awake . . . and yet it is as real,
As tangible, as these.

(Pulling free of Roderick's grasp.)

If you could see it,
Roderick, if you could penetrate my heart
And see it lurking in the crimson darkness there,
You would not touch the least infected part of me.

RODERICK

We each have our familiars, Edgar, and they live
Where it is darkest. Let them hide
In their congenial filth. No need for us
To seek them out. Let us, you and I, enjoy
The mathematic pleasures of the mind,
In which they cannot share—those hidden monsters
Of the heart. Let us, like voyagers in the airy void,
Entwine the fibers of our thoughts in labyrinthine knots
Of perfect counterpoint. Or, if you are tired
And that seems too high and arduous a task,
Let us retire to the twilight of Pomponius Mela.
Or there is this—

(Picking up the fallen book.)

The quaint romance
You started yesterevening.

EDGAR

It was a foolish book.

RODERICK

Folly has no terrors. I'd rather listen to
Relics of ancient poetry than to the raging
Of the storm. Look—I open it at random.
Here, where the wax has made a virgule—read!

EDGAR

(Reading.)

The rain beats down, and Ethelred,
    His heart made bold with wine,

Awaits no more the hermit hoar
But lifts his mace against the door.
   Alas (alas) for that good knight!

The blow is struck, the timbers crack,
   The dry wood breaks like glass—

(*A SOUND startles both men. Edgar pauses, but only the storm is audible now. He resumes reading, though Roderick's attention is now fixed elsewhere.*)

No hermit hoar finds Ethelred
   Behind the shattered door;
Instead a dragon dread and old
With tongue of flame, with scales of gold
   Alas (alas) for that good knight!

With iron mace he smites its head—
   O hear the creature's cry!—

(*Another, louder SOUND interrupts Edgar. As if compelled, Roderick approaches the half-opened doors center stage, behind which a faint glow can be discerned. The light increases till the end of the scene, though it is never other than dim.*)

RODERICK

(*Moans.*)

EDGAR

Besmirched . . .

RODERICK

Continue. To the end of it.

EDGAR

Besmirched with blood, the weary wight
   Beholds a brazen shield;
Upon its face enamelèd:
I am the shield of Ethelred.
   Alas (alas) for that good knight!

For see—the shield eludes his grasp
   And crashes to the floor—

(A SOUND, the third and loudest. Edgar lays the book aside. A convulsion overcomes Roderick at first hearing the sound. Then, momentarily, he is calmer.)

RODERICK

Do you hear it now? Surely you cannot help
But hear. Long—long—long—
For endless hours, for entire days,
I heard. But dared not, dared not speak
For fear that speech would summon her,
For fear she could draw strength
From this intolerable vigil we have kept.

(The light within the room begins to fade.)

Always, always, while I sat beside her bed,
Telling our best-loved lies—that she would never die
Alone—that we would leave, as we had come, together—
Always then she'd fix her eyes on mine, like manacles,
Compelling me to witness each single sinking
Downward step into her death. She'd draw a breath—
But could not breathe. She'd claw the sheets as though
They were her shroud. I loved her, Edgar:
How could I bear to go on witnessing. . . .

EDGAR

I did not know.

RODERICK

(Solemnly, tenderly.)

We have put her living in the tomb.

EDGAR

I never knew.

RODERICK

We put her living in the tomb.
And now . . . those sounds that seemed so near:
Is it not clear? The breaking of the hermit's door—
Shall we not rather say: the rending of the pine,
The coffin's raw, rugged planks. And then,
The dragon's cry—what might it be unless

The screaming of the rusted hinges as she forced
The vault? And when the shield fell to the floor—

EDGAR

I did not hear!

RODERICK

An hundred times I've seen
The high winds of her malady tear through her limbs
Until her wasted frame could bear no more and she
Collapsed. But always, always to arise again.
As she has risen now, and mounts the stairs.

EDGAR

(*His hands on Roderick's shoulders. Imploring.*)

She's dead. The Lady Madeline is dead.

RODERICK

(*Fearful, rapturous.*)

Dead? The Lady Madeline will never die alone.
Our lives—our deaths—are indissolubly one.
Would you still deny? Madman! Do you not hear
The slow inexorable progress of her naked feet?
Does not the heavy beating of her heart transfix
Your own? Feel—feel the floor's reverberation!
Can the very atoms of these walls comprehend—
And you not know? Madeline is with us now.
She stands at this moment beyond this door.

(*The curtain falls.*)

ABOUT THE AUTHOR

THOMAS MICHAEL DISCH became a freelance writer in 1964 after working in advertising. He was born in Iowa in 1940, and educated at New York University. His first published science fiction story, "The Double-Timer," appeared in *Fantastic* in 1962. His novels include *The Genocides, Echo Round His Bones, 334, Camp Concentration* and, most recently, *On Wings of Song*. He has also published several short story collections, such as *Getting into Death* and *Fundamental Disch*. Thomas Disch was involved with the popular television series, *The Prisoner,* and has edited several anthologies of short fiction.

OUT OF THIS WORLD!

That's the only way to describe Bantam's great series of science fiction classics. These space-age thrillers are filled with terror, fancy and adventure and written by America's most renowned writers of science fiction. Welcome to outer space and have a good trip!

☐	13179	**THE MARTIAN CHRONICLES** by Ray Bradbury	$2.25
☐	13695	**SOMETHING WICKED THIS WAY COMES** by Ray Bradbury	$2.25
☐	14323	**STAR TREK: THE NEW VOYAGES** by Culbreath & Marshak	$2.25
☐	13260	**ALAS BABYLON** by Pat Frank	$2.25
☐	14124	**A CANTICLE FOR LEIBOWITZ** by Walter Miller, Jr.	$2.50
☐	11175	**THE FEMALE MAN** by Joanna Russ	$1.75
☐	13312	**SUNDIVER** by David Brin	$1.95
☐	12957	**CITY WARS** by Dennis Palumbo	$1.95
☐	11662	**SONG OF THE PEARL** by Ruth Nichols	$1.75
☐	13766	**THE FARTHEST SHORE** by Ursula LeGuin	$2.25
☐	13594	**THE TOMBS OF ATUAN** by Ursula LeGuin	$2.25
☐	13767	**A WIZARD OF EARTHSEA** by Ursula LeGuin	$2.25
☐	13563	**20,000 LEAGUES UNDER THE SEA** by Jules Verne	$1.75
☐	12655	**FANTASTIC VOYAGE** by Isaac Asimov	$1.95

Buy them at your local bookstore or use this handy coupon for ordering:

Bantam Books, Inc., Dept. SF, 414 East Golf Road, Des Plaines, Ill. 60016

Please send me the books I have checked above. I am enclosing $_____ (please add $1.00 to cover postage and handling). Send check or money order —no cash or C.O.D.'s please.

Mr/Mrs/Miss_____

Address_____

City_____State/Zip_____

SF—9/80

Please allow four to six weeks for delivery. This offer expires 3/81.

FANTASY AND SCIENCE FICTION FAVORITES

Bantam brings you the recognized classics as well as the current favorites in fantasy and science fiction. Here you will find the beloved Conan books along with recent titles by the most respected authors in the genre.

☐ 01166	URSHURAK	
	Bros. Hildebrandt & Nichols	$8.95
☐ 13610	NOVA Samuel R. Delany	$2.25
☐ 13534	TRITON Samuel R. Delany	$2.50
☐ 13612	DHALGREN Samuel R. Delany	$2.95
☐ 12018	CONAN THE SWORDSMAN #1	
	DeCamp & Carter	$1.95
☐ 12706	CONAN THE LIBERATOR #2	
	DeCamp & Carter	$1.95
☐ 12970	THE SWORD OF SKELOS #3	
	Andrew Offutt	$1.95
☐ 14321	THE ROAD OF KINGS #4	$2.25
	Karl E. Wagner	
☐ 14127	DRAGONSINGER Anne McCaffrey	$2.50
☐ 14204	DRAGONSONG Anne McCaffrey	$2.50
☐ 12019	KULL Robert E. Howard	$1.95
☐ 10779	MAN PLUS Frederik Pohl	$1.95
☐ 11736	FATA MORGANA William Kotzwinkle	$2.95
☐ 11042	BEFORE THE UNIVERSE	$1.95
	Pohl & Kornbluth	
☐ 13680	TIME STORM Gordon R. Dickson	$2.50
☐ 13400	SPACE ON MY HANDS Frederic Brown	$1.95

Buy them at your local bookstore or use this handy coupon for ordering:

Bantam Books, Inc., Dept. SF2, 414 East Golf Road, Des Plaines, Ill. 60016

Please send me the books I have checked above. I am enclosing $_____ (please add $1.00 to cover postage and handling). Send check or money order —no cash or C.O.D.'s please.

Mr/Mrs/Miss _____

Address _____

City_____State/Zip_____

SF2—9/80

Please allow four to six weeks for delivery. This offer expires 3/81.

Bantam Book Catalog

Here's your up-to-the-minute listing of over 1,400 titles by your favorite authors.

This illustrated, large format catalog gives a description of each title. For your convenience, it is divided into categories in fiction and non-fiction—gothics, science fiction, westerns, mysteries, cookbooks, mysticism and occult, biographies, history, family living, health, psychology, art.

So don't delay—take advantage of this special opportunity to increase your reading pleasure.

Just send us your name and address and 50¢ (to help defray postage and handling costs).